MAKEUP AND MOCHAS
BOOK 2

# The Man For You

# NIKKI GRANT

Casey at the Bat by Ernest Thayer, 1888
The Frost is on the Punkin by James Whitcomb Riley, 1911
Daffodils by Robert Frost, 1916
The Love Song of J. Alfred Prufrock by T.S. Eliot


Book Cover by Designs by Charlyy
Cover Photographer CJC Photography
Cover Model David Wills
Final Edition Interior Artwork and Formatting by Designs by Charlyy
Proofread Kendra with Spice Me Up Editing
Sensitivity Read by Lo Morales @wellreadnurse
First edition 2024

To the ones sitting in their sadness
understanding the depth of the emotion,
and knowing that there is still beauty in this season.

# LETTER FROM THE AUTHOR

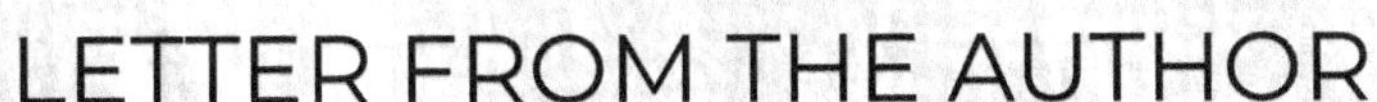

Things like depression and stalking are more common than we sometimes like to talk about. This book deals heavily with both of those. I was first officially diagnosed with depression during the Covid years and it was a hard thing for me to come to grips with. Medication, new routines, and therapy all became a part of my story.

As you dive into Ashley's story, please keep in mind that even though it is fictional, this is a situation that is happening to many every day. Ashley doesn't always ignore her stalker and she has a hard time talking to others about what is happening. It can be easy, as those outside of the situation, to criticize the way she handles everything with "him." Please approach her situation with the grace you would if this was someone you know. Because it might be.

My early readers, as well as myself, include several people that have dealt with very similar circumstances. And through this story, I hope to help even more readers name what they have gone through and help them continue on their healing journey. Sometimes knowing you aren't alone is enough.

If you are dealing with depression or stalking - virtual or IRL - your feelings and reactions are valid. And know that you aren't alone. There are resources listed at the back of the book that I hope will continue to help on your journey. Thank you for reading.

Love and sparkles,
Nikki

# CHAPTER BREAKDOWN (WHERE TW AND CW HAPPEN)

Feel free to skip this page if you want to go in completely blind.
This list is here for you to use as you see fit. The chapters are also
listed so you can skip certain things if you want or need to.

**Attempted assault (on page)**
Chapter 51, 52-53 (aftermath)

**Kidnapping (on page)**
Chapters 48, 49, 51

**Stalking/Hacking (on page, any time "he" shows up)**
*Chapters 4, 5, 7, 9, 11, 12, 13, 15, 16, 17, 18, 22, 23, 24, 26, 27, 28, 30, 32,
33, 34, 35, 36, 39, 40, 41, 43, 44, 46, 48, 49, 51, 52, 53, 54, 57, 62*

**Stalker POV chapters**
*Chapters 7, 11, 13, 18, 23, 28, 34, 40*

**First time FMC and other intimate partners besides final
MMC(on page)**
*Chapter 10, 21, 22*

**Sexually Explicit Scenes (on page and/or referenced)**
*Chapters 12, 21, 22, 58, 59, 60, 63*

**Mental Health: Depression/Anxiety (on page, referenced)**
*Includes talk of therapy sessions, active panic attacks, negative self talk,
medication*
*Chapters 8, 21, 32, 35, 36, 38, 39, 41, 43, 46, 48, 51, 52, 54, 55, 57*

**Chronic Health: Renaud's/Fainting (on page)**
*Chapters 12, 13, 14, 21, 27, 32, 35, 38, 51, 54, 55*

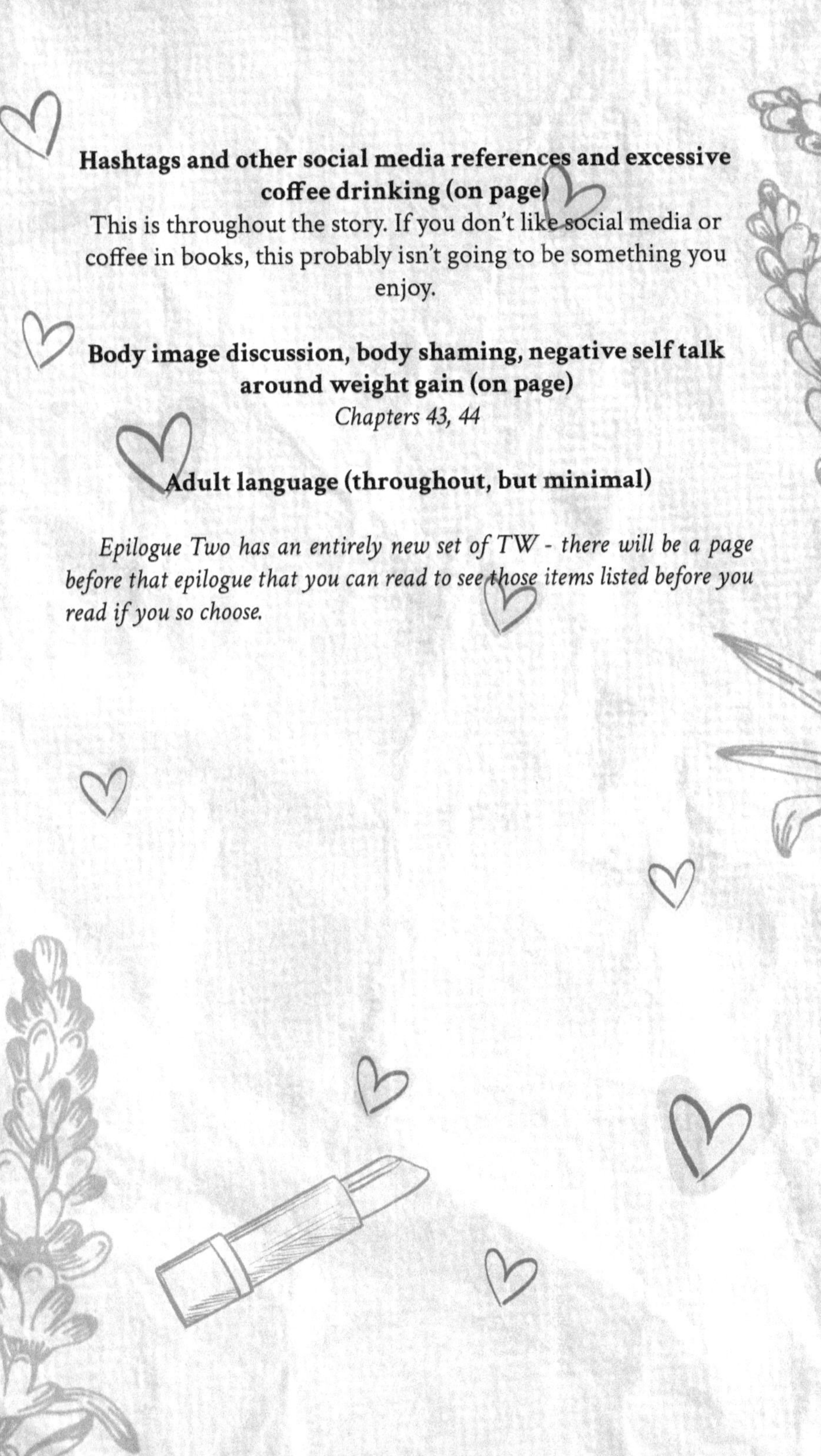

**Hashtags and other social media references and excessive coffee drinking (on page)**
This is throughout the story. If you don't like social media or coffee in books, this probably isn't going to be something you enjoy.

**Body image discussion, body shaming, negative self talk around weight gain (on page)**
*Chapters 43, 44*

**Adult language (throughout, but minimal)**

*Epilogue Two has an entirely new set of TW - there will be a page before that epilogue that you can read to see those items listed before you read if you so choose.*

# PLAYLIST

Shackles - Steven Rodriguez
For the Girls - Aston
Take Me to Church - Hozier
So What - Pink
I Wanna Thank Me (feat. Niecy Nash) - Meghan Trainor, Niecy Nash
Fight Song - Rachel Platten
This is Me - Keala Settle
Love Myself - Hailee Steinfeld
Trust Issues - Emei
…Ready For It? - Taylor Swift
Sit Still, Look Pretty - Daya
Last Man Standing - Livingston
Vampire - Olivia Rodrigo
Plot Line - Emlyn
Bones - Imagine Dragons
Troubled Waters - Alex Waters
But Daddy I Love Him - Taylor Swift
Looking at Me - Sabrina Carpenter
Cinderella Snapped - Jax
Dirtier Thoughts - Nation Haven

# GET TO KNOW ME: VLOG POST 1

Hey there, besties!

My name is Ashley, and I just finished my senior year in high school. I am super excited to go into my freshman year at Colorado State University (CSU) in just a few months. I decided to start sharing a few vlog posts on top of my other social media content this summer so you can get to know me better. I figured now is a good time to change up my social content a bit as I start preparing for my college journey. If you've been following me for a while, you know I love makeup, fun drinks, and exploring all things Colorado. I've lived here my whole life and absolutely love being here. If you're new here, hi! Glad you're here and I hope you stick around for a little while.

I'm planning to stay at home for school for at least my freshman year, but I want to know what you loved or love about your college experience. Did you stay on campus? Did you get an apartment close by or did you stay at home? Did you do partially online or all on campus? What did you enjoy most about your time as a college student? Give me all the deets. Luckily, I'm staying close to home but I'm still nervous to start a new chapter.

Most of my friends from high school are either taking a gap year, jumping right into their careers, or going elsewhere to study. So, I'm going into this year with a clean slate. At least, that's how I'm looking at it. This summer is pretty standard for me as far as what's already planned.

Farmer's Market days with my parents.

Gardening with my mom.

Makeup content, duh.

And hopefully lots of hikes with my older brother.

Oh, and I'm going to do some of the Summer Concert Series nights this year. I wasn't able to go to any of those last summer and I was seriously bummed I missed out. If you're one of my local besties, make sure to let me know if I am going to be able to see you there.

Okay, I think that's it for now.

Talk soon besties!

Ash

Ashley

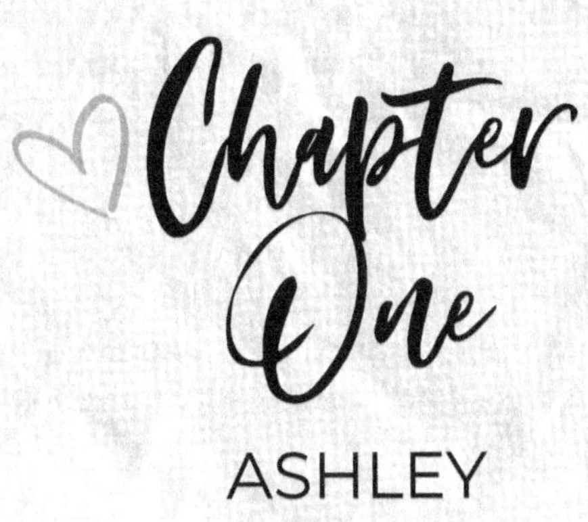

# Chapter One

## ASHLEY

### SUMMER BEFORE FRESHMAN YEAR IN COLLEGE

**CINNAMON BUN COLD BREW**

*Social Post: I think I may be ready to choose my major. I've been debating between business and marketing for a while but I think business will help me more in the long run. Now that's one thing off of my infinitely huge list that needs to happen this summer #ashleydoesmakeup #dailythoughts #collegeprep #csu #coloradogirl #checklisttime #businessmajor*

*Image Description: CSU brochures next to my coffee mug from a local coffee shop.*

I close out of Instagram and then open the email from the admin offices again. I've been bouncing between these two options for months. I think going with the business major

and adding in the marketing classes that will benefit me most will be my best option. I can always adjust things in a semester or two—or five—if I need to. I'm already planning to add in my esthetician license once I graduate. I'm not 100% sure what my career will look like in five years, but I know it's going to have something to do with makeup and skincare.

Shocker, I know.

But seriously, I'm so ready to turn this into a career. And something I can build up more than just a few social media posts a week. My older brother, Matt, has told me he is going to help me with the marketing side of things once I decide what I want to do. He's absolutely brilliant at what he does, so I'm excited to have his support. He's a genius with technology and pretty much any online platform. I just need to figure out what *I'm* doing first.

Summer is going to absolutely fly by and I want to focus on one more summer of not worrying about "adult responsibilities."

And I think I'm okay with that.

I was right: the summer flew by, and now I'm heading to the admin offices of CSU to finalize my class schedule. The drive is pretty easy from my parent's house in Windsor to the campus in Fort Collins. I love the mix of older buildings and the "old town" feel of Fort Collins within the newer buildings and updated signage. There's so many restaurants and places to explore by the campus. Not that there aren't plenty of those in Windsor too. It'll be fun to have an excuse to be down here several days a week. Especially since the schedule I'm going with includes a few gap hours between classes, so I'll have some down time that I can go to a coffee shop or one of the parks close to campus.

"Did you need to bring anything with you to this meeting today, or did they get all of your info online already?" my mom asks me as we pull into the huge parking lot in front of the administration offices. Most of the rest of this college experience will be solo, but

Mom really wanted to come with me today. And it's nice to have her by my side when trying new things.

Don't get me wrong, I am not shy by any means. I can talk to anyone and rarely feel overwhelmed or out of place. Pretty much the exact opposite of my brother. Our parents are both a happy medium to that, so we are well balanced with their reactions and encouragement to find our own comfort levels.

I make myself busy by pulling up the emailed appointment from the admin offices to double check where we are heading on campus. "It looks like everything is already set up," I explain. "We need to head to the main building, check in, and then we will be able to meet with my advisor. After we confirm the schedule, we will get anything else I need before the semester starts. After this initial semester, I should be able to do most of this fully on my own unless I have questions or need something else."

Mom parks the car and we just sit for a moment before she turns off the car. Yay for air conditioning, because it is absolutely gross outside. "Are you sure you want to stay at home for this first semester?" she asks gently. "I know we've talked about it, but I don't want you missing out on any of the college experience. You thrive when you are with other people and experiencing new things. And I don't want you to feel like you're missing out halfway through the year." She pivots to face me in her seat so she can gauge how I am feeling about all of this. I take a moment to think it over again as well as the reasons she just gave.

"I really appreciate that, Mom. Truly. But I think I want to keep this first semester light. There's going to be so much to get the hang of, and I want to be able to disconnect from 'school brain' a bit if I need to by coming home. I'm definitely up for discussing other options next semester. But I want to be home this year. The drive isn't far and there's plenty of places on campus and around the area that I can use to have that 'college experience' if something changes." I rest my hand on hers and give her a light squeeze to cement in what I said.

My parents have always been super supportive, and they have taken the time to make sure we think through decisions and their potential results of those decisions. I know not everyone has this and I'm super grateful that I do. "Let's do this and then go find some lunch in one of these places that are outside of walking distance. I have a feeling I'll be eating at the Subway across the street often."

We chuckle together as we get out of the car and start walking toward the building. "I can always dig out your unicorn lunch box from when you were in elementary school and pack you a lunch every day." Mom bumps her shoulder with mine as she places her keys inside of her purse.

I make a face like I'm actually considering her offer before I respond, "maybe after a few weeks. Don't want all the cool kids to feel out of place because they haven't had the chance to show off their cool lunch boxes and backpacks first."

We have to hold back the laughter once we get to the heavy glass doors at the front of the building. I am a college student now and want to make a decent first impression. I smirk at my mom as I notice she's trying to also put on her "official business" face too.

Check-in is simple and soon we are waiting for my appointment. The waiting area only has a few other students waiting and a handful of faculty members going over class preparations at the end of the room. The space is open and has lots of windows. At least it doesn't feel like a doctor's office waiting room.

I find a couple of open seats within the eye line of the receptionist so I make sure I will hear and see her when she calls for our turn. Mom settles between me and another parent. I'm assuming it's a parent anyway; they're sitting next to a guy around my age and frantically shuffling through papers and folders in their bag. Mom turns her phone on silent before tapping my phone as a reminder to do the same. No clue why I forget to do that all of the time.

"Is it your first year too?" Mom immediately starts up a conversation with the mother next to her.

The lady smiles at her and sighs a bit. "Yes, how can you tell?" she laughs lightly in response. "I just don't know how they're supposed to get all of this figured out in eight semesters. There's so many options and specialties to choose from. It's overwhelming."

The guy next to her leans in to enter the conversation. "They do this every day for hundreds of students. They know what they're doing. And the options won't feel as overwhelming once I pick a focus area or what I'm wanting to do after graduation."

"He's definitely right," my mom encourages. "This first semester is a great starter to the routines of college and seeing what the basics of their chosen major is. Ashley went with a really broad major so we went through and picked things that will work with her pre-requisites as well as with a variety of career paths."

I lean myself forward so I can make eye contact with the two sitting next to us. "I'm Ashley and a business major. What about you?"

The guy around my age leans over to stretch out his hand to shake mine. "I'm Sam and same. Are you from around here?"

"Yep. I live about twenty minutes away from here so I am living at home this semester. What about you?"

"I live here in Fort Collins so I'll be staying at home, too. I have a job close to my house most afternoons and weekends, so I wanted to keep some of my routines the same."

"Totally get that." I'm just about to ask to exchange information when the receptionist comes out from behind her desk with a folder of papers in her hand.

"Samuel Jones, Miss Chelsea is ready for you."

"Good luck! And maybe I'll see you around." I smile up at him while he stands and helps his mom get her papers together. He's tall—like, really tall. Up against his mom and seeing him stand in front of me, Sam has to be at least 6'4". His green eyes pop behind his dark-rimmed glasses and even though his eye color doesn't fit the mold, he reminds me of Clark Kent. I have to bite my tongue to avoid saying just that when I realize he's noticed my staring.

"Sounds good, Ashley. If we finish up around the same time, maybe we can compare schedules and meet up some time," he offers with a smirk.

I smile in response as they walk to the office together. As soon as the door closes I feel a sharp jab in my side.

"Oww, what was that for?" I don't even need to look at her to know that Mom is smiling and she has just poked me in the side with her finger.

"He's cute..." she trails off, obviously waiting for me to respond.

"I have been a college student for literally negative days. Let me chill for a bit before you start asking about a boyfriend, Mother," I joke with her. "I wasn't in a rush to date in high school and I'm the same now. It'll happen when it happens and he may just be a good friend."

"Your brother would call him Clark Kent. I wonder if his hair curls a bit if it gets just a little longer."

"Ashley Carter? Mr. Johnson will see you now."

"Saved by the receptionist." Mom smiles down at me as she stands and offers me a hand. I have no clue why. We are the same height at 5'4". I love standing next to my mom. It's like looking at an older version of myself. She has light brown hair, which matches my natural color when I'm not all bleached and highlighted. And her brown eyes match mine and Matt's. She's got the beginning signs of aging with the laugh lines around her eyes and a couple of light age spots on her forehead. We really do need to have a discussion about daily sunscreen application.

"Let's go get signed up for the semester," I say brightly, linking my arm through hers as we make our way to the office and officially start the college years of my life.

Ashley

WED   THU   FRI   SAT   SUN        DATE

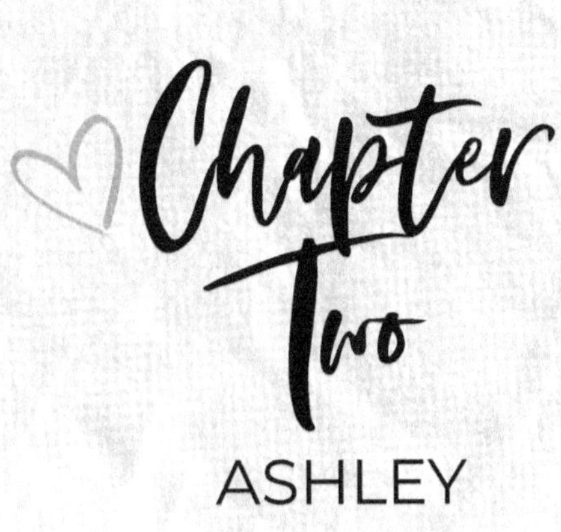

# Chapter Two

## ASHLEY

### FRESHMAN YEAR

**MEDIUM COLD BREW LESS ICE; EXTRA, EXTRA WHOLE MILK**

*Social Post: It's orientation day! I'm officially a college student and can't wait to see where these next four years take me. Super nervous but super ready to tackle this thing. Have a great day, besties! #csustudent #nocogirl #justme #makeupandmochas #ashleydoesmakeup*

*Image Description: Mirror selfie in my full-length mirror in my bedroom. I'm wearing a pair of straight leg jeans and an oversized mauve tee.*

Why are there so many cars in this parking lot? Okay, that's a stupid question. Everyone is here for the same thing as me. Of course it's a full parking lot. I need to make sure I get here earlier than fifteen minutes before class moving forward. I don't want to park all the way next to the street and have to take the two minutes before class catching my breath instead of socializing.

I circle the parking lot again before finding a spot close to the staff parking. This should work okay. I back into the spot and then take a second to touch up my lip gloss.

Me: Hey mom. I'm here. Heading inside for orientation. I'll text you when I am heading home.

Mom: Sounds good. Have fun.

I smile at her message before putting my phone in my back pocket. Car is locked. Keys in purse. Purse on arm. Okay, that's everything. I am halfway to the building when I hear my phone "ding" with another incoming message.

Mom: Put your phone on silent. ;)

I laugh out loud and turn my phone on silent before returning it to my pocket. I am definitely going to be the one person in class that gets in trouble for their cell going off at some point this semester. I tend to leave my phone laying around at home and can never find it afterwards, so I keep the sound on so we can find it.

Once I get inside, I follow the flow of students wandering toward what I'm assuming is the space where we are supposed to be meeting.

"Are you here for freshman orientation?" I ask the guy standing next to me while we are waiting to be funneled into the doors ahead of us. I should probably confirm I'm in the right spot before sitting through the wrong meeting.

"Yeah. I was here yesterday getting my schedule and my advisor walked me through the building as part of our tour. There are way more people here than I thought there would be," he comments to me as we continue walking. I'm about to respond when someone pulls him away into a loud conversation and lots of excited back slapping. Okay, guess he has friends here already. I quickly find a seat about halfway up the bowl of theater style seats, all the way on the left so I can be close to a walkway when it's time to leave, but still a good space to see everything.

"Is this seat taken?" The voice sounds familiar, even though I've only heard it once. I smile up at Sam standing next to me.

"Does that line usually work for you?"

"Oh good, it is you," he chuckles as he places his phone in the pocket of his messenger bag.

"That could've been really awkward for you."

"So…can I sit?"

"Oh yeah, sorry about that." I scooch over to the next chair so he can have the one on the end. His legs are long enough that the extra stretch space will probably be a necessity for him. "Did you get your schedule all figured out the other day?" I try to keep the conversation going as Sam sets his bag on the floor and pulls out a notebook.

"Yeah. I have five classes this semester and they are all the basic ones we each have to take for our major, so I'm hoping there's some flexibility if I end up changing my mind down the road. What about you?"

"I've got six. But I'm not working this semester and one of them is a class I kind of already took in high school as an elective, so it should be easy for me. Can I see your schedule?" He passes over his notebook and I take a quick glance at the classes listed. "It looks like we are both in the Tuesday/Thursday lecture class with Professor Johnson for Online Business Marketing. That should be a fun class."

"I had a friend take it last year and they really enjoyed the content and the presentation. I was hoping to get Professor Johnson for that one. He's been here for like ten years and does a lot of the marketing classes. He's super hands-on and up to date with current market trends, so we won't have to listen to classes on how to use Clip Art or Word Art."

I don't catch it in time. I laugh. Out loud. Louder than what would be considered ladylike. I slap my hand over my mouth and look over at Sam, my eyes wide with mortification. This room is so full of people, and I don't even want to know how many eyes are staring at me right now. He just smiles at me before using his pointer finger to link with my hand and pull it away from my face.

"And now you have lip gloss all over your hands." He smiles at me before reaching into his bag and pulling out a tissue for me. I nod a "thank you" and wipe off my hand and lightly around my lips, just in case I smudged that too. "And they're already preoccupied with their other conversations. No need to be embarrassed."

"Thank you. I tend to be a little on the 'too loud' side of things so I try to be aware when I'm in spaces that wouldn't exactly like that. And this is definitely one of those spaces."

"I think you're good. And apparently you feel the same way I do about Clip Art. The newspaper that I work for still has one editor who insists on using it for his sections and it drives me nuts. Do we not have the budget for Canva yet?"

"Completely agree. And that's awesome that you work for a newspaper. I'd love to hear more about what you do and how you got into that." I place the used tissue into my bag at my feet right as several aids come down the aisles passing out packets. We take the packets and continue passing them down the aisle.

"I have to leave as soon as this is over to get to an interview I have set up with someone across campus. Can I get your number so we can maybe sit together for class next week?" Sam opens his notebook to a blank page, and part of me absolutely loves that he didn't pull his phone out.

"Guess we're doing this the old-fashioned way then?" I pull out my gel pen from my bag and jot down my number and email. "That way you have it in case we need to share notes for class." He smiles back at me behind his glasses as he pulls the papers out of his packet. And then the faculty arrives, and it's time to fully pay attention.

Ashley

WED   THU   FRI   SAT   SUN        DATE

# Chapter Three

## ASHLEY

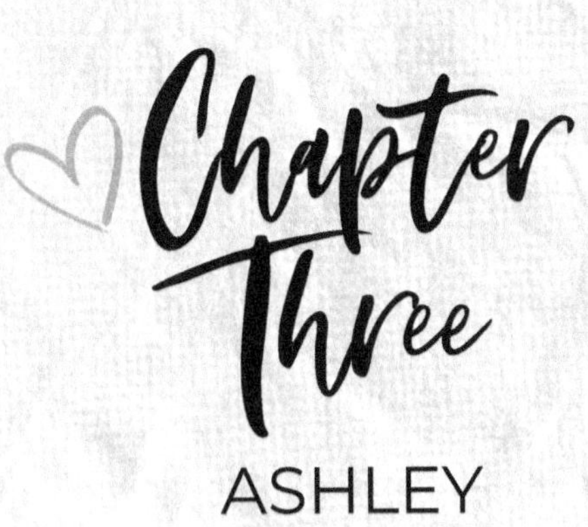

**BROWN SUGAR LATTE**

*Social Post: What does one wear to a college football game? I don't know any of the players personally and I really don't want to wear a jersey. Help!! #csu #footballfit #collegefootball #coloradogirl #nocogirl*

*Image Description: Random clothes all over my bed. And I mean all over my bed. I can't even see my cute blue bedspread under all of this.*

"Ugh, I don't want to do this." I'm pouting and I know it. I flop myself onto my bed. Well, I guess the more accurate description would be onto my clothes on top of my bed. My bed is somewhere under here. "Why is picking out an outfit for a college social event so hard?" I ask the room. I fish my phone out from underneath the copious amounts of sweatshirts next to my pillows to text Sam.

Me: Seriously, what am I supposed to wear to this thing tonight?

Sam: It's a football game, not a fashion show. Wear jeans and a sweatshirt. Dress comfy and warm. It's oddly cold outside today.

Me: You're no fun.

Sam: Then why are you texting me these questions? I'm a guy. I wear jeans and a T-shirt most days. Except for when I have an interview or presentation at work then it's slacks and a button down.

Me: No tie?

Sam: We're getting off topic. Show me three options for a sweater or something and I'll pick. How's that sound?

Me: Fine

<Sends pictures>

Sam: Go with the green sweater. It's school colors and you look good in it.

Me: Just good?

Sam: Finish getting ready. I'll be there to pick you up in thirty minutes.

Me: You're still no fun.

Sam: Muting my phone now. See you soon.

I toss my phone back onto my bed and quickly strip out of the blue camisole I was wearing temporarily. He's right, it's weirdly cold today. Mid-September usually means we are still in mostly summer temps, but it's in the fifties today and a little windy. After putting on the green sweater, I take a look at the finished fit in the full-size mirror on the back of my door. He's right—I do look good in this. Emerald green is one of my best colors. It contrasts beautifully with my light hair and brown eyes. I need to add a bit of green to this eyeshadow look to pull it all together. And it reminds me of Sam's eyes too. He does have really pretty eyes.

Fifteen minutes later, I am ready to go. I toss some emergency cash into my purse and a couple instant hand warmer packets. I really hate being cold. I debate grabbing a pair of gloves, but then decide that I should be fine with my jacket and pockets. It's only September. I do not need my winter coat yet.

I head down the stairs to grab a water bottle from the kitchen before Sam gets here. My parents are both in the kitchen, chopping up veggies for dinner and sharing a bottle of wine.

"Date night tonight?" I ask them as I pull my reusable water bottle from the dishwasher and fill it with water. I lost another sticker in the last wash and this thing is seriously looking rough. I need to check my stash to see what else I can put on here, or maybe it's time to clean off the whole thing and start over.

They wait for me to turn back around before they continue the conversation. "Yep, it's Friday night. Nancy and Charles from next door are coming over for dinner and then we are going to watch the game from the comfort of our living room," my mom adds onto her response. She doesn't like being cold either.

"That'll be fun. Their son is going to school out of state, right?"

"He's going to the University of North Carolina for pre-med."

"If any more of your friend's kids start college, there's going to be a lot of info for you to keep track of." I have to hold in my laughter as I continue my train of thought.

"I think there's five schools total between all of the families in the neighborhood, as of right now anyway," Dad offers. "Three of them are in Colorado so that makes it easy to remember." Dad takes another sip of his wine before adding the sliced peppers to the bowl he's working out of. "Sam is coming to get you for the game tonight, right?"

"Yep," I respond as I snag a couple bell pepper strips from the bowl. "He should be here pretty soon and then we are heading over. He was in Windsor for some newspaper things earlier this afternoon, so our house is on his way to pick me up before we head to the stadium. And he said it's no biggie to bring me home. I don't know if we are staying for the whole thing, but we wanted to check out a home game before it gets so cold that I won't enjoy it."

"I trust you and I know you can take care of yourself, but he won't be drinking right? It's Friday night and you'll be close to campus. I need to make sure you will be safe to come home." The "dad voice" is out in full force now.

"Yes. He's the same age as me so neither of us can legally drink anyway. And he writes enough stories about local DUI cases that he says he won't ever risk it. If something changes, I have your number and Uber. I've got this, Dad. No stress." I lean over to kiss him on the cheek and snag another pepper from the bowl before Mom has a chance to slap my hand away.

"You're my little girl—I will always stress." And with that, the doorbell rings.

"He's just a friend, but do you want to come meet him before we leave?" I offer before picking up my things and heading toward the front entryway.

"If he steps in, I'm happy to say hi, but I don't want to be too much the first time you bring a boy home." Dad winks at me as he stands with me to walk me out.

"I've brought guys home before," I counter just as we reach the door and I lean to unlock the deadbolt.

"Your brother's friends that took you to prom because you didn't like any of the other offers you received don't count."

"Um, hi, Ashley. How many offers are we talking about here?" Sam doesn't miss a beat in the banter between my dad and myself.

"I honestly don't remember. They were all jocks and way too full of themselves and I don't have the time for that. I much prefer the Clark Kent thing you have going on."

"There's something that makes that reference not quite work, though. Unfortunately, I need to keep my glasses on all the time or I am practically blind, and the eye color is wrong too." Without hesitating in his response, he leans forward to shake my dad's hand. "It's nice to meet you, sir, I'm Sam."

My dad nods his head in greeting back to Sam as he shakes his offered hand. "Nice to meet you too. Are you all good for tonight? We will be home watching the game so if anything changes, don't hesitate to call and we can come get you both."

"I appreciate that, but we should be good."

And I wait for it. Because I know my dad, and any moment now he is going to do his weird little quirk to see if Sam is going to pass the "test." I pretend my shoes are super interesting as the "prolonged eye contact" begins. I hear my mom stifling laughter behind me and then I totally lose it. My dad rests his hand on my shoulder and squeezes lightly, "Have fun you two."

I give him a side hug and wave to my mom as I lead Sam outside.

"I feel like I just missed a major inside joke in there…" Sam trails off as we make our way to his car. He pulls my door open for me and I smile at him as I get settled into my seat. I wait until he's in the driver's seat next to me and has the car started before I respond.

"My dad has this weird, quirky thing where he gives new people awkward levels of eye contact. It's to see if they match his energy or something like that. And it's an easy little marker to see if someone can still be respectful even when moderately uncomfortable." I rub my hands together to warm them from just those few short moments outside. I really should have grabbed a pair of gloves.

"So, does that mean I passed?" Sam asks as he reaches in front of me to open the glove compartment and pulls out a pack of new light colored gloves.

"What are these for?" I ask as I take a look at the gloves. These aren't cheap ones. They have the special finger things so you can still use your phone but aren't too bulky so I can keep them in my purse easily, or my coat pocket. And they're the most perfect taupe color. They're going to go with everything but are dark enough that they shouldn't show some little stains that are inevitably going to happen, like coffee drips.

"I've only known you for a couple of weeks, but I already know how cold you get. It happens when you are on your laptop for a long time too. Figured you needed a new pair of gloves and tonight would be a good chance to break them in. But you didn't answer my question yet—did I pass?" He smirks at me as he stops at a light.

I smile back at him as I slip the gloves on my hands and then drop the label into my purse to throw away later. "Yes, you passed. It's a privilege though, so don't get too cocky. It can be revoked." I pretend to be serious as I point my finger at him like I'm scolding him.

Sam throws his head back and laughs. "Noted. I will carry the responsibility with the appropriate amount of reverence and expectation."

"Nice vocabulary there, Superman." I chuckle to myself and then we settle into comfortable silence until we get to the stadium.

There are so many people here. I knew there would be, but this feels excessive. It's the first home football game of the season. And our team is shaping up to be a pretty strong contender this season—at least, that's what Dad was saying earlier this week. I'm not usually one to follow sports, but I want a well-rounded college experience this semester, so here I am. Sam doesn't play sports either, but he was more than willing to check it out with me tonight. He talked to his paper to see if he could do a small column on a weekly look at CSU and student life. This week the topic was pretty much set for him – football. It made our plans for tonight easy, but really, football? Yay.

I normally have zero issue being around people and crowds, but this feels overboard, even to me. "I don't think I've ever seen this many people in one space before," I lean over to tell Sam as we grab our things from the security check at the doors before heading to where our seats should be.

"I got to go to a few pro games last year with my dad. That beat out this crowd in terms of size but knowing that there are this many people within a short drive of here…" He trails off as he shakes his head. "You're right, it feels overboard." Sam smiles down at me. "Let's find our seats so we can start people watching."

"You do know me so well!"

The game is uneventful. I was honestly expecting more, but I'm glad we went. It was a fun night and we got to see our team in action. We ended up sitting next to a few other freshmen that are in one of Sam's classes, so the conversation flowed well most of the night. They're probably not people we will be hanging out with on the regular, but not people I want to run away from either. Our team wins the first home game 21-17. By the end of the fourth quarter, I am cheering and getting excited for our guys to add that win to their record for the year.

"I'm going to head to the bathroom before I take you back home. Do you want to meet me at the car or do you want to walk with me?" Sam holds his hand down to me to help me up from the bleachers.

"Next game, do not let me sit that long. My butt hurts." I laugh as I walk in place for a few steps to bring circulation back into my legs.

"Well, it's killing me," he winks down at me and I groan.

"You did not just say that!" I shriek at him. I playfully slap his arm closest to me but reach over to link my arm with his as we make our way down the steps. We head back to the bathrooms—him to go right inside the door, me to wait in line, typical.

I pull out my phone to go through a few of the photos that I took tonight to pick something for my stories. I settle on a cute pic of my gloved hands holding my cup of hot cocoa with the field in the background—not bad for a phone pic. I add a quick caption and post it before heading into the bathroom. I've been working on being more consistent with posting since the beginning of the summer with a mix of makeup and skincare content and then things from daily life. I'm finding my "social media voice" and really enjoying it. I started the summer with 5,000 followers and a halfway decent engagement rate and I'm already up to 10,000. I'm excited to see where it goes from here with continued consistency.

I finish up in the bathroom and touch up my lip gloss again before heading out to meet Sam. He's waiting just outside holding up his CSU sweatshirt for me. "Put this on before you start shaking please."

"Ooh, the dad voice," I joke back at him, "I really am okay." My arms are covered in goosebumps, despite the sweater. I was fine until I got up from my seat and wasn't under the stadium lights anymore.

"You'll be more okay once you're in the warm car, but that's still a few minutes away. I'll feel better if I know you aren't uncomfortable. Please." He holds it up again and helps me into it as I concede.

"Thank you, Sam. You're gonna have my perfume on this jacket for days now. You've been warned." I link my arm in his offered one again as he tucks his notebook into his other hand along with his keys.

"You say that like it's a bad thing."

The walk to the car is in comfortable silence and I am thankful for the heated seats in Sam's car as we make our way back to my house.

"Did you get enough to work on your story for this weekend?" I ask Sam as I pull my phone out of my bag to check the notifications from my last post.

"Yeah, I should be all set. I have a few photos that I can include for the web version of the story and then a few different ways I can take the story depending on what my editor wants this week. Being able to follow along with my own college journey this year is going to make this process a lot easier. At least, that's the hope."

"I like that you have the freedom to do that right now while you figure out what you are wanting to do. It's like your own platform to share your interests and explore what works for you."

"Exactly. Like what you are doing on social media. I love seeing the different things you share. Not everything is for me, no offense to your cut crease tutorial, but I enjoy how you show up online."

"Hey—you can listen to the skincare videos and content. Everyone needs skincare, even if they don't wear makeup," I scold back at him, "but I'm glad you are enjoying my content. You don't tend to share a lot on social media, so I will have to make do with our study sessions and your weekly stories."

WED    THU    FRI    SAT    SUN              DATE

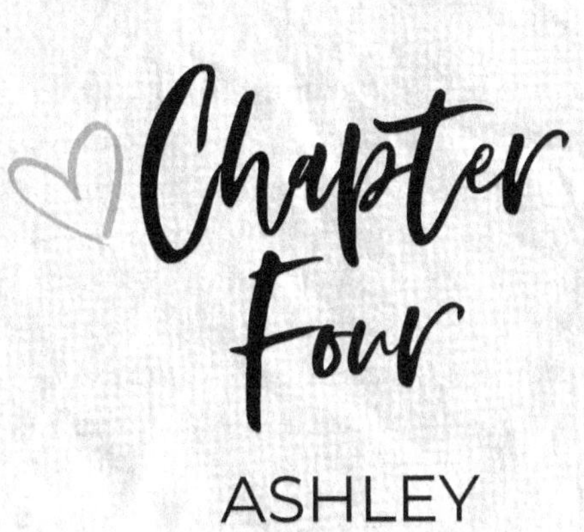

# Chapter Four

## ASHLEY

**KOREAN APPLE TEA WITH GINGER AND CINNAMON**

*Social Post: Get ready with me to head to a full day of classes on campus. Dressing in layers is a must since the temperature outside is so different than inside. And even different classrooms are different temperatures too. Add to that my school and snack bags. It's a process to make sure I'm ready to be on campus for several hours for my classes. Tuesdays are my full days with three classes and a study session in between with a few friends. What do you think? #ashleydoesmakeup #coloradogirl #dailyfit #collegefit #csugirl #mirrorselfie*

*Image Description: Full-mirror selfie of me in my bedroom. Black leggings with a black tee and oversized baby blue cardigan. My blonde hair is pulled up in a messy ponytail showing off my simple diamond stud earrings.*

This semester is seriously flying by. I knew the school schedule would be a different pace to get used to, but between family things, school, extracurricular activities,

and my content—it's been a very full few months. I'm loving it though and am definitely glad I went with staying at home this semester. If nothing else, that twenty-minute drive home has been helpful to have some unplugged time to decompress and get ready for the next thing. My parents let me have my own space when I'm home, but I like being around them. So it tends to be a little of my time working on projects and then seeing what they are working on.

Right now, our time has been spent getting ready for Halloween. And Halloween is not a small holiday to my parents—or anyone on their street actually. It's a big event for all of the families and a great chance to see everyone again. We live on a quiet cul-de-sac so kids are able to go house to house safely. And we usually have some tables of apple cider and hot cocoa too so parents can chat while the older kids go to each house on the street. With two weeks until the holiday, décor is in full swing and we are finalizing the extras that we will have with a few other families.

This year Nancy and Charles, along with my parents, are hosting the refreshment tables. Baked goods, drinks, and a couple first aid kits will be there for the families that come to our street. I cannot bake to save my life, so I'm going to help man the table and make sure everyone is taken care of. I'm hoping Sam will come hang out with me, but we haven't talked about it yet. I wouldn't say we are "dating," but I wouldn't be upset if it moved that way. I enjoy spending time with him and things have started getting flirty with our conversation.

I get to campus early so I have a few minutes to check notifications and breathe before I head in for my first class with Professor Johnson and Sam. With the posting consistency, the comments have started growing pretty steadily too. Nothing too crazy yet, but I try to stay on top of it. It helps me see what is being engaged with so I know what is working and what people want to see more of. So far, people seem to like the mix of college and makeup content. Which works for me.

There are a few more comments to go through than I was expecting with that last post based on the notification number when I open the app. Weird. It was just an OOTD post.

CO2478: This color looks really good on you, Ashley. You should wear it more often.

Samtheman62: Don't forget your gloves in your car again before coming in for class. It's freezing in here today.

I smile at the comment from Sam. He loves to moderately troll me in the comments—usually with things that only partially relate to my post. There's a few more comments asking about outfit details or which class I'm loving the most—basic stuff that is pretty much always there. I scroll through the rest of them really quickly before heading inside to class.

Sam was right, it is freezing in here!

"Is the heater broken or is this man from Antarctica?" I aggressively whisper to Sam as I find my seat next to his. He has to stifle his laughter as he passes me a coffee cup from the on-campus coffee shop.

"I think he's from the North East somewhere, so not Antarctica. And this is one of the older buildings on campus, so the heater doesn't always cooperate. Hence my reminder to grab your gloves before coming inside." He smiles approvingly as I pull them out of my bag and put them on my hands. I must have poor circulation or something because I seriously get so cold. I will need to start doubling up my socks soon because my feet get just as bad as my hands.

"What are your plans for Halloween?" I ask Sam as I get my laptop powered up and my notes for the class ready to go. He gets to class earlier than I do so he already is fully settled and just waiting on me. It's kind of cute.

"I hadn't thought about it. The paper has a few events they are going to report on, so I will find out tomorrow if I'm handling any of those. What about you?"

"I'll be at my parent's house. Halloween is a big neighborhood event for them so I'll be helping out with the first aid kits and just overseeing things. If you don't have a story to cover, would you like to come hang out with me?"

"Welcome back to class, everyone. Please make your way to your seats if you aren't already there. We have a lot of material to cover today as we begin our breakdown of the difference between paid and organic marketing on social media." Professor Johnson does not waste any time. He always jumps right into what he is going to be covering the second his business shoes cross the threshold into the room.

As he powers up his laptop and gets it connected to the smart board, Sam looks over at me, "I'd love to come hang out with you for Halloween. I'll text you after the meeting tomorrow to let you know what the plan is."

"Perfect." And then the worst thing happens. Well, not the actual worst, but it feels that way. My phone dings. Multiple times! What the heck? I dig in my bag to find it and turn it on silent before taking a quick look to see what on earth that was for. It's just more Instagram notifications, those can wait. I slip my phone back into my bag and pray that no one else heard the obnoxious notifications.

As I look around the room, I realize I was not so lucky. It feels like every single person in this room is staring at me. Like no one has ever forgotten to turn their phone on silent before. Geeze, guys. But Professor Johnson is also looking at me. Borderline glaring at me. He takes his class time very seriously and I just disrespected him by not being "fully ready to listen and learn." He is a little militant, but he does an amazing job, so it's something no one pushes him on. Except me today, apparently.

"I'm sorry, sir," I tell him, loud enough that he can hear me, but hopefully quiet enough to convey my remorse. I feel awful.

"Please be sure your devices are powered off or on silent before next class, Miss Carter. You aren't the only one in this room and it's no one else's business what others need you so desperately for this morning."

And I feel like I'm about four years old now. Awesome. I bow my head to look at my laptop and take a few deep breaths. I'll have to apologize to him after class because that was humiliating. And I don't want him to think I was trying to be disrespectful on purpose. He's an amazing educator and I have loved his class so far this semester.

At the end of class, I tell Sam to head over to the library and I'll meet him there in a bit so I can talk to Professor Johnson. Class went well, but I'm a bit of a people pleaser and don't handle it well when authority figures are disappointed in me. Especially over something that I can so easily take care of like putting my phone on silent. A few other students are waiting to talk to him so I hang back by the first row of chairs to wait my turn.

Professor Johnson definitely has that "greying gracefully" thing going for him. And I'm not the only one that has noticed it. He's probably in his late thirties, and there's a few girls in class that give him a little extra eye contact or the subtle touches on his arm while asking questions. Like the one talking to him right now. This girl is trying *hard* to get his attention. It's almost comical how disinterested he is. I'm actively trying to force back a laugh when he looks up from his desk and sees me waiting to talk to him. I quickly sober up my look but am surprised when I see a small smile on his face.

Oh, he knows what she is doing and he thinks it's funny too. Okay, then. I guess this isn't a new thing that he deals with. I notice the lack of a wedding ring on his hand as he hands the student he is talking to a paper from the stack in front of him. He picks up his bag from the end of his desk and begins packing up his things before he raises his head to look at me again.

"Can I help you, Miss Carter?" His tone is smooth as he calls me over. I walk the few steps to stand next to his desk.

"I just wanted to apologize for earlier. I am so bad about turning my phone on silent and I cannot believe that happened right at the beginning of class. I didn't mean to be disrespectful and I know that frustrates you. I really am sorry. I enjoy your class so much so I hope that didn't come across as disinterest because that could not be farther from the truth." I stop to take a breath and notice his dark eyes on my own.

The slight smile on his lips is mirrored in his eyes. He doesn't wear glasses so the smile lines around his eyes accentuate the amusement he expresses. "I didn't think it was done maliciously. Please make sure your phone is silenced before you enter my classroom in the future." And with that, he puts the strap of his bag over his shoulder and motions for me to walk with him out the door.

"I appreciate your understanding. I promise it won't happen again."

"Was it anything important? Usually when it's back to back sounds like that, it's more urgent," he inquires as we walk toward the library and admin offices.

"It was just Instagram. I don't usually get notifications like that from social media, so it confused me for a moment. I'll check what it was once I get to my study session with Sam."

"I hope everything is okay. I will see you Thursday." He pauses at the library door and I do the same so I can head inside for my time with Sam. "Thank you for coming to me to apologize, Miss Carter, not many would." I can't help but return the smile he offers me.

"You're welcome. I'll see you Thursday."

I quickly find the table where Sam is set up and already working. We only have about an hour together to get things done and we usually buckle down pretty quickly so we don't waste time. We have our fun hang out time after classes are over and sometimes on the weekends too.

I pull out my phone to clear those notifications before I start working on my own assignments. They're all from the same user as this morning.

> CO2478: Have you thought about letting your hair go back to its natural color this fall?

CO2478: The blonde is lovely on you, but I am curious how your features will pop against the brown hair that likes to peek through your roots when you wait too long between hair appointments.

CO2478: I do like that you keep it longer though. There are a lot more options that way.

I don't know why, but I feel uncomfortable. I block the user and delete the comments. I have enough comments that feel good and are from people I know. I don't need to have any weird energy on my page. Goodbye, strange Colorado man.

"How did the conversation go with Professor Johnson?" Sam finally asks as I put my phone down on the table in front of me, upside down.

"It was fine. I think everything will be okay now, but that was so embarrassing."

"I can imagine." He smirks at me a bit. "Maybe add a reminder to your phone to have the notifications turned off before you leave your car in the morning. I need to go grab another book really quickly, be right back." He stands up and heads toward the librarian's desk. I pull out my bag to see what I need to work on this hour. I should have gone up with him. I need another book too. I leave my bag on my chair and pocket my phone before heading to the periodical section.

It doesn't take me long to find the copies that I am needing for Professor Erickson's Colorado History class. It's both a required history credit and something I am really enjoying. Total win-win in the class department. I'm still flipping through the articles when I get back to the table. I set them down next to my laptop and go to move my bag from my seat when I notice an envelope sitting on the top. It's a plain white envelope that you would use for a bill or other random business letter.

I glance around to see who might have left it here. Sam is

perusing the periodicals where I had just been, and there are a handful of other students in the area, but no one is looking over here. I use my fingernail to pop the seal and see what's inside. There's a small note card and then a second piece of paper. I look at the note first. It's handwritten with dark ink, and the handwriting is clean and easy to read. Not gonna lie, I'm impressed by the neat print.

> *"I wanted to leave you a little pick-me-up and thought you would appreciate this. Have a great rest of your day."*

No signature. No other markings to let me know who it might be from. I pull the second piece of paper out and see it's a gift certificate to one of the coffee shops close to campus. Nice. I won't say no to free coffee. This must have been one of those "random acts of kindness" things. I'm glad I left my bag here.

"Why are you so happy?" Sam chuckles as he comes back to our table.

"I got free coffee," I reply smugly. It's mine and I'm not going to share.

"Has anyone ever told you that you have a coffee problem?"

"Yes, regularly. And I don't believe them either." I stick my tongue out at him before sitting back down and getting to work.

Ashley

WED   THU   FRI   SAT   SUN        DATE

# Chapter Five

## ASHLEY

**PUMPKIN COFFEE CRUMBLE FRAP**

*Social Post: Good afternoon everyone! Thanks for tagging along while I get ready for the Halloween festivities this evening. Do people still use that word? Festivities. It feels kind of old-fashioned but fitting for the holidays. I am going with a CSU cheerleader inspired look this year with white, gold, and green. Join my live to hang out while I get all covered in school spirit. #iglive #ashleydoesmakeup #festivities #makeupandmochas #csugirlie #coloradogirl #halloweenmakeup*

*Video Description: Makeup drawer opening to show eyeshadow palettes and blushes.*

I love doing live videos. Well, actually, I'm learning to love live videos. Especially now when there are more people actually tuning in that I'm engaging with regularly. That's why I like scheduling my lives when I can, so that way I'm not just talking to myself for thirty minutes. I finish getting my base foundation and other complexion products on before I set up to go live. I'm just going to do my eyes and finish my hair on the video.

I'm already wearing a really cute white turtleneck shirt and green pleated skater skirt. The gold is my hair as well as jewelry. White tights and black ankle booties finish off the look. I don't have an actual cheerleader outfit, I am not that athletic, so I went for a cosplay version of it. And I think I did a pretty good job. Sam should be here in about an hour, so I have enough time to go live and finish getting ready.

I take a deep breath and then hit the go live button.

"Hey everyone. I wanted to come on and hang out with you while I do my eye makeup for tonight. Thanks for tuning in. Make sure you let me know if you are watching live or catching the replay. I'd love to hear what you are doing tonight to celebrate!"

I continue with the small talk as viewers join and begin chatting with others and answering my questions. There's the few random no profile pic users that hop on to leave the random "you're so beautiful" and "I'll take you trick or treating." No, thank you. I'm just putting the finishing touches on my lashes when a familiar username pops up on my screen.

CO2479: Good afternoon, beautiful.

Did this guy seriously just create a new account with the next numerical number? I ignore his comment and grab my hairspray to tame down the baby hairs before I finish the live and head downstairs. Sam should be here soon.

CO2479: Are you going to be warm enough in that tonight?

CO2479: You haven't had the chance to get any CSU sweatshirts yet, have you?

CO2479: The color does look stunning on you, Ashley.

I can feel the chills move up my arms as the comments continue. My other followers don't seem to notice because the chatter is the same among them about their plans or the eyeshadow palette I used tonight that they want to check out. The comments are standing out to me though, and I don't like it. I need to be done for the night.

> CO2479: Will you be safe tonight?

> CO2479: I don't like the idea of
> you being out tonight.

And I'm done. I don't even say goodbye. I hurriedly stop the live stream then pull up the CO guy's account. No profile picture. No pictures posted. One account following. No accounts following them. And that's definitely a block. I make sure to press the button to block future accounts that this user creates. What a creep.

Halloween is another neighborhood success. My older brother, Matt, doesn't live far away so he drove over to help out tonight too. Last year he passed out candy at his house, but he wanted to be with us this year. I like having him close. He reminds me of a big teddy bear and I need the feeling of security he brings with me tonight.

Don't get me wrong, Sam definitely gives off the "Superman vibes" with how tall he is and how confident he comes across. But he's not my brother. Where Sam is taller and obviously muscular, he is on the lean side of things. And my brother is built like a football player. When I was little, I used to call him "Matty Bear." He does not appreciate that nickname anymore so I only use it when I need a hug or want to tease him. Matt and Sam fell into a comfortable silence together after they did the obligatory guy handshake where they both tried to appear bigger than they actually are. Again, kind of funny considering they're both big in their own ways.

They didn't have long to get to know each other before the

kids started coming and the neighborhood started buzzing. We got our first families around 5:30. The ones with little kids or those visiting their grandparents before heading back to their own neighborhoods. It doesn't slow down until after nine, and by then, I am ready to go inside and warm up. It is too cold to be out here while trying to be cute. I really should have gotten a sweatshirt to go over this turtleneck. It's thick, but not that thick.

Sam and Matt both seem to realize this at the same moment and the next thing I know, they are on opposite shoulders both reaching for me to settle their jackets on me. I start laughing hysterically while they just glare at each other.

"Okay, you've both marked your territory sufficiently. Sam, I'll take yours while we pack up if you don't mind. It's a bit warmer than Matt's." I wink at my brother before picking up a tote full of paper goods from the table and begin walking back to the house. Once I get to the front porch, my mom comes outside with a knowing smile on her face.

"How are the two of them getting along?"

"They both have been pretty quiet. I think I'm having more fun with the tension and awkwardness than they are. I can only imagine the conversation they are having now that I've walked off in Sam's jacket and not Matt's." I smirk at her as she eyes the pair over my shoulder. We can see them at the table from here, but hopefully they can't see our faces since the lights inside the house are bright behind us. They are talking, but neither is very animated. Not that either usually are regularly, but still.

"So, have you two decided to try being more than friends yet?" Mom prompts as she takes the tote from me and leads me inside.

"We haven't talked about it, honestly. I mean, I like him as a friend, but I'm not sure if I can see myself marrying him." We start putting the items from the tote away as mom turns her head to level her gaze at me.

"Who said anything about getting married? You're eighteen, Ash, you're allowed to date to have fun enjoying each other's company while going to college. You've never been impulsive exactly. Don't be stupid about decisions you make together, but you can enjoy the season of life you are in. And I think your dad and brother would agree with me."

I take in her words for a second before I respond. I don't know why I had that thought in my head about only starting to date if I felt it would be serious. I can just enjoy a relationship with him. If he even wants to take that step with me.

Apparently, my mother can now read my mind because she doesn't miss a beat in her response. "Yes, he wants to be more than friends. I think he's just waiting on a sign from you that you want to as well."

WED   THU   FRI   SAT   SUN          DATE

# Chapter Six

## ASHLEY

**SUGAR AND SPICE MOCHA**

*Social Post: Is it bad that I'm already repeating outfits for class? There's just something about having those "go to" outfits that I know I feel good in. #classfit #csu #coloradogirl #collegelife #ootd*

*Image Description: Full-mirror selfie of me in a pair of black leggings and oversized green sweater, hair is in a high ponytail and I finished off the look with black booties.*

The final weeks of the semester feel like they are flying by and dragging along all at the same time. And I hate it and love it. Finals are fast approaching, as are many of the end of semester projects. Sam and I have found a steady flow of classes, coffee dates, study sessions, and weekend brunches with my parents. It has definitely felt casual and comfortable, and I feel like I've needed that to ease into the dating world.

When I told him after Halloween that I never dated in

high school, he wasn't all that surprised. "You seem to be very comfortable hanging out with everyone. You're outgoing and can talk to anyone, but you tend to press the brakes a bit when you start getting too close. I'm happy to stay friends if that is what you would like, but I would be lying if I said I didn't want to be more with you, Ashley."

And I was a melty puddle. How was I even supposed to respond to that? So, after picking my jaw up off the floor, I simply nodded and laced my fingers in his as he pulled me in for a hug. I was already in his jacket, again. I loved that thing and never wanted to give it back. And having the smell of his cologne, a mix of whiskey and wood, wrapped around me in his arms and the jacket, was the best way to end that conversation.

Since then, there have been lots of cuddles on the couch while watching a movie, holding hands while walking around campus, and late-night phone calls. And kisses. Lots and lots of kisses. Kissing Sam is like getting lost in the best kind of daydream. I loved the feeling of him holding me close while he explored my mouth with his own. Him being so much taller than me is amazing. And a little awkward too. I learned quickly that just leaning my head back while he kissed me got to be really uncomfortable really quickly. So now, I usually end up halfway on his lap while we are on the couch watching something after dinner and studying.

And that's where we were right now. We just finished up the final project due in Professor Johnson's class. A full marketing breakdown of a brand we follow on social media. It was a really cool project with a very practical application. Seeing what the brands we love are doing and how it works in real life is probably more beneficial than some of the other outdated textbooks that the other marketing professors taught out of. I had done my breakdown on a woman-owned makeup brand based out of New York and Sam chose an online newspaper that's been putting out more social media content to appeal to younger readers.

The projects were interesting to both of us, so it didn't take us long. And now all that stands between us and the end of the semester is turning in this project and taking the last few finals tomorrow.

I lean back in Sam's arms to look at his face once the movie finishes up. "You have one other class besides Professor Johnson's tomorrow, right?" He replies with a nod and a soft humming sound. "I just have that one tomorrow and I am done. I'm so ready to have a break from all of the class requirements. Even if it is just for a few weeks." His hand stroking my hair relaxes me back into his shoulder as I snuggle in and just enjoy the settled feeling he brings me.

"Can I still come over and see you over break?" he whispers into my hair. I almost headbutt him in the nose from turning my head so fast and immediately adjust so I can see his eyes with my own.

"Did I give you some impression that I don't want you coming over once classes are done for the semester?"

"Not at all. But I wasn't sure if your family had plans or what you wanted to do before we do this all over again in January." His smile is reassuring as he starts playing with my hair. He loves doing that. I've taken to leaving it down so he can run his fingers through it when we are at my house.

"I would like to keep doing this over break. We tend to have quiet holidays. Well, not quiet. You can see how much Christmas threw up all over my parent's house," I say as I motion my arms to show all of the everything that is set up for Christmas. My mother loves Christmas and it becomes Christmas at our house on November first every year. Decorating usually takes us a full weekend, at least!

Sam just chuckles in agreement with me. "Okay, Ash. I'd really like that too." He places a chaste kiss on my lips and then my cheek before he helps me stand as he does the same. He packs up his bag as I bring my papers to the table to get ready to call it a night.

"Can I pick you up tomorrow for class? You would have to wait until I get out of my other class before I could bring you home, but I would like to take you to lunch before I go to work if that works for you," he asks as we make our way to the front door.

"I'd like that. I'll be ready."

"No, you won't," he chuckles into my lips. "I'll call you when I leave my house so you have a fifteen-minute warning. And I expect you to be bundled up and ready to go when I get here."

"Or what?" I tease back at him as he kisses me again before stepping onto the front step.

"You aren't ready to play that game, Ashley." And then he winks at me before walking to his car.

Well what the heck is that supposed to mean? And why do I kind of like the sound of that?

I surprise pretty much everyone when I am already awake and getting ready when Sam calls me in the morning. I even have time to make myself, and him, a cup of coffee before he gets to the house. I had unlocked the front door when I came downstairs a few minutes ago and let Sam know via text so I'm not surprised when the front door opens.

"I'm in the kitchen. What do you want in your coffee today?" I holler over my shoulder as I hear his footsteps inside the house.

"Just whatever you are having today is fine," he smiles at me and I immediately notice the box he's holding.

"If that is already my Christmas present, I hate to tell you this, but you still have a couple of weeks."

"Well, this one isn't from me. It was on your front porch. Amazon must have left it late last night after I took off or has already been by this morning. Why don't you see what's inside while I keep the car running. It's cold out there today." He sets the box on the table and then takes the travel cup from me as he leaves a quick kiss on my forehead. I love forehead kisses. And he knows it.

I pull the kitchen shears out of the knife block on the counter to slice through the tape on the box. It's addressed to me and I don't recognize the company sender. It probably is Amazon, but I don't remember ordering anything. It was probably Matt. That man is always online and tends to just buy me stuff if he sees something he thinks I will like or I can use. And he's almost always right.

Inside the box is the standard brown packing paper and below that is a garment bag. Like one of those really nice garment bags that gowns and expensive sweaters come in. I do a little happy dance before reaching inside to pull it out. Inside is the most gorgeous purple jacket I've ever seen in my life! It's pea coat length and insanely warm. I quickly put it on and already know this is going to be a favorite winter wardrobe item for me for years.

I peek back in the box as I grab my coffee and bag just to see if there is a note inside.

"I saw this and thought of you. Hopefully you don't have to borrow other people's jackets anymore."

Yeah, this was definitely Matt. I chuckle to myself and then hurry outside to a warm car, enjoying the warmth of my new jacket the entire sixty second walk.

"I guess my brother got tired of seeing me in your jackets and got me another one of my own," I joke with Sam as I get settled into the car. "I'm going to live in this thing this winter. It's so insanely warm."

He just laughs at me. "I guess I can't be mad that he's taking care of you, but I'd be lying if I said I won't miss seeing you in my clothes."

It doesn't take long for us to find a parking spot close to the building and make our way inside. Students have already started going home for the break so the parking lot has more empty spaces than usual. As we make our way into the building and to Professor Johnson's class, I am once again thankful for the new jacket. It's perfect for the colder temperatures and isn't too bulky. Finding seats is seamless since it's the final day. We turn in our final projects as we get into the classroom and then make our way to the end of the second row of desks. This final should be pretty easy since its basic marketing and online strategies. And turning in our brand breakdowns is a big piece of this grade too.

I'm going over a few of my study cards when Professor Johnson makes his way into the classroom. I quickly pull out my phone to make sure it's on silent and Sam chuckles quietly as he notices. I had posted a selfie of me in my new jacket on the way to campus. There's just something about car lighting that makes for amazing selfies.

"You're not going to let yourself be embarrassed by that again, are you?"

"Um, no. That was so awkward. I don't want any professor to think that I don't appreciate them or their classes. It feels super disrespectful to me."

"I don't think it's that serious, Ash. He deals with kids our age all the time. I'm sure you aren't the first one to forget to turn off your ringer on your phone and you absolutely won't be the last."

"I get that. I still don't want to do it again." By then, I've started warming up from the outside chill, so I slip the coat off of my shoulders and settle it on my chair. I shiver slightly with the temperature change and decide to put the coat on my lap to cover my legs. I'm in jeans, but I still feel a little cold.

"I may need to see about getting a pair of light gloves for next semester. The taupe ones you got me are great for outside, but I think they might be too thick for typing. I don't like how cold my fingers get when I'm typing."

"I'll add it to your Christmas list," Sam jokes before putting away his notes and motioning for me to do the same.

Ashley

# Chapter Seven

## HIM

She looks amazing in my jacket.

I knew she would. I don't understand how she always forgets her own jacket and insists on wearing one from that boy she spends time with. He seems alright enough, but he's not taking care of her as well as I can.

As well as I plan on doing.

As well as I need to.

As well as I am going to.

As well as I am.

The picture she posted shows just how well it fits her. The colors do wonderful things for her and I know it will keep her warm this winter. And hopefully out of his clothes.

If she insists on wearing clothes that don't belong to her, I will find a way to gift her more things.

With the semester coming to a close, I'm not sure what her plans are for her social media content. I hope she takes a break. I don't like all of the attention she is getting from other men online.

She needs to be able to enjoy her time with her family and take a step away from classes. And I don't enjoy spending hours each week going through profiles of other men in her comments – making sure they don't plan to escalate their flirtatious comments beyond the harmless nature they share right now.

That's all I'm trying to do.

Take care of her.

WED   THU   FRI   SAT   SUN          DATE :

# Chapter Eight

## ASHLEY

### NUTELLA CREAM COFFEE

*Social Post: I will never get tired of taking pictures of the snow. #coloradowinter #january #noco*

*Image Description: Selfie of me in front of the snow covered street with the street lights on in the background.*

Winter break goes by way too quickly. Before I am ready, it's time to start classes up again and get back to the reality of the collegiate routine. I have missed the daily expectations of knowing what I needed to be working on. Content wasn't as much of a priority over these past few weeks, and to be honest, it's been nice to have a bit of a break. I was still posting, but it was less "face content" and more product and cute photos I've taken. I didn't want to take a full break from content and lose my momentum, but I definitely needed a change.

This semester, Sam and I are diving more into classes for our major rather than just the general ones. As of right now, our focus is the same, so we have three classes together this semester. Another branding and online marketing class with Professor Johnson, an English class with Professor Summer, and an Introduction to Business Finance class with Professor Jackson are the ones we will get to take together. And then we each have two additional. It's going to be another heavy semester, but at least I'll have Sam for a study buddy.

The first day of classes is a whirlwind. There aren't a ton of new students on campus since only a few transfer in for the spring semester. Most of us know where we are going and how to find the right buildings. Just like last semester, the first class of the day is with Professor Johnson. I drove myself today so I gave myself a few extra minutes to get my things and head inside so I can wait for Sam before we find our seats for the semester. The wind chill makes it absolutely freezing outside, so I'm thankful again for my purple jacket. Sam found me a super comfortable pair of fingerless knit gloves to use for class. We found over the break that even having my hands warmer, but my fingers being able to move over the keys unhindered, made a big difference in how cold I tend to get.

Today was the first day I posted a selfie on social media since Christmas and I've been purposefully avoiding the app to see the comments. I have had to remind myself that I am posting for myself as much as I am for those that enjoy my content. And having creepy dudes in the comments comes with the territory. I have just moved my phone to silent and put the device back into my bag when I feel a hand rest on my shoulder gently.

"Good morning, beautiful. Ready for round two?" Sam smiles down at me as he pulls me in for a quick side hug and a gentle kiss on the top of my head.

I extend my arm like I'm going to escort him into the classroom. "*Après vous.*"

"Since when did we learn French?" he jokes as he takes my arm and matches my stride.

"No clue. I'm pretty sure that's the extent of what I know unless there's a makeup brand that also uses French terms, but it's too early to think in anything besides basic English."

"Noted," Sam nods his head before helping me out of my jacket as we settle into our seats.

The classroom is less than half full, but it is still a good ten minutes before class begins. I recognize a lot of the faces around us, so hopefully this won't be a big jump from last semester. It's still a 100-level class, so it's mostly freshman here. The accounting class we are taking is a 200-level, so I'm a bit worried about that one. My brother is definitely going to be on speed dial when it comes to assignments on that one. He loves numbers. Not me. I love makeup and coffee and branding. I love analyzing different marketing plans that brands use and how different colors and themes can elicit responses, emotions, and change within an audience. It's fascinating to me. Hopefully, we will get to do a bit of that this semester. But I know for sure it will show up next year. I might have found a few of the syllabi of the 200-level classes with Professor Johnson and I cannot wait! It may change between now and then, but I'm still excited.

"Can I please get a few volunteers to help pass out these packets as we get started this morning?" Professor Johnson has zero problems speaking over the hum of students in the space. Sam gets up to help pass out packets as I finish getting my laptop set up for additional notes I may need for this class. Professor Johnson wastes no time passing the different papers to the handful of helpers and then begins glancing over the classroom.

He takes his time checking to see who is here and it feels like he is trying to match them up to students from last semester with the way his eyes travel over each row of seats. He's in his traditional shirt and tie today with a nice navy-blue combo that gives him that effortlessly put together look that he always seems to have. Did he grow his hair a little longer over break? It's still fairly short, but there's enough there that I can see a slight wave in the texture of dark brown and grey. He pulls his phone out of his pocket and messes with a few things just as Sam gets back to his seat next to me with a stack of papers for each of us.

"I have a feeling this semester is going to be a little more intense than last semester," he whispers to me as I leaf through the papers to see why we have more than just a syllabus this semester.

"Yeesh. Yeah, a little bit. What are these outlines and briefs for?"

"Now that everyone has their packets, let's dive into what we will be working on this semester. Marketing changes every few years, and with the rise of social media, those cycles have shortened even more. So, this semester, we will be doing some practical projects that you can use with your resumes for internships or job interviews. I don't want to waste your time and I trust that you will offer me the same consideration." He settles behind the desk and begins the slideshow on the screen to go over expectations, schedules, his office hours, the whole thing.

"Are we going to actually be creating campaigns?" I whisper to Sam as I glance over the attached briefs again.

"I'm not sure, but each packet has different briefs. So that is very possible. What did you get?"

"A spa here in Fort Collins. You?"

"A baby food company in Colorado Springs," Sam scrunches his face up in response and I don't have enough time to school my own features before I hear my name being called.

"Miss Carter, do we already have a problem with the course work for this semester?" *Shit.* I hate being called out for unintentional stuff like this.

"No, sir. I'm sorry."

"Thank you. While I have your attention, do you mind explaining the purpose of a brand brief like the one attached to your packet for the rest of the class? And stand please if you don't mind." He gives me the look of a disappointed dad and I'm already kicking myself for messing up in one of his classes with him two semesters in a row. Professor Johnson heads up several of the intern programs as well as mentorships that have gotten students job placements upon graduation for the last six years here at CSU. And I do not want to be on his bad side. I'm not a complete people pleaser, but I don't like it when I mess something up, especially when it's fully in my control, like turning the ringer off on my phone.

I take a breath and grab my packet as I stand. I glance over the description one more time before diving into the purpose of a brief and how it can be applied to many different areas of marketing from influencers to brand strategy to full-blown marketing companies. It's the outline of a promotion and the requirements the brand needs in order to fulfill that promotion.

"Basically, it's the recipe that the brand is utilizing for that marketing campaign. They want to have those items done to their specifications to make sure their desired result is achieved." I wrap up my explanation and take my seat. Only minorly shaking as I let myself breathe and take in that I just spoke in front of 200 students. I hope I didn't mess that up.

"Correct, Miss Carter. You each have a brief in your packet. Over the course of the first three weeks of this semester, your job is to familiarize yourself with your company and brand. Learn everything you can about the product, customers, staff— everything. Thirty percent of your grade will be attached to those briefs. Don't waste the opportunity of a lighter assignment load by waiting until the last minute. It will show."

The rest of the class goes by smoothly with a few more instructions. And one very nervous student in the back of the class asking how they could drop the class. Jaws dropped on that one. I understand being overwhelmed, but the middle of class is not the time to ask that. Email your advisor, dude. I shake my head and look over at Sam, who is mirroring my reaction. "Not cool," he mouths to me and I nod in agreement.

Professor Johnson handles it much better however, "If you are a business or marketing major, this class is a requirement. If you feel like you need to wait until next spring to dive into this particular requisite, you are more than welcome to follow the instructions of the papers in your lap on how to do so." If we were back in junior high, several of us would be laughing and breathing "burn" under our breaths. But we are all adults, so instead I see a few faces glow with phone screens as they text it to others in the room instead.

"As we end this class period, just a reminder, phones should be on silent and away while you are in this room. I am respecting your time and I expect the same from you. That is all for today." The class moves as one as they pack up their things and start moving toward the front of the classroom.

Luckily, the next two classes go off a little more as expected. No students calling out inappropriate questions and more traditional syllabi. I can work with this. Tomorrow we will have our other two classes and I'll have a good idea of the full course load for the semester. And I'm just crossing my fingers that I won't have to drop a class. I tend to place pretty high expectations on myself, which shows with this semester's course load. I don't want to let myself down, but I also don't want to fail a class because it's too much. I have the ability to take summer classes if needed, so I don't need to squish all of the classes into eight semesters if I feel I need to do it in nine or ten.

Sam walks me to my car in the early afternoon as we finally finish everything on campus for the day. "I have to work tonight and tomorrow after classes, but can we do dinner or something Thursday? There's a new Poke place in Berthoud that I've been wanting to try with you."

"Poke sounds perfect. Text me after you're done with work tonight." I set my bags in my car and turn to face him. His body is close to mine, but I don't feel crowded. I lift my head so I can make eye contact with him just as he rests his hand on my waist while the other one props on the car frame behind me.

"Are you sure? It might be late," he whispers as he tucks my hair behind my ear and sets a kiss at that spot right below my ear and I shiver in response.

"Yes, I'm sure. I'll be up." I smile at him and then gently start pulling away. "But I need to get in this car before I freeze. I forgot my outside gloves this morning and I've hit my limit of outside time before I start turning into a popsicle." He just shakes his head at me as he leans in for one last kiss before he waits for me to get buckled and my car to start.

"Be safe. I'll talk to you tonight." Sam gently closes the car door and waits until I have backed out of my spot before he walks away.

Ashley

WED   THU   FRI   SAT   SUN          DATE

# Chapter Nine

## ASHLEY

### CHOCOLATE STRAWBERRY FRAPPE

*Social Post: Glitter is amazing, but the clean up afterwards is not an easy project. Good thing my coffee cup blends right in! #coloradogirl #valentinesday #crafting #alltheglitter #sparkles*

*Image Description: My sparkle-covered coffee mug sitting on the aftermath of crafting: cut up papers, sequins, glitter, hot glue gun, and scissors on the kitchen table.*

It's approaching ten in the evening by the time I finish packing little Valentines for the neighborhood with my mom. She started doing this a few years ago, and it's fun to create the little notes. The morning of the fourteenth, we slip out and place them on the windshields of the cars that park outside or we tape them to front or garage doors for those that don't park outside. It's not anonymous, but it's a nice little smile for people first thing in the morning. Last year, a couple of the other neighbors did the same thing too. So, our whole area had cute pink and purple hearts and notes throughout the day. It's a fun tradition we've started and this way we don't have to host a big party. We may still be recovering from Christmas over here.

I have a few of the notes left over that I plan to leave on Sam's car and in his bag tomorrow when I see him. Just little things to let him know that I'm thinking about him. I have another one for my brother that I hope I can put on his car or in his laptop bag without him knowing. Probably not going to happen, but I can hope. I'm about to slip into my jammies when I feel my phone vibrate in my pocket.

I fish it out to see that Sam texted me. Wow, he had a late night tonight.

Sam: Hey, gorgeous. How did craft night with your mom go?

Me: It was perfect. We got a lot done and my fingers are beautifully decorated with glitter. I think I even have some in my hair lol.

Me: How was work tonight?

Sam: It was really good. I got to finish the feature for the Valentine's Day cards that Loveland does each year. I had the chance to do some behind the scenes interviews so I'm hopeful that this article will get some good online reach.

Me: That's so awesome. My parents get me the card every year. I have them in a shoebox in my closet. Dad always reminds me that he is my first Valentine so he can't slack off now that I have a boyfriend.

Sam: Would he be upset if I got you the card too? Or do you want to keep that just something between the two of you?

Me: Honestly, I don't know. They only do one design each year, don't they?

Sam: Yeah. And there's only a few places to buy the card and then mail them out to get the special stamp. I should have checked before now on this.

Me: Did you already mail it out?

Sam: Yeah. But you can use the front as a bookmark so it's not kept with your cards so it still is something special for you and your dad.

Me: Sounds like a plan. Are you still at the paper or are you on your way home already?

Sam: Already home. We have class early tomorrow and I need to run a quick errand before I meet you on campus. You need to get to sleep too, Ash.

Me: I know. What time do you want to meet on campus tomorrow?

Sam: How does 7:30 sound?

Me: Gross, but I can do that.

Sam: I'll have coffee.

Me: You better. Lol.

Me: Sleep well

Sam: You too <kissing face emoji>

The next morning comes too fast, but Mom and I have work to do before I leave for school. I dress warmly and quickly before taking a quick mirror selfie holding up several of the little notes from last night. I post it and then hurry downstairs to grab up my stack of notes to sprinkle all over the neighborhood. Matt, our mom, and dad are already at the table, finishing parsing out the stack and putting finishing touches on a few for specific people.

"What area do you need me to do? I want to get mine out so I can get to campus before Sam does if possible." I check in with everyone once I fill up my travel mug with some coffee. Yes, Sam is bringing coffee to school for me, but that's still like an hour away and I need some now. It's cold outside. And Dad picked up some more of the Breakfast Blend I love. And I am not wasting the opportunity to enjoy it while it's still fresh.

"Can you do this stack here? It's for Nancy and Charles next door through the end of the road on the same side. You should have enough for all of the houses and then an extra in case someone is out walking around." Dad passes me a small stack of cards and a little baggie of chocolate truffles. "Your mom decided she couldn't sleep last night so she ended up making truffles after we went to bed apparently." Mom playfully swats him with the dish towel on her shoulder at the tattling.

"I couldn't sleep. So, I might as well be productive. And there's more in the fridge for you all later today. Ash, can you put those truffles next door for Nancy? They're Oreo Raspberry and she is going to love them. I have another bag in the fridge for you to bring to Sam if you would like too." I lean over to kiss her cheek in response.

"Perfect! I'm going to get these taken care of so I can warm up before I need to leave." I turn to Matt before I walk over to the front door. We have a small, elevated bench there that has a basket for all the winter layers: scarves, gloves, headwraps, etc. I need to cover my fingers before I go outside, but hate being over bundled if it's not absolutely necessary. Extra layers mean extra frizz and static with my hair and clothes—no thank you. "How bad is it outside right now?"

"You're going to want to layer up, Ash. It's cold out there. Your car had a nice layer of frost on it when I got here. I'll scrape your windows and start your car when you get back so it's prepped for you before you leave. Do you want to wait a couple minutes and I'll head out with you? I need to do my section and then I'll be hanging out here today. Mom is finally ready to take down the Christmas décor so I'll be busy with that today."

"You act like it's going to take you all day," my mom replies, slightly exasperated. We all just look at her. "Okay, fine, it's going to take you all day." We just laugh in response.

"Mom, if Sam and I come over after classes, we could probably jump in to help and still be working on cleaning it all up until ten tonight. Christmas threw up in this house and it's amazing. But there is a lot." I press a kiss to her cheek and then head back to the door, now sufficiently bundled up and resigned to a messy bun for my hair today because knit hats may be warm, but they don't play well with my hair.

"I should be good, Matt." I almost forgot about his question, "I only have like five houses and they are all easy drop offs. I'll start at the end and work my way back. Maybe start another pot of coffee though." I smirk at him as I step outside.

"I am not making you more coffee!" I hear Matt scold as I close the door behind me. That man is going to end up with someone who likes coffee more than I do just to show him that it could be worse and I am going to enjoy it so, so much.

It doesn't take long to drop off my notes, but by the time I finish at Nancy and Charles's house, my face hurts from the cold and I know my lips are chapped. I need to pick up an overnight mask to help combat the cold this winter. And probably a humidifier for my bedroom too. I get to the front door right as Matt opens it from the inside, all bundled up to come outside.

"I saw you coming up the walk so I wanted to start your car. You should be good to go in like five minutes, right?"

"Yep, I just need to grab my things and switch out my gloves and I'll be leaving soon." I step inside and toe off my shoes on the rug inside. It's not snowy outside, but there's some leftover gross slush on the sidewalks from the last storm and I don't want to mess up my mom's clean floors. We are going to make them enough of a mess with glitter and pine needles in a few hours.

I hear Matt holler something from the front stoop as I'm taking off my coat and other layers. "What was that?" I poke my head outside to hear him better.

"It looks like you got gifted in the time from when I got here this morning until now." Matt is holding up a little red envelope and small box. My windows are also all cleaned off.

"Can you bring it in when you come in please? I already took off my shoes."

Matt huffs a laugh in reply and walks the items back inside. "I think they cleaned your windows too. Let me know when you are getting re-layered up and I'll go start your car."

I take the items from my brother and bring them over to the table where I have a bit more room. I may have slightly taken over that front bench with all of my layering things. I have to have options for different outfits and situations. I cannot wear my bright pink gloves with my purple jacket. It just doesn't quite work. They look great with my black one though. Anyway, back to the letter.

It definitely could be from Sam because he loves leaving me little notes in my bag or car for me to find later. My dad does it too. This one has a really pretty lipstick sticker on the back of the envelope. I am going to have to find out where he found those because they are so cute! The note inside is handwritten in a beautiful dark blue ink. It's that elegant mix between black, blue, and purple. I have a few pens with that color ink and they are my favorite to use for journaling because of the contrast in color against the blush pink pages of my journals.

> Ashley,
>
> I hope your day is as sweet as you are. Happy Valentine's Day, my love. Wear something that you feel amazing in today. Hopefully this gift gives you something to smile about, even in the cold.
>
> Sincerely,
> Yours

Okay, that was adorable. I shoot a quick 'thank you' text to Sam before pocketing my phone again and opening the box. I can't hold back my gasp and mom immediately comes to see what I'm holding.

"Are those diamond earrings?" she whispers from over my shoulder.

"It looks like it." I pull the holder out of the jewelry box to look at the information underneath. "Yeah, they're each ¼ carat apparently. Are they pink?"

"Those are beautiful. You picked a good one, Ash."

"From our conversation last night, it sounded like he was just going to give me a special card. I was not expecting this. But I am not complaining," I practically giggle.

I make quick work of running the card and box up to my room and then switching out my earrings. The light pink of the stones is the perfect subtle bit of color. I add a thin black headband to my hair after throwing it up into a messy bun to add a little bit of sophistication to the overall look. I text Matt to let him know I'm almost ready so he can start the car and then go to the window to take a few selfies in the diffused sunlight that it offers.

I do a quick edit to a few of the shots that highlight the textures of the head band against my hair, the earrings, and the shimmer of my eyeshadow. This post is going to be adorable. The black long sleeve shirt I'm wearing just makes my features pop even more.

By the time I'm in the campus parking lot waiting for Sam, the comments have started filtering in. I take a couple of minutes to filter through a few and respond to the names I recognize. I've been doing this recently so I don't feel as guilty for turning off notifications and ignoring my phone while on campus.

Samtheman62: Love the subtle pink you chose for today. <heart emoji>

Chelsea_blushes_32: Girl, those earrings are stunning. Happy heart day.

Lippiesfordays_plz: I'm loving the subtle Valentine's Day nod today. Any plans tonight?

LVLNDhearts4you: Way to celebrate the holiday.

NoCoevents365: Happy Valentine's Day!

COProP33: A classic but elegant choice today, Ashley.

Fallisbetter475: I think I like the purple on you just a bit better, but this is such a cute look. You look like a professional Barbie!

I chuckle at that last one and then squeal at the knock on my window. Sam is standing there with two to-go coffee mugs in his hand. I silence my phone before putting it in my bag. I turn off my car as Sam sets the coffee on the roof so he can open my door without spilling. That would not be a fun day.

"Do you have your gloves?" Sam asks as I step outside and button my coat up. I respond by pulling both pairs out of my pockets.

"Inside and outside." I smile up at him before going up on my tiptoes to give him a kiss. "Thank you so much for my card and gift this morning. It was such a wonderful surprise."

"It got to you already? Nice. I'm glad you like it. Do we have anything planned tonight? I don't have to work since I submitted my story last night."

"The end of Christmas."

"That sounds absolutely horrifying," Sam responds almost incredulously and I can't help the laugh that I let out. That did sound really bad when I put it that way.

"We are taking down the Christmas décor at the house today. Mom wanted to know if you could come help too."

"It's a date."

WED   THU   FRI   SAT   SUN        DATE :

# Chapter Ten

## ASHLEY

**BUTTERSCOTCH VANILLA LATTE**

*Social Post: Someone remind me that I actually like glitter please. #cogirl #noco #christmasdecor #cleanup #glittereverywhere*

*Image Description: Open totes in the background half full of Christmas decor. My hand holding a nutcracker and absolutely covered in glitter in the focus of the picture.*

Classes this morning go surprisingly well. Coffees in hand and little envelopes on top of books show that most couples met up before the first class of the day. Even those that aren't necessarily in a relationship seem to have spent a bit more time than normal this morning getting themselves ready for the day. Assignments are turned in, everyone pays attention, and we even get out of classes a little early too. I think some of our professors had early date nights planned, because we end up getting to my house at the same time as we would normally get out of classes for the day. Nice.

I park in the driveway and Sam finds a spot on the side of the street. He comes up before I'm even out of the car to open my door and take my bag from me.

"Such a gentleman," I remark to him and he answers with a wink and quick kiss on the top of my head before closing the door behind me.

"It looks like someone left something on your front stoop. Do you want to get the door and I'll grab it?" And yep, there's another package right by the front door. It looks like a gift basket filled with a whole bunch of goodies.

"It's probably from the neighbors down the street. We always do a lot of random gifting today to the neighbors and it's caught on recently with a few of them." I use my key to let us inside and then toe off my shoes. "It doesn't look like anyone is home at the moment." I pull my phone out to see if they have an ETA on getting home. I hear Sam setting the basket down in the kitchen and then our bags at the dining room table.

> Mom: We will be home around five with dinner. Matt had to meet one of his friends to move a finished piece of furniture to the buyer's house. If you get home before we do, can you take the chicken out of the freezer so I can make that tomorrow? Love you and have a great afternoon with Sam.

> Me: Thanks mom. We just got home and brought in a package. See you in a bit.

"It looks like we have the house to ourselves for a few hours. Do you want to get started on packing things up, get some homework done, or just watch a movie and chill for a bit?" I make my way into the kitchen to move the chicken as requested and Sam follows.

"How about we grab something little to eat and then head upstairs for a little while?" I can feel his breath on my neck before his lips meet the space where my neck and shoulder meet. Okay, that feels amazing. "What do you think?" And then I realize I didn't answer out loud because I'm seriously enjoying where his lips are right now.

"I think I like the sound of that, but I think the food can wait." I tilt my head back so it rests on his shoulder as his hands come around to grip my waist to hold me steady.

"Yeah?"

"Yeah." I turn around and smile up at him before grabbing his hand and leading him upstairs to my room. As I close my bedroom door behind us, I'm glad that I took a few minutes to tidy up last night. My room is hardly ever "messy," but it was definitely a little cluttered last night. I set my phone down on my nightstand just as I feel Sam come up behind me.

"Have I told you how much I like it when you wear your hair up like this?" he whispers in my ear as he places kisses from the top of my ear and begins trailing down my neck, back to that spot on my shoulder that drives me absolutely crazy. My only response is a small hum. He chuckles against my skin before asking, "have you forgotten how to use actual words, Ashley?"

"Only when your lips are on me, apparently. Why do I like that so much?"

"Can I find what else you like?"

I nod and raise one of my hands to cup the back of his head as I lean back again. I want more neck kisses because I'm officially addicted to this.

"I'm going to need actual words from you, Ash." Okay, now that was hot.

"I'd love for you to find out what else I like, Sam." I smile up at him as he turns my body to face his. And then his hands are holding my face still as he leans in to kiss me. His kisses send sparks through my body and I have to make myself not immediately jump into his arms. I rest my hands on his chest before traveling lower to begin unbuttoning his shirt.

"I like when you wear button shirts. They make you look all professional."

"I think you just like unbuttoning them."

He smirks down at me as he assists me in pulling it off of him and laying it on the edge of my bed.

"You're not wrong." I never used to think that an attractive guy looked better without his shirt on until I met Sam. Again, Clark Kent. He goes from handsome and professional to strong and confident just by removing one article of clothing. I let my eyes take him in before my hands are in his hair. "I love that you keep your hair long enough for me to play with." I let my nails drag down to the back of his neck as I keep playing with what I can touch.

"You know I love it when you touch me like that," he responds as his hands trail to the bottom of my top. "Can we start figuring out what you like now?"

"You don't have to be so polite all the time," I answer as I reach down to meet his hands, helping him pull my shirt up and over my head. I'm in a simple pink lace bralette today and am glad that I took an everything shower last night. Before I can fully take in his reaction to me, his hands are on my shoulders and tracing down my arms until his fingers lace with mine. He leads me until I'm sitting on my bed and he's standing in front of me. My hair tie comes loose next as he gently pulls it free from the mess on top of my head. I have no idea when he took off my headband, or maybe it came off when my shirt came off.

"I thought you liked it when I had my hair up," I am a bit snarky with my response, but he loves my sassiness.

"I do, but you look stunning with your hair down like this, and I have a feeling I'm going to love seeing it spread out on the bed behind you." With that, he shifts me backward so I am laying on the bed, his hand holding the base of my head, and the other one playing with the strap on my shoulder. His lips follow suit, focusing first on my lips and then traveling down my body. I am not prepared for the feel of his mouth on my nipple through the lace. The added texture of the lace is pure pleasure and I can't stop my hips from coming up, trying to find pressure.

Sam keeps up his work on my nipple while humming his approval. "Need something else there, Ash?" Oh, he's being the snarky one now.

"I really like what you are doing, but I need more." I arch my chest into him further as his hand that was on my strap goes down to pinch and then massage my other nipple through the lace.

"What do you need, Ashley?" He stops for a moment to make eye contact with me.

"Make me feel good, Sam."

"How do you want me to do that?" Our voices are just shared whispers even though we are home alone right now.

"I think you're the one that knows more about that than I do…"

"Are you telling me that you haven't ever done this with a partner before, Ashley?"

"Nope." I have to force myself to maintain eye contact. Why is the 'I'm still a virgin' thing such a hard conversation to have?

"You good with this?"

"Very. I want to do this with you." I smile up at him. "You're the first one I've wanted to do more than make out with and I want you to be my first."

His answering smile gives me all the warm fuzzy feelings. "I'll do my best to be gentle."

"Just make me feel good, Sam. Don't worry about the other stuff."

"Anything you know you don't like?"

"Not at the moment – but can you please stop asking me questions and just get me naked already?"

He laughs in response but listens to my direction and stops asking questions. "Just tell me if you need me to slow down or stop something, okay?"

"I promise, now please kiss me." And he doesn't make me wait long at all. Being in his arms, kissing Sam, is the most amazing place to be. I feel beautiful and safe and wanted. His trailing hands have me feeling needy all over again and I know he is exploring to see what I like. It's almost like he's trying to find those special places that will drive me crazy and he just found one.

"You ticklish here, babe?" He trails his fingers over the top of my leggings, just barely slipping his fingers under the elastic.

"Nope, just incredibly sensitive." He grips me a little harder along my waist as he pushes himself up onto his knees next to me. Before I can fully comprehend his eyes moving from mine, he is sliding my leggings down off of my legs. He left my matching lace panties behind and I'm kind of glad he's taking his time with this. He stands once he gets the leggings down and removes his own jeans. Then his body is back on top of mine, our closest layers the only thing that separates us from being fully skin to skin.

I trail my fingers back up and over his shoulder again and feel the muscles of his upper back under my hand. Sam takes the time to mirror my movements, trailing his hands up my side then down to cup my breast through my bra. I push up a little bit so I can reach behind and unclasp the material. I'm getting a little impatient apparently.

"You are so gorgeous, Ashley," he breathes before his mouth is directly on my nipple and I cannot believe how worked up I am getting as he alternates sides, with his fingers and hand manipulating the other. I need just a bit more, and he must know I'm close because his hand is sliding under my underwear to explore.

"That feels so good, Sam. Don't stop." I arch into his touch and he presses harder–everywhere. I feel a finger dip inside of my entrance as the heel of his hand puts pressure on my clit. His mouth begins sucking on my nipple and my nails dig into his shoulder as I shatter around him. The orgasm takes my breath for a minute and I just focus on his finger moving subtly in and out as I come back down.

"You are breathtaking when you let go for me, Ashley." He smiles down at me as he brushes my hair from my face. He slips a second finger inside of me and starts gently pumping in and out, all while continuing to massage my breast with his other hand. "Got to get you ready for me, babe. You are so wet already, but I want to make sure you are stretched a bit."

"That feels incredible. I've played with some toys before so I have had some penetration before." I arch into him again. I am going to turn into a needy little girlfriend with his hands on me if it's always going to feel this good.

"Are you wanting me to try now or keep playing with you some more?"

"I think I want you to grab a condom out of my nightstand and stop being so gentle with me, Sam." He sits back a bit to check my expression and sees that I am absolutely serious. I am not prepared for the sounds that come when he removes his fingers from my pussy though. I am a lot wetter than I was expecting based on what I just heard. Sam doesn't let me get self-conscious though, because he's bringing his glistening fingers up to his lips.

He stands to grab the foil packet from my bedside table as he cleans his fingers with his tongue. Now, *that*, was hot.

"Next time, I'll get you ready with my tongue, because you taste amazing." I can feel the blush creeping over my face at what he just did, but I can't focus on that long. My panties are on the floor along with his underwear and then the condom packet is being torn open.

"Can you show me how to help put it on?"

"I love how you go from sassy and telling me what you want to being my Ashley and asking for what you want. Both sides of you are my favorite." He smiles as he shows me how to find the right side and then gently roll it on. He then leans back over my body and uses his fingers to collect more of the wetness he drew out of my body earlier. He's using it as lube on his cock and I have no idea why that is so sexy.

"I'm going to go slow, it probably won't feel amazing at first, but I'll make sure you feel good, Ash."

"I trust you, Sam."

And then his lips are back on mine as he begins working his way inside of me. The stretch is more than I was expecting. Even with getting me ready with his fingers, his dick is thicker and doesn't provide as much give as his fingers did. He stops when he's a few inches in, giving me time to adjust to his size.

"I'm halfway there, Ashley, how are you doing?"

I nod back up at him. "Just push all the way in, this is torture and I need to feel you fill me."

"As you wish," he whispers in my ear before lightly biting down at the same time as he pushes home. I gasp in response and tilt my head up and back. God that feels good.

"You are squeezing me so tight, Ashley. This is not going to last long."

"You feel so good, babe. I need you to move, please."

"Are you asking me to fuck you?"

"Yes, Sam. Stop being so polite and fuck me."

He doesn't answer with words and I lose myself in his movements. The way I feel his thighs contract next to mine as he pivots in and out. The grip of his cock against my inner walls as he moves. His lips moving over the skin closest to where he's braced over my body. And then his fingers are roving down my body to begin exploring my clit. He slips down further to gather some of the natural lubrication coming out of my body from the pleasure he has already given me and then he is back on my clit, rubbing small circles in time with his movements in and out of my pussy.

"How close are you, Ashley? I want to feel you come again while I'm inside you."

"So close, just a bit more," I practically whimper at him because I am so close. And it's only a moment or two later when he puts his mouth back on my breast and I detonate. It's a good thing that we are home alone, because I am not quiet. The pleasure hits me everywhere and the feeling of Sam tensing over me keeps the orgasm going. I can feel his body shudder as he finds his own release.

Moments later, his eyes meet mine.

"Happy Valentine's Day, Ashley."

"You too, Sam."

Ashley

# Chapter Eleven

## HIM

That wasn't his gift to take.

WED   THU   FRI   SAT   SUN        DATE

# Chapter Twelve

## ASHLEY

**IRISH CREAM COLD BREW**

*Social Post: Anyone else have to color coordinate their classes/study materials? #studytime #midterms #csu*

*Image Description: Stacks of notecards on top of color coordinating notebooks and pens, two lip gloss bottles and a coffee mug in the middle of the mess on my desk.*

Apparently, I fell asleep after we finished studying for midterms. I had met Sam over at his house after classes today so we could study and get some time together. The last few weeks have been insanely busy—me with balancing content and course work and him with balancing work assignments and classes. We get to start some of our more practical assignments and even some intern applications after midterms, so doing well on these tests is critical. I've decided to wait on any internship or teacher assistant positions. Maybe for next summer or for my junior year, but I still don't fully know what I want to do after graduation, so I might as well take my time.

Sam is going to see about taking on a summer-long series for the paper so he can really build out his portfolio. He's also applied to TA for Professor Erickson with building out another Colorado History class this summer. Maybe that will mean a few "field trips" for the two of us hopefully. He has some meetings with Professor Erickson after spring break to go over some ideas and then mapping it out from there. Part of me is a little bummed that I don't have something similar to be working on. I have my social media platforms, but that's hardly comparable.

I'm woken up with a gentle kiss to my forehead and then the feel of a smile pressed up against my skin.

"I fell asleep." I open my eyes to see a satisfied smile on Sam's face in response. "What time is it?"

"A little after ten. Do you want to stay here tonight or do you want me to drive you home?" I take just a moment before responding to his question.

"I think I need to go home. I didn't pack a bag and we have class first thing tomorrow. I don't really want to rock the boyfriend chic look tomorrow for exams."

"But you look so cute in my clothes." Sam pouts like a petulant child and it's beyond adorable. I do pretty much live in his sweatshirts when I'm with him – and when I'm home too.

"I may look cute in your clothes, but it's not the put together look I tend to go for on campus. Even my legging days are thought out. I like picking out my clothes and coordinating accessories each day." I scooch off the bed and start putting my things back in my bag. At least it's a clear night out and I don't have to drive through rain or snow. Driving in the dark is going to be bad enough.

"And you do such a good job with your daily outfits too. I'm going to have to take a peek at your accessory drawer next time I'm over," Sam trails off as he comes up behind me to place a kiss on my neck.

"And why is that?" I hum back at him as I melt into his arms and just enjoy him holding me for a moment.

"So, I know what you are missing for colors and styles. I feel like you hardly ever repeat accessories and I want to get you something you'll enjoy wearing." I step out of his arms and shoulder my bag as we start making our way to the front of the house. His parents have already gone to bed for the night so the house is quiet.

"You can never have too many pairs of earrings or tubes of lipstick," I smirk up at him as we make it to the front door. "But you have already done really well with the jewelry you've gotten me so I am pretty sure I'll love whatever you get for me." I turn toward him on the front stoop to push up on my toes and meet his lips with mine.

"Jewelry? I must be tired because I don't remember getting you any jewelry yet, babe." He kisses me gently and then pulls back to meet my eyes.

"The gift from Valentine's Day," I prompt, seeing if that helps. He's thinking it over just as my car alarm starts blaring.

"Shit, where are my keys?" I begin digging frantically in my purse until I find them and silence the alarm on my car. "What the heck prompted that?" I start to walk toward my car, but Sam grabs my wrist to stop me.

"Let me go check really quickly. That was weird."

"I'm a big girl, Sam. You don't have to go check my car first to make sure no one is hiding in the backseat."

"I know I don't have to, but I want to."

I concede and let him go be the protective macho man. He takes my keys and takes his time opening and checking my trunk, under my car, and in the windows before he opens the driver's side door and starts my car for me. I pull on my gloves and walk from the porch to the car now that he's shown I'm safe from the boogeyman.

"All good?" I ask as he unfolds himself from my car.

"All good. Can you text me when you get home please?"

"Of course, I can. I always do." He gently shuts the door after I buckle in and adjust my mirrors. I plop my phone into the holder and turn the sound back off so I'm not distracted while I drive.

"Lock your doors," comes the muffled request from Sam. I just smirk at him and shake my head incredulously, but I lock them anyway. He did a story last year about someone avoiding a carjacking by having their doors locked at a traffic light so he's a little paranoid. Can't blame him.

t's a quick drive home with minimal traffic on the roads. My radio plays quietly and apparently, I went on autopilot a little bit, because I end up turning into the coffee shop parking lot instead of the turnoff to my neighborhood a bit further up the road.

"Well that's new," I murmur quietly. I need to plan a "sleep all day" day this weekend. Good thing I'm not going anywhere for spring break. I need some rest. A ding from my phone startles me as I turn around toward the plaza exit.

"Didn't I silence this?" I have got to stop talking to myself. I decide to ignore it, and double check the locks on my doors, before pulling back out onto the quiet road. A few minutes later, I'm in my driveway. The porch light is on as is the kitchen light just inside. One of my parents still stays up until I get home each evening. I love our nightly chats when it happens. And knowing they care and want to have that touch point each night is super comforting too.

I send Sam my check in text to let him know I'm home before I grab my bags and head inside, locking my car just as I get to the front door. I'll clear the rest of the notifications once I'm inside and warm in my bed.

You know that feeling you get when someone is trying to get your attention? Like they're watching you, but you don't know who it is and if you have your skirt tucked into your underwear or if they just really love your shoes? That's the feeling I get as I put the key into the lock. I take a breath to decide if I'm going to turn around or just pretend that I'm not suddenly terrified that I'm about to be kidnapped. I decide to peek over my shoulder as I push the door in.

Several things happen at that moment.

My car alarm starts going off again.

I drop my keys from being startled by the noise.

My phone then starts beeping like an Amber Alert or Storm Warning is going off.

My mom, just behind the front door, screams in surprise at both abrupt noises.

And I make eye contact with a man standing in the shadows just

outside the glow of the street light.
   And then apparently, I pass out.
   Yeah, I need some time off.

# Chapter Thirteen

## HIM

She almost spent the night at his house again. I need to find a way to remind her that isn't where she belongs. At least her *boyfriend* is about to get busier if his calendar is any indication. That will give me more time to show her that I'm a better fit for her.

And seeing her tonight, I wasn't expecting the thrill of seeing her eyes connecting with mine, even from across the street. She knows I'm watching. That I'm making sure she's safe. She needs to pay better attention to her surroundings though. The phone notifications and car alarm startled her today, but at least it showed her that she was zoning out instead of being aware of what is happening around her.

She isn't a child playing in the playground with Mommy watching to make sure she won't get stolen away. She's a young woman who draws attention everywhere she goes. And it's not hard to see why. She's so oblivious to it though. And my jealousy can only be held back for so long.

At least her mom was close to her when she went down outside of the house. I wasn't aware she had a medical condition that predisposed her to fainting spells. I need to make sure that doesn't happen again. I want her to know she's safe and being taken care of. Not that she needs to be scared or worried. I may have pushed too far tonight.

Hopefully she gets some rest tonight and sees a doctor soon. I can't have my girl not being healthy. My attention is already split.

And it will continue to be that way until she is in my arms and in my bed.

WED    THU    FRI    SAT    SUN         DATE

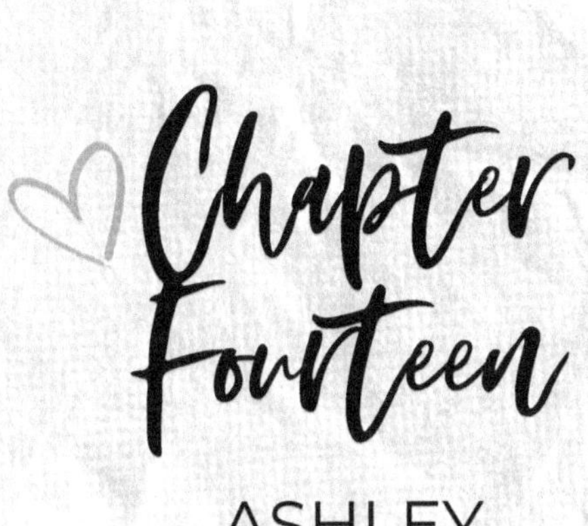

# Chapter Fourteen

## ASHLEY

**WHITE CHOCOLATE RASPBERRY LATTE**

*Social Post: Hospital chic is not looking to be a trend for this year. But just a reminder, take care of yourself and listen to your body. Hopefully getting some answers today as I continue to recover from my episode the other night. #coloradogirl #hospitalchic #noco #selfcare #mentalhealth #restday*

*Image Description: Selfie while waiting for the doctor to come back in to review tests with me and my mom. Wearing a blue hospital gown and a blanket because it's freezing.*

Since the fainting episode outside of my house a few months ago, I've learned a few things. One, I'm really bad at making sure I've had enough to eat and drink when I get busy. Two, I was really bad at realizing what was happening around me and now I'm borderline paranoid. Three, I have a bit of a creepy follower online and I might have one in person too.

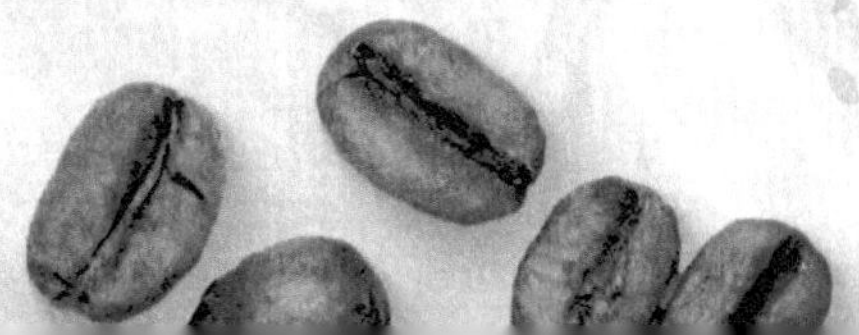

I haven't seen the mystery man in person since that night, and even then, I'm not sure if I actually saw him. I didn't hit my head when I fainted, but I was really dazed when I came to on the couch in the living room. My dad had come running when he heard Mom screaming and carried me inside. They were just debating calling an ambulance when I came to. I was really confused and woke up already crying and shaking. Apparently it was from the adrenaline rush, and my dad just held me until things settled down. I didn't bring up what I thought I saw outside, chalking it up to sensory overload or something similar. I'm surprised my parents let me wait until the next day to go to the doctors instead of running to the ER right away that night.

Thus, started the flurry of the next month. Doctor's appointments, schedule adjustments—I dropped a class—and my brother getting a bit more involved in my social media. He put a few filters on my platform to preemptively block spam accounts and filter comments and messages. I haven't gotten any more creepy messages on Instagram and with the limited time on campus, I haven't had other notes left in my things either. Maybe whoever it was got tired of the pranks and has decided to leave me alone.

The doctor also told me that I have to wait on any strenuous activities, i.e. sex, until I've been episode free for six weeks. I made it a whole five weeks before I fainted again. That time it was strictly dehydration. Sam and I had gone for a short hike and I hadn't had enough water before we hit the trail. By the time we realized I wasn't doing well, it was too late. Luckily, we hadn't gotten very far and were able to get to the trailhead before I passed out. So now the timer has started over again and we are at four weeks this time around.

I've missed a few classes too. It's only been twice, but they've both been on Mondays. My professors have been really understanding with it all though. I was able to turn everything in on time, even with a few weekend days turning into rest days instead of coursework days. I'm thankful for the chance to take a step back and make sure I'm taking care of myself though. I had been really good about supporting those around me, but not taking the time I needed for my own self and what I needed. Through the doctor's appointments, we found out that my perpetually being cold is actually an underlying medical condition and not just a weird quirk.

Raynaud's syndrome means I have poor blood circulation in my extremities: my hands and feet. So, I get cold easily and stay cold for longer. Wool socks and insulated gloves have been added to my wardrobe rotation as a result. Sam also found rechargeable hand warmers for me too. I keep one in my bag and one in my car now. Those things are amazing! 10/10 highly recommend.

We are now only a week away from finals and from our brand projects along with our other coursework being submitted. I've been steadily working on them and feel really confident with the direction I took with everything. Sam even found a creative way to do his baby food project while still enjoying it. I know this is the perfect project for me since I'm focusing on a lot of social media growth right now and many brands are using influencers to grow their visibility and sales. It's also been a chance for me to connect more intentionally with other influencers doing similar content. @sashaloveslipstick, @ChelseaWearsPink835, and @everydaynatalieshines are just a few accounts that are on my daily check list to engage with.

Matt has even started helping more content creators over the last six months so he was able to help both Sam and myself with our projects. Analytics, hashtag research, and brand comparison weren't required for this assignment, but I'm glad we dove into it. If nothing else, it's good practice for pitching to brands when the time comes. I'm meeting Sam at a coffee shop close to campus this afternoon so we can review each other's proposals and then have dinner after we get them printed out. Most of our "dates" have turned into work sessions, but he doesn't seem to mind the low-key evenings.

I get to the shop before he does so I quickly find a table tucked into the back corner before ordering my drink at the counter. All the local coffee shops around town have made it easy for us to try a new location for almost every coffee date. And that means more local places to support. And more coffee to try. I order a white chocolate raspberry latte and happily sip through the foam while I sift through the files on my laptop. I jot down the order they need to be viewed in and am just starting on the final design page for the cover letter when Sam settles into the seat across from me.

"Hey, beautiful," he smiles at me as he shrugs out of his light jacket and sets his laptop bag on the floor next to his seat. "I see you already grabbed your coffee."

"Of course I already grabbed my coffee, did you really think I could be in here smelling the grounds and not get a cup? This latte is fabulous by the way. What are you going to get?"

"They have a drip coffee from Boulder today. I may try that one out."

"Keeping it simple today?"

"Can't go wrong with a classic." He winks at me as he stands back up and places a kiss on the top of my head. "Do you need anything while I'm up there?"

"I think I'm good for now…" I take a moment to think over what I've eaten today. "Actually, can you get me some avocado toast? I need some protein."

"You got it, babe. And then we can dive into these proposals so we can go to dinner and have a proper date night."

I am so ready for a proper date night. It's been too long.

"So, are you happy with the final printout?" Sam and I are sitting on the couch at my house, thumbing through our projects and putting the printed materials in the appropriate folders. Portions of each proposal will be digital, but we also have to turn in some paper copies of our proposed emails, brand research, and slides with notes.

"I think so. It's helpful to see a lot of this in paper form and not just digitally. It really shows how much work goes into every brand partnership. It's not a quick 'hey work with me' email, but actual thought and research needs to go into the big deals that you see online. The right partnership can be super beneficial for both the brand and the influencer or the consultant that is brought on to help. What about you?"

Sam puts the last of his papers in his folder and then pulls out a jar of baby food from his bag to set on the coffee table in front of me. "If I never have to see that label again, it would be too soon." He chuckles. "I learned a lot with this project, but I kind of hate that I had baby food as my brand."

"Are you bringing actual jars with you for the final?"

"I can only jazz up baby food so much. I figured props would help with a few extra brownie points." He shrugs his shoulders before gently taking the folders off of my lap and resting them on the table next to his project and baby food jar. He turns his body a little so his back is in the corner of the couch then maneuvers me so I'm on his lap, my back to his chest. The throw blanket that had been on the back of the couch is now on my lap as I settle into his hold.

With more strenuous activities off the table for us for a little bit, this has become our comfy go-to place to be. Sitting on the couch, under a blanket, just being with each other. More often than not, we put on a movie and I fall asleep within the first hour. But I love being held and having him close to me. Sometimes it turns into a pretty hot and heavy make out session, but as soon as Sam realizes I'm getting "too worked up," he backs off. Sometimes I don't like how considerate he is.

I tilt my head back so I can see his face. "Do you want to stay over tonight?"

"We haven't hit six weeks yet, babe," he gently reminds me as he rubs up and down my arms, probably subconsciously making sure I'm warm enough.

"I know. And I'm not asking for more than snuggles and kisses, but I need that right now I think. You don't have work tomorrow, so we can have a later morning...what do you think?"

His smiling response tells me I won this one and I do an internal happy dance. We bring our things to the dining room table so we don't misplace anything and then I go to lock the front door before we head upstairs. The dead bolt gets stuck sometimes, so we only lock it when we leave the house or are going to bed usually. And tonight, it is really stuck. I finally relent and call Sam over to me to help.

"Do we need to start talking about upper body strength training?" he jokes with me as he jiggles the lock and pushes on the door to get the deadbolt into the slot.

"My brother already gives me a hard enough time about not going running with him. Please don't add to the peer pressure," I whine at him. Don't judge me. I don't like running.

Sam lets his head fall back in laughter and I quickly poke him in the side to get him to shush. My parents are already sleeping and his laugh is almost as loud as mine.

"Okay, no healthy peer pressure, I relent."

"You don't need to be a drama queen about it," I pout back at him before starting up the stairs. "Can you turn on the hall light really quickly please? It's too dark on these stairs without it on."

"Drama queen? That's a new one." He laughs quietly as he flips the light on and then follows me up the stairs. It doesn't take long for me to wash my face and get changed, setting a pair of sweats and T-shirt out for Sam so he can do the same. He left a change of clothes over here last month when he fell asleep on the couch while we were watching a movie and then we overslept. Meaning he couldn't run home to change before classes. Not cool.

"I much prefer it when you're Clark Kent, but as long as you keep the drama queen moments to a minimum, I think I'll keep you." I settle under my blankets and nestle into his arm so he can hold me close.

"You think you'll keep me?"

"You okay with that?" I look up at him, so content in this moment.

"Very. Get some sleep, Ash. I'll see you in the morning."

Ashley

# Chapter Fifteen

## SAM

### CARAMEL MACCHIATO

*Social Post: Someone get me a barista badge, because I'm getting pretty good at this. #athomebarista #coffee #formygirl*

*Image Description: Picture of several flavored syrup bottles next to the stainless steel French press and standard coffee maker.*

I am so gone for this girl. When I saw her at the beginning of our first semester, I knew she was amazing. But seeing all that she has worked through so far this year, her strength and determination, just floors me. My work this summer with Professor Erickson means I won't be able to spend as much time with her, so I'm enjoying anything I can get right now. With finals just around the corner, I'm trying to remind her to rest and take care of herself. If that means a few text messages throughout the day to remind her to eat and drink, I can do that.

I am enjoying the few quiet moments this morning, feeling her in my arms, running my fingers through her hair, before she wakes up. The quiet of the morning has always been one of my favorite times, and I love that I get to share some of them with Ashley now. She actively looks for the beauty around her. And seeing life through her eyes has been incredible. I hear a light tap on the door before hearing her dad on the other side.

"Good morning, coffee is done and there's breakfast in the oven staying warm whenever you guys are ready to get up. We are heading to the Farmer's Market. Text if you need anything."

"Thank you, sir. Have fun," I say back and hope it's loud enough for him to hear without waking up Ashley. No such luck. She stirs in my arms and squeezes my torso a little as she stretches and wakes up.

"Good morning, handsome. What was that?" Her voice is a little scratchy with sleep, and I have a small drool spot on my T-shirt, and I love seeing her like this. She isn't always picture perfect on social media. But I feel like I get to see the "behind the scenes" Ashley, and it feels special to be a part of this side of her life.

"Just your dad. Your parents are heading to the market and there's coffee downstairs. Did you sleep well?"

"Mmmm, yep. Sleep was great. Coffee is better though." She rolls over so she can sit up on the side of the bed.

"I thought you were cutting back on the coffee," I tease her as I get out of the bed and round to her side so I can stand in front of her. She tilts her head back so she can see my face.

"Who told you these lies? Because that is just an awful thing to even think about." She over exaggerates a full body shudder before she maneuvers around me to get up. She slips her feet inside of the gray slippers I got her a few months ago when she started spending more time resting at her house. The floors are mostly hard surfaces and with the Raynaud's diagnosis, it makes more sense why she always feels so cold.

"Okay, no more talk of smaller amounts of coffee. Do you want to head to the market today or is there something else you would like to do?" We begin making our way downstairs to the kitchen.

"I think I need a sleep day before finals. I'm as ready as I can be study-wise. But I can tell my body is tired. I don't like how hard it's been to adjust my body to the needed rest around school this semester."

I pour her a cup of coffee and then one for myself. With all of the coffee syrups and extras on the counter, I've been learning how she likes her coffee when at home. I keep it simple today with just a pump of caramel syrup and a splash of cream before setting the mug in front of her by the kitchen island. The plates of egg casserole are still warm from being in the oven and I'm glad that I don't have to figure out breakfast. Cooking hasn't been a high priority for me before, but I should probably start working on that.

"Do what you need to do. It's been an adjustment and that's okay. I'm here for whatever you need. You needing some extra sleep just means extra cuddles or quiet days in with you and I'm not complaining about that."

"Do you have things to do today?"

"I need to run some errands for my mom. But I can come back later this afternoon if you are feeling up to it."

"I'd like that," she smiles up at me and I begin calculating how many stops I need to make before I can be back here with her again.

My last stop of the afternoon is an event space not far from the college campus. My mom is a florist and she needs a key for a wedding she has here tomorrow. The plan is to drop off the flowers early so she can then meet up with a friend for brunch. I was already in this area of town to pick up some folders from Professor Erickson since we will start working together in just a couple of weeks.

Picking up the key is easy and the venue director hands me a few papers so Mom knows how to get in and out of the venue tomorrow. I will probably be able to go with her for the drop off, so I'll flip through them when I get home to make sure we know where to go in the morning. New venues mean new processes and procedures, but it also means new opportunities for my mom.

Back at my house, I sort out the papers from Professor Erickson and the ones from the venue. There's also a bag from another Fort Collins business that is trying out a new wildflower business card and wanted to see what Mom thought about the designs. They're talking about doing a collaboration together which hopefully means a couple of articles that I can write and some new clients for both businesses.

I am toward the bottom of the papers I need to sort out when I see a plain white business envelope. I don't remember which stop this one came from, so I open the seal to see which pile it needs to go into. The letter inside is typed and leaves me more confused than I was before I peeked inside.

*To Whom it May Concern,*

*Thank you for doing your best to take care of my girl over these last few weeks when I couldn't be there. Your services are no longer needed. I respectfully ask that you step away from your relationship and your time spent in her company. Again, thank you.*

There's no signature. No return information. I'm not even 100% sure this is for me. But I think it is. Which means this is about Ashley. She never mentioned another guy. She would have told me if there was someone else. I slip the envelope back inside of my school bag. I'll ask her about it after finals. I don't want to add to her stress level right now. But this is definitely weird.

Sam

WED   THU   FRI   SAT   SUN        DATE

# Chapter Sixteen

## ASHLEY

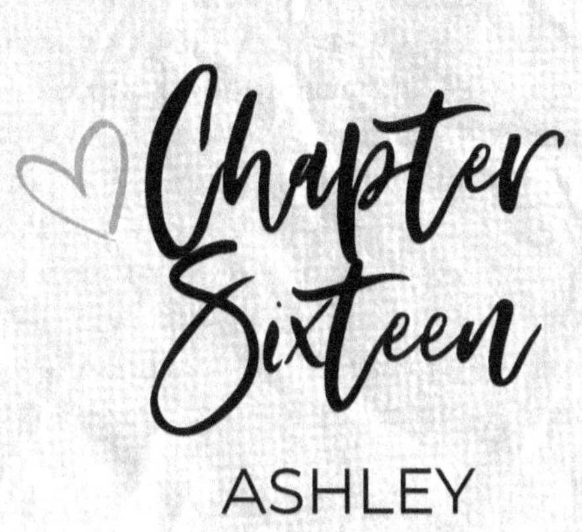

### COOKIES AND CREAM COLD BREW

*Social Post: I had to pick up this eyeshadow palette after seeing @ sashaloveslipstick use it a few weeks ago. What do we think of these colors? #pinkmakeup #sashaloveslipstick #cogirl #nocogirl #prettypictures #aestheticpictures*

*Image Description: Product flat lay of sunscreen, pink eyeshadow palette, and pink lip gloss on a white soft fabric background.*

Summer has started much like all my high school summers have. Originally, I was going to get a part time job this summer, but with the fainting and the stress issues there, I decided to take it easy at home instead. This way, I can do more with my parents with their Farmer's Market days and maybe start working with my brother on things too. And spending time with Sam, that's another high priority for the summer. He's going to be busy with his TA work with Professor Erickson, but I hope we can do some downtown concerts or drive-in movies together.

I'm just coming down the stairs to refill my coffee mug when I notice that Matt is already here. He's not usually here in the morning, but I'm not quite ready to be a person this early. It's summer and I was up way too late reading last night. And I just need to refill this cup so I can go do my recording for the week and then work on editing and posting the content.

When I notice him just standing there staring at me I finally talk, "Why are you awake and out of the house this early in the morning? It's summertime and you work for yourself – sleep in while you can." I do not understand this man.

"You are never going to guess who I have a business proposal call with tonight." Am I supposed to? He places his water glass in the sink and turns to face me. I don't have enough sleep in me to even begin guessing. Why are we talking about business proposals? Apparently, he takes pity on my frozen face because he offers a bit more information.

"I'll give you a hint – 'Always keep your purse full of happy pens and pretty lipstick.'"

He pulls out his phone like he could care less if I figure it out. And then I do. And I am not too big of a girl to admit that I screamed like a total fangirl and barely remembered to set down my coffee before jumping up and down.

"Shut up!! You do not! Sasha? Seriously?? How is this happening? What is the plan? What does she need? Can I help? Can I meet her?" Okay, this may be too much, but I really do not care.

"I do. Yes, it's Sasha. I'm totally serious. I have a pretty good website and she asked for a consultation. I spent several hours last night and then some time this morning working on her proposal and I don't think you can meet her yet. It might be weird to start off my proposal by asking for a favor." I can tell he's trying to make sure he answered all of my questions and I don't remember what I asked so I just continue on.

"I cannot believe this. Sasha is one of my favorite influencers! I would love the chance to collaborate with her as I continue growing my own channels. She's got amazing content, but I know she doesn't have a ton of time to devote to her content while she works full time. What are you planning to talk to her about tonight?"

"Yes, I know. Hence why I think she is reaching out—she wants this to be bigger too. And I really hope I can help her get there." Matt smiles at me in that 'aww, you're so cute' way and I have to hold back the urge to flick his nose or something.

"I have a plan worked up for our conversation tonight but wanted to see if you had any other things to share that might be helpful. You have been following her for a while and I want to make sure I help her where she most needs it right now." he shares, maybe seeing my annoyance with his earlier expression.

"Okay, so you already know that makeup is something she first started playing with as something to do for herself when she got out on her own. She started working at Home Depot in college and enjoyed working at the store but kept getting passed over for promotions—honestly, probably because she's a girl. She didn't have the best home situation from what I can gather from her content. But she focuses on a lot of 'ready to go' looks."

"And remind me what that means?" He knows this stuff; I'm not sure why he asks but I humor him.

"She does a lot of things that fit with an everyday girl's budget and time table. Most of the products she uses are from brands that are affordable and last a long time and have a lot of versatility to them."

"That makes sense. So why hasn't she gotten brand deals or a huge following? It seems like she has a great niche there."

"She had to stop posting for a while. She didn't announce an actual break on her social media, so when she went quiet, it felt a little abrupt, and she didn't let her followers know what was happening until she came back. Work was too demanding and then she had to take a mental health break. She's made a few videos talking about her anxiety and how that has affected her content and her job. She hit burnout trying to do everything so she had to find a better balance. Since she stopped posting for close to a year, she lost a lot of momentum and has struggled with getting back on top of things again. She also doesn't hop on trends quickly, again because of the anxiety. She's done some posts about the longevity of classic makeup and it isn't sustainable to jump on every trend or every collection drop from a brand. That might have gotten her pulled from a few lists for free stuff."

"That makes sense. Knowing that background helps because I can focus on brands that target classic looks and everyday collections rather than trendy collaborations."

"Exactly. You got this, Matt. You're going to do great tonight."

"I am going to head home and shower and then get ready for my call. I've got a Zoom meeting booked for five tonight. Wish me luck. And no," he stops talking for a moment and makes eye contact with me, "you may not come home with me to listen while I have my call with her."

I hold back from throwing an actual temper tantrum before going to give him a hug and then realize that he ran here instead of driving because he is gross with sweat.

"Okay, you are gross—definitely take a shower. But thank you for telling me. I can't wait to hear how it goes. You are going to cut her a deal if cost is a problem, right? I'd seriously love to see her account take off. She deserves it. Especially with all the crap she's had to deal with over the last few years at work and starting out on her own."

"I'll do my best. Love you, Ash."

And with that, he heads out the door and I run upstairs to work on this skincare video. If I'm going to have the chance to meet with Sasha, I need to make sure my content is ready to go. I haven't been doing this as long as she has, but we have similar vibes. Ready to wear college looks and skincare essentials for dorm living are surprisingly very similar to ready to wear work looks and skincare essentials for every budget.

Today is my big content day, so I'm holed up in my room doing product and application photos and videos all day. I started doing these bulk record days when I wasn't feeling well earlier this year. It helps me plan out my content a little better and then take advantage of the days where I am feeling well. I never know when things are going to spike and I won't be up for recording or trying new things. And when it's a video record day, I need to be in a good headspace. If I'm fighting a headache or stressed over an assignment, it's hard to get excited over a new glitter eyeshadow palette. Those are good declutter the makeup desk or organizing the décor closet days. Or soak in a bath days.

It's early evening by the time I am wrapping up my last video and finally cleaning up. I have open products all over my makeup desk, my bed, and the bathroom counter. I really should find a better way to organize these full content days. It's a good thing I don't have a cat, there would be glitter all over everything. As it is, there's already random eyeshadow powder on my white and pink comforter and streaks of lipstick on my desk. I hear my phone notifications going off, but I am determined to get this put away before I see what's happening. Sam should still be at work and my parents are downstairs, so, unless it's Matt saying that he's on his way over with Sasha, it can wait. And I seriously doubt that's happening. He has to get her to say yes to working with him first. God, I hope she says yes. That would be absolutely incredible.

With me actually focusing on cleaning up and putting everything back where it belongs, it's only twenty minutes until my room is back to normal. Well, my normal. There's a few sweaters on the end of the bed that I tried on this morning and then decided I wanted to wear something different, hair ties all over my desk from slight hair changes between videos, and a notebook with notes and hashtags and check marks all over it to make sure I got everything recorded today. I do need to find a more organized way to do this.

The picture for the day has been uploaded and I'm thankful it was just a cute product flat lay today. I've been limiting my face content to just once or twice a week. It's minimizing the creepy comments and messages asking if I need a sugar daddy. No, Bob, I'm all set, thank you very much. I make a cursory glance at the notifications to see if there's anything I actually need to check out after I text Sam to see what his plans are for the evening.

Notifications come in batches at this point. And most of them are just fluff. Matt's filters make it a lot easier to sort through and I usually start with the messages and story replies. Especially after I post, I like to interact with the accounts that are genuinely there for my content. I love that I'm starting to recognize some usernames and have some accounts that I feel like I've started forming an online friendship with. After those messages are answered, I look at the tagged photos. This is the section that isn't perfectly filtered, and thankfully, it isn't utilized much. I've had a few followers recreate my looks or do collaborations with me for themed days, but there have been a few spam accounts that tag me too.

My account is still pretty small, compared to other makeup accounts. I'm sitting at 25k followers right now, which is a whole lot bigger than I was expecting. But it's still "micro influencer" status to a lot of brands and other creators out there. Today there's just two new photos that I need to check. The first is obviously a spam photo with dollar signs all over the image and promises of free phones and followers. Yeah, let's just block you.

The second photo takes me a moment to even figure out what I'm looking at. It's blurry, like how it looks through a window when it's been raining. The colors are spectacular, and I don't recognize the username, CoNoCo27win; it could just be another sweepstakes account. The caption just says, "looking for the beauty." I go to the user profile to see what else is there and find a few more photos of a similar style. It all looks like rainy portraits through a window or windshield. Pictures from both day and night and different backgrounds. These are beautiful. Maybe the tag on that one was wrong. I leave it for now and save one of the pictures that gives a pretty winter feel. Not sure why, but it's calling to me. I may see if I can get a print of it for my room.

Ashley

WED   THU   FRI   SAT   SUN        DATE

# Chapter Seventeen

## ASHLEY

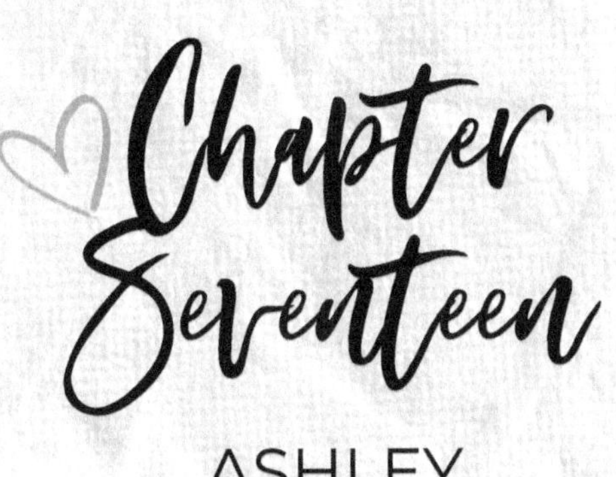

### HORCHATA ICED TEA

*Social Post: Good morning! What time do you usually get up during the summer break? I sleep in whenever possible, usually. Unless my brother wakes me up with unnecessary text messages. Insert side eye emoji here. LOL. But seriously, it's too early. #summertime #coloradogirl #justme*

*Image Description: Photo of my sheer white curtains letting the light in through my window.*

The next morning, I wake up to a message from Matt asking if he can chat through something with me. Well, that's not ominous at all.

> Me: Why are you sending me cryptic text messages at five in the morning?

> Matt: It wasn't cryptic. I have something I want to run by you when you are awake and human.

> Me: I'm pretty sure I'm always human.

> Matt: Have you had coffee yet?

> Me: No. I'm still in bed. It's barely light out.

> Matt: It's eight in the morning, Ash.

> Me: Don't judge me.

I send him a gif of one of the Pixar monsters asking another character to go to sleep so he understands I am not happy. I can already picture his deadpan response. That man does not understand summer vacation. I quickly get myself up and ready and then make my way downstairs. Sam is going to come over in a bit so we can go walk around downtown for a little while today and try out a new brunch place. And then we are going to see the concert on the green tonight. Maybe with the parents. We'll see how that goes.

I immediately go to the coffee pot to fill up my mug when my phone rings. I shoulder the device while hunting for the right syrup to match my mood this morning.

"Good morning, I don't have coffee in me yet. You've been warned," I mutter into the phone and now hope that it was my brother or Sam calling and not some random person. No clue why I didn't double check that before I answered. Oh yeah, coffee.

"Hey, Ash. I'm driving by to drop off some stain options for Mom. Wanted to see if you are up and functioning so we can chat about my call with Sasha last night," Matt responds on the other end. He's a little distant so the phone must be connected to his car

Bluetooth. I seriously hate that option. Just get a headset.

"Yeah, I'm up. And actively working on my coffee so I'll be human momentarily."

"I thought you were always human." I can hear the smugness in his voice so I just hang up on him. He should know me better by now. I can't actually logic through conversations this early. College really pushed my comfort zone, but I adjusted my sleep schedule to make sure I was awake at least an hour before that first class.

Sam found out the hard way that I am not fully coherent when I first wake up. Don't ask me questions because I will not understand how to respond properly. He had asked if I wanted to go skiing with him over the winter break. Yeah, I did that once and never again. I'm a stay at the lodge with hot cocoa and a good book girl. I'll stay off the slopes. I had mumbled an agreement and he didn't clarify later so, I completely forgot the conversation within moments. And then had to find a nice way to tell him to find someone else to take with him for the ski afternoon he had purchased as a date with me.

I hear the door unlock and open and move so I can see the front door. Matt steps inside and toes off his shoes by the bench. "Can you go grab a notebook? Or do you want to use one of mine?" he asks when he makes eye contact with me.

"Am I going to want my own notebook for this?" I am getting excited, not sure why yet, but he seems excited.

He just smiles at me before answering, "You're gonna want your own notebook for this." I squeal and run upstairs to pick something cute out. Matt and I both got our parent's love for stationery. Notebooks, pens, note cards, highlighters—they're all amazing. I am not the most organized person, except when it comes to office supplies. I have different notebooks and pens for different purposes. I decide on a notebook with an amethyst design and a few black, purple, and deep blue pens for this conversation. A small bag holds the pens, purple page tabs, a couple neutral highlighters, and some generic line stickers.

I come back downstairs to find Matt at the table, his own mini office setup already laid out in front of him. "So I have an idea that I want to run by you before I fully send over the final details to

Sasha."

"Okay, whatcha got?" I open my notebook and wait for his idea.

"Would you be open to a mentorship with Sasha?" He immediately holds up his hand in a placating gesture that tells me to chill out a moment, "I haven't talked to her about this yet so hang on. If she is open to it, would you be interested in working with her this summer? That way you can work on your content and she has someone she can work with for the bigger campaigns she is wanting to focus on. And then you both have that additional experience moving forward."

"Not sure why you felt the need to ask me. That's a hard yes."

"Okay, let's see what she says and we will go from there."

"Can I do my happy dance now?"

"Have at it," he just chuckles at me as I stand up and start giggling like a five-year-old with a sprinkle ice cream cone.

"So, you are going to get to work with Sasha this summer on content?" Sam is laid out next to me on the picnic blanket. The Beach Boys style band is about halfway through their set and the sun is finally thinking about setting. Families and couples are enjoying the music and the food trucks while checking out the few new stores downtown. Doors are all opened and it's a great chance for people to connect with neighbors and businesses. I love the vibe downtown during summer events.

"Yep," I let the 'p' pop a bit as I grab my cream soda from the cooler at our feet. "So, I will have some more structure for the summer. Which means, hopefully less stressful moments since I will have a plan and can be working on some of the bigger projects with Sasha. We have our first meeting next week and will be able to map out the big collaborations and goals. And I'll be able to see if any of the work we are doing will translate into projects for the fall. Maybe I can get a head start on some of the research or reports for next year."

"I can tell you're really excited about this. And maybe we can do some library work days this summer while I'm writing and you are working on content or brand reach outs."

"As long as we still get some time where we aren't behind screens."

"At the risk of breaking our no screen rule while we spend time together, can we get a quick picture before it gets dark?" Sam scoots his arm over so he is propped up behind me a little bit and I can rest my head on his shoulder.

"Not for the paper, right?"

"Nope, just for me." He smiles at me before placing a soft kiss on my lips and then pulling his phone out. He takes a few pictures and shows them to me. I ask for a couple of them and then give the okay on two of them to post.

"Make sure you tag me in those. They turned out really well. It must be the lighting and the good news of the day."

"Not that you're spending time with me?" Sam teases me as I pull my phone out to accept the tag request.

"And because I'm spending time with you. That's a given." I share the photos to my stories and then add another slide of the stage in the background from where we are sitting. It's generic enough and only in my stories, so I don't mind posting something a little more specific. We'll be heading back soon anyway. I think the set is almost over.

"Oh, I need to show you this account I found yesterday. How neat are these pictures?" I pull up the rain photos and show them to Sam.

"This is a really neat concept. I haven't messed around with water photos like this before, but this is really good. There's just enough detail shown that it feels like you're getting a peek behind the glass. It looks like he just posted a new one." He passes the phone back to me so I can see what it is.

It's obviously taken as sunset approaches. So he's probably in the same time zone if this was taken recently. The bottom of the photo has grass and several colorful sections throughout. The top half of the photo has an outline of buildings and then the sky with the colors of the sunset behind it.

"I wish I could see more of this photo to know what he saw behind the glass and the water droplets."

"Maybe he'll show more details with more content shared. It looks like he hasn't been doing this very long."

"I'm curious to see what he focuses on as he keeps posting. He's already got several thousand followers so I'm not the only one. And I already have one bookmarked that I want printed out."

"I wouldn't be surprised to see him offering prints or canvas art at some point. He's got a good eye."

Ashley

# Chapter Eighteen

## HIM

Twenty-five posts until she found my account.

I had to resort to tagging her in one of them, but I wasn't sure if she would see the tag as someone sharing something for her to see or another unwanted advance.

I want her to see the effortless beauty of life around her. She has been too focused on stress and things that are not for her recently. Giving her something to smile at brings me such great joy. And I put that smile there. Not the boyfriend. Not her family. Me.

She even saved one of the photographs. I'll have to set it aside to give to her later.

I'll give her some time though.

It's been a while since her last episode and I want her to keep getting better. It won't be long until she's back on campus where I can easily see her more often. In person.

Although, she is quite beautiful behind my lens.

WED   THU   FRI   SAT   SUN       DATE

# Chapter Nineteen

## ASHLEY

White Chocolate Mocha with a pump of Caramel topped with Whipped Cream

*Social Post: Have you ever had that moment that you feel like is going to change everything? I think that might just happen today. Also, what do you wear to meet your favorite creator? Help!! #sashaloveslipstick #summer #nocogirl #ootd #coffeeshopday*

*Image Description: Open journal and planner next to coffee mug and an excessive amount of pens and lipstick. Planner date is covered in stickers and smiley faces.*

How many times can you theoretically text someone within thirty seconds? I'm going for gold here this morning texting Matt as I get ready for this meeting.

Me: What the heck am I supposed to wear?

> Me: Do I need to bring anything else besides what she asked me for?

> Me: Am I paying for both of us or just myself?

> Me: Should I bring a portfolio?

> Me: Crap. I don't have a portfolio.

And now I'm hyperventilating. I don't have panic attacks, what the heck is happening. My phone ringing pulls me out of it before it fully starts.

"Hello?"

"Hey, Ash. First, breathe." My brother takes a pause so I can do just that before continuing, "Second, your meeting isn't until like 1:00 today. Why are you freaking out so much about this? It's coffee." He did not just say that. I walk down to the kitchen so I can grab more coffee while trying to temper my response so I don't come across too crazy. It's too early for this.

"Because I'm about to meet with Sasha! She is my version of a mini celebrity and she wants to meet with me. Granted, it's because you worked your persuasive magic, but still. I'm allowed to freak out a bit." I take a breath and a sip of my coffee.

"Do you want me to come over for a bit? I can work on my end of things a bit more while you get your things together so you can ask me questions as they come up and then I can drop you off at the coffee shop." Um, duh.

"You are the best!" I practically scream into the phone. "Yes, please! I'll go take a quick shower and see you in twenty minutes." I hang up before he can even respond and head up to my room. I take a longer shower than normal—enough to wash my hair, but not quite enough to classify as an everything shower. I pop downstairs to get another pot of coffee going before figuring out makeup and outfit for today.

I settle on a pair of denim shorts and a pink sleeveless top. I feel put together and cute while still casual enough for a coffee shop meeting. I throw a little product in my hair so that way it won't dry all frizzy before pocketing my phone and going back downstairs for more coffee. I've been up for a few hours and need a top off, don't judge. I'm not surprised to see Matt at the dining room table, already having things spread out and organizing everything for his meeting with Sasha.

"Are Mom and Dad out for the morning?" Matt asks as I put the creamer back into the fridge and then make my way to the table next to him.

"Yeah, I think they are heading to the farmers market and then I'm not sure after that. There are some new artisan vendors they've been following on Instagram that are showcasing things today and they aren't done with Christmas shopping yet." I roll my eyes and then pull out my phone to see if I can find which ones they are looking for. Yes, our parents shop for gifts all year. It means they can focus on each person individually and not just on what they find in the weeks leading up to the holiday. It works for them.

"Have you been with them to the farmers market recently?" My brother does not ask questions just because; he has something he is thinking about.

"Not for a while...why?"

"Just thinking..." he trails off and starts working on something on his laptop. He drowns himself in whatever he is working on and I immerse myself in my own things—editing the videos and pictures from yesterday and engaging with my followers' comments from this morning.

"There it is." My brother breathes out and sits back in his chair. I had almost forgotten he was working next to me.

"What did you do?" I ask him, leaning over to see what he just did.

"I'm not showing you anything. I'm working my magic." I just glare at him and then abruptly stand up to bring the extra stuff back to my room. We need to leave soon. By the time I get back downstairs, Matt is packing up too. I do a little spin for him at the bottom of the stairs to show off my outfit.

"How's this?"

"What am I looking at here?" Again, I just look at him. You would think he's never around me.

"You look fine, it's just a coffee meeting." I sigh, I don't have time for this. I take a look at the mirror by the front door before grabbing my things.

"Ready to head out?" Matt asks as he shoulders his bag as well. I don't even respond, just grab his keys and head outside. I need to just get there. My anxiety is through the roof. I hate afternoon meetings. Too much time to stress over all the possibilities.

Matt comes inside with me and finds a spot to sit by the front windows while I order a drink and head to the fireplace in the back of the shop. It's cozy and quiet and there isn't as much walk-by traffic around here. I have a few minutes before she gets here to check notifications and pull out my notebook for the meeting. Okay, deep breaths, Ash. This is going to be amazing.

Sasha may just be the easiest person to talk to. It helps that I've been interacting with her content for a while. I can tell I'm a little less nervous than she is when she comes over to join me, coffee in hand, of course. But once we have a chance to start chatting about our favorite brands, products, and what we want to work on this summer, we both fall into easy conversation. Because of my school schedule, we have to work intentionally on things this summer. And we don't want to overwhelm either of our schedules.

"So, how do you feel about doing a mix of collaborative posts and then working on a few specific series' for your channel over the summer?" she suggests as we move from overview to specific planning.

"I like that. I know you already have several things in the works from what you've shared on your socials, but I would love to be involved in some of the new things that you'll be working on once you start working with Matt. My schedule will be limited once I go back to school, so I'd like to take advantage of the extra time to have additional videos recorded." I sip my coffee and frown a bit when I realize it's empty. I'm gonna need to grab more once we wrap up.

"I completely agree with that," Sasha nods in agreement. "We have to work with your schedule and make this work for you when you go back to school. Are there any specific things you want to work with me on this summer?"

"I'll look over the tentative content plan and see if there's anything that overlaps with things I was thinking for myself as well. And then we can chat later this week?"

"Perfect. I have a rough plan for the summer but I don't know how much your brother is going to adjust things yet."

"Very fair," I laugh at her comment. "He does tend to rework a lot of things when he starts working with a new client. It always comes out perfectly in the end though."

"Good to know." She smiles at me and then pulls out her notebook so we can finish up a few more things before we fully wrap up at four. We are going to meet up on Monday nights and then Friday mornings until school starts back up.

"Do you want to meet my brother in person before you head out?" I ask her as I place the last of my things in my bag.

"Oh, I didn't know he was coming..." I can tell she's a little nervous and don't want to stress her out more. I give her a second to see what she wants to do, not wanting to come across too eager to add more onto her day.

"Yeah, sure." She looks at me and smiles. "Is he already here or is he picking you up?"

I motion to the front counter where he's been working. "He's over by the front window. He's been working here while we were meeting. I don't love being places by myself and we got here a bit before you did." We start walking toward his table as I finish telling her.

"Hey, Matt. We are all done. I didn't know if you wanted to say 'hey' to Sasha before she took off." I head to the counter to grab more coffee and let them have a minute.

After a few more moments, I head back to the table with my

coffee. Okay, they're cute together. My brother has been way too content working behind computer screens. Maybe this will be the push he needs to start seeing someone. They wrap up their conversation as I send over a couple photos to Sasha so she has some of the brand info that we talked about today. It's going to be so fun working with her this summer.

Things definitely just got a lot busier, but I cannot wait!

Ashley

WED   THU   FRI   SAT   SUN          DATE :

# Chapter Twenty

## ASHLEY

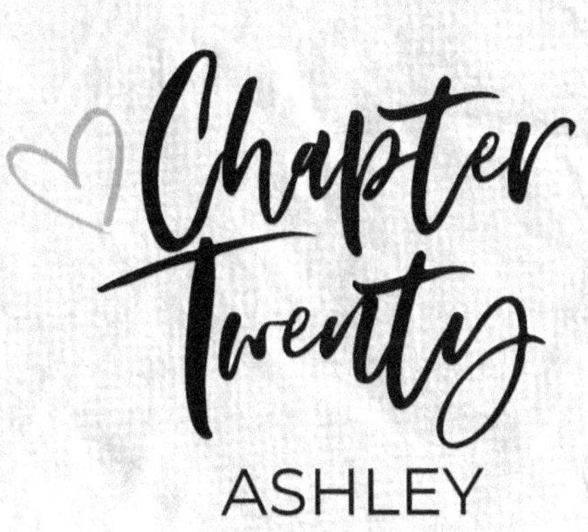

### WHITE CHOCOLATE MOCHA FRAPPUCCINO

*Social Post: Look at the new pretty I just got!! It may be incredibly early, but I'm excited to check out the new studio this morning with @sashaloveslipstick and @kyliethrives #yoga #yogaflow #yogamat #sashaloveslipstick*

*Image Description: Yoga mat strap over my shoulder, grey strap layered over my pink tank top.*

"Okay, but why are we going to a yoga class instead of sleeping in on a Saturday morning?" It is seven in the morning on a Saturday and I am out of my bed, outside of my house, and in a car with Sasha and her friend, Kylie. And we are going to a yoga class. It's barely light outside. Okay, that's an exaggeration, but it's still too early for this. I haven't had enough coffee for this yet.

"Because it's a new woman-owned business in the area and we

told her we would film some content about workout proof makeup today," Sasha reminds me. Oh yeah. There is a reason for this.

"As long as it's nothing too intense. I haven't taken a yoga class since college," Kylie adds in from the front seat. All of us have travel cups from the local coffee shop in hand as we make our way to the studio. It just opened up last month and we met the owner at a farmers market just after she opened up. She's such a sweetheart and I hope that we get some visibility for the studio while we get some content today. And apparently, a workout.

"It's supposed to be a recovery yoga session today. Lots of deep stretches and a focus on restorative breathing and increasing circulation. Something for each of us," Sasha lets us know as she pulls into the parking lot. The strip mall has a few other businesses, nothing that's open though. Maybe we can find somewhere for brunch after this. The class doesn't start until eight, so we are planning to finish makeup here, taking advantage of the gorgeous natural lighting and soft greens and blues of the studio, before we transition to the class.

"Did Nicole let you know how many people will be here this morning? It sounded like a new type of class that she just started offering on the weekends." I ask Sasha as we get our bags and makeup cases out of the back. Kylie grabs the phone stand and ring light, just in case. I'm glad I have a new yoga mat for this. Mine was starting to look pretty ratty. I've had it since a yoga phase I had in junior high and the Lisa Frank pattern just isn't the vibe I'm going for right now. Sam found me a really simple purple gradient one and gave it to me earlier this week while we were talking about the classes I'll be attending this summer with the girls.

"I think only about ten others. We will have to see if anyone is okay with their picture or video being taken before the class starts. We can always set things up to only shoot on us, and I just want some basic footage that we can splice into the longer promo video for the studio and then our vlog posts about workout ready makeup. I have zero desire to showcase our downward dog form in any social media content." We all laugh at that as Nicole greets us at the door, helping with a few of the more awkward pieces of equipment.

"I am so glad you ladies could make it this morning. I have a small table set up for you to use in the corner by the window. Let me know if you need anything else while you get the content shots before class starts. Other class attendees should be here in about half an hour, so hopefully that's enough time to get things going."

"That should be perfect. The beauty about workout ready makeup is that it's simple and the natural lighting is going to make this so much easier. Do you want to put on your music though? That way it helps with the flow of the video and we have a bit of background noise." Sasha hands Nicole a little bag we had prepared for her earlier this week. It has some of our favorite skin and makeup products as a thank you for letting us use the space during the class today.

This is the part of working with Sasha that I didn't realize I would love so much. Being able to partner up with local businesses and female entrepreneurs. We get to connect with so many of them now, helping them make connections to other people and businesses so they can grow. We even have some spa nights planned as a way to help support some moms and caregivers in the area. We get to share some practical skincare and makeup tips with those that attend and they get to have a night to take care of themselves. I didn't realize how often moms just get into a routine of surviving and taking care of everything else that they don't always have the time or energy to do a new skincare routine, a face mask, or even a foot soak. These events help us remind them that they can schedule in time for themselves and give them the tools to do so.

We just need to find a nail salon and spa that offer childcare during services. That would be the absolute dream. That way they can fully relax knowing their kids are being taken care of in the same building. Why isn't this already a thing? This has turned into so much more than just makeup tutorials and aesthetic photos. It's actual impact and community involvement. And it's amazing.

Two hours later, my body is deliciously sore and I definitely need a shower. I had no clue that a more chill yoga class could be that intense.

"Well, at least we can definitely show that this routine was sweat proof. My bra is soaked but my makeup still looks amazing."

I dab at the back of my neck with my towel. "I think we need to skip brunch because I need a shower."

"I can drop you off at your house and then we can plan to meet tomorrow afternoon to work on edits if that works for you. I think we have enough content to get some blog posts done too if we have the time and energy tomorrow." Sasha picks up her sticker-covered water bottle to drain the rest of the water before she fills it up at the station by our makeshift photo and video recording stand. We've gotten good at recording with the tools we have and yoga blocks made the perfect prop for our phones during the class.

"That works for me too. My boss just texted me and they need me at the restaurant early. So I'll need to go shower and head out soon. Thanks for letting me tag along for this." Kylie pockets her phone before helping to pick the rest of our equipment up.

"If we can't go to brunch together, we are too busy," Sasha laughs. "We need to plan a non-work related thing soon before you go back to school, Ash."

"That is going to come up way too soon. I'm not ready for more early mornings."

Before long, it's time to start getting ready to go back to school. Sophomore year, here we come. Sasha took me out shopping last night and it was nice being able to hang out with her while we shopped and had dinner. And of course, having conversations with people out and about. I was super excited to meet Tilly last night too. She seems super sweet and hopefully, I'll be seeing her around campus starting in just a few weeks. She'll be a year behind me in classes, but with similar majors and interests, we'll see what happens. I already have it in the back of my mind that I may see if we can room together next year if I decide to stay on campus. Need to see if this is going to be an actual friendship or just the "oh yeah, I know her," type of relationship first.

Ashley

WED   THU   FRI   SAT   SUN       DATE

# Chapter Twenty-One

## ASHLEY

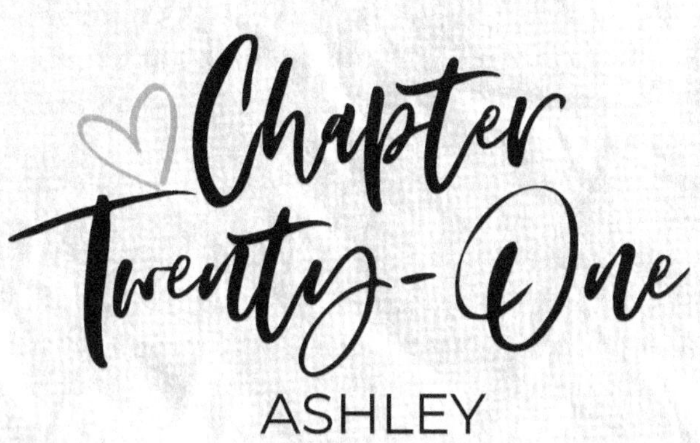

### CARAMEL BRULEE LATTE

Social Post: "Control what you can and leave the rest." Can I have a mantra? I think I should be able to have a mantra. Today is my 19th birthday and I can't wait to spend the day with my brother. It's tradition – no judging. I'll show you how we spend the day later, as long as I don't chicken out. I think going into this year that is going to be what I focus on, though – controlling what I can and leaving the rest. Leaving it out of my thoughts, my intentions, my emotions. I hope this isn't coming across doom and gloom. It feels that way a bit. But with a new year beginning in college and this platform continuing to grow, and as I get to keep working with Sasha, I need a focus for myself. Hopefully this is an encouragement to at least one of you. Do you have a mantra or saying that you hold to? I'd love to hear them if you do! #birthdaygirl #happybirthdaytome #nineteen #control #personalmantra

Image Description: Journal page opened up with "Control what you can and leave the rest" written in cursive at the top of the page along with a "Happy Birthday to me" sticker.

"So how are we celebrating your birthday this year, Ash?" my brother asks as we drive around town. It's my birthday and we started going out together to celebrate when he turned sixteen and got his license. We've done everything from skipping school to go to the zoo, getting pedicures, and he even took me to get a new piercing a couple years ago. Last year, he was the one with me when I got my first tattoo: a simple Columbine flower on my ankle. I wanted it to be something little for my first one and he definitely got the tattoo bug after then. He's rocking almost a full sleeve at this point.

"Are you okay with brunch and another tattoo appointment?" I may have already booked us a spot at a place I love in town. I've known what I've wanted this time around since the spring, but wanted to wait until my birthday so I could go with Matt. In those moments where things felt outside of my control, I needed a reminder that I am the one that has the final say in how I react to the situations around me.

With all the changes in this last year, I feel like I'm constantly reminded how much I can't fix. How much stuff just happens to me without my approval or consent. With the fainting, Raynaud's, and the creepers lurking online—it just feels overwhelming. And I hate that this is something I just have to let run its course. I need to see how it continues to play out. I can control my sleep and stress, to a degree, but not fully. I am in college. And I pretty much have to live online and social media for what I am doing with Sasha.

"Is that how you want to spend the day? I didn't get an appointment at the studio, but I can call my guy and see if he can squeeze us in."

"I already have that taken care of. You have about an hour to choose what you're getting this time though or I get to pick for you."

"As long as it's nothing coffee related, that may be an interesting way to spend the day. But I don't really want you choosing permanent ink for my body." He smirks at me as we pull into a breakfast place to grab something quick before we head to our appointments.

A few hours later, we are heading home, new wrappings in place, and I am ready for a nap.

"I do not understand why I get so tired after getting a tattoo," I murmur to Matt as I rest my head on the window. The drive home isn't long, but I'm struggling to stay awake.

"It's the adrenaline and endorphin rush from the pain levels. It gets easier the more you do. Do you need anything or are you okay until we get home?" He has a bit of concern in his voice. I really hope I don't pass out again. Waking up confused is not a good look.

"I should be fine. But if I fall asleep, I'm just sleeping, not unconscious. Okay?"

"Okay. But if you can wait until we get home, I'll feel a lot better. I can't fully check in on you while I am driving. And even though the tattoo is small, it's still a shock to your system. Mom knows we did this today, right? She said it was okay with the fainting episodes?" Yeah, he's definitely concerned now.

"I might have forgotten to run it by her. The spells aren't happening enough that I think how different activities will affect them, you know? And it's a small tattoo. I think I just need a nap and I will be okay. And probably some water."

"And protein," I see him shaking his head incredulously out of the corner of my eye. "You can't survive on coffee, Ash."

"Of course, I can. You just haven't tried it yet. Sasha does it too. Do you give her a hard time about her coffee consumption?"

"Every damn day."

"Do I get to see?" Sam asks me that night. Luckily, I didn't have an episode after the tattoo appointment. I did take a pretty heavy nap though and I was so glad that my parents planned a quiet night in with Sam and the four of us instead of going out.

"It's not healed yet. So, it's not going to be pretty."

"Well, you're gorgeous, so let me see. You said you designed it?"

I nod at him as I start pulling up the hem on my skirt so he can see the tattoo on my upper thigh of my right leg. "I wouldn't say I designed it. It's pretty simple, Sam," I laugh at him as I peel the wrap back so he can see the healing lines on my leg. Yeah, that hurts a bit. The script is simple, but it's a message I hope I can keep focused on this year *"I am Mine."* It has a simple lavender stem next to it to remind me of tranquility and peace.

"It's beautiful. And a good reminder for you this upcoming year." His hands settle on my waist as he kneels down in front of me to get a better look.

"I thought so. And it's simple enough that if I want to add to it later, there's some options."

"So do I get to have some fun with you while I'm on my knees?" His eyes practically sparkle with mischief as he looks up at me.

"I won't say no to that." I give him the green light he was looking for and then I'm being hoisted into the air so he can lay me down on the bed.

"Does your leg hurt? Do I need to avoid touching it?" he checks in with me as he peels off my sweater and follows the movement with kisses.

"Just right around the tattoo marks. Let me cover it back up, just in case. And you may want to go lock the door. My parents are still up."

"You don't think you can keep quiet while I give you your birthday present?"

"When you say it that way…absolutely not."

Ashley

WED    THU    FRI    SAT    SUN         DATE

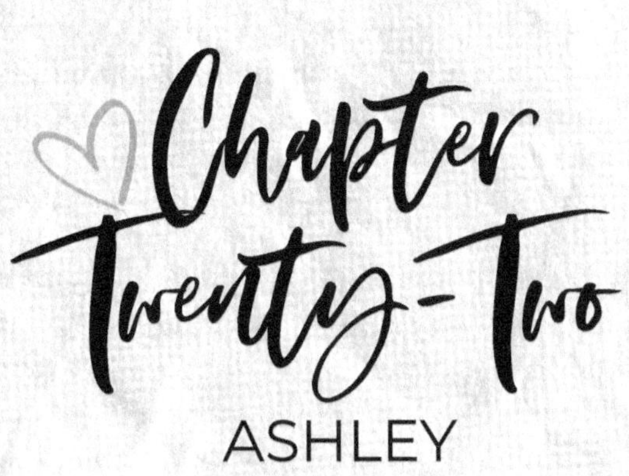

# Chapter Twenty-Two

## ASHLEY

**MOCHA MUD PUDDLE**

*Social Post: Back on campus. Year two, here we go. How do we feel about totally leaning into the Barbie aesthetic? #pinkeveryday #sashaloveslipstick #coloradogirl #csu #firstday*

*Image Description: New stack of colored notebooks, tabs, pens, and highlighters for the new year on my vanity desk in my bedroom. All in various shades of pink ranging from neon to blush. My coffee mug sits empty next to the stack along with my watermelon lip balm.*

I am more excited about this year than I thought I would be. Sam and I don't have any classes together this semester, unfortunately. But I do have one with Tilly. And I have Fridays off from classes this semester so I will be able to have a day to work on things with Sasha too. I am loving what we have planned for this fall, so that additional time will be needed, especially as we get closer to our campaign for October. Luckily, most of the work for the Pink Every Day campaign is already done, so it's just prepping the content now and getting the longer videos recorded.

Sam is meeting me on campus this morning so we can have a quick minute together before we go our separate ways for classes. He already sent me a cute text this morning after I sent him the mirror selfie with my new green sweater he bought me for my birthday. It was only part of my birthday gift, but this was the only thing I could wear outside of the bedroom. (insert winky face here).

"So, does the Barbie aesthetic mean that I have to be Ken? Because I don't think my aesthetic is going to match with the vibe you have going on here, Ash," Sam jokes with me as he greets me in the quad on campus.

I can't help the laugh that comes out. I'm at least outside for this one, so I am not embarrassed by the noise level or the glances my way. People can deal with it.

"You don't have to be Ken," I reassure him. "I just meant that most of my stuff for the new year is very pink and sparkly and happy colors. I'm still rocking the greens this year. I can only wear so much pink before I start turning into a valley girl."

"There is so much to unpack in that statement, I don't even know where to start," he shakes his head as we start walking to the building that houses most of our classes.

"How is your schedule looking with juggling school, work, and your TA stuff now?" Not gonna lie, I'm concerned over the load he has this semester. I'm not sure when we are going to have time together outside of mornings like this, but that also means I will have to get up earlier to meet him on campus before classes. Gross.

"It's going to take some adjustments, but I think it'll be okay. I'm only taking four classes since what I'm doing for Professor Erickson is going to count for a few credits. And I have a few more long term stories I'll be working on for the paper instead of traveling every week for new stories and connections. I think our biggest schedule variable is going to be any events you have with Sasha, so we will have to stay connected on that to make sure we get time together."

"I definitely think that's doable. I don't think we have anything bigger than spa nights planned this fall, so we should be able to sync up pretty easily. You have to head right into meetings after classes today though, right?"

Sam holds the door open for me as we enter the building and begin making our way to my lecture hall. I have Professor Summer for a Creative Writing Online class first thing this morning. And I'm excited to start branching into copywriting and other avenues of online writing. It's so different from even what we were learning in high school. We get to the class before I'm ready to say goodbye.

"How do you feel about making out in the hallway like a couple of horny teenagers before I head inside class?" I ask as I press my back to the wall next to the door. I know my face is filled with mischief as his eyes meet mine to see if I'm being serious.

"Are you sure that's how you want to start off the semester, babe?" he jokes back with me, but still leans in to kiss my lips. Definitely not the make out sesh I was aiming for, but his lips feel so good on mine.

"Probably not, but I do enjoy kissing you."

"I like kissing you too. But we do need to remember that these professors are there to help us with those business and professional connections too. I don't really want their visual of me to be pressing you against the wall with my hand under the hem of your shirt and my tongue down your throat."

"Well, that's an interesting mental picture," a voice joins in from behind Sam and he groans quietly before pulling away a bit.

"Good morning, Professor Erickson," he greets his advisory professor as he grins at me in a 'see?' way.

"Am I interrupting here or am I good to steal you away, Sam?" Professor Erickson looks at both of us as he waits for a response. At least he isn't treating me like I'm invisible like some of the other male teachers on campus.

"I have to head into class, so you are good to steal him away." I give Sam's hand a little squeeze before I turn to head into the classroom.

"Oh, I have something for you, Ashley," Professor Erickson raises his voice a little to make sure I don't run off too fast. I turn and know I look confused. I'm not taking any classes with him this semester. I must forget my manners for a moment because I don't actually respond, I just look at him and wait. He moves his messenger bag to the front of his body so he can reach in and get what he is looking for. He pulls out a letter envelope and hands it over. "This was with my mail this morning. Not sure how it got there, but figured I would get it to Sam if I didn't see you this morning."

"Oh, thank you. No clue why something for me would end up with you. I didn't even apply for a TA spot this semester so I shouldn't have anything going to any teachers. Are you sure it's for me?" I look down at my full name printed on the envelope and realize that yes, it is for sure for me. Now I just need to try to convince myself that this is completely normal. Nothing to worry about. Nothing weird is happening. Maybe it was a note from last semester with the projects we completed and it didn't get passed out in class and it got put with another professor who has a similar name. There has to be someone with a similar name, right? Ashley Carter isn't exactly super original. Okay, I'm spiraling a bit here.

I take a deep breath to settle my heart rate and thank Professor Erickson again. I slide the envelope into my bag to check once I sit down inside the classroom. If it's class info or grades or anything official, I want to make sure I can read it when I can give it my full attention. I give Sam a quick peck on the cheek and then slip into the room. It's only about half-full, so I find an open seat halfway back and at the end. I can see the full front of the room, but I won't feel crowded if this ends up being a full class.

I get my planner and notebook for this class out and decide to open up the envelope from Professor Erickson while I wait for class to start. I slide my nail under the seal and pull out the printer paper. The letter has my name at the top and a simple sentiment typed below it.

*"I can't wait to see you again."*

I don't understand. The comments on social media are one thing. It's something I fully expected to happen when I started building up my platform. But this has gone beyond that now. There have been times when I felt like someone was watching me, but nothing has been confirmed. So I thought I was just being paranoid. I thought I saw someone earlier this year when I had my first fainting spell, but when I came to, my mom had said she didn't see anyone and then it never happened again.

I only got one note on campus last year, and I definitely thought that it was just a student being funny or kind with the coffee card. This doesn't feel innocent though. This feels scary. This feels like an invasion of privacy. I don't understand. And I don't like it.

I take a picture of the letter and send it to Matt.

Me: <Image Attached>

Matt: What am I looking at?

Me: A note that one of the professors gave me this morning.

Me: This is weird right?

Me: Like, I'm not overexaggerating?

Matt: What professor?

Me: Professor Erickson. The one that Sam TA's for. But I don't think it's from him.

Matt: What do you mean?

Me: He said it was in his stack of mail this morning, but he wasn't sure where it came from.

Matt: And do we believe him?

Me: I think so.

Matt: Can you put it back in the envelope and give it to me after school today?

Me: So, you're worried too?

Matt: I don't know yet. But I want to check.

Matt: Be careful today and let me know if I need to come get you.

Me: Will do. Love you Matty.

Matt: Love you too.

The day passes quickly, but I feel exhausted. My mind was racing all day wondering who sent the letter and why, looking around for someone who may be watching or taking notice of me. I just hope this is actually just a harmless prank or a misunderstanding and not someone trying to scare me.

Matt is working at the dining room table when I get home. He has a bunch of stuff pulled up for Sasha's fall campaigns and follow up messages from farmers market events we attended this summer.

"Let me know when you are at a good pause point to take a look at this. I'm going to go get changed real quick and then I'll be down." I run upstairs after depositing my bag on one of the chairs across from where Matt was working. I swap out my green sweater for a Luke's Diner T-shirt and an oversized black cardigan that I pretty much live in when I'm home. This thing is so comfy and I will actually cry when it falls apart. And considering I've had it since ninth grade, that day is probably coming sooner rather than later.

I debate leaving my cell phone upstairs. I don't want to deal with the social media notifications, but Matt may have to reset some of the safeguards on my comments if this person found me through social media. I thought it was already filtering things pretty well, but there's always room for improvement, I guess.

Matt has switched over to my socials by the time I get downstairs. He has my Instagram and webpage pulled up on his laptop and is going over traffic details. I've stopped trying to figure out how he gets access to all of the little things he does online. If he's doing it to keep me safe or help get Sasha more visibility, good for him.

"Can I see the letter?" he asks quietly as I sit down and pull out my own laptop. I need to get some school stuff plugged into my digital calendar and to-do list tracker so I can stay on top of these assignments. I pull it out of my notebook and hand it over.

"It looks like a pretty basic piece of paper and envelope. No return info at all and no signature. Just the message to me. I am very confused with why it was given to Professor Erickson though. Why would they do that? Did they assume he would give it to Sam? Was he hoping Sam would see it and go all Alpha Male on me or something?"

"Do you really see Sam doing that?" my brother asks in a 'are you serious' tone.

"No, but I don't know what the purpose of this was supposed to be. Just tell me what you want already. If you want to see me so badly, wouldn't it make sense to tell me who it is so I can see them?"

"You are not seeing whoever sent this, Ash. This person may be completely harmless or totally unhinged."

"I'm nineteen, not nine, Matt. I know that. I'm just thinking out loud here."

"Well, until we know who this is and what their intention is, I'm going to put a few more filters on your social media sites and on your phone. That way if someone starts tracking you or starts spamming your messages, it will start tracking on my end and I will be able to see who it is and hopefully find out why too."

"Don't you have better things to do than babysit my phone all day?" I tease him. But honestly, I'm glad he is listening to my concerns and taking them seriously.

"That's the beauty of technology. It babysits your phone all day, I just have to read the data. Now, how was day one of your sophomore year?"

Ashley

# Chapter Twenty-Three

## HIM

She got the letter from me. So at least she knows I'm still here. I didn't mean to scare her, but she was obviously spooked from what she read. And then she ran home to her brother who promptly locked down her social media and her phone. The basic tracker I had hidden in her apps was disabled before he even realized it was there. But now I am going to have to try even harder to keep a watch on my girl.

The semester has just begun, and at least her boyfriend will have a busier schedule this time around.

WED    THU    FRI    SAT    SUN         DATE

# Chapter Twenty-Four

## ASHLEY

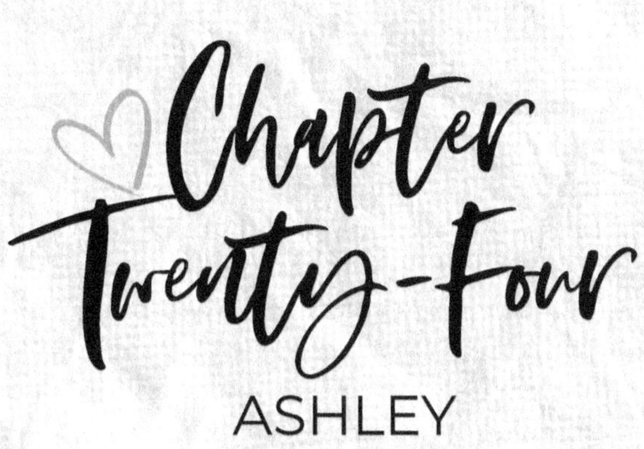

**APPLE CIDER CHAI**

*Social post: Just because it's Halloween doesn't mean it can't be pretty. #spookydecor #spookyseason #alltheglitter*

*Image Description: Dining room table filled with random Halloween decor—black glitter pumpkins, spider webs, candy, gold glitter vases, etc.*

Knock on wood, but things have been quiet. Really, really quiet. School is going well and I am loving my schedule this year. One class with Professor Summer, one with Professor Johnson, and two with Professor Jackson. I really want to get these finance and math classes out of the way so I can enjoy the other content we will be covering. The assignment load is lighter this semester in terms of quantity, but there is a lot more time going into each one.

Before I even realize it's time, we are planning a Halloween party at my brother's house. He volunteered to host as long as I could help. No problem there. I am definitely the more outgoing of the two of us. He has the space for it though. It'll be weird not helping out my family at the neighborhood party this year, but maybe this will be a new tradition for us. Sam unfortunately has to work, but Tilly and her roommate, Corinne, will be joining us.

Tilly and I stopped by the store to grab more candy and fake spiderwebs before heading over to finish decorating. The party is tomorrow so we are taking this afternoon to get ready for the festivities.

"So how many people are coming to this thing?" Tilly asks as I pull into Matt's driveway.

"Um, like ten I think? Matt and a few of his friends, Sasha and her roommates, you and Corinne, and I think a couple people from the restaurant that Sasha's roommates work at. It should be pretty chill. And we can be on candy duty too. My brother likes to give out the good stuff." I smile at her as I reach behind to grab the bag of candy on the floor behind her seat. She waits for me to pull it into my lap before she reaches back to do the same. The spider web package gets caught on my chair and tears the bag though.

"It probably would have been better if we got out to grab those," she chuckles at me.

"Yeah, but it's cold, and I don't like being outside longer than I absolutely need to."

"Completely get that."

We hop out of my car and I grab the spiderwebs and other small décor pieces from the back seat while Tilly grabs our backpacks from the trunk. We brought our stuff in case we finish early so we can get started on our Q2 projects for the semester.

"What are the chances your brother already has things set up and we just have to make it sparkle a bit?" Tilly asks as we make our way up the walkway to the front door.

Matt opens the door before we even have a chance to knock, the stress is obvious on his face without even having to glance into the house behind him. "Absolutely none."

Four hours later, the house is transformed—at least the main living spaces—and pizza has been ordered so we can eat. The boys handled most of the heavy lifting and we got to just "add the sparkle" like Tilly said. We also prepped a few snacks and the candy bowls so we can just show up tomorrow and have a good time. Luca and Jonathan moved some furniture around and went to the store to buy more pumpkins for the front yard. Matt only had like three when we got here and that was definitely not going to be enough.

Unfortunately, we weren't able to bedazzle anything this time around. Tilly and I are already plotting how we can sneak in around Christmas to get back at Matt for saying no. Glittery pumpkins sounded amazing, but Matt didn't want to deal with the lingering glitter after the party. Rude. Glitter makes everything better.

Luca is one of my brother's friends and he makes beautiful wooden furniture, and décor too. And he promised to give me some leftover snowflakes that he doesn't use for other projects so I can "bedazzle to my heart's content." My brother didn't do too bad in the friend department. And I definitely didn't miss the fact that Jonathan caught Tilly's eye when he came in with an armful of pumpkins earlier. The two of them would be cute together. But I am not playing matchmaker this weekend. We have pizza to eat and then I need to get Tilly back on campus. We still have to do our nails tonight too.

"So, remind me again why there are more than one type of Barbie?" Luca teases me as he places the pizza boxes down on the kitchen island.

"Because there is a Barbie doll for every occupation and event and we are in our Barbie era right now," I taunt back at him and stick out my tongue for added effect. I swear I've known this guy since I was in sixth grade and he still thinks I'm twelve.

"And because we said so, and that should be reason enough,"

Tilly taunts back. This girl seriously gives as good as she gets. I was not expecting the sass on her when I first met her this summer, but she is quickly becoming my spirit animal.

"Have I told you that I want to be you when I grow up?" I ask her after I finish laughing at her previous comment.

"Considering I'm a year younger than you, no," she laughs back at me. "Can I bring a box of this back to the dorm if there's enough left over? Corinne had to work tonight and leftover pizza is practically gold right now." She directs the question to Jonathan who had run out to get the pizzas. He just stares at her for a moment, trying to figure out how to answer her apparently.

"If you need it, that's totally fine, I have other food, not trying to be a problem if you needed it, just figured I would ask." Her backtracking is not a normal response from her and I immediately glare at Jonathan, silently communicating to him to fix it.

"You can take as much as you want. Sorry, I was just thinking about if you wanted any other food besides the pizza and couldn't figure out how to offer in a way that didn't sound creepy." He shrugs it off and starts preparing a box for Tilly to take with her. I just shake my head.

"We gotta run, but we will be back tomorrow night at seven for the party," I holler back to my brother as I put the rest of my things in my bag. Including my glue gun and bag of sequins that didn't get to be used tonight.

"Leave the glitter at home tomorrow please," my brother practically pleads as we head outside. I just laugh at him in response. He hasn't seen our costumes, and they give the Lover bodysuit a run for its money. Not exactly, but it's close.

The air is cool and it finally feels like fall. Tilly is already down at the car by the time I stop sniffing the air and enjoying the change in temperature. She pulls open the back door to set the pizza on the backseat and her bag on the ground. I go to the other side to drop off my things too and then notice a flyer on my windshield.

"Are they seriously flyer-ing neighborhoods now? I thought they just did this in shopping plazas." I grab the flyer and throw it in the backseat before we both get in the car and buckle up. The doors automatically lock as I pull out of the driveway and make my way back to campus. It's later than I like being out, especially on a night where the high school kids think it's fun to play pranks on other people. I am not looking forward to heading back to the house tonight. There's a bunch of teens on our street so it's not unusual for them to have their own version of "mischief night" the evening before Halloween.

Usually it's just harmless pranks like TP'ing the trees or Saran wrapping cars. And they always come back to help clean up the next day. It could be worse. I've heard stories of other neighborhoods that have property destroyed or things stolen. I just have zero desire to get potentially caught in the cross hairs of that mess.

By the time I get home, it's almost midnight, and the teens must have already visited our street because it is a mess. There are chalk drawn neon lines all over the road and individual driveways. At least that will wash off with the first rain, or a power washer. Our house also happens to be covered in pink paper hearts. Someone seriously spent some time on this. The front porch, door, windows, and garage have several of the hearts attached.

I text Mom as soon as I park in the driveway.

> Me: Do we know which teen is responsible for the Valentine's Day imitation outside?

> Mom: What do you mean?

> Me: <Image Attached>

> Mom: lol that's awesome.

> Mom: No, I don't know. We'll deal with it in the morning.

Mom: Do you need help bringing things inside?

Me: Nope. I'll be in momentarily.

Mom: Okay. Dad has the front door unlocked
and is waiting for you downstairs.

I kind of love that they have done more to help me feel safe since the fainting episodes earlier this year. Matt also told them about the letter I received earlier in the year, so I think that played into things a bit too.

I get out of the car and make my way inside, beeping the car lock behind me as Dad opens the door and helps me with my bag. I see cookies cooling on trays in the kitchen behind him.

"Sorry I missed baking night tonight," I tell him. I had a lot of fun with Tilly and my brother, but it still feels weird to miss out on the family things we always did together.

"Don't worry about it, Ash. There will be plenty of other opportunities to bake cookies. And apparently we will get some good time together tomorrow removing pink paper from the house."

"I hope it doesn't rain tonight. No clue if that paper is going to stain the house if it gets wet."

"I'm not concerned," he places a kiss on my forehead as we reach the bottom of the stairs. The master bedroom is on the main floor while my bedroom, an office/library, and my brother's old room is upstairs along with a full bathroom. "Sleep well, and I'll see you in the morning."

"Good night, Dad. Don't stay up too late with those cookies."

"I just pulled the last ones out of the oven," he smiles back at me as I head upstairs. My outfit is already set aside for tomorrow so I don't need to worry about that tonight. I can just take off my makeup and go to sleep.

Except there is a pink heart placed on my pillow alongside a pink glitter pen. "Please let this be from Sam and my parents were just playing along," I whisper to myself. I have to believe this is from Sam. Nothing else makes sense.

I walk over to my bed to see if the heart says anything. In simple print writing, a note is written on the heart.

"Have a wonderful holiday tomorrow, even if it's
not your favorite one."

So random. Christmas and Valentines are definitely my favorite, but Halloween has a bunch of good memories attached. Did I talk to Sam about this? I must have.

I send him a thank you text with a picture attached of the house and the note on my bed before turning off notifications so I can get some sleep tonight.

## MARCUS

**TETLEY'S BRITISH BLEND**

*Social Post: I may be moving back to the States, but I am not giving up my tea appreciation. #ukprofessor #gradprogram #coloradobound #csuprof*

*Image Description: CSU letterhead sitting on my kitchen table next to a cup of black tea.*

It's official, I'm moving to Colorado to take on a position in the spring. They are massively expanding their business department as they add on more digital classes. By coming on board, they are hoping to give the students some practical tools to move into job positions and internships as they graduate. I've been looking for a new place to call home now that my temporary position in the UK is coming to a close.

I've been teaching at a small university in Scotland for the last three years and I am ready to come back to the States. My family has been pressuring me to find a new position closer to home so I can settle down. I have my siblings to thank for that. Both of them have gotten married and started their families over the last few years. And my mother is loving the Grandma title.

The email from the admin department of CSU came through this morning, but I was in lecture so I haven't had the chance to let everyone know yet. I have a few other things to settle before I can make the move official. I send off a notice to my supervisory professor at the local admin offices to schedule a meeting later this week before I log out of my email account. After everything is taken care of with my pending resignation, I can start looking for an apartment in Colorado and see how much time I will have in between terms.

Going from teaching grad students in the UK to teaching underclassmen in northern Colorado is definitely going to be a shift. At least the weather will be similar. And I will have more opportunities to connect the students with internships and positions. The area has also stayed partially remote with job positions since the pandemic so that's also a huge perk to those entering the job market right now. More flexibility and better balance between work and home means happier employees and less wasted time too.

These next few months are going to go by quickly. I need to book another flight or two while I am local. Who knows what extra licenses I will need to qualify for in order to fly recreationally in the mountains of Colorado. Nothing beats the views out here though.

It feels like just a few days later, but in actuality, it's been weeks since I got the email from CSU. I have the employment contract printed out and added to my moving folder, making it all that more official. I was able to rent an apartment in a new building not far from the CSU campus. My class schedule for the spring semester has also been finalized and I will be able to have a few student assistants as well as a full time secretary once I get to the area. I have a proven record of my students that I've mentored going on to fill high ranking positions at established companies as well as startups. I am just waiting on the tentative list of potential students that may want to work with me. I don't think the school has announced that I will be coming yet, so that means I can go through social media and sift through their content before they have a chance to tailor it to what they think I will like.

That happened at my position before I came to Scotland. Students went in and altered their online content to what they felt I would appreciate. I ended up picking students that weren't my best fit, and I was not their best fit either. It was a huge waste of time and I did not appreciate it at all. The university that I had been employed at received my notice alongside some strongly worded letters about said students. I don't like being taken advantage of. My name alone cannot guarantee a job. I may be successful in my field, but not every student is going to enjoy working in the online marketing space. And if they aren't willing to put in the work, they will not hold a position with the companies I am affiliated with for very long. Laziness is intolerable. And manipulation is highly unattractive.

Luckily, I only have one mentor student this semester, and I plan to continue working with him remotely once I move. He isn't quite ready to graduate and take on the position we have been working toward. There is a large winter sports resort that he has interned at over the last few breaks that is looking to add on an online class catalog once they can hire him full time. Sean has an amazing presence on camera and is going to do well teaching virtually, as well as heading up the enrollment process. Turning online resources into recurring revenue is one of my specialties. And the course catalog that I now have had the chance to help build out covers everything from digital resources to woodworking tools to choosing the right equipment for winter sports.

I'm curious to see which students I am able to partner with over the coming months and what other industries we will be able to make an impact in. So far, it's been mostly sports, home, hobby, or similar industries. And even though I enjoy it, it's lost the challenge.

# ASHLEY

I'm going to New York City with Sasha!!! At least, that's the hope. As long as the meeting goes well with Natalie, we will be heading to NYC in a few weeks to launch her first collaboration. Natalie owns a makeup brand that we've wanted to connect with, and this collaboration is so much more than we could have imagined. It combines the work we are doing with the Pink Every Day campaign with an actual product line. This has seriously grown to so much more than just a makeup account, and I love that I have had a part in it all. She has the meeting with Natalie in two days, so I need to head over to Matt's house to meet with her and see what she needs help with before the conversation. I am just packing up my bag from the desk I use at the library when I notice someone standing close by. I look up to see Professor Johnson standing next to my chair. He has his winter tweed coat on and is holding his messenger bag. The jacket makes him look older than he is, but I like the distinguished look it provides.

"Hi, Professor Johnson, I was just getting ready to head out. How's your afternoon going?" I greet him as I stand and finish putting my notebooks and laptop into my own bag. And then I start fishing for my gloves so I can go outside. I spent too much time typing this afternoon and I can tell that I am borderline too cold already.

"It's going well. I wanted to run a couple of things by you if you have a moment."

"Sure, how can I help?" I pull out my phone and open the notes app. I hate taking notes on my phone rather than a notebook, but I don't want to take everything out of my bag again. Too much of a chance I will get distracted and will end up staying here working for another hour instead of heading to my brother's house.

"First, I saw your submission regarding the color theory project. I would like to hear more before I approve the thesis so you don't waste the time on the project if it won't be a good fit. Do you have time now to go over that or do you want to set up a meeting?"

"I wasn't quite ready for that conversation tonight. Can I swing by your office during office hours tomorrow morning and show you what I am wanting to do?"

"That will definitely work. Thank you. Will nine work for you?"

I nod in agreement and add the note to my app and then my calendar, sending him the calendar invitation so it syncs up and nothing gets forgotten. I hate showing up for meetings when the other person forgot to write it down and then it's awkward. Don't waste my time and I won't waste yours. It's common decency, really.

"What else did you need to run by me? Or was that the main thing?"

"That was the main thing, but I also wanted to let you know that we will be adding to our faculty next semester. Professor Williams will be coming from a grad program in the UK. He has a proven record of helping businesses launch online programs and pairing the right students with those positions. I think you would be a good fit for his mentorship if it's something you are interested in. I also will have a mentorship program launching in the spring, but I wanted you to have both options so you know what to apply for and what to work on over the coming weeks."

"I have no clue what business I could help with his program, but it does sound interesting. What mentorship program will you be working on?" I shoulder my bag and begin walking toward the doors with Professor Johnson. He holds the door open for me so I can exit first and keep my hands in my pockets. No arguments from me there.

"Can I walk you to your car?" He asks quietly as we step outside. Why is it so cold out here? I know it's November, but I seriously hate the cold.

"That would be great. I can't be outside for long, but I'd like to hear a bit about the program so we can talk in detail in the morning." The parking lot is dark and there aren't many cars or students about, so I'm glad Professor Johnson is walking with me. I hate being outside in the dark by myself.

"I can get the information ready for you tomorrow when you come in. I have a few ideas, but what I was originally planning is going to have to shift with Professor Williams coming to join us." He seems almost a bit dejected with that last bit of information.

"Are you not looking forward to Professor Williams coming to campus?" I hope I'm not prying, but I'm definitely curious.

"We worked together a long time ago, not directly, but we were on the same faculty. I'm not necessarily upset about him coming, but I had some things planned out for the next few years that will now need to change. He will add a lot to the department and I think it will benefit the students in the long run. We'll see how it plays out." He smiles down at me to confirm his sentiment as we get to my car.

"I'll see you in the morning. And I'm excited to hear about your program as well as what you think would be best for me for the coming semesters. I really appreciate your help with this."

He leans forward and holds my door as I slip inside and start the engine, placing my phone in the holder on the dashboard. "You are a good student, Miss Carter. I'm excited to see where your career takes you. Be safe and I will see you in the morning." He gently closes the door and stays in the spot until I lock my doors and start backing away.

I hate early mornings, but hopefully this will be a good meeting tomorrow.

Marcus

WED   THU   FRI   SAT   SUN        DATE :

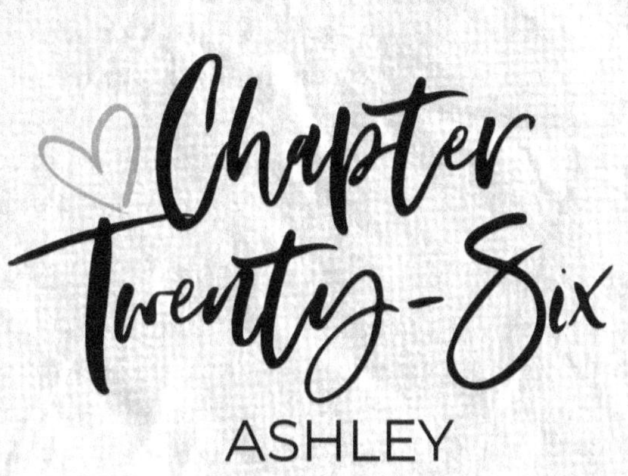


# ASHLEY

**VENTI ICED CARAMEL MACCHIATO, EXTRA SHOT, LESS ICE, EXTRA WHOLE MILK, EXTRA WHIPPED CREAM**

*Social Post: Meeting ready—heading to campus first and then I have some other things planned this afternoon. So ready for everything coming up!! #justme #meetingprep #professionalBarbie #noco #csu*

*Image Description: Stack of notebooks next to my travel coffee mug, a tube of lipstick, and several pink pens on my desk.*

The next morning feels weird. I don't know how else to describe it, but something is off. I shoot a text to Sasha letting her know I will be by the house after my meetings this morning so we can prepare for the conversation with Natalie for the makeup collaboration. I don't get a response back from her in the time it takes me to get ready and head to campus, which is a bit weird. She normally gets back to me pretty quickly. Sam is working with Professor Erickson today, so he is planning to meet me after I'm done with Professor Johnson before I head to my brother's house.

I don't normally skip classes, but I'm planning to today with the meetings. Way too much stress to try to listen to business finances and SEO trends in detail and actually hope to retain anything. I definitely left the house too late to grab a coffee though and I am not happy about that. I will have to text Sam to see if he can grab me one or just stop somewhere on the way to Matt's.

I get to the admin offices of the business department a little before nine and make my way to the receptionist desk. Checking in for my meeting is pretty seamless and I don't even have time to sit down before Professor Johnson comes to his door and calls me inside.

"I wasn't sure what your coffee preferences were, but I got you a hazelnut latte from the main coffee cart. I know it's an early morning for you and you have some big things planned for today." He passes the cup to me and I take in the smell. There's something amazing about the smell of fresh coffee, especially when it's cold outside.

"This is great, thank you. Yes, we have the collaboration meeting with a pretty established beauty brand out of New York this afternoon. There's a lot of possibilities that may come with this for Sasha. I'm so excited to see how it all plays out."

"Is this going to benefit you as well? I know you are enjoying working with Sasha, but I want to make sure this is going to translate to your own career growth as well." He takes a seat in his chair behind the desk as he pulls out a folder and waits for my response, sipping on his own to-go coffee cup.

"It will. I'm learning a lot of very practical behind the scenes things for collaborations and collections as well as having conversations with businesses and owners that will turn into some solid connections depending on what happens after graduation. I still don't one hundred percent know what I'm doing for a full career, but I feel like I am setting myself up for a lot of great options as we get closer. And that's part of why I want to go over my project ideas with you."

I jump into my full pitch for the project and he counters with a few options that will fully round out my research and proposal. We end up taking up the full slot with the project details so we can't talk further about the mentorship programs. I get penciled in for an appointment next week so we can talk about those options. He will have a better idea what Professor Williams will be offering by then so I will have more information to make a well-rounded decision.

"Thanks again for the coffee and your time today. I really appreciate it." I stand and shake his hand as I begin walking with him to the door. "Do you have a pretty full day today?"

"You are very welcome. I'm glad it worked out and I'm excited to see what you come up with for that assignment. It'll move nicely into some of the research you will be working on next semester as well. And yes, I have a full day of meetings today. I will also be meeting with the faculty team and admin staff to go over the plan for next semester. The additional classes mean additional requirements. So, I may be adding a few TA spots sooner than I was originally planning."

"Can you pencil me in as interested if you do end up needing someone? I think it would be helpful to TA for you if you think I would be a good fit. But let me know what the requirements would look like and we can talk more about it later too."

"I appreciate that, Miss Carter. Have a great day and I can't wait to hear about the meeting with Natalie."

Well, my brother is an idiot. What did he think was going to happen when he told Sasha all that he had been doing? I mean, I knew he was keeping tabs on my stuff, but I thought that was strictly for safety reasons. He's been on her socials in the background to help her reach more people and get into new opportunities. Of course, she feels like her trust has been violated.

After getting what info I could from Sasha and then heading to my brother's house to rip him a new one, I'm finally at Sasha's to commiserate on the poor choices of my brother as we get ready for the Natalie meeting. I won't be the one talking on the call, but I am here for moral support. And ice cream. Because again, my brother is an idiot.

Fortunately, the meeting goes well and Sasha has officially been brought on board with the Natalie x Pink Every Day collaboration. And we are heading to New York City in just a few weeks! My brother has some serious groveling to do if he wants to fix this. And I just hope this isn't going to hurt my position or relationship with Sasha.

The next few weeks are an absolute blur. Assignments, classes, coffee dates with Sam, planning meetings with Sasha, and trying not to yell at my brother too much take up my days. Thanksgiving comes and goes and it's only a bit awkward when Sasha isn't at my family's table like we had been planning. But apparently, we are starting the groveling full force now. Matt has a lot of work to do to make up for his colossal overstepping.

With the schedule of when we will be traveling, I will need to do a few finals early and those teachers are all happy to be flexible with me on those requirements. I've built up a really good relationship with all of my teachers so far this year and I think that definitely helped when I went to them to ask about the schedule adjustment.

It's all about the connections, right? That's a big piece of what I am doing with Sasha and with my classes on campus. Especially with not fully knowing what career path I will be taking, I need to take advantage of these opportunities.

We leave in just a few days for NYC and I am nervous about everything we will be doing there, but also super excited. The packing content and the "travel skincare essentials" videos I put out have been a big hit. I even got a small PR package from Natalie with some travel goodies so I was able to show that off in the video too. The comments were all to be expected and it gave me a good idea bank for future travel content.

BusyMom2735: Okay, but I need that bag for my car for touch ups when I actually remember to do my makeup.

Chance2Run: How are you planning on doing your makeup for the airport? Full face or keeping it simple?

GlamBabe426: Have you seen the videos of the girls doing a full skincare/spa routine on the plane? You should totally try that!

CObabeHart35: I love that we got to see your travel essentials, do you have hotel essentials too?

MasonCanGlam: Aren't you worried about traveling to the city this close to the holidays? It looks like it's going to be super busy and it's just you and Sasha going...

Samtheman62: Do you need anything else before you leave? I don't think I can fit in your luggage, though.

Chance2Run: Why are you and Sam so cute, though? We need more #couplecontent!

CollegeDailyCSU35: How did all of your professors take you leaving during finals?

Ugh, finals. I was able to finish my last one on campus earlier today, and I am now officially done with this semester! Yay me. My bags are packed—my brother is an early packer and so is my dad, so we spent the afternoon getting the bulk of everything organized and in my luggage so I don't have to go shopping tomorrow. With it being this close to Christmas, we try to avoid the stores when we can. Another huge benefit to shopping year-round. I log off of Instagram and start my nighttime skincare routine. I know the flight and travel is going to really throw off my schedule and systems, so I need to do a little extra in preparation for that.

I have an extra hydrating mask on my face and a thick body butter layered up while I enjoy a cup of raspberry leaf tea about twenty minutes later. I make my way to my bed so I can relax a bit while the mask sits. I will need to rinse off some of it and then add on my lip and under eye products before I can go to sleep. Reaching for my phone on my nightstand, I pull up Spotify to find a calming instrumental playlist. I am way too keyed up to go right to sleep.

I find one that has mostly Taylor Swift and similar artists but all on piano. The main overhead light is off in my room, but the fairy lights surrounding the room are on. It's the perfect setting for a reset night at home. I am just settling into my mountain of pillows when I hear a text notification come in. I pick my phone back up wondering who is texting me so late, Sasha is probably already sleeping and Sam has an early meeting tomorrow.

Unknown: What time do you leave for New York?

Unknown: I really don't like the idea of you going by yourself so far away.

Me: Who is this?

Unknown: Do you really not know?

Me: No, I'm sorry. I don't have this number saved.

Unknown: <image attached>

It's one of the photos from that photography Instagram account I follow—the one that looks like it's raining and everything is out of focus. I save the photo so I can zoom in and see if I can figure out what this one is. It's almost become a game to try to guess each photo when they are posted. The account posts sporadically, sometimes it's every day, and sometimes there's weeks between posts. This one is dark, with some light shining at the top of the picture and then something dark underneath. It looks like the exterior of a house. Hold up, is that my house? There's no way. How do I handle this? Play it off? Get upset? I don't even know.

Me: I really enjoy the pictures you post, but this feels a bit weird. How did you get my number?

Unknown: I wanted to make sure I could check on you when you are traveling. I didn't mean to make you uncomfortable.

I don't want to respond. Can I leave this alone? I get up to wash the rest of the product off my face and then finish up with the additional products. I hit the remote to dim the fairy lights so only every other one is lit up. I slip on my fuzzy pink sweatpants over the boy shorts I had been wearing. I feel cold, but I don't want to turn up the heat if I don't need to. I really hate that I'm always so cold.

I am going to turn off my phone notifications for the night though. I don't have the energy to message random people that I don't have names for.

Unknown: Good night, beautiful. Sleep well.

**<blocks number>**

WED    THU    FRI    SAT    SUN         DATE

# Chapter Twenty-Seven

## ASHLEY

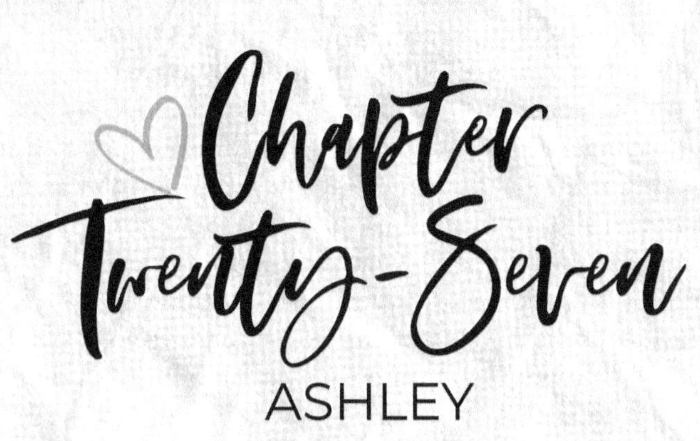

**PEPPERMINT HOT CHOCOLATE**

*Social Post: Insert Taylor Swift singing here! #welcometonewyork #holidaytravel #airportday #sashaloveslipstick*

*Image Description: Photo of the "Welcome to New York" sign in the airport.*

We are in New York City!! And besides being freezing cold, this place is amazing. Seriously, I don't know what I was expecting, but it's way colder than I thought it would be. Apparently, the humidity in the air and the proximity to the water means that the temperatures feel colder here. We haven't even made it to our hotel yet and I'm already debating trying to find a store where I can buy some thermal or wool leggings and better socks and gloves. I will not survive here.

I decide to wait until we get to the hotel. There may be a small store in the lobby or right next door and then I won't have to ask about adding a stop to our evening. And Sasha needs some decompress time. I thrive on being around people, but Sasha needs some down time in between "peopling events.". And I feel like I need to walk around a bit before I go to bed. The plane was cramped and loud and I still can't quite feel my toes. It's been a while since I've flown anywhere, but I definitely thought they kept the planes warmer. Maybe it's just a symptom of the Raynaud's getting worse. I make a mental note to ask my doctor when I get home.

"Are you okay if I pop out for a bit once we get to the room? I need to find some warmer layers. I was not prepared for the humidity change," I check in with Sasha once we find our floor and start looking at the signs along the hallways for our room number.

"Yeah, that's totally fine. Can I give you some cash to grab me a scarf and hat of some sort? That wind is going to kill me if that keeps up when we do our walk with Natalie tomorrow."

I grab the key card out of my pocket and wave it over the door lock. The room is large and we each have our own bed. And apparently a goodie basket on them too!

"Or I may not need to go out," I chuckle. This has my brother written all over it. Sasha has an even larger basket on her bed with some of her travel and hotel essentials, and some winter wear to add to her wardrobe for the trip. My basket is filled with similar goodies, including some wool lined socks, the good ones that backpacking campers use. The coordinating gloves and wool lined tights are an amazing added touch. I've been wanting a set of these but couldn't justify how much money they were.

I don't camp, so it would literally just be for the few days out of the year that it got cold enough for them. I don't go outside for long when the weather is cold anymore, so I didn't see the need to spend fifty dollars on a pair of socks. I love my brother though. He doesn't care how much something is, he's going to take care of his girls. I can tell that Sasha is feeling a bit overwhelmed so I offer to let her take the bathroom first, maybe a bath will help her reset a bit. And I brought stuff to give myself a pedicure tonight. Self-care time makes everything a bit better. And tomorrow is going to be insanely busy!

New York has been such a whirlwind. And now we have to figure things out for what we are going to wear to an actual gala. We got told at dinner tonight that the event we had listed as a "dinner" is actually a full-blown gala with presentations, press, and a red carpet. Understandably, Sasha is freaking out. She is going to have to present during this thing and we weren't prepared for any dress up event, let alone a gala where she has to present at the end of our trip.

I was able to get us an appointment for a dress rental place tomorrow. And that will take the bulk of the crazy details off of our plate. I'm so glad that I brought things with me to do my nails. We may just have to stop to get some different polish options depending on what we find for dresses. Sasha has calmed a bit since we got back to the hotel, but I can tell she isn't doing well. And I would hate for her to have an anxiety attack.

"Take a few minutes and breathe. It's going to be great. You know what you are doing and why we are doing it. I know this was a surprise, but you are amazing and the fact that they asked for you tells me that they have every faith in you that you can do this," I try to encourage her a bit. I'm not sure what she most needs right now to stave off the panic attack. She visibly takes a few deep breaths and then gathers her things to head into the bathroom.

I shoot a text to my brother as soon as the door clicks shut behind her.

Me: So, Sasha may need a virtual hug
if you have a way to send her one.

Matt: What's going on?

Me: She has to present at the gala on Friday night. In front of like 1,500 people.

Matt: A gala wasn't on your itinerary.

Me: You would be correct.

Matt: What do you need?

Me: I have a dress appt booked for us for tomorrow already. I don't have to present so I'm planning to pull some numbers and some talking points for her tomorrow. We have less than 48 hours before we have this gala. Not much time for her to be comfortable with it.

Matt: Yeah, let me see what I can do on my end. I'll email you some things tonight and then we can make a game plan tomorrow.

Me: Anything you need from me?

Matt: Nope. I'm just hoping she is ready to talk to me soon. Not being there for her is killing me.

Me: So maybe you will stop interfering with our devices and social media then?

Matt: Do I have to answer that?

I send him a gif of someone sticking out their tongue and then turn the notifications off on my phone, except the alarm for the morning. It's going to be a busy day tomorrow and I need to get some sleep. It doesn't take me long to find some Gilmore Girls reruns on the TV so I turn down the volume and dim the room lights. I did my skincare right when we got to the hotel so I don't have to wait for Sasha to finish in the bathroom. Just as I'm getting settled in bed, my phone lights up.

"Leave it alone. The notifications are off for a reason. You need to go to sleep," I whisper to myself. I am so bad about "just checking really quickly" and then being on my phone for the next hour. The screen goes dark and I try to go through a breathing practice that Sasha shared with me last week. Some of the meditation and breathing exercises she uses for her anxiety have been really helpful for me too. I have a hard time shutting off my brain at night, so giving me something to work through definitely helps.

My screen lights up again. Another notification, really? Maybe I need to adjust this so I don't get anything except for messages from certain contacts after nine at night. It's not even eight here right now, but my body is exhausted. I pick up my phone to fully turn off notifications when I see the missed text messages.

Matt: I will email you some things tonight to go over with Sasha tomorrow. Let me know if you get other information about the event that I should know. I'll look on my end too. Sleep well.

Matt: Let me know if your schedule has changed for tomorrow since the itinerary you gave me last week. I know you have the dress appt, but I'd like to have the new one so I can know where you are and what's going on.

Me: Has anyone ever told you that you are a bit on the overprotective side?

Matt: Yes.

Me: LOL, goodnight Matt. I'll send you everything tomorrow. I'm turning off notifications now. All the dings and lights on my phone are making it hard to fall asleep.

Matt: Sounds good. Sleep well.

Matt: Love you.

Me: Love you too.

I quickly find the setting to turn everything off on my phone and set it on Do Not Disturb. And then I'm finally able to fall asleep.

Dress shopping in NYC is an experience I won't soon forget. Luckily, the sales associate we worked with found some stunning options for us and we didn't have to be at the store for long. Sasha went with a simple but stunning black gown. She is going to have some great options for her hair and makeup. And part of me really hopes that Matt buys it for her so she doesn't have to return it before we head back to Colorado.

I chose a jewel toned green dress. It really brings out the highlights in my hair and will make my eyes pop. It's going to be hard to decide what I'm doing with my makeup—gold, green, or pink. Maybe a light combination with all three...I'll have to do a few trial runs tonight. That'll make for good content in the hotel room.

We did call it an early night after we finished with the dresses and I am so glad for a night in. Matt had dinner delivered to the room for us again. This time it's from a Vietnamese place not far from here, and the Pho may be the best I have ever had. NYC has some of the best varieties of authentic cuisine from so many cultures. I definitely need to come back here for a week and do nothing but eat.

Both in our jammies, we are working on our laptops on content, emails, and finalizing things for tomorrow. The conversations we have had with Natalie and the Pink Every Day collaboration team have been amazing. But there are a lot of notes to sort through.

"I'm looking forward to when this is all working and we can just enjoy the creativity side of things again, and not be taking up hours of our down time sorting through contracts and deadlines," I huff out as I uncap a water bottle from the basket still sitting next to my bed. The headache since we landed has just not gotten better, and I just hope it's an elevation change issue and that I'm not fighting off a sinus infection or something.

Sasha laughs as she reaches for her own water bottle. "I totally get that. Maybe we can see about bringing someone on to handle contracts and things once we get this one up and going. Because I am not a lawyer or a business manager, and this is not a fun part of the process."

"Maybe it's something Matt can do, when and if you want to bring him back into the conversation," I offer hesitantly. I don't want to push her back to him before she is ready. And my brother definitely crossed some lines. But I miss having him here working on things alongside us.

"Maybe," she muses a bit as she stares off into nothing for a moment. She misses him. It's super obvious.

It doesn't take long to get to our stopping point for the evening. We both have found that once we hit a certain level of fatigue that we are no longer beneficial in any work we get done. So, it's better to stop, get ready for bed or take a break, and look at it fresh the next morning. And we definitely have hit that point.

I lay down, but filter through the emails and texts from the day. There's info from the dress place with the rental details and all the fees that we may incur if the dresses aren't returned in pristine condition. I'm wearing a $1,500 dress tomorrow night—trust me, it's getting returned in a bubble wrap sleeve if needed. I cannot afford that thing, although I wouldn't complain if one day I can have dresses like that in my closet.

We had both posted some behind the scenes info today of Natalie's factory, offices, and then dress shopping. So, the comments and messages are all over the place. There is no way that I will get through all of them. I've been going to the rainy image account a couple times a week, just to see if there's an update and to see if he messaged me again. There haven't been any new messages, but I am still super intrigued by his photos.

The latest one was posted earlier today, it looks like a city scape in the background, a dark car in the front. The street lights and signs blink in and out around the rain drops. "City schedule" is the caption. And it already has over 1,000 likes and 500 saves. I see why this account is getting the attention it is. I feel like it's a snapshot into someone's daily life, but with an artistic flair that seems to say that I'm missing something important. And I have the hardest time looking away.

I send the picture to Sam with a quick message.

Me: Where do you think he is?

Sam: It could be Denver, or even downtown Fort Collins. The rain really makes it hard to decipher where he is.

Me: That's probably on purpose.

Me: Do you want to see the dress I picked out for tomorrow?

Sam: Do you want to show me now or send me a picture when you are all done up?

Me: Both?

Sam: LOL, let me see.

Me: <Image Attached>

It takes him a minute to respond and I start getting worried. It is a dressing room photo so the angle and the lighting are horrid, but I do look incredible in this gown.

Sam: Ash, you look incredible.

Me: I thought so.

Sam: What time do you have to be at the venue tomorrow?

Me: Not sure, I need to coordinate with Natalie in the morning. There may be some press things we have to attend before the event. But I need to call it a night. My phone is going to yell at me to go to bed soon.

Sam: Good night, beautiful. Sleep well.

I smile down at my phone before I reset everything to the Do Not Disturb settings I used last night. It was so nice not having my screen constantly light up. The settings must take a minute to fully take this time though because I get a text message right as I go to set my phone down on the nightstand next to me.

Unknown: Sleep well, beautiful. I can't wait to see pictures from tomorrow.

Me: Who is this?

Unknown: Still haven't figured it out?

Unknown: I'm hurt, Ashley.

Me: I don't know what game you are playing, but I am not enjoying it.

Unknown: That was never my intention, Ashley. I'll let you get some rest. Enjoy your day tomorrow.

I don't even bother to respond, I just block the number and delete the thread. Who the heck sold my number and what are they getting at with these cryptic messages?

Ashley

# Chapter Twenty-Eight

## HIM

She chose the green dress. I knew she would. It is stunning on her. I had contacted the store earlier today to see what they had available for my love to try on. When they mentioned they had the newest collection from a few local designers, I knew the green floor length satin gown would be just the one for her.

She is going to look like the royalty she is. I wish I could be the one on her arm, showing her off for this event. She isn't ready for me to take on that role yet. So I will gladly wait in the shadows, making sure she is happy and taken care of, and given every opportunity to shine.

She needs to come home soon though. The last week has been so off without her here. And now that campus is emptying out, I have more moments that aren't filled with work. Moments where all I think about is her. And how much longer I will have to wait to call her Mine in public.

I don't want to keep waiting.

I want her.
She is already mine.
She just doesn't know it yet.

WED    THU    FRI    SAT    SUN        DATE

# Chapter Twenty-Nine

## ASHLEY

**SWEET VANILLA COOKIE BUTTER**

*Social Post: Glam makeup nights mean over-the-top skincare routines afterwards. Do you have a favorite skincare item that you use on nights where your skin needs some extra love? I love this hydrating overnight mask for that extra step during the winter months. #skincarelove #newyorktrip
Image Description: Skincare bottles and containers on the hotel bathroom counter next to a white washcloth and lip scrub.*

Of course, my brother showed up last night. I shouldn't have been so surprised. Him turning the stage into Sasha's own vanity desk where she records content, though, I was not expecting that. He knows her so, so well and seeing them back together makes me so happy. I hope she plans to make him grovel a bit more though. He deserves it. And she deserves to be fully pampered. It also helped to have him here today to bring back the dresses and get ready to go back to Colorado.

He ran to the dress place to return the gowns while we got checked out and met Natalie and the others for brunch in the hotel lobby. We still have a few things to finalize before we leave as we continue working on the collaborations together. Hopefully, this is just the first collaboration in the line of many more to come. And Sasha has mentioned turning this into an actual full-blown organization as "Pink Every Day." And if that happens, I may have a full time position running certain aspects of it. It's still in the daydream phase right now. But it's not out of the question.

We are just finishing up the last of our coffees when Matt gets back, motioning that the car is ready when we are. Hugs and a few final photos later, we are ready to head out. I dig my new wool gloves out of my purse and layer up before we go outside. Not sure how it's possible, but it got even colder today than it had been when we arrived on Tuesday. And it's windy. I am not built for winter in the North East and I think I am okay with that. I wonder if they make heated coats. And hats. And scarves. And boots. Ugh, I hate being cold.

I slip into the backseat of the SUV Matt rented when he got to town. At least it's warm in here. And it should be an easy drive to the airport. As I find my seatbelt, I notice the big black garment bags next to me.

"Was the dress place not open when you went to return the gowns?" I ask as I peek inside one of them. Yep, that's my dress from last night. "I don't want to get hit with the late return fees. That place has gorgeous options, but they charge for literally everything."

Matt just shakes his head as he meets my eyes in the rearview mirror. "The dresses are yours to keep, Ash. You too, Sasha. You both deserve something nice in your closets."

Sasha covers her mouth with her hand in an audible gasp. "Matt, that's way too much. Those dresses aren't cheap, and they're brand new. I don't need something that extravagant in my closet."

"I'm not complaining about it, but she's right. Those dresses are expensive. I am more than happy with the formal gowns I already do own, and maybe we can plan ahead for the next gala and can buy something for that one."

"Will it make you feel better if I tell you I only paid for one of them?" he asks us as he merges out into traffic, turning down the music so it's barely above a whisper.

"Only one? How did that work?" I ask. I know how much mine was. And I'm pretty sure Sasha's dress was comparable in price. It wasn't as high end as mine, but it was newer. And from a smaller collection.

He just shrugs his shoulders and I know that's the only answer I'm going to get. Matt always wins. And more often than not, I will benefit from it too. And Sasha now too. I better not complain. That whole gift horse and his mouth or however the saying goes. Now to figure out when I can wear it again. Because there is no way it is going to be living in my closet for the next year without anywhere to go.

The next few weeks are way busier than a break should be. But starting new collaborations and pitching to other companies and manufacturers for the coming year, means the Christmas break is super full—for all three of us. Matt, Sasha, and I have virtual meetings several times a week with other business owners. And we were able to set up Pink Every Day collaborations and initiatives with six beauty brands, one clothing company, and three other Women-Owned Colorado businesses for the new year.

Which also means that we have an invitation for the Gala next December in New York again. They are already planning for next year and are wanting to continue to highlight the work we are doing. And even though we haven't put a lot of things into practice yet, there is a lot that is in the process. And the number of businesses contacting us asking how they can support us is staggering.

Not every business is a good fit for a full collaboration, but they are willing to run content for us, host a fundraiser, or sponsor pieces of the collaboration. Travel, printed materials, advertising, photo shoots, merchandise, branding, test products, the list is huge of what we need to make this work. And to make it work well. We have a lawyer now too. Like I said, this break has been insane. But it's official.

Pink Every Day is now an actual organization with a non-profit and a for-profit branch. Sasha is the first employee and she is able to draw a salary from what we have set up already. If everything goes according to plan, Matt will begin drawing a paycheck by the summer. And I will be right behind that. Right now, I am in the "intern" role, so I can add a lot of what I am doing to college credits or future projects. And then we hope to bring Tilly on as the next major intern.

With school starting back up soon, our schedules are going to need to be very well laid out. But it looks like I know what I'm doing after graduation now. Head of Product Development at Pink Every Day. I think I like the sound of that.

Ashley

WED   THU   FRI   SAT   SUN        DATE

ASHLEY

### EGGNOG LATTE

*Social Post: New semester, here we go! This break wasn't exactly restful, but I'm excited to get back into my routines of classes and content. What are you most excited about in this new year? #justme #schoolsupplies #csugirlie*

*Image Description: Pink Every Day pen on top of my new pastel pink and purple notebook.*

Sophomore, Spring Semester—Here we go.

Okay, but seriously. Does the first week of college classes ever get easier? I feel like I'm figuring this out all over again. New faces, new classes, new schedules, new teachers. So much of it is new this semester. With Professor Williams joining the faculty this semester, several classes have been added to the options of what we can take, and a few of the outside programs have been adjusted too. That also means that several of the professors in the business department are taking on mentor students in addition to their TA's. So, there's a lot more opportunity for us to work with a professor one on one or in small groups. I really need to take a look at all that is being offered this semester and see if anything aligns with what I will be doing with Sasha and Pink Every Day.

Especially now that it will more than likely be a full time position, even before I have my degree. There's even the possibility that I may have employees underneath me before I have a degree at this rate. How is this real life? And how am I the one doing this? It's amazing though.

I slide into the lecture hall of my first class. It's with Professor Williams and I am so excited to finally see what's so special about this guy. Everyone was talking about him this morning. Okay, not everyone, just the girls ahead of me at the coffee cart. Apparently, he gives Professor Johnson a run for his money with the Zaddy vibes. I am just getting my laptop up and going when I see why he was given that descriptor.

Professor Williams enters the hall with a steady authority. The vibe of the room immediately changes, like even the air knows that he is here. He is tall and walks with a confidence I've only ever seen in movies. He's good at what he does, and we all know it. No convincing is going to be needed on his part. His very presence commands respect and attention. His dark hair is neat, just long enough that he had to style it this morning, but not so long that it will get messed up in the wind.

His face isn't fully clean shaven, he has some scruff on his face. But his jaw line is still very clearly seen. He is wearing a white dress shirt with a dark green tie that coordinates beautifully with our school colors. He is wearing a sports coat, not a suit jacket with a heavy wool coat over it. He carefully takes off the coat and rests it on his chair as he hooks his laptop up to the stand at the front of the room. I finally take my eyes away from him to realize that everyone else has been doing the same. Everyone is absolutely transfixed. Who is this guy and why do I need to know everything about him?

Class begins moments later as Professor Williams calls over two students in the front row to pass out the syllabi and other printed materials, probably his class expectations, office hours, and the outline for his mentorship program. It wasn't something that I was going to look at this year, but I'm curious what it looks like.

"I heard that he only takes two seniors for his mentorship program each term," a student whispers behind me.

"Any chance he has room for a junior willing to please?" another one asks suggestively in return. Gross.

"You did not seriously just ask that?" a third voice pipes up and I have to hold down the laugh trying to break free. Do not call unnecessary attention to yourself, I chide internally. I do not need a repeat with Professor Williams that I had with Professor Johnson last year.

He stands at the front of the room, surveying the space and seeing the progress of the students passing out the papers. At least he's not trying to talk over everyone moving around right now. As soon as the papers are distributed and the students are back in their seats, Professor Williams begins his presentation.

"Can I get pregnant just by someone's voice? Because I think I'm pregnant," the junior behind me whispers and I bury my head in my hands in embarrassment. Is she serious right now? I hear a muffled slap and an "ouch" and hope that means her friends just showed her how massively inappropriate that comment was.

"Welcome to The Ethics of Small Business, I'm Professor Marcus Williams. I know I am new to this campus, but I am not new to teaching in a collegiate setting and I am excited to be here. I am originally from New England, but have been teaching abroad in the UK, more specifically Scotland, for the last few terms. My goal with this class is not only to provide you with a practical education, but to give you the critical thinking tools necessary as we continue to grow business alongside technology and a changing global workspace.

"The papers in your hands outline my class expectations as well as the extracurricular offerings that will now be available. I have worked with the dean of students and the business department to bring you some very practical new opportunities beginning this semester. I hope you take advantage of them." He shuffles a few papers on the stand and then clicks to the next slide.

"Now, let's talk about ethics when it comes to small businesses."

The next thirty minutes absolutely fly by. I was mesmerized by the smooth, deep voice of Professor Williams, but also the way he carried himself around the room. He is confident, but in a quiet way. He commands the space around him. No one talks out of turn. No one asks questions just to get a reaction out of him. The respect that is generally earned only after countless hours with a student body is automatic with him.

I really need to figure out what I want to do this semester for the mentorship opportunities. Because deciding between applying for working with Professor Johnson and Professor Williams is going to be really hard. I have a meeting with Professor Johnson after classes today to go over my options. And I really hope we can make a good game plan. It looks like there will be a lot more competition for these positions than I originally thought.

"Okay, but seriously, how am I supposed to choose?" I know I'm being dramatic and I absolutely do not care. I just got out of my meeting with Professor Johnson and am having our first library work date of the semester with Sam. Tilly and one of Sam's roommates, Brock, are also with us. So, it's not fully a date. But we are calling it that. With how busy things are going to be this semester, it is very, very possible that this is how our dates are going to be for most of the semester.

"What are your main options again?" Brock asks as he pulls out another syllabus to add dates into his paper planner. He has all of his classes color coordinated like me so we've been sharing our highlighter and pen collection as we get everything sorted on paper.

"Okay, so I can TA for Professor Johnson and start helping him with some basic admin tasks. But that isn't really going to help me with my roles at Pink Every Day with Sasha. It'll look good on my resume, but I don't want to go into a teaching role. But many of the teachers like seeing the TA role before they look at the mentorship opportunities. And I really, really want to get into the mentorship with either Professor Johnson or Williams next year."

"Is there an in between? Not necessarily a TA position, but maybe an advisory role that you can do? So you can help out with some of the admin tasks or research or things that would be beneficial for you to start learning how to do, and then have time with them to ask your questions or get the support you need with what you are working on for Sasha?" Sam asks, his hand rubbing light circles on my thigh underneath the table. I love how he gives me the attention I need, even when we can't be fully on our own together.

"Oh, I like that. And it would be a bit easier to get into something like that with Professor Johnson since he already knows me and what I'm doing with Sasha. It sounded like he might have been hinting at something like that in our meeting, but he needed to figure out what that would look like before he asked me. Let me email him before I forget about it."

The next thirty minutes pass quickly, with me emailing Professor Johnson about Sam's idea and then checking our master to-do list for Sasha, Pink Every Day, and school tasks. We switched over to a master overview of our tasks at the beginning of my last semester. There are things on here that don't necessarily apply to me, but it helps seeing what Sasha, Tilly, and Matt have going on as we continue to build out what we are working on together. It also will help as we add to what we do and know who has the space and capacity to add on those tasks.

With all of that updated, it's time for us to go our separate ways. Sam is working with Professor Erickson again this semester, Tilly is still working at Ulta alongside being a student, and Brock, I don't know where he needs to go. I don't really know him yet. Note to self: ask Sam about Brock, especially if he's going to be joining us this semester. I seriously know nothing about him, other than that he lives on campus and may have some OCD tendencies.

Sam walks me out to the lobby of the building—he has to meet with Professor Erickson for their first planning session of the semester and I need to get home to record some content while the lighting is still good in my room.

"What all do you have planned for recording today?" He shoulders my bag alongside his own as we make our way to the large glass doors at the end of the space.

"As long as the weather holds up, I will be doing my recap of products I finished last month and then ones I bought for this month. Those videos always do well. And then I am going to do a few B-roll type videos of my nighttime skincare routine. I want to do a skincare series for 'back to school' budgets and spaces and that will give me some good background content to play with. It'll be good educational content for the website and then it'll help pull in some of the current searches around dorm life."

"Perfect. I'm excited to see what you are working on. If you ever need a new face to work on for content, let me know."

"You would let me do stuff to your face for content?" Sam laughs and I immediately cover my mouth. I said that way too loud. "I did not mean it to come out that way. I meant skincare. And washing your face. With cleansers. Oh God, you know what I meant, right?"

"You are too cute when you get embarrassed. And I would love for you to do whatever you want to my face—skincare or otherwise." He leans in to brush a kiss against my lips and I have to fight the urge to deepen it right here on campus.

"I miss spending time with you. I hate how busy things are right now," I whisper against his lips as he holds me close.

"I know, but it's only a season. And we are both getting things set up for a solid career after college. It's going to pay off." He places another kiss on my forehead before linking his fingers with mine. "Text me when you get home, okay?"

"Will do. Don't stay too late. You tend to get way too busy with Professor Erickson that you leave too late and then you have stuff at the paper to get caught up on. Can I call you at some point to politely remind you that it's time to check out for the day?" I make it a point to pout and give him my best impression of puppy dog eyes. He just smirks at me as he runs his finger lightly over my bottom lip until I release it from the pout.

"I think that sounds great. I may not be able to get away right at four, but if you can call to check in at that time and then that will help me pace myself and stay on track with work today."

"You got it. Chat soon. Have fun today."

I step outside into the frigid January air. The wind makes it feel so much colder than it actually is. And I rush to my car and struggle to get the door open and the engine started. My fingers do not like working right when I'm cold. A buzz in my pocket alerts me to a new text message and reminds me to pull it out of my jacket before I start driving home.

Sam: Everything okay?

He must still be in the lobby watching me.

Me: Yeah, just trying to warm up my car and myself. I forgot to wear my gloves outside.

Sam: Are you good to drive home?

Me: Yep, my fingers are almost not blue anymore?

Sam: Blue? Seriously?

Me: No. Not blue. Just stiff and cold. Color is normal. I'm going to head out now. I'll call you at four.

Me: Get to work. ;)

Sam: Yes ma'am.

Me: Don't do that, it's weird.

Sam: LOL. Drive safe

I replace my phone onto the holder and rub my hands together before adjusting my mirrors and shifting into reverse. Once I get to the light to get out of campus, my phone buzzes again.

Unknown: Please don't forget your gloves again. It's too cold with your condition.

Note to self, ask my brother how to have my number unlisted.

Ashley

# Chapter Thirty-One

## MARCUS

### BARRY'S IRISH TEA

*Social Post: Just because it's a coffee cart, doesn't mean it can't also have a decent tea selection. #goodmorning #morningroutine #coloradomorning Image Description: Open wooden box with a few tea bags inside, obviously needing a restock because three teas is not a "selection."*

My office on the CSU campus is right in the middle of the admin offices. I don't have a window, and the heater makes noises that tell me it hasn't been upgraded or even tuned in many years. This building may be older than me. Actually, I take that back. This building may be older than my grandfather. I need to get my work finished so I can go to my apartment and get some more things accomplished. I need to rethink my office hours. I knew it was going to be an adjustment coming to the new school this semester. There's a lot of new responsibilities and new faculty to figure out.

Some things haven't changed though. The undergrads all thinking that they can flirt their way to a better grade aren't as prevalent as some years, but they are still here. The upperclassmen who want to try to talk about who their daddies are in order to move their position up in the mentorship application have also made it a point to introduce themselves already too. And we haven't even officially started reviewing those. I need a TA. Maybe more than one. No, definitely, more than one.

My laptop dings with an incoming email just as I log out of the campus system. It's from my TA back in Scotland. I had passed him along to the new professor that took over my position. I make a mental note to check in with him during my office hours tomorrow. It's the middle of the night over there right now, he shouldn't be working anyway. And I'm not sure how else to tell him that he doesn't need to be available 24/7 to be good at his job.

I'm not surprised to see many of the staff still working in their offices. Meetings with students, organizing semester projects, reaching out to local businesses to partner with, and more than one coffee date being solicited by students all are happening in the conversations around me. I shake my head incredulously. Some things never change no matter what campus you're on.

Good professors won't adjust grades for students just because of some flirting. I've dealt with it on every campus I've taught in. It's one of the big reasons why I keep to myself. I stay quiet and unassuming. The flirting still comes; I guess it's the appeal of the unknown. I don't date students, other faculty, or campus staff. It's definitely easier to say no to students now. I'm thirty-five, not the twenty-four-year-old taking on his first assistant teaching position. I was way too young for that position, but I was the best one for the job.

I enjoy teaching. It's not just a role that I fill in the classroom. It's an opportunity to help the next generation find the jobs they love and help them be fully prepared for those positions. Over the years, my students have gone on to enter positions in the job markets rarely opened to brand new graduates. Ten years into teaching, my students now hold two CEO positions, five CMO positions, one hospital director, and twenty leadership positions at Fortune 500 companies. And that's just in the States.

CSU is the first school in the United States that has wanted to incorporate the mentorship program that I piloted overseas. It will probably be another year or two before it's fully implemented. Especially because they want to expand it to more majors besides just the business one. With the market in Colorado, adding the program to the agriculture and veterinary services programs was a no brainer. But we need to bring in other experts for those fields. I know how to sell products and services online. I don't know a thing about different varieties of peppers or when the best time to breed cattle is.

I'm almost to my car completely unbothered when one of the other Business Professors stops me with a wave and a jog over to me to avoid yelling.

"Professor Williams, I am so excited to have you join us this semester. I'm Professor Johnson. We have a few overlapping specialties. Do you have time this week to meet for coffee and go over some of the TA and mentorship details? I know you had mentioned in your email that there are things we should implement this semester in order to get students ready for those opportunities in the coming months." I have to pay close attention to what he says. It's obvious that he ran over to me even before he caught my attention. The cold mixed with the bags he is carrying means he is out of breath and winded, even though we aren't more than twenty yards from the front doors. The elevation may be different from my place in Scotland, but the weather is mild comparatively.

"Can you email me when you get in the office tomorrow and I will check my calendar to see what we can make work? I don't work when I am out of the office and I haven't fully synced my calendar up yet. I would also like to find some time to sit in on a class of yours so I can get a feel for the department. But we can talk about that tomorrow. Drive safe tonight." I extend my hand to him in a silent indication that this conversation is over. It's below freezing outside and I have zero desire to be out here as long as this conversation has already been.

"Will do. Thank you, Marcus." He must only be a year or two older than me but he simultaneously puts himself in a position of authority over me as well as seeking my approval with his mannerisms. I'm not sure what he's getting at or what he wants from me, but it's not going to work. I have nearly a half foot on him, and at least, fifty pounds in bulk too. And I use every one of those numbers to look down at him. It's not an outright challenge, but I will not put up with whatever bullshit he is trying to pull with me.

After a moment of holding his gaze, he looks away, nodding his head in acceptance of my silent taunt. He walks back to his vehicle and I shake my head. This is going to be fun.

"Chelsea, can you please get me the most updated list of faculty and course catalog when you have a moment please?" I ask the admin office secretary as I make my way to my office the next morning. I need to get a feel for who is on campus with me and who all I can connect with for the projects I am working on—for the school and myself. The demographic here is almost completely different to what I dealt with in the UK and I need to get a better feel for what I am working with.

I internally hold back a groan when I approach my office door and find two students already there waiting for me.

"I don't have office hours this morning, you can email me with your questions," I let them know as I slip my key into my door and begin pushing my way in. The male student holds the door open for me and slips in behind me before I can set my things down and close the door behind me. I look at him and compose myself before I address him. It is way too early for this.

"If you are needing my email address, Chelsea has a stack of my cards at the desk in the lobby." I round my desk and set my things down as I begin preparing for my day, not giving the student any more of my time.

"I wanted to ask you about the mentorship program. I know it hasn't been fully announced yet, but I think I would be an excellent candidate. My father went to school with you in undergrad and wanted to invite you to dinner this weekend to discuss it further."

I just hold his gaze in response. I knew his ask was going to be selfish, not caring for my boundaries or what I have clearly laid out as expectations. But there is always the one, or five, that push it.

"You are welcome to email me with your questions, comments, and concerns. But you are not welcome in my office during this hour as this is my time to prepare for those paying for my time. And I do not believe you are paying for my time right now, are you Mr...." I let my voice trail off, showing him that he didn't even have the decency to introduce himself when he barged uninvited into my space.

"Mr. Casey Strikes, sir."

My control slips and the corner of my mouth neglects to hold back a smirk. "Seriously?"

"Yes, sir?" He doesn't know why that's funny. And that just makes it so much better.

"I have a project for you and then if you complete it satisfactorily, we can discuss the *possibility* of you applying to the mentorship program."

"Okay?" He's nervous. Good.

"Read through Casey at the Bat, then write up why I find it ironic that you come in here acting like you own the place, when in reality, you just struck out."

He shakes his head, clearly confused by my verbiage. If he was in any way educated on American literature, he would have caught that reference. He nods once then leaves the room, silently closing the door behind him. And I spend the next ten minutes before leaving for my class listening to James Earl Jones recite Casey at the Bat. I will not strike out at this position. Because, unlike Casey, I am fully aware of my capabilities and my limits. And I don't make promises I cannot keep.

WED    THU    FRI    SAT    SUN         DATE

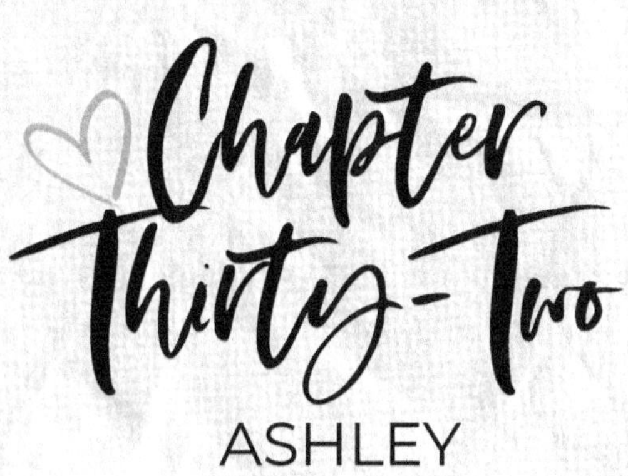

# ASHLEY

**CHAI GREEN TEA**

*Social Post: When the frost is on the pumpkin...or everything actually. The frost on the windows and everything outside is gorgeous, but I'm over the cold. I think doing some makeup inspo by the fractals in the ice would be super fun. What do you think? #americanlit #poetryinspo #frost #makeupinspo*

*Image Description: Ice and frost pattern on the windshield of my car.*

Unknown: Good morning, beautiful.

Unknown: It's cold outside today. Don't forget your gloves. Please let me know if those are no longer sufficient and I can see about getting you a better option.

> Me: Thank you, but please stop texting me unless you are going to tell me who you are.

> Unknown: Part of the fun is you trying to figure it out.

> Me: I don't like this game.

> **<Blocks Number>**

Is this ever going to stop? The messages are innocent enough, but this is seriously annoying. I feel like he's watching me. And I don't know who it is or what they want. Is it a classmate just trying to play a prank? Or someone who doesn't understand boundaries. No, I know they don't understand boundaries. This guy will not leave me alone.

I've pulled back from sharing face content on my profile. Only doing so when there is a group shot or it's for a specific work thing. I've also stopped doing live videos. It's harder to monitor those comments and where the video is going to be pushed on the internet. At least with prerecorded videos, I can filter the key words and the hashtags to make sure the bulk of the audience is intentional. And then the filters my brother implemented keep most of the creeper comments away.

I wish I knew how my phone number got linked to my account though. I can't find it anywhere online or on the Pink Every Day website. We have private numbers and separate work emails to help avoid the wrong people connecting with us. And hopefully soon we will be able to hire someone to help filter through the comments and emails even more. Running a business primarily on social media is a totally different beast than the way our parents ran their marketing campaigns.

At least the teachers and course load on campus aligns with the current market needs. We aren't learning about newspaper ads and commercial spots anymore. It's social media ads, trending videos, and how to optimize SEO on every social media post, blog post, and meta data behind photos. There are so many ways to get in front of the right audience. And with that comes the problem of social media. Once it's out there—it's out there. It never fully goes away. So whoever has decided that they should have access to me as a person, as well as me as an influencer, they aren't going to just go away.

If I knew who it actually was, we could block them fully. And if they escalated to being in real life with what they were doing or causing harm or making threats, then I could get a restraining order. But I can't exactly go to the police and say, "Some random person is texting me good morning every day." I don't think that would go over well. And seriously, how many phone numbers can this guy actually have? It's excessive.

Now that I have managed to settle down from the morning anxiety attack from Mr. Unknown, I'm ready to be on campus and find myself back into my regular routine. I get to meet with Professor Johnson today to finalize the TA and mentorship plan for the next few semesters. Apparently, he got together with Professor Williams earlier this week and they made a short list of students who were interested and who they thought would be a good fit. Sam made the list too. He is taking a bit of a different approach for his career planning, so he will be continuing with Professor Erickson for this semester.

Altogether, there are seven professors taking part in the program. Each one will have at least two TA's this semester. Next semester, one student will be upgraded to mentor student and one or two more students will be added to the TA slot. Depending on the success and how many local businesses partner with the program, there will be more mentor students added. Ideally, this will allow students to have real-world practice with the roles they are wanting to fill. In real time. So as the industry changes, we will have front row seats to the new technology and how it applies to our individual fields.

It's going to be amazing.

This has gone way beyond makeup already and I cannot wait to see where things go. I get to campus with enough time to get coffee before meeting with Professor Johnson, but I decide to post a quick story to Instagram and engage with a few of my followers instead. Especially with the shift in my content, I need to make sure I am checking in with my followers a few times a week. I want to make sure they know that I am not stepping away from social media, it just looks a little different right now.

I get a simple story posted of a screenshot of the weather—cold, no surprise there—and then jump into my group chat in my Insta DM's. These girls have been part of my online "squad" for over a year now. We've never met in person, but they are so encouraging. And I definitely feel like I know each one of them. Maybe at a future event we can finally meet in person.

ShinyLips427: Girl, the eyeshadow palette from Natalie and Sasha this month is incredible! When are you going to do some tutorials and looks with it?

ChelseaWearsPink835: Yes!! With all of the greens and golds, it is going to look stunning against your skin tone. I wish I could wear those colors.

ANC272: Girl, you absolutely can wear those colors! You just need to lean heavier into the browns for the base and then blend it out. I'll try to get a video up for you. One of Sasha's friends has similar coloring to you, I'll see if I can borrow her.

ShinyLips427: I've missed your live tutorials. Is creeper dude still making himself known?

ANC272: I wish. I still have no clue who he is, so I can't do anything about it. Maybe we can set up a private online community and that way I can keep doing the videos but it's to a smaller group.

ChelseaWearsPink835: Like a subscription only thing?

ANC272: Maybe. Ugh, I'm going to be late for my meeting. I'll chat with you guys later. Have a good day. Make good choices.

ShinyLips427: Never!

ChelseaWearsPink835: And we really do need to set up a new username for you babe, it's super beyond basic. You have a platform now, you need to build your own brand, not just Sasha's.

I send a heart emoji and close out of the app. Did I seriously forget my gloves again? Ugh, this just is not my day. I bundle up as well as I can and brace myself for the walk to the front door. Since I am not here before the first class, I had to park quite a ways away from the building. By the time I get inside, my throat hurts from breathing in the cold air, and my hair is literally crunchy from freezing. I guess it wasn't fully dry before I left the house this morning.

I rush to the admin offices so I'm not late for my meeting with Professor Johnson. I know I look windblown and flustered. I hate that I won't be walking in there ready to pitch myself for the spots, but hopefully my work speaks for itself. The receptionist let me know that he's ready to see me and I can just go in. As I get close to the mostly closed door, I hear two male voices talking. She did say I could go in, right?

"Knock, knock," I tentatively say as I knock my fingers against the wood and push it in a little bit, making eye contact with Professor Johnson and Professor Williams. Why do professors in their thirties just look so damn hot? They're both tall. And where Professor Johnson wears glasses that draw your eyes up to his commanding gaze, Professor Williams has the facial hair that draws your eyes to his jawline and his lips. It's not fair how good these two look.

"I was told I could come in, but I can wait in the lobby if you need to finish up. I can go grab coffee for us, Professor Johnson, if you need me to make myself scarce for a few minutes." I am not one to shy away from conversations, but I am intimidated by the two of them. I feel like I walked into a serious moment. The tension between them is THICK. Emphasis made on purpose there.

"Nonsense, Miss Carter. We have a scheduled meeting." He motions for me to have a seat and then hands me a travel coffee mug from his desk that I hadn't noticed before. "I know this wasn't originally part of your schedule, so this one is for you. I wasn't sure what you would want for coffee this morning, but figured a vanilla latte was a safe choice. You can warm up while I finish going over a few things with Professor Williams."

"Oh, thank you." I happily take the travel mug and take a sip. This is way too good for a simple latte. "Did you make this?"

"Yes. I'm glad you like it." With that, he turns back toward Professor Williams and hands over a folder. "This is the last student that I am nominating for the program. He is new to the area, but I think he will be staying local after graduation if given the right position. He's at least open to talking about it." Professor Williams flips through the pages and nods as he reviews the information inside. I wonder who it is. And if it's someone I know.

"Thank you, Professor Johnson. I'll let you go so you can have your meeting with Miss Carter. I will email the team with my thoughts later today and we can get this finalized by the end of the week." He shakes his hand and begins making his way out the door. I try to avoid eye contact, but he lingers in the doorway. I look up to see him looking at me, specifically at my hands. "Do your fingers usually turn blue, Miss Carter?"

Crap, are they really? I look down quickly and sure enough, they have a teensy bit of a blue tinge to them. "I have a medical condition that makes it hard for my extremities to get enough blood flow. I forgot my gloves this morning and wasn't able to park close." Professor Johnson is by my side before I have a chance to finish talking, holding a pair of black wool gloves. They're obviously his, because they're huge compared to mine.

"Please put these on. I wasn't aware that the Raynaud's has started progressing to this level." Professor Johnson takes my coffee mug as I slip on the gloves and then place them under my legs, trying to speed up the process of bringing circulation back to my fingers. "Do we need to check your feet too?" He's already on his knees in front of me and has his hands on my laces of my boots before I can comprehend what is happening.

"No, it's okay. I'm wearing a few pairs of socks and my boots are lined too. My toes feel fine. Really, it's okay. I don't need all of this attention. I can come back later if now isn't a good time. I know you both are busy and I've already taken up more time than intended." I don't think he heard me though because he continues unlacing my boots. Now I feel awkward. And I just want my coffee and to go back home.

"I believe she told you 'no,' Professor Johnson," the deep voice from next to me has the best kind of shivers coursing through my body. There is no room for argument in his statement. Professor Johnson is still on his knees in front of me, hands on my boot and my calf. When did he slide his hand up my leg?

"I really am okay." I stand and move so I'm out of his reach, sliding the gloves off of my hands and passing them back to Professor Johnson. "I'll see you both in class. Can you just email me about what you need from me to move forward in the program?"

I am so flustered and I don't know why. Probably from the blue fingers. And interrupting the conversation. This is quickly spiraling toward an anxiety attack. I need to sit before this escalates and I pass out. I hurry to the front of the building, seeking a space to sit and reset a bit. Why are there people everywhere? There are seriously no open seats anywhere. I am going to have to sit on the floor. And I need to sit soon because I am actually going to pass out now.

I turn around to make my way back to the classrooms, library, and study rooms. At least those places will be quieter. The buzzing of my phone in my pocket just adds to the chaos I am feeling right now. And someone is calling my name. I look up to see both Professor Williams and Johnson staring at me. I'm back in front of the office I just left. Did I totally blank out for the two minutes it would take to come back here? What is happening?

"Are you okay, Miss Carter?" Professor Johnson's voice is worried, alarmed.

"I think I need to sit down." I'm barely able to form the words. Everything is spinning. And I'm so hot. And then I'm being held close. I look up to see Professor Williams holding my bag and my coat and then notice that Professor Johnson has his arms around me.

"I've got you, Ashley," he whispers against my hair and I know he does. I'm okay here. And I let the darkness take me.

Ashley

WED    THU    FRI    SAT    SUN        DATE

# Chapter Thirty-Three

## ASHLEY

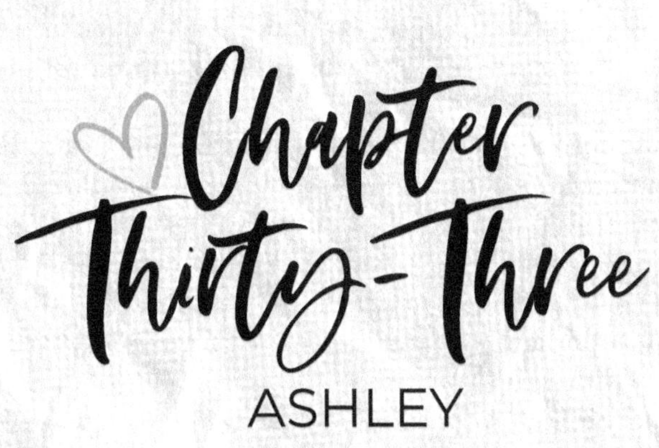

**ICED WHITE MOCHA, VANILLA SALTED CARAMEL COLD FOAM, CARAMEL DRIZZLE**

*Social Post: Note to self, take anxiety triggers seriously. Sometimes, all you need is to take a moment to breathe, but don't ignore it. #csugirlie #colorado #mentalhealthawareness #control*

*Image Description: "Breathe" written in cursive at the top of my notebook page in pink marker.*

"What happened?" The words come out before I even fully open my eyes. Everything hurts. Did I get hit by a truck?

"You passed out again, Ashley." Why is my mom here? "Professor Johnson was here and kept you comfortable until I could get here. What do you remember?"

I force my eyes open to see my mom kneeling next to me. I'm on a leather couch that I hadn't noticed before in the corner of

Professor Johnson's office. This really is a nice space. "I came in to see Professor Johnson. I was cold. Like really cold. And then I got all flustered. I had a hard time saying what I wanted and got overwhelmed. And I couldn't get on top of it. And then it all went black." I don't have time for this. "Does this eliminate me from the program? I really want that spot, Professor Johnson."

"You're not out of the running for anything, Miss Carter." That isn't Professor Johnson's voice. I turn my head to look behind my mom to see Professor Williams sitting in a chair against the wall of books.

"We just need to see what you will be up for and then make the necessary accommodations. Your program may look different than the others enrolled, but your spot is secure. We both want to work with you through the TA and mentorship program, especially with what's planned for Pink Every Day in the next year or so. You focus on getting better and we will figure it out from there," Professor Johnson adds to the conversation.

"Thank you both so much." I look at my mom, trying so hard not to cry, but I feel like I need a massive emotional release right about now. "Can you take me home?"

She nods and smiles at me. "Sam is going to drive your car home after classes and you've been excused from classes through the end of the week. Hopefully some rest is all you need." I begin sitting up, reaching for my coat so I can bundle up before heading outside.

"If you want to bring the car to the front, I can help get her outside, Mrs. Carter." Professor Williams is standing next to her now. He is seriously so tall. Mom looks to me to make sure I'm good and I nod my approval. These are my teachers, and I think they're both old enough to be my dad. Okay, that's a funny thought.

"Something funny, Miss Carter?" Professor Williams asks as he kneels in front of me, tightening my boots and then sliding my coat around my shoulders.

"Nope. Just thought of something. If you can carry my bags, I should be able to get up and walk out of here without causing any more of a scene." I try to stand up and immediately realize that my legs haven't gotten the memo that it's time to work yet. This is seriously so frustrating. I let my head fall back on my shoulders as I try to hold back the tears again. I don't win this time. And they fall across my cheeks, spilling onto my neck. Well, this is an attractive look.

"Hey, you are going to be okay. We will work the school stuff out. You just get better." Professor Johnson sits next to me, holding my hand and stroking the back of it lightly. "A few days off will be good, and classes and programs will still be here when you get back. And you can email or call if you need anything while you are home. I'm here to help you, Ashley." His voice is comforting and reassuring. I really enjoy being in his classes. I look up to see Professor Williams holding my bags.

"Do you want to try standing again? Your mom is waiting at the front door."

"Yeah, I don't know why I had issues with that before. This spell must have hit me harder than the others. It's been a while since I passed out." I stand slowly and let my body adjust to the change in elevation. I wobble a little, but Professor Johnson is right there, offering an arm for me to steady myself with. I take a few tentative steps and then I'm able to start walking toward the hallway.

I know people are staring, but I can't bring myself to look at who else is in the hallway. The people that need to know what's going on are on my side. And the main professors that hold my career at CSU are wanting to help me. I just need some sleep and a few days to disconnect and I'll be fine. The wind hits my face aggressively as Professor Williams props the door open. He positions his body to block as much as he can and I am thankful for his build and height right now. Having him to my left and then Professor Johnson behind me, steadying me, I'm blocked from most of the eyes and the wind.

Moments later, I'm tucked into mom's car and my bags are settled into the backseat.

"Can you please let us know if you need anything? And I'd like to check on you tomorrow if that's okay," Professor Johnson seems worried. And it's kind of nice to have that concern from another adult in my life besides my parents.

"Yeah, that's fine. I'll probably sleep the rest of today but will try to get some homework done tomorrow. I can email you when I'm online and check in." I nod my agreement as I bury my hands under my legs. The heated seats are amazing in here.

"Sounds good, get some rest, Ashley. I will see you soon." He smooths my hair away from my face and then gently shuts the door next to me.

I let my head hit the back of the seat and look over at Mom. "Can we get ice cream on the way home please?"

"It's below freezing and your fingers are blue, and you want ice cream?" she asks incredulously. And I know it's a crazy question, but I want ice cream.

"My 'extracurricular activity' calendar just reset again. I think I deserve ice cream." I'm pouting and I know it. And I don't exactly care.

She just shakes her head and laughs at me. "You have an incredibly attentive and patient boyfriend. Is he giving you a hard time about the doctor's recommendations around the fainting spells?"

"Not at all," I hurry to defend Sam. I did not intend to come across that he might be the one pressuring me. "I just enjoy being with him and we've barely been able to do more than make out sessions in months. He puts up with a lot from me between work commitments and the health stuff."

"The right guy will never look at it as something to 'put up with.' It's part of your journey. And he's there to enjoy it with you. Even if it's not what you originally thought it would be." She reaches over to pat my thigh as the tears start up again, why do I keep crying? "Why don't we get home and I'll have your dad run out to get ice cream in a bit when you have had the chance to rest and fully warm up. Do you want me to call your doctor about the progression of the Raynaud's or do you want to do that after we get home?"

"I think I can call when we get home. They said this was a possibility. I just may need to make a few adjustments."

"And stop forgetting your gloves."

"I need to sew them into my coat pockets or something so I don't forget them anymore."

"I do have a sewing machine." She winks at me as we continue our way home. I don't even want to look at my phone. It will be just my luck that someone saw me pass out on campus and has taken or shared pictures. Hopefully they left off the tags though. Sometimes college kids are worse than they were in junior high when it comes to how mean people can be. Luckily, I've missed most of that. I've never had a designated group that I've hung out with. I get along with everyone and have good relationships with my teachers. Never the top of my classes, but far from the bottom, active in social things at school, but nothing where I would steal the spotlight.

I'm happy where I am. And I think that's what set the episode today off. I was the center of attention for a moment. And I felt like I had interrupted something important. Were either one of them mad at me? Had I misread some body language or nonverbal signal that I wasn't supposed to be there? The receptionist had said I could go in, right? Or did she tell me to wait outside the office until I was called in? Did I assume it wasn't a problem? Why did I think I had the authority to make that decision? Just because I have a social platform and a job position that includes travel and some news coverage, that doesn't give me any extra privileges.

My mind keeps running in these circles until we get home a few minutes later. I have to force myself to unbuckle and grab my bag from the backseat. My bed looks like the best thing ever, but I know it can wait a few minutes. Water, comfy clothes, remove makeup—those things need to happen first. And then, I need to put my phone on silent on the charger. I need to unplug for the rest of the day. My mom will touch base with Sam and Matt. I can go offline for the rest of the day.

My blankets feel amazing and I'm glad I added another layer to my bed last week. My room is fairly warm, but once I get cold, it's a battle to warm up. The extra layers definitely help.

I roll over one more time to clear my notifications before sleep takes me.

> Unknown: You scared me today.

> Unknown: I want to take care of you, Ashley.

Unknown: Can you please let me be there for you?

Me: I don't know what you want from me.

Unknown: Just you, Ashley. I want to take care of you. I don't expect anything in return. Please let me take care of you.

Me: That isn't your job.

Unknown: It could be. I want it to be.

Me: Please stop.

**<Blocks Number>**

Ashley

# Chapter Thirty-Four

## HIM

She's tired of "playing these games." Well, I am too. She has to know it's me. I've seen the way she looks at me. She just doesn't know how to tell her boyfriend that it's over. I can help her with that.

She wouldn't want to upset him though. I can make sure that he isn't hurt unnecessarily. But she needs to be mine. I have to take care of her. She isn't taking care of herself. And seeing her fall apart today, seeing her tears, was more than I could handle.

Her putting everyone else first stops now.

I can put her first.

WED   THU   FRI   SAT   SUN        DATE      /      /

# Chapter Thirty-Five

## ASHLEY

**HONEY CHAMOMILE LATTE**

*Social Post: This has become my "work from home" view—I don't hate it, but I miss being out and about. #workfromhome #collegelife #chronicillness #mentalhealthawareness*

*Image Description: Photo of my bedroom window, light streaming in through the sheer curtains.*

I don't like my 'new normal.' That's what we are calling it, but it's not what college was supposed to look like. I was supposed to be on campus, having study dates, going to sports events. I had a full course load of classes I was so excited about, with professors that were there for me, my studies, and my career. And my boyfriend. I was supposed to be exploring that relationship.

But my days are now filled with adjusted schedules. It's a slow morning, and a class on campus if I'm "feeling up for it." Some days

I can't get out of bed. The doctors say it's partially the Raynaud's progressing and my body figuring out how to manage it. But there's a part of it that I don't like talking about. I have a good home and a good family. I am taken care of. I get to go to school for what I want. I get to go shopping for the new makeup I like. I have privilege and friends and consistency. Depression isn't supposed to hit someone like me. I have no reason for it. But here we are.

And it has gone from a few days of uncertainty a month to days where it hurts to get out of bed. The escalation of symptoms is concerning—to me and my family. My therapist thinks that something triggered it and that it may be both hereditary and situational. Apparently, my mom dealt with depression when she was pregnant and when my brother and I were younger. She's been on medication since then and manages with a mix of medicine, therapy, and some lifestyle changes.

I don't want to give up what I'm doing with school and with Sasha, but adjustments had to be made while my body figured out how to deal with medication. News flash—depression meds make you seriously sleepy. At least, that's how my body handled it. There were a few weeks there that I struggled to stay awake during the day while we had to "trial and error" the dosage.

I had to pass on the TA position this semester. Kinda hard to do when I can't even go to campus most days. I was able to finish my classes and get everything submitted. And I had virtual meetings weekly with Professor Johnson so I could stay on track with my assignments and goals. This does mean I am behind on the full mentorship plan, but because I am local and already a part of a growing company, Professor Johnson says I shouldn't miss out on this opportunity.

The semester goes by without my approval, but here we are. Summer in Colorado. And Sam is traveling this summer working on a project for a larger newspaper out of Denver. Professor Erickson was able to get him connected for this internship. And I hate how much I cried when he told me. I should be happy for him, right? This is a huge opportunity for him. And all I could think of was how much I would miss him. There's only so much career growth he could experience at the small paper he's been at for years. I hate how I felt like he was leaving me, when he was doing something that brings him joy and will help him long term. Depression seriously sucks.

I am in the middle of another rough day when my phone dings. It's mid-July and I haven't had the chance to talk to Sam in about a week. He's backpacking somewhere in the mountains right now with limited signal. Survival groups are really big right now and Sam gets to document it while also learning survival skills. I could not go that long without a shower, but I'm happy he gets this opportunity. My content has also shifted since the beginning of the year. I'm only blogging now, and then sharing some cover photos to my social media. I don't have the energy for more. Or the joy anymore either.

Which means, the social media notifications are few and far between. So having one pop up mid-morning, when I didn't post anything today is weird. I don't want to look, but I make myself grab my phone. I need to try to get out of bed today. And maybe this will give me a reason to do so.

It wasn't a social media notification, it was an email. From Professor Johnson.

Ashley,
I trust that you are having a restful summer. I know the semester did not end how you originally planned, but I am proud of you for continuing to show up for yourself and your classes. I have the opportunity to attend a new four-week course this summer. It will cover some new technology that will streamline search engines and help those platforms become more intuitive for each user. I am able to bring an assistant with me to these seminars. There is only one in person seminar, being held on the CSU campus. The rest are all virtual.
Please think about attending. I think it would help your career and the opportunities you missed this last semester. And we can talk about what you are wanting to do this fall.
I look forward to hearing from you,
Professor C. Johnson

I take a few deep breaths. I am not going to let this summer totally pass without doing anything. And this will fill up the last few weeks before classes start up again.

> Professor Johnson,
> I'd love to attend this with you. Can you send me the details please? Thank you for thinking about me.
> Ashley Carter

"I am so excited to get to attend this seminar with you, thank you again so much for thinking of me for this." I'm gushing and I know it. But I've spent the better part of the summer in my bedroom and I desperately needed something to get me out of the house. I was only able to do a few of the farmers markets with my family and I seriously missed that. At least with this, it's something I will enjoy and it's college credits too. And hopefully, I can get in some of the mentor stuff that I missed since I was home most of last semester.

"Absolutely, I had a few students on my list but wanted to reach out to you first. I know this will be beneficial for what you are doing in your role at Pink Every Day as well as the growth you are hoping to implement after you graduate. And with how fast technology is developing, there is a lot that you need to be aware of or there is a good chance you will be behind the curve."

"Completely understand that. I feel like I'm already behind the curve, but hopefully this will ease me back into things for the fall semester. I need to finish reviewing the things my advisor sent over this week. I can't believe it's already time to pick my classes." We head into the lecture hall on campus. Of course today is the day I get a close parking spot, when it's pushing 100 degrees outside and I don't have to worry about blue fingers.

"I wanted to ask you, would you be interested in me taking over as your advisor? It might help simplify some things on your end, especially with the mentor program."

"Um, that would actually be great. I don't ever talk to her except for the class schedule. And you've been so helpful with the adjustments I've needed and getting me into this seminar schedule too. Yeah, I'd like that. Thank you, Professor Johnson." He holds his hand in front of him in a "you first" motion as we find our seats halfway back in the room. There's got to be over two hundred people here.

"I think you can call me Charles when we aren't in a classroom setting, Ashley," he mentions to me as we pull out our laptops and get ready for the lecture to start.

"Well, we are in a classroom setting right now, technically speaking, Professor Johnson," I smile up at him. He just shakes his head and chuckles lightly, adjusting his glasses a bit.

"Pay attention so I can quiz you later." He taps my laptop as the room quiets and the projector turns on, signaling things will be starting soon.

"Yes, sir."

Halfway through the three-hour seminar, I need to pull my gloves out of my laptop bag. I caught it early, so I can still type, but my fingers have started getting stiff and harder to move. I hate how cold I get. And I can tell I'm getting frustrated. I'm approaching twenty, not sixty-five. My fingers should work properly. I force back the tears and make myself focus on what is being said, retracting my hands into fists to try to will them to work.

I close my eyes, trying to settle myself down before this spirals further. I feel a hand on my own. Professor Johnson leans in to whisper as he holds my hand in his own. "You are strong and fully capable of taking this class. Take a break from the notes. I'm right here and I've got this. Do you need to step out for a minute?" The care in his voice is obvious. He wants me to succeed—both academically and mentally. And I didn't know how much I needed to hear that until he finished his question.

"I think I'm okay, thank you, Professor Johnson." I take a few deep breaths and reach for my water, giving myself something to focus on outside of my fingers and the weight on my chest.

"Care to try that again?"

"Thank you, Charles." He smiles at me as he continues taking notes. I close my laptop and focus on the teacher at the front of the room. Having someone here to take notes so I can fully pay attention to what is being discussed has its perks.

Unknown: You seemed happier today. How was the seminar?

Me: It was good. And I think I needed that class today.

Me: How's your summer going?

Unknown: Better now.

Me: How come?

Unknown: You're not ignoring me anymore.

Me: I still don't know who you are though.

Unknown: That's okay. Are you planning anything for your birthday yet?

Me: Probably just another tattoo appt with my brother. My boyfriend is still "off the grid" so we'll keep it simple.

Unknown: When does he get back?

Me: Later this week. So he'll be back before we have to prepare to move in on campus.

Unknown: Is staying on campus the best choice with how you've been feeling?

Me: I don't think that's anything we need to talk about.

Unknown: I just want to make sure you are safe and being taken care of.

Me: I'm fully capable of taking care of myself.

Unknown: I don't doubt that.

Unknown: Just be careful, Ashley.

Unknown: I'm worried about you.

**<Blocks Number>**

Who does this guy think he is?

WED    THU    FRI    SAT    SUN         DATE

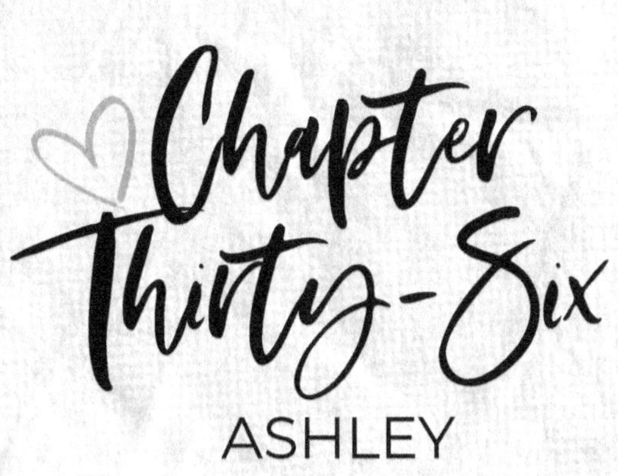

# Chapter Thirty-Six

## ASHLEY

**CARAMEL APPLE SPRITZ MOCKTAIL**

*Social Post: Insert cliche "happy birthday" post here, but seriously, here's to another trip around the sun. #justme #birthdaygirl #coloradogirl*
*Image Description: "Birthday girl" coffee mug on my nightstand.*

"Are you sure you just want to do tattoos for your twentieth birthday, Ashley? We could go do something else," my brother asks as we head to the car. It's my birthday and I had to force myself to get out of bed again today. If we didn't already have these appointments booked, I would have probably canceled.

"Yeah, I want to go to our appointment and then probably come home. Maybe we can order in for dinner tonight. I don't want anything major."

"Is Sam coming over later? He got home from his trip earlier this week, right?" The car starts and we begin making our way to town. It's August and usually that means it's super hot outside. But today is overcast and chilly. The weather matches my mood, and where that would have upset me in previous years, it just confirms my attitude about today.

"I don't think so. He has to get some things finalized with Professor Erickson from the trip and then he has something planned with Brock for moving in together for the semester this year."

"And you're sure you want to stay on campus this fall? Is that really the best decision with everything that's been happening with your health?" I know he's concerned and he has every reason to be, but I don't want to be babied anymore. I can do this. I know my body and my limits and I don't want to feel like I'm isolated at home.

"I talked it over with my therapist and it's what I've decided to do this fall. I'll have Tilly with me and Sam won't be far away. I'll be okay," I let my voice trail off while I track the raindrops on the window next to my face. The glass is cool, but not too cold that it hurts my cheek. Just enough discomfort that it helps me focus on the sensation and not the steady overwhelm that just doesn't go away anymore.

"Do you know what you're getting done today?"

"Another affirmation. I like the simplicity of them and I don't want to commit to a bigger piece yet. You?"

"I'm getting a lipstick kiss added to my sleeve for Sasha. She left me one on an envelope last month and I kept it. I'm hoping it will fit into some of the blank space I have left so I can have something of her with me."

"If you guys weren't so adorable together, it would be gross. You do know that, right?" He just laughs at me, but he knows it's true.

A few hours later, we are on our way back home, my new wrist tattoo wrapped up and hopefully will be healed before I have to start wearing my gloves again.

"I am Enough" is the sentiment on this one. I like that I have affirmations on my body reminding me that I'm in control and I can do hard things. Control what I can and leave the rest. If that one wasn't so long I would probably get that added next. Maybe I'll be ready for something different next time and not just another script or print tattoo. I sit in the car for a moment after the engine cuts out, listening to a few kids up the road throwing a ball around or playing tag. I'm not sure what they're doing, but hearing the giggles and shouts is something to focus on outside of myself.

"I think I'm just ready to get back into the normalcy of going to classes, meeting with Sasha for work, and being a college student. I hate that I haven't had control over anything the last few months and I just need to be able to feel normal for a bit." I take a deep breath and blow it out slowly, feeling my chest expand to the point it hurts before I release it. "I don't know how to make it all better, Matt, and I hate that I can't fix it because I don't even know what is wrong half the time. What do I do to make it better?" The last question comes out as a sob because I can't hold it back anymore. Between the tattoo and the weather and my birthday, the release I've needed finally hit and my body is done holding it back.

I feel my brother unbuckle and adjust in his seat so he can wrap his arms around me and pull me as close as the seats will allow. I let him hold me as I cry and let it all out. He doesn't try to talk or tell me everything will be fine. He just holds me and rubs my back gently, stroking his fingers through my hair and letting me know he's there. He sees me. And it's not going to feel like this forever.

I don't know how long I stay there, long enough for the car to get cold and my body to be tired from the tears. Do you know the cry sessions where your entire body needs a rest afterwards because you just let everything out? That's what this feels like.

"Do you think it's okay if I'm not up for anything tonight? I just want to go to bed." I pick up my purse from the floor and stare out the front windshield. I am not ready to go inside.

"I think that's fine. Just don't push us away, Ash. We are here for you. Even if all of the craziness at school and online doesn't change—we are here for you. Let's go in before they think something happened." He squeezes my hand and then opens his door. Hopefully I can make it to my room without getting caught in conversation.

Luckily, my parents took the hint that I needed some space tonight. I hate thinking I've disappointed them, but I need a night of quiet where I don't have to be happy and talkative with everyone. I need a night where I don't have to be ready for content or conversation. I need a night to just lay in my bed and be still. Maybe cry some more. But just be still. I'm moving on campus next week and I won't get the chance to have fully quiet nights. So, I'm trying to enjoy the quiet while I can.

After a while, my body feels lighter and I can breathe again. The digital clock on my nightstand says I've been sleeping for four hours. I can probably roll over and sleep all night honestly. I check my phone to see what I've missed, already deciding that I'm not going to let myself be online for long.

Sam: I hope you're having an amazing day today, I miss you.

Sam: Your brother just let me know how you're doing. Please let me know if you need anything. I can bring over some ice cream or sushi or something else.

Sam: Sleep well, Ash. I'll see you on campus in a few days.

Unknown: Happy birthday, beautiful.

Unknown: I can't wait to see what you chose for your tattoo this year.

Tilly: Happy birthday, gorgeous!!

Tilly: Can we go room shopping later this week? Target got some new storage things in for the college locations and I want to get a few things. Let me know what your schedule looks like.

Sasha: Hey lady! Happy birthday!

Mom: I have dinner in the fridge for you if you get hungry and a new book for you on the table downstairs too. I'm here if you need anything. Your dad and I are going to go to dinner with some friends but will be home around nine probably. The house is locked up and the alarm is set.

Me: Hey mom. Just woke up. Thank you so much. Not sure if I'm going to get up yet or not. Where did you go to dinner?

Mom: We went to the Mill in town. They just switched the menu over and figured it would be a good chance to check it out. Do you need anything before we come home?

Me: I'm good. Have fun tonight.

Mom: Love you baby. Happy birthday.

Me: Love you too mom.

It's only seven, so they must have left early for drinks or something based on the first messages from her. I don't have it in me to respond to anyone else. I do want to grab something to eat though. I haven't eaten since this morning and I don't think coffee counts as breakfast, unfortunately. The bowl inside the fridge with my name on it makes it easy to see what's for me. Leftovers are seriously the best sometimes. Yay for comfort food.

While that heats up, I look for the book she left for me. There's a few gifts wrapped on the island in the kitchen so I leave those alone for now. Not sure if anyone wants to actually see me open them, so those can wait. I find the book that Mom was talking about though. It's a new romance from one of my favorite authors, set in Scotland. Why is an accent just the hottest thing ever? Even when it's in print. I've already read this one on my Kindle and in Audio, but this one is a special edition and it's seriously so pretty!

The next envelope has a little note on the outside. *"You don't have to wait to open this one."* I smile, wondering what is inside. The envelope has several coffee gift cards inside, yay me!! There's seriously several hundred dollars' worth of coffee gift cards in here, for a couple different places too. There is a small black box that had been attached to the envelope. It's not wrapped, so I might as well peek inside. I don't have to wait, the note said.

Inside are several 4x4 photo squares, the kind that you can use to create a collage on your wall. They're all the photos that I liked from the photo account I follow on Instagram. They're my favorite ones too. All the rainy images, different backgrounds. The photos bring me a peace but also a sadness. A sadness that feels familiar. This is how I feel about outside of my body right now. It's beautiful, but I can't see it clearly. There is comfort in the sadness. I feel seen. I flip through the tiles, seeing which ones were picked for me, not even thinking about where they came from. I had shared the account with a lot of my online and IRL friends, so it's not out of the question that someone got these printed for me.

When I get to the one at the end of the stack, I gasp. The rain has cleared, but not fully. It's still foggy and dim, but I can see the image through the water droplets. It's a bench in a park, just off of a walkway. There is a familiar rose bush next to the bench and a bag that goes with me every time I leave the house. I sit on the bench. My head in my hands. And although I can't see the detail, I know

I'm crying. I'm broken. And I'm seen in that brokenness. I flip it over to see if there's a note on the back. The others were all blank, but part of me wishes that this one will be different.

*"I see you, beautiful. I wish I could take the tears away"* is the simple note written in that familiar script on the back.

I take the book from my mom and the pictures up to my room. I arrange the photos on my wall next to my window. These beautiful images bring me emotions that I'm not ready to name. Once they are all arranged, I sit on my bed to admire them. I take a quick picture and share it to my stories. No caption. No music. Just the image. Moments later, my phone dings, and before I even look, I know it's him.

Unknown: They look beautiful.

Unknown: Happy birthday, my love.

I don't block him this time. Something is keeping me from doing so. And I'm too tired to question it as I cry myself back to sleep.

# Chapter Thirty-Seven

## MARCUS

**LYON'S TEA GOLD BLEND**

*Social Post: A new semester is just around the corner. #csu #csuprof #collegelife*

*Image Description: Academic planner sitting on top of my laptop.*

"What do you mean, you get first pick of the TA students? You've been here for one semester. I've been working with these students for months and I already had a plan for who I was going to select this semester." Professor Johnson comes storming into my office this morning. I level my eyes at him. If he's going to throw a tantrum, I'll wait until he acts with the decency that calls for my attention and respect. He takes a few deep breaths while I sip my tea, waiting.

"Are you going to respond to me?" This man.

"I will respond when you approach the matter in a way that shows you are a nearly tenured professor and not a high school student who was just grounded on homecoming weekend." My words are filled with disdain and I don't even try to hide it. Something is off about this guy and I don't know what it is. I felt it the first time I arrived on campus, but we didn't have much interaction, so I brushed the thought aside. But with the new semester starting, and our classes, assistants, and mentor students needing to coordinate with each other, he's here, in my office, again.

I can tell he's angry. He may be older, but he is not my superior.

"I got the email from admin this morning saying that you have first choice for your students. Before me. I had a plan for my TAs this semester and I don't think you should have the first pick of students."

"What plan?"

"Excuse me?" Oh, did he really think I wouldn't question him on this. I stand and button my suit coat, fixing my cuffs before raising my eyes to look at him again.

"What do you have planned with your students? And why wasn't this added to the agenda at our summer meetings when we were discussing the requirements for our programs and classes? If you had additional input, you had ample time to submit that information. Now things are set and classes begin next week. We can't make adjustments to the program at this time. By not following proper procedure, you dismiss the needs of the students and disrespect the professors that did follow protocol." I do not stutter. I do not back down. I pick up my laptop bag and motion for him to walk in front of me as we exit my office. I have a lunch meeting with admin to finalize things for the semester and I will not be late.

His tail is obviously between his legs and I don't know why I feel such satisfaction from that. I can tell he's used to getting his way. He has the classic attractiveness that demands attention and it's obvious that both students and faculty notice him. But I will not be pushed over. I've earned my respect and status for more than my size and build. And it's time he understands that.

"I apologize. I should have looked over the details more clearly when it was time to submit suggestions and needs. When will the list be posted?" He walks alongside me as we exit the building.

"Tonight. I have a meeting with admin to finalize a few last spots and then we will be sending out the placements this evening. Are two TA's and one mentor student sufficient or have your needs changed?" My bag settles on the back seat as I open the driver's side door to allow the oppressive heat to leave the small space. I'm not a total dick. I can provide some accommodations.

"My needs haven't changed. I just hoped to work with Brock Shale and Ashley Carter. They've been in several of my classes and I had been preparing for them to be my TAs and then transition to the mentor positions in future semesters." He's hopeful with his request.

"I believe Mr. Shale is set to be one of your assistants. Miss Carter will be paired with myself and Mr. Masters for this semester. Mentorship positions are not guaranteed with the professors they TA for though, so there's an opportunity for her to move to you next semester." I lower myself into my car and start the engine, effectively telling him that the conversation is over. He had his chance. And I have a program to run.

That evening, the list is posted. Six professors are participating this semester. Twelve students will be assistants this semester. All twelve of them are good candidates for the mentor program. Once the semester is underway, each professor will meet with their students to set a plan until they graduate and what they want to accomplish before they graduate. Many of them already have their placements for after they finish their studies. Several with startups, and a few with more established businesses. This program is designed to stretch the students as much as the professors. Hence the variety of placements. We each have a student that grew up preparing to take on a company role with their parents or family companies and one student that recently found their calling or company fit.

Mr. Shale has grown up doing different positions with his

parent's marketing company. His final position is not settled yet, but he is preparing for a few different roles. His boyfriend is already working there full time as his father's executive assistant. I've known Mr. Shale Sr. for several years, and I hope his son has a good experience with Professor Johnson.

I will be stretching myself with my main placement. Miss Carter is going into a field I know very little about. The majority of the work that Pink Every Day accomplishes is makeup and skincare related. But they are also committed to working with women-owned businesses and nonprofits that directly impact the communities they reside in. It's a big picture company. And I want a part in it.

My other placement is the younger brother of my mentor student back in the UK. I'll be working with Sean remotely, but Rowan has transferred to the States to attend CSU for at least the first two years. I already know him from my time with Sean and know that this will be a good fit for both of us.

I'm just waiting for the complaints to come in from both students and professors. Favoritism, crushes, and politics have played a big part in who applied to these programs. But those have no place in the workforce, especially with some of the companies represented by these students. I want students that are actually going to do something in the industry, not just sit at a desk and look pretty for a few hours before heading to the country club. That's why the students that were chosen all have a hand in a non-profit or similar organization. We are doing more than marketing products with this class. We are making actual changes within our classrooms and businesses.

I send off a letter of introduction to all of those in the program as well as the placement instructions. We will have a meeting at the end of the week to prepare for the semester ahead. And we have several students lining up to fill spots if any of these drop out. I've spent the last semester getting to know these students, and I don't think any of them will walk away from this opportunity. But I've been wrong before.

Marcus

WED   THU   FRI   SAT   SUN        DATE

# Chapter Thirty-Eight

## ASHLEY

**PEAR CINNAMON MOCKTAIL**

*Social Post: New notebooks: check. New pack of pens, highlighters, and other pretty writing utensils: check. Dorm room unpacked: check. Coffee bar stocked: absolutely. Schedule posted by the door and on my calendar: check. Still losing my mind over the first day of classes outfit choices: absolutely!*

*Help me pick my outfit for meeting with the business professors and the rest of the TAs! I can't pick!*

*Also, what do we think of the new handle? I thought it was time to set something up more officially than the generic one that was chosen for me when I started this account forever ago. #csugirlie #coloradogirlie #coloradogirl #collegelife #dormlife #dormessentials #newschoolyear #junioryear #sassyashleysmiles*

*Image Description: Photo slides of different outfits laid out on my bed.*

I end up going with a sundress that I feel amazing in. It's a soft yellow color and pairs beautifully with my oversized navy cardigan. Thick socks and canvas shoes finish out the fit. I can't really wear sandals anymore. My feet get too cold too quickly. And I can't bring a lap blanket with me wherever I go. I keep one in the car and bring it with me to some places, but it's the first day meeting many of these professors and students, and I don't want to announce that I'm basically an old lady that can't keep herself warm as my introduction. This is my chance to start over and have a really solid semester.

Especially when I will have to ask for a few "favors" this semester with meetings for Pink Every Day and then the NYC trip in December. At least we have more of a heads up this time around so I can make plans with my professors and assignments early on. I was surprised when I was placed with Professor Williams. I definitely thought he would pick only seniors or those going into a more "masculine" field. Yes, I know how ridiculous that sounds. But that's where my mind went. He just gives off "Daddy energy." Okay, enough with the quotation marks. You know what I mean, right?

He commands every space he is in. You can't help but look to him for approval or input when someone else speaks. He's the one running this program, and I was completely baffled when I was chosen to work with him. I'm looking forward to working alongside Rowan, an exchange-ish student from the UK. Men with accents, right? Sam, Tilly, Brock, and I had a little laugh about that last night when we were reviewing things. Brock got placed with Professor Johnson. Tilly opted out this semester. And Sam is with Professor Johnson too. I was surprised when I wasn't added to that group. I've worked a lot with Professor Johnson and was looking forward to continuing what we had started talking about last semester.

Part of this program is having a Professor advisor though. And Professor Johnson is mine. So I'll still get to see him for those meetings and conversations.

"The goal of having professors in this department overseeing the TA program, mentor program, and being your academic advisors is to facilitate interdepartmental relations. This way, you get to build relationships with many professors and departments within the business building. Many of you have different fields you will be entering or have already begun working in. We want to give you the tools needed to advocate for yourself, find the necessary resources, and make things happen. We are here to help you do just that. We don't just want you grading papers. We want you to partner with your professors to submit inquiries, meet with local businesses, do research, and make things happen. It's your choice how the next few months will play out.

"Take the rest of the time we have to meet your groups and set an initial meeting plan with your professor. Classes start next Wednesday. Don't waste your time. And thank you for being a part of the first group participating at the CSU campus here in Fort Collins, Colorado." Professor Williams finishes his speech and then makes his way to the table that I've been sitting at alongside Rowan. I'll have to let Tilly know when I meet up with her later that Rowan does indeed have an accent.

"Good morning, Mr. Masters, Miss Carter," he regards each of us as he pulls out the third chair at the small table. Eyes from around the room are on us and I don't like the attention. I subtly, intentionally slow my breathing and focus on the papers that he placed on the table in front of me. I can see my name. I can read the title on the page but can't make my brain make sense of it. More eyes. More whispers. My phone vibrates in my pocket. Why isn't it stopping? I am not going to do this again.

I can feel the tears tracking down my face. The whispers feel like shouts and I'm too hot. I feel steady pressure on my hand, on my knee. I know someone is here trying to calm me down, but I can't tell who. I'm deep into a panic attack and it came out of nowhere. I didn't have time to get on top of it. And if I'm not careful, I'm going to pass out.

"What do you need?" I hear the whisper.

"I wish I knew. It's too much. Too loud. Everyone's looking and I already messed it all up." I'm practically sobbing now, but I'm able to get the whispered words out.

The man holding me steady cradles my head into his shoulder

and picks me up, carefully tucking my skirt under his arm so I don't flash the world. Small mercies. Moments later, I feel the energy in the room shift. I can take a full breath again and I can smell the cologne that rests gently on the arms that hold me. Spicy, like cinnamon and tobacco. Strange combination, but it works. I let my fingers trace the stubble on the neck up against my own. Letting the sensation ground me. The cushion next to me shifts and I realize I must be on a couch and someone just sat next to me, and whoever I'm sitting on apparently.

I feel the steady up and down movement on my back, the pattern and pressure bringing me back down to the present. "Thank you. I'm sorry about that," I'm able to breathe out. I'm not crying anymore, but I feel exhausted.

"Does that happen a lot, Miss Carter?" Professor Williams is obviously concerned with his question. I force myself to bring my eyes to his, noticing Professor Johnson and Sam standing in the doorway.

"The panic attacks started earlier this year. I have been really good with my triggers and don't have them as often anymore. Today came out of nowhere. I don't know what happened. I am so embarrassed. Did you carry me out of there?" Now, I'm absolutely mortified.

"I'm sorry if I crossed a line. You were having a hard time breathing and I needed to get you out of that room. I hoped a reset would help you get back in control." Professor Williams gently repositions so I can sit on the cushion and he can stand back up, fixing his suit. It's then that I'm able to look over and see Rowan sitting next to me, obvious concern on his face.

"I thought it's been a while since you've had an episode like that, baby," Sam's voice is gentle, but I don't miss the extra pet name. It's adorable that he's staking his claim next to Rowan. I'm not interested in the cute little Scottish puppy, but I like that he's acting like that. I smile at him in appreciation for his concern.

"It's not happening as often. I thought the group today would be smaller and I'd be able to handle things. I think once I have a clear plan for the expectations on me this semester for classes and for what I need to do for the program, I'll be okay. I'm so sorry I lost it in there. Did I mess up that whole meeting?" Ugh, way to get booted from the program before it even begins, Ash.

"You didn't mess up anything. I knew you were having some health concerns, but I didn't realize that meeting was going to set you off. Can we spend some time going over some of the options for classes and requirements for the semester once you get your syllabi next week so we can avoid these incidents in the future?" He says it with concern, not like he's bothered by it.

"My mom deals with anxiety and panic attacks. It's something we've seen before, so it didn't surprise either of us," Rowan pipes up. "I'm happy to connect the two of you if you want to talk to her about what may help you. I know it's embarrassing but know that you've got people here who want to help."

"I think I'd like that. I have a friend who deals with social anxiety and anxiety attacks, but they don't show up like this for her. So, besides my therapist, I don't have someone who fully understands what's happening."

"You're not alone with this, Ashley. Let us help you, okay?" Professor Johnson's voice is pleading. And I know I totally freaked him out. He's been there for many of my episodes and it always rattles him. He's fine in the moment, but he is obviously shaken at the end of them. I hate that I cause him pain, even in this thing that I can't control.

"Okay. Can we jump into the paperwork now? And then I think I need a nap."

"Sounds like a plan, Miss Carter. Gentlemen, thank you for coming to check, but I do need you to go find Mr. Shale and finish your meeting as well, please."

"Yes, sir." Sam smiles and then shoots me a wink. They leave the office and the three of us get settled into the office to work through our requirements for the semester.

WED    THU    FRI    SAT    SUN        DATE :

# Chapter Thirty-Nine

## ASHLEY

### NUTELLA COLD BREW

*Social Post: Because every dorm room needs a bit of sparkle #sassyashleysmiles #dormlife #dormroom #csugirlie #coloradogirl #collegelife*

*Image Description: Four square canvas art prints—all are different makeup items in dark pink sparkles over a light pink background: two lipsticks, an eyeshadow palette, and a brush set.*

"There goes any chance at a social life this semester," I huff out as I plop myself onto my bed.

"Like you had any plans for a social life anyway," Tilly chuckles from the bean bag chair on the floor under the window. She's editing some content on her phone I think as the same fifteen second loop of a song keeps playing over and over again. I get it, it's hard to line those transitions up.

"True, but this course load is going to be insane. Between

the actual classes, stuff with Pink Every Day, and now Professor Williams's requirements, it's going to be a lot. And then my therapist wants to bump up how often we have visits. He wasn't happy with how severe and abrupt my last episode was during the meeting last week."

"At least he isn't dismissing it."

"True again. I just feel like I'm going to be missing out on the full college experience here. You know? I haven't felt up for any of the mixers or extracurricular events since early freshman year. And I'm practically months away from taking on a full leadership role with the company. And I can't be 'boss babe' and 'party queen' at the same time." And yes, I did actually use quotation marks there.

"When have you ever wanted to be a part of the party scene?" Tilly is actively holding back a laugh right now and she's doing a good job, but she's not wrong.

"You know what I mean, I haven't even had the opportunity to shoot down an overly handsy guy at a house party. I went from friends to more with Sam and then I got sick and we haven't been able to go out. I want to tell people, 'sorry, I'm taken,' when they try to ask me out. Not just get the pity eyes when I pass out on campus."

"Do you want me to be looking for party opportunities this semester?"

"You know what, yeah. Let's go shopping so we are prepared and take advantage of a good day while I have it."

"Are you sure about this?" Sam picks Tilly and me up at our dorm before we head out to the house party just off campus. "You haven't really been interested in the social pieces of campus life, especially a house party at one of the frat houses."

"I need to do this, Sam. I want to let loose for one night and just enjoy feeling good. Please. I need this. And I want to have you with me in case an episode starts up." My body is turned toward his, my hands resting on his hips, playing with his belt looped through his jeans. His hands mirror my own, and his thumbs shoot heat through my entire body. My cropped green sweater pairs beautifully with these leggings and I know I look good. My hair is pulled back in a matching headband and my makeup is a little bolder than usual. But the green makes my eyes pop and I know it.

The pink diamond studs in my ears are worn almost every day, a reminder that simple things are beautiful and that I am worth it. All of it.

Sam leans in and places a kiss on the corner of my lips and then up against where my ear meets my neck, pushing his body into mine a bit. I miss feeling his body on mine. I miss sex. I miss sex with him.

"I'm here for whatever you need, baby. I just want you to be careful and not overdo it so early into the semester. You'll let me know if it's too much, right?"

"Yes, Dad." I roll my eyes at him and he just shakes his head.

"Let's get this over with."

It's not long before we get to the house hosting the party. It's ten at night, but the house and lawn are packed. It's loud and there are so many people here. When do they go to sleep? Yes, I know I sound like an old lady again, but seriously, it's a Tuesday! We have class tomorrow.

"Okay, so Ashley is DD, we only get one drink and only something we open ourselves. And we are back to the car by eleven. Is that the plan?" Tilly pockets her cell phone and leaves her purse in the car and I follow suit.

"Yep, I can't mix alcohol with my meds, and that way I can make sure I stay aware of what's happening around us. But please, don't leave me alone. This is actually insane."

Sam settles his arm through one of mine, resting his hand on my opposite hip. His arm behind me gives me the support I need to make my way to the front door. "Please tell me we know some people here."

"I think you'll recognize a few," Tilly smiles at me as she grabs my hand and pulls me closer to the wide-open door. And I wonder briefly if I will even fit inside the crowded space, much less have a good time in there.

It doesn't take long to realize that parties may not be my thing. But at least we found a corner in the kitchen. Tilly dug through one of the coolers to find a seltzer for herself and a beer for Sam. I'm more than happy with my Diet Coke. Brock and Hunter are here somewhere too. They grabbed drinks with us when we got here and then went off to "see who else is here." We are, why not stay with us?

"So, whose house is this?" I ask Tilly, practically shouting over the music from the main space.

"One of the professor's brothers I think. He graduated last year but kept the house. He rents it out to the football team or lacrosse team, I don't know. But they throw a party a few times a year."

I lean my body back into Sam's, enjoying his arm wrapped around me. It centers and grounds me—his touch. I know that he is here with me. And I focus on that, willing my mind not to spiral. I'm safe. I'm having fun. At least, I'm out with my boyfriend and my friend. I'm being a college student. Yay me.

"I like the new handle, Ash," a very loud male voice calls out from across the room. Could he seriously not be bothered to walk over here to talk to me?

"Who is that?" I ask Sam and Tilly while holding eye contact with the blond guy in some sort of jersey across the room. Did he not change after practice? There's grass stains all over it. Gross.

"I think he's on the football team, not a starter though," Sam comments.

"And apparently, he follows you," Tilly giggles.

"Okay, no more of that for you, go dump it in the sink." I tap the drink in her hand. She is not a giggler so I know when she's had a bit too much. Even though that was less than half a can, she's already feeling it.

"Ugh, I need to find a bathroom, and then can we head out?" I pass my drink to Sam as I start peeking around to see where a bathroom might be. It's not a long drive, but my stomach hurts and I need to make sure I haven't started my cycle early. The antidepressants are really messing up my periods and how they show up. I've bled through enough of my pants this year, I don't need to do it while I'm out and about.

"Do you want me to walk with you or do you want to wait for Tilly?"

"I think I'm okay. She's talking to Brock and I need to go. Keep an eye on her, that drink hit her harder than they usually do. I'll either meet you back here or at the car, okay?" He places a quick kiss to my forehead and then I'm off through the group of college kids. And a few graduates, if I had to guess. Some of these guys look seriously old. Well, not too old, probably late twenties. Definitely not students though.

The bathroom isn't hard to find considering there's a line of girls waiting to use it. This seems typical and I have to force back a laugh. There has got to be a better system here. Is there seriously only one bathroom in this whole house? My stomach gets hit with another punch of pain and I know I need to take some ibuprofen and check my underwear, fast. I take my chances and head toward the stairs.

I know this is probably a bad idea, but I need to find a bathroom.

"Can I help you with something, Ash?" It's the football guy from the kitchen.

"Oh, hi. I don't think we've met before. Just looking for a bathroom." I scooch past him to peer down the hall. All the doors are shut and I really don't want to take the chance of seeing someone having a bit of sexy time in one of those rooms.

"I'm Drew. We met before class one day last year, but I know it's hard to keep everyone straight. Especially when you're juggling the whole social media thing too."

"Yeah, it's a lot. Nice to meet you again, Drew." I look the other way down the hall just to find more closed doors. "I'm sorry for cutting this short, but I really need a restroom. Do you know where one is?"

"Oh, of course. You can use the one down here. It is the shared one for me and another one of the players, Nathan. My room should be open so we'll go in that way. But I think he has someone with him in his room." He leads me to the end of the hall and the quiet of his room is a surprising reprieve from the commotion outside. He shows me the bathroom door and then motions to both locks. "Just in case." Yeah, definitely do not want anyone coming in, either door.

I take care of business quickly, adding a tampon just in case. I'm not spotting yet, but my body is so weird right now, I don't want to chance it. Luckily, I have some pain meds with me so I take those and use my hand to cup some water from the sink to wash them down. I let myself take a few more deep breaths before I head out to brave the crowd again. The bedroom is dark when I come back out. Did he seriously leave me in here? Jerk. Or maybe he thought I wanted some privacy. Okay. Not the end of the world.

I pull out my phone to let Sam know where I am and that I'll meet him at the car. Then I use my phone as a flashlight to find the door. I haven't made it halfway across the floor before my phone buzzes in my hand.

> Unknown: Please tell me you are being safe there tonight.

> Me: How do you know where I am?

> Unknown: Are we really playing this game again?

> Me: I'm fine. I'm sober. I'm leaving.

> Unknown: Good girl.

I shake my head at my phone and then pocket it again. Because I'm at the door to the hallway. And I apparently need both hands to open it because it's seriously stuck. No, not stuck. Locked. I'm locked in Drew's bedroom. His very dark bedroom.

> Unknown: Don't worry. I'm coming.

> Me: What do you mean?

Nothing.

I can't bang on the door because of the noise downstairs. I try to text Sam to let him know where I am, but the messages keep coming back as undeliverable. I try to go to Instagram and message him that way, but the app won't even load. I sit on the edge of the bed, facing the door, settling my breathing and trying to stave off the panic attack. I cannot pass out in an unfamiliar place, surrounded by drunk college kids. Not happening.

I don't know what happens, but I must lose several minutes because then the door is unlocking. Not the one in front of me, but the one from the bathroom. I feel him behind me, but before I can turn around, I get insanely dizzy. And then everything goes black. Not again.

# Chapter Forty

## HIM

Her boyfriend seriously brought her to a party here and then left her by herself. Let another man, that he doesn't know, take her to his room. I'm glad she was smart enough to not touch one of the drinks. Several of them were spiked, even through the cans. Her friend got one. And with her response to me entering the room, hers might have been as well. At least the boyfriend stayed downstairs with the friend.

I can take care of my girl.

I'll bring her home.

She has been pushing herself too hard.

And tonight, was a really horrible idea. If she wasn't so weak, I'd punish her for it. But right now, she needs comforting and care.

She passed out when she heard me behind her. It makes it easier to bring her across campus to her dorm and then to her room. It was way too easy to get a key to her room. It's easy to tell which bed is hers. The soft pink pattern of the bedding shows her femininity. The pillows show that she enjoys nice things. The earrings she wears are keeping me close, even if she doesn't know it. I think she does though.

I lay her on the bed and take off her shoes. I need to make sure she's not too cold. Her fingers look fine, but she wasn't wearing socks tonight. Just a pair of black flats. I look at her toes and feel them – they're cold. I grab one of her fleece blankets and tuck her in. I am so tempted to look at the tattoo she got last year. The one that's always covered. I promise not to touch, I just want to see.

WED   THU   FRI   SAT   SUN        DATE

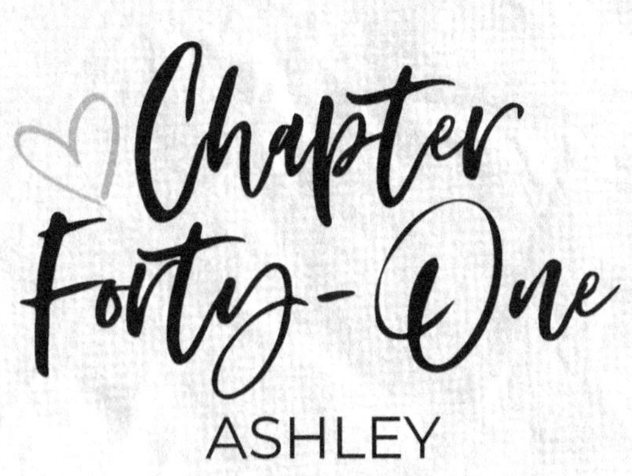

# Chapter Forty-One

## ASHLEY

**RASPBERRY ALMOND LATTE**

*Social Post: And this is why I take off my makeup every night...*
*#makeup #dayafter #skincare*

*Image Description: Mascara stains, green eyeshadow smudges, and*
*red lipstick marks on my light pink pillowcase.*

The next morning is here before I'm ready for it, but my alarm on my phone didn't get the memo that I feel like death today. And I have to get ready for class. So stupid. My head is pounding and my body aches, much like it does every time I have an episode. I don't remember what triggered this one though. Ugh, I feel awful. I grab my phone to check messages and see if I have time to go back to sleep.

Sam: Where are you?

Sam: I'm by the car.

Sam: Are you okay?

Sam: I'm getting worried.

Me: She's okay. She had an episode. I got her back to her dorm and she is resting. I emailed her professors for tomorrow so she can take the day off and sleep.

Sam: Um, okay. Who is this?

Sam: Hello?

Sam: Not cool...

Sam: Tilly just let me know that you are okay and sleeping and your phone is charging. Get some rest when you wake up. I'll come check on you after class.

What the heck? I don't remember any of this. At all. Who brought me back here? And how did they contact my teachers? I scramble to find the icon for my email and login to my school account. There is nothing in my sent folder from last night. And nothing in my calls or texts to indicate that whoever it was messaged from my device or accounts. I text Sam and Tilly to let them know I'm awake and then email Professor Williams to check in. We weren't supposed to meet today, but I don't want to check out on a day that he may have needed something.

I am debating on whether I want to get up to take a shower or go back to sleep when my phone dings.

Unknown: <picture attached>

This time the picture isn't blurred out. It's very, very clear. It's a tattoo. "I am Mine." But the first part is crossed off with a red Sharpie and the "Mine" is circled.

Unknown: Please don't forget.

I whip the covers back to look down at my leg, covered in red ink that wasn't there when I went to the party last night. I scream at the markings that aren't supposed to be there.

Me: What did you do?

Unknown: I took care of you.

Unknown: That's all I've been wanting to do, Ashley. I'm just waiting for you to let me.

Me: I don't belong to you. You need to leave me alone.

Unknown: And that's where you would be wrong, my love.

Two hours and an entire bottle of rubbing alcohol later, my thigh is a lovely shade of pink instead of being covered in glaring red marks. I called Tilly freaking out the second the last text came in. I don't love that she ditched classes to come over here to help me out. But I needed his mark off of my body. I don't think he did anything else. My underwear was still on as were my bra and shirt from the party. My tampon was still in and unsurprisingly, I started my cycle at some point overnight. And my leggings had been folded at the end of the bed.

"I honestly thought it was a follower with a little bit of a crush. He's always been harmless, a little over the boundary lines a few times, but nothing too intense. This was crazy though." I blow on my cup of tea before bringing the warm steam closer to my face. The warmth of the mug centers me and the peppermint is doing wonders to settle me too.

"Do you think it's a student?" Tilly asks. She's sitting on the couch next to me, nursing her own mug of peppermint tea. She's the tea addict to my own coffee obsessed personality. And I'm starting to appreciate a good cup of tea. I'm not giving up coffee any time soon, but I enjoy our growing tea collection.

"It would have to be, right? To get me back to my dorm. Are there cameras or something we can check?"

"Do you want to see if your brother can get that information?" Tilly is hesitant with her question, and I don't blame her. We are gearing up for another Pink Every Day campaign. October is our busiest month content-wise, which means September is our busiest prep month. And Matt does so much to make sure we are ready for everything that we will be sharing and supporting in the coming weeks. Plus, we have the New York trip just around the corner, practically. This time, we are working on our company collaboration partnerships earlier, so we will actually have products and initiatives to unveil during the event.

"I think we can probably subtly look into it ourselves. Maybe talk to campus security, or something like that. I don't want to bring him into this until it's necessary. I blocked the guy again and I'm thinking about changing my number and unlisting it. I'll get a public Google number or something that can be associated with the school and the organization. Maybe a reset will be good."

"What are you going to do about the social media thing?"

"I don't know, Tilly. I've already seriously pulled back on what I'm doing. I can't pull back too much more or I'll lose the momentum that I've built. If I was fully running the Pink Every Day socials, it would be different. But I'm still a separate entity from the organization. I may have to limit comments and engagement even more though. And just pray that it doesn't completely kill what I have going on."

"A platform isn't worth your safety, Ash. If you need to take a break, your brother, Sasha, and those that you are working with aren't going to fault you for that." She sets her mug down on the coffee table in front of her.

"I know that. But I feel like stopping will be quitting. And I'm not good at much else besides content creation and curating an online platform and community. If I lose what I've built, I won't have anything that is solely attached to my name. I need this, Tilly. I can't walk away just yet."

"Just please be careful. This guy is crossing both virtual and physical boundaries at this point. And he's increasing the risk of getting caught. Which means he's escalating. I'm worried for you."

"True crime much?" I chuckle, trying to ease the tension.

"I know it sounds like something we would watch on Lifetime, but it's a popular trope in movies for a reason. He saw something he liked. He formed a para-social relationship with you. And he thinks that you belong to him. Is he going to see your lack of reciprocation as a personal attack? These are real situations, Ash. Don't dismiss it. I know you're worried. The guy literally wrote on your body last night, in your bedroom. We can file a police report and shut down your social media while an investigation happens. I'll back you up and support you. And your family will too."

"I appreciate the concern, really, I do, Tilly. Let's just see what happens after this incident. Maybe he'll see my response to this and realize that I'm not interested." I try to shrug it off. But even I know that my argument is weak and massively unrealistic.

"And what if he takes it as an attack against the relationship he believes the two of you have?"

"I don't know. But I'm sure he'll make me well aware."

He definitely made me aware. Over the following weeks, I would come back to my room to find notes and gifts on my bed. They were all simple enough. Small things like new pens or a notebook, a new cardigan, something for my hair. Lots of coffee gift cards and a special card with a note during the Ulta sale so I could go splurge. Most of the gifts I donated or passed on to others that I thought would like them. I didn't want to have anything from him. But he knew me so well. And some of the things were hard to not keep.

After the first really bad cold spell on campus, a set of rechargeable hand warmers showed up in my school bag. The ones Sam had gotten for me had died the week prior, so I needed a new set anyways. I don't know when they got in my bag, but they were definitely appreciated. I had mixed feelings about using them, so I convinced myself that Sam must have gotten them for me, and I wasn't going to ask because I didn't want to spoil the surprise. Delusional? Probably. Needed? Absolutely.

I found myself drawing further and further into myself. I didn't want to give this guy any more opportunity to connect with me. Especially because we didn't know who he was. Tilly was looking out just as much as I was at this point, but we hadn't been able to find out how the gifts were making it into our room or my things. No one with lingering glances or weird responses on campus. It was just normal. Except for the growing anxiety in my chest. I had canceled more plans than I had made and found it harder and harder to work past that.

I met with Sasha, had lunch with my family once a week, went to class, met with Professor Williams for TA things, and Professor Johnson for going over my schedule and assignments. That was it. I wasn't doing anything extra anymore. I just didn't have the energy or the desire. What if he saw me? What if he was there? What if it was the time when he would decide to do more and escalate further? Tilly and I had been able to talk to campus security about the gifts showing up in our space, but they didn't have any answers for us. After a few meetings with admin and finance, we were able to get the security cameras upgraded in and around our building. And hopefully the other buildings on campus will be upgraded soon too.

I think whoever was leaving the notes realized that things had been upgraded, because nothing has shown up this week. Part of me hopes he has stopped. Part of me is concerned it's the calm before the storm. Classes are finally done for today and it is just a few days until the end of the semester. The sky is overcast and gloomy, really out of the normal for Colorado, and it feels like winter even though it's still in the fifties outside. It feels like the outside matches my inside. And I find comfort in that.

I walk across the campus, my hands holding onto the hand warmers in my pockets of my purple coat. This thing is still a favorite of mine. My feet are in two layers of socks inside of my lined black booties. I've gotten good at cute layers these last few months. Even with my mood, I still try to put myself together every day. I have a meeting with Professor Johnson to proctor two of my final exams today. The last two I need to take before I can be done with my requirements for this semester. Both are my hardest exams too, probably not the smartest thing to make them both happen this afternoon. But I wanted to give myself a few days to finish reviewing some extra notes from Professor Williams's class and then my last finance class from Professor Jackson. Luckily, Professor Johnson said he had the space to help today as he has the last batch of projects to finish grading so will be in his office for a few hours.

I lightly tap on his office door after I check in at the receptionist's desk. "Good afternoon, are you ready for me?" I poke my head in a bit to the open door to find Professor Johnson sitting at his desk, papers neatly stacked in front of him. Music is playing lightly from the speaker in the corner, it's a pretty instrumental track that seems familiar, but I can't place it right now. There is a CSU throw blanket on the couch in the corner and a small space heater too. I don't remember those being in here last time I was in here.

"Good afternoon, Ashley, come on in. I'm almost done with this paper and then I can get you set for your first test. Which one do you want to start with?" He motions to the seating options in the office and I need to decide if I want the couch or the smaller table with a chair. I decided on the chair to start with. I may need to switch in a bit, but I need to focus on this one.

"Professor Jackson's please. Let's get the scary number one out of the way, please." I force a smile as I set my bag down and get my pen case out. I need to have a pencil and pen for this one, and probably some scratch paper. I thought I had some smaller pieces in here somewhere specifically for this. Why is this bag always so messy? I quickly drop to my knees so I can rummage through my bag a little better. After taking out all of my books, my laptop, and my extra gloves, I find the small notebook that has my loose paper in it. "That was quite unnecessary," I mumble to myself.

"Do you need anything before I give this to you?" Professor Johnson is standing in front of the little table, holding onto the papers for the exam. Great, now I'm embarrassed again. On the floor digging around like a child searching for the last Halloween candy in her mom's purse. I take a few deep breaths before shaking my head and replacing the items into my bag.

"All good, I just couldn't find my loose papers for the work I need to do for the exam. How long do I have to work on this one?" I get settled into my seat and pull my favorite writing instruments out.

"You have ninety minutes for this first one. I will be sitting at my desk if you need anything. Once you hand it in, we can't make any changes, so take your time. Does the music bother you or do you want me to turn it off?"

"Actually, I kind of like it." I listen to the soundtrack again and have to hold back a laugh when I recognize the song. "Is this an instrumental version of 'This is Why We Can't Have Nice Things' by Taylor Swift?" His smile is knowing and kind behind his glasses. I love it when people smile with their whole face and not just their lips.

"Yes, I found this instrumental compilation earlier and thought you might enjoy it while working. Was I right?"

"Yes, thank you. Okay, let's get this one done." Professor Johnson places the papers on the surface in front of me and I get to work. He goes back to his desk and grabs a cup I hadn't noticed before. "Here's a raspberry almond latte for you, I picked it up just a bit before you got here, so it should still be warm."

"Oh, thank you. That's a new combo for me, but it sounds great." I take a little sip and this may be a new favorite. The flavors combine so well together and free coffee always tastes better. "Okay, this is amazing. Was this from the on-campus coffee shop?"

"Yes, they just got some new syrups and I wanted to experiment a bit. I'm glad you like it." There's that smile again, but then it's quickly replaced with a mock stern look like he's trying to rein it in a bit. "Now get to work, Miss Carter. I'm starting your ninety minutes now." He presses something on his phone as he resumes his place behind his desk.

"Yes, sir." I smile back at him and then start working through the papers in front of me.

# Chapter Forty-Two

## MARCUS

**LONDON FOG LATTE**

*Social Post: Almost done with grading projects for this term. The creativity and ingenuity shown this semester was incredible and I can't wait to see how these students continue to develop their skills in the coming months. #csuprof #colleglife #teacherlife #gradingpapers*

*Image Description: Cup of tea sitting next to a stack of papers along with several pens and highlighters.*

Rowan and I are finally done with grading the projects this semester. I'm glad we decided to stay and get this done tonight. We are supposed to have a winter storm come through tonight, and I didn't want to risk a snow day and not having this stuff done. We've polished off the pizza I ordered for dinner and are getting grades and notes uploaded in the system before we call it a night.

"Nights like this remind me of home, hearing the wind outside, seeing the cloud cover earlier. I'm already looking forward to going back this summer," Rowan notes as he packs up his bag. I hum in agreement. Scotland was beautiful. And it didn't take long to get used to the overcast weather. Colorado is a totally different world. It's sunny here for 300 days every year, and cloudy days are very abnormal. It almost feels like the sun is brighter here than anywhere else I've been. I definitely got burnt from being outside a few times before I started getting good about sunscreen application and staying in the shade when possible.

"I miss it too. I do like being back and teaching these classes again though. Grad programs are great, but I get to reach a broader group of students with the undergrad classes. And I got to bring over a piece of Scotland with me this time around," I joke with Rowan as I lock up my office door. We begin heading toward the main door to leave when I see Professor Johnson's door open and his light still on.

"Snow is supposed to start soon, are you about ready to head out?" I ask as I poke my head into the classroom. I knew that Miss Carter would be taking some exams tonight. She has an out of state trip with her company, and it's more important that she be there for that event than sitting in a class for an exam she's already prepared for. I'm glad her advisor worked with her on that, and it wasn't any problem to move around a few TA responsibilities to make it happen.

"Yes, Ashley just finished her last exam. I'm just getting the information put into my laptop and then we will be heading out. She asked that I walk her out since it's dark outside. You two can go ahead. We won't be long." Professor Johnson slips on his overcoat and powers down his laptop before rounding his desk to pull a purple coat off the coat tree and slide it onto Miss Carter's shoulders. She looks absolutely exhausted.

"Are you doing okay, Miss Carter?" I know my voice sounds concerned, but hopefully the alarm I am feeling isn't showing. She told me that some of her episodes are triggered by stress and I don't want to send her into a dip unnecessarily.

"Oh, yes. I am a bit cold and tired. Today was a long day. I don't have to go anywhere tomorrow though, so I'm hoping that I can take a rest day and be ready to leave for New York at the end of the week. We get to be there for a few extra days this time and I don't want to miss out on anything we get to do with Natalie and the other brands we get to meet with." She smiles, and it is so obvious that she loves what she does. Not many people find their passion so young, and it's incredible to see her step more into her role with the company alongside Sasha.

"Can I walk you to your dorm, Ashley? Mine is right next door so it won't be out of the way. And that way these two can head out right from the main parking lot and can get out of the cold faster," Rowan asks as we step outside. The temperature has dropped significantly since even a few hours ago and I know Ashley will not be able to be out for long.

"Um, yeah, that would be great. We need to kind of hurry though. I forgot my heavy gloves and my hand warmers died during the last test." She buries her hands in her pockets and I can see her wince. Her fingers must already be colder than what's comfortable for her.

"Can I hold your bag for you or do you have it?"

"I have it, thank you. Have a good night Professor Johnson, Williams. Thank you for your help this semester. I will email you both tomorrow to check in and if you can let me know when we need to finalize things for the spring semester, that would be great. Good night." She practically buries herself in the collar of her jacket as she and Rowan make their way through the pathway to their dorms. Part of me is concerned with how she is doing and if I should wait, but Rowan is with her. He'll call if there's a problem.

I decide to wait in my car for a little while and check in to make sure they got back okay. The only time I see her excited about things or showing any joy at all is when it comes to her work with Pink Every Day. She works hard and has an incredible eye for design and brand consistency. She is going to do great things for that company and I already am looking for other opportunities that she may enjoy for smaller projects.

Once I learned more about what she and Sasha and a few other students too are doing with the organization, I did what I could to donate. Since most of what they do on the non-profit side of things is for single moms and young families in the area, and they are just getting started with the practical outreach too, there isn't much that I can do besides support financially. Ashley mentioned that they are looking at some other events for the spring and summer and will be posting some job boards and volunteer options on campus once they start planning. I told her to get me dates as soon as they are decided so I can make sure to be there.

Part of me feels that she used to be a lot more outgoing. Something is holding her back and I don't think it's just her health concerns. Yes, stress is a big factor, but there's something else. I get to my car and hit the remote start button as the car next to me does the same. I must not have been paying attention and hope I didn't miss any conversation on the walk back to the cars. He looks just as deep in thought as I had been.

"Have a good evening, Professor Johnson. I will see you in the morning." I tip my head and duck into my vehicle. The heated seats help me warm up quickly as I take out my phone to answer emails and check notifications while I wait an appropriate amount of time before reaching out to Rowan and Miss Carter to make sure they got to their rooms okay. It's only eight at night, but it's a campus that's pretty close to downtown. And I worry about the students that are here. Even though it's a relatively safe place, we don't generally have incidents on campus, or even off campus, among students. Things happen and people are stupid. And even I saw tonight how easy it is to be oblivious when preoccupied with other things besides your own surroundings.

I need to get with admin tomorrow to see which students are staying on campus over the winter break and see if any of them would potentially be interested in a holiday get together. I'm not sure what, if anything, the campus has planned for those that stay here. Some are international students and some just don't have good family situations back home, and this is their reprieve from that, even for a few extra weeks. I text my two assistants to make sure they are good, glad we have a group chat already set up from the few times we needed to coordinate times to work together on a project.

Me: Did you both make it to your rooms okay?

Rowan Masters: Yep, see you tomorrow Professor.

Ashley Carter: Yes, sir. Thank you. I will email you tomorrow for info on finishing my assignments this semester.

Me: You are all set, Miss Carter. I don't have anything still open for you.

Ashley Carter: I know I am all set with my assignments, but weren't there still some projects you needed help with before the close of the semester?

Me: We finished the last of those tonight, Miss Carter. You are done until we start preparing for the spring semester.

Ashley Carter: I'm sorry I missed tonight. I could have scheduled a different time for my tests with Professor Johnson. I didn't mean to put more work on the two of you.

Rowan Masters: Girl, who didn't treat you right? LOL. It didn't take long and you have a major trip to prepare for that is attached to your career. Don't apologize for that. And I'm pretty sure you cleared that time with Professor Williams anyway, right?

I chuckle to myself at Rowan calling her out on that. She does apologize a lot. And Rowan is right, it's almost like she has been taught to apologize for things outside of her control.

Me: Rowan is correct. You were excused from the session this evening so you could finish those exams. I will talk to you when you get back from your trip. Have a wonderful time.

Ashley Carter: Thank you, sir.

Ashley Carter: And you can call me Ashley. It doesn't have to be Miss Carter. I know you call your students Miss or Mr. generally, but you call Rowan by his first name…

Rowan Masters: That's because he's known me since I was like ten. LOL. But yeah, he does do that. He generally only calls me Rowan when we are outside of a class setting. In class, he still calls me Mr. Masters.

Me: If it would make you feel more comfortable, I can call you Ashley when we are not in the classroom.

Ashley Carter: I would like that. Thank you.

Me: You're welcome.

Me: Good night you two.

As I set my phone on the stand and prepare to back out of my spot, I notice that Professor Johnson is still sitting in his car next to me. The reflection of the glow of his screen on his glasses shows he is scrolling social media. I tap on my window to get his attention and then give him a thumbs up to ask if he's okay once he makes eye contact. He nods his head and shows his phone, showing me that he is working on some things. Maybe he was waiting for me to leave so he could make sure my car was working okay or something.

I pull out of my spot and begin making my way to my apartment. Thinking again that while I love being in this position, it's getting harder to come home to an empty apartment each night. I'm looking forward to seeing my family for a few days over the break.

WED    THU    FRI    SAT    SUN        DATE:

# Chapter Forty-Three

## ASHLEY

**CRANBERRY SPICE MOCKTAIL**

*Social Post: Help me pick my dress for the gala in NY next week! I won't be on stage during any of the events, but I still want to look nice. I went with the green dress last year so you'll recognize that one. And then I bought a new one too. Based on the dress choice, I'll start working on accessories, shoes, and hair and makeup options. Thanks in advance! #sassyashleysmiles #galatime #tripprep #blacktieaffair #gownsandsparkles #nytrip #sashaloveslipstick #pinkeveryday*

*Image Description: Side by side images, green gown in one and floor length red gown in the other, both are satin in material and texture and very simple without added embellishments.*

Is it bad that I am literally counting down the hours until the New York trip? It feels like I've been waiting for it for months and it's finally just a day away. I just need to finish packing and then we will be on our way. Matt and Sasha are going to come pick me up in the morning so we can head to the airport.

We have an early flight, but not stupid early. I refuse to fly before eight in the morning unless it's absolutely necessary. Waking up before five in the morning in order to get ready and to the airport on time just to wait is not my idea of ideal before a work trip. They want me to be professional, right?

I turned my phone on "Do Not Disturb" after posting the photos. It's the first time I've posted a full body picture in a long time and I don't want to deal with any of the comments. I've put on a little weight in the past few months. Thank you, antidepressants and a crazy schedule. I feel better overall though. Having a set routine between my classes, TA responsibilities, and work with Pink Every Day has really helped. I have become resigned to the fact that I won't have a traditional college experience. I tried that once and it did not go well. I still wince every time I see the tattoo on my thigh. It's like he tainted it, even though the red ink has been gone for weeks. I still see the marks he left on me. The fact that he was in my room, with his hands on me, and I had no clue.

I make myself busy with packing up the rest of my things while I wait to see which dress I am bringing with me. One bag for travel, sight-seeing, and lounge wear in the hotel is already fully packed. My bag that will have everything for meetings, corporate events, and the gala still needs a few things. My business professional and business casual wardrobe has grown and I love the pieces I've gotten. Luckily, most of them still fit me. There're just a few shirts that I had to pack away this semester. My dress slacks and my pencil skirts still fit though. And that's why I invested in those staple pieces. I'll have those until my kids go to college if I don't change weight too much more.

"Have I waited long enough before I see how bad this is?" I whisper to myself as I settle on my bed, amidst sweaters and socks that still need to be packed in one of my bags. I unlock my phone and pull up Instagram. I don't even look at the messages or shares—I go right to my profile page and pull up the picture. I only posted it thirty minutes ago, but it already has over one hundred comments and 400 reactions. It's ten in the morning on a Thursday, why are they all online right now?

ShinyLips427: Babe, both of those look stunning on you! But you should go with the red to have something different from last year.

ChelseaWearsPink835: You can't go wrong with either. Take both and see how you feel that day. You should be able to adjust accessories and hair/makeup easily with either dress. And since they're both floor length, you can wear the same shoes.

ShinyLips427: Oh yes, shoes! You should wear the strappy silver ones! So sexy and you don't get the chance to wear them nearly often enough.

Samtheman62: Who is that knockout?

Samtheman62: But seriously, either looks amazing on you. Bring them both with you. And then I think we need a date night when you get back so you can wear the other one. Maybe a show in Denver?

I find myself smiling at Sam's comments. I miss him. Things haven't been the same for a while with us. I still see him as my closest friend, and my boyfriend, but I am struggling to let him in to see everything I'm dealing with. He didn't sign up for this. He signed up for bubbly Ashley. Happy Ashley. Not depressed Ashley or nervous Ashley. I don't like how I am right now, how can he? I haven't been able to tell him any of this though. With our schedules right now, dates have been pretty much impossible. And I don't want to come across as needy and asking for him to give up any of his time off. That's not fair of me to ask for that.

Chelsea_blushes_32: Red for sure!

Lippiesfordays_plz: Which one are you happier in?

Sparks12thy: I think I need to see options once you're in shapewear so you aren't filling out the dresses improperly

LVLNDhearts4you: Gorgeous! Red is our pick!

*Sm2365CT: Been a while since you showed a pic and I think we know why now. Freshman fifteen hit a little late there, Ash?*

*HNT762: Okay, those new curves though! Ma'am you are lookin' good!*

NoCoevents365: We need to coordinate some things for the spring! Our vote is green with some statement jewelry!

Carn3476: Are you asking for some shapewear for Christmas?

Fallisbetter475: Go green. It's a classic look and you can change up how you style it compared to last year.

CoNoCo27win: The red is stunning on you.

Okay, I was expecting the comments, but they still hurt. I've gained a bit of weight, but I also know that I don't look the same. I feel tired, and it shows. It's been a long year. And I'm just ready for the reset that this trip is going to provide. I put both gowns back in their bags and pack them both into my luggage. An hour later, my two roller bags, backpack, and carryon bag are ready to go. I just need to reorganize my purse and pack my meds and I'll be good to go. Luckily, my jewelry case and travel makeup bag are pretty set so I didn't have to adjust those too much. Maybe I can talk to Tilly about hitting up the campus gym once I'm back. I don't want to necessarily lose a bunch of weight, I like the curves I've gotten with the change, but I don't feel good overall. And exercise produces endorphins, right? At least that's what Elle Woods said and there's nothing that proves she was wrong about anything else.

The next morning comes too early. It may be seven and not five, but I got lost doom-scrolling on social media last night on ways to lose weight while taking medication. There are way too many experts out there. Now I know how Sasha felt when she was trying to find someone like my brother. And even without me filling out a single inquiry, I already have a few messages in my inbox offering services or tips on losing weight. Not all of them were super kind either. Do people read how they sound before they hit the send button? Rude.

I force myself to get up and take a quick shower. I will want another one after the travel day, but I need some help waking up. At least it smells like coffee is already brewing in the other room. Tilly really is the best. After a quick morning routine, I bring my bags in the main space of our dorm room and sit at the little counter to have a cup of coffee with my roommate.

"What time are you taking off?" Tilly asks as she sits across from me, sipping on her own cup of coffee. She picked up some whipped cream and added that along with crushed candy canes to the top of her cup. She may just love Christmas as much as my mom does, and that's not an easy thing to say.

"Matt and Sasha should be here within the next fifteen minutes I think. They texted me when they left the house. They need to make a quick stop at the gas station and then they'll be on the way. They'll text when they park outside so I'll grab my hand warmers and put on my second pair of socks then. Matt will come up to help with my bags, so that helps."

"Having the time away will be good, I think. No worries about the photo guy or school. You can just focus on what you love and all that you will be able to do in the next year. Only a little over a year until you can fully take on your role at the company and one step closer to getting to do this full time." She's always so encouraging. What would I do without this girl?

"I'm looking forward to it. And we have a planned rest day tomorrow. I'm debating treating myself to the hotel spa if I can get appointments for a pedicure and a massage. Probably not a facial, bad idea to do that at a new place right before big meetings. I should have gone to my esthetician here in town earlier this week. Oh well."

"Maybe we can go when you get back. I get to start working on some of my hours for my esthetician license over the break, and part of that is me receiving some of the services and seeing how they feel. Do you want me to get something scheduled with Monica?" My phone dings and I stand to go rinse out my mug before grabbing my hand warmers off the charger.

"Yeah, that would be great. Text me what the options are so I can see what I want to do this time around. I'm definitely going to need some heavy moisture after the travel."

"Will do, do you need anything else? Have all your meds?" There's a light tap on the door and she heads over to let my brother in.

"Yep, everything is packed and ready to go." I smile over at my brother as I shrug on my coat.

"You managed to keep everything in just two luggage bags? Good job, Ash." He acts impressed, but I'm actually a very good packer, thank you very much.

"You act like I am a horrible traveler," I smirk at him. "Thanks again for your help, Tilly, I'll see you when we get back. Make sure you don't spend your entire break working on your license. Have some down time too." I give her a quick hug and then we are on our way to the airport and to our second New York trip as Pink Every Day.

WED THU FRI SAT SUN        DATE

# Chapter Forty-Four

## ASHLEY

### CHAI SPICED HOT COCOA

*Social Post: Have I mentioned how much I hate being cold? Anyway, we're in NYC!! So glad we have a rest day today and then next week is filled with things with Natalie, Pink Every Day, and a few new collab partners that we will be sharing soon! Who do you hope to see us meeting with? @sashaloveslipstick @pinkeveryday @cobeauty #sashaloveslipstick #sassyashleysmiles #makeupqueen #lippie #newyorktrip #christmasinnyc #pinkeveryday #pinkcollabs #womenowned*

*Image Description: Me bundled up in a knit hat and scarf, blowing into the cold air. NYC in the background.*

The week in New York goes by way too fast, but it's amazing! We are able to meet with our partners at Natalie HQ as well as CO Beauty from last year too. I'm so glad they were able to come back out. And now that Pink Every Day is an actual organization and not just a social media campaign, we were able to coordinate meetings with four other beauty brands too! Two of them are looking at collaborations during the new year and the other two are still thinking about it. But this is the kind of visibility we need in order to get more funding and help more local organizations. We've been focusing on makeup but are hoping to start some skincare collaborations once I come fully on board after graduation.

We have the gala tonight and then a rest day tomorrow before going home the following day. My hair and makeup are done and I'm staring at the two dresses on my bed, along with the dreaded shapewear. I really hate wearing those things. I have the super heavy duty one and then the smoothing one. I will be so much more comfortable in the smoothing one, and I'll actually be able to eat in it too. And breathe. Breathing is kind of an important thing. I don the smoothing shapewear before I can talk myself out of it.

There's a light knock on the door before I hear Sasha's voice. "Hey girl, do you need help zipping up? We've got to head down in a minute here." I make sure that all of my important bits are covered and open the door for her so she can come in.

"You can zip me up once I decide which one to wear." I go back to staring at the dresses.

"What are you debating with them? Maybe I can help," she prompts as she fixes a stray hair into a bobby pin at the nape of my neck. I went with a braided bun that screams elegance and sophistication. And also allows for the dangly diamond earrings I'm wearing to get the attention they deserve. Mom had given the early Christmas gift to me before we left so I could have them for tonight. And I'm glad she did because they are stunning. The silver smoky eye look that I went with is mature and sophisticated and makes me look closer to twenty-five than the twenty I actually am. It's not much, but it makes me happy. I feel good tonight.

"I love the red one, it's elegant and makes me feel incredible. And I wore the green one last year. But the green is also slimming and more of a classic piece." I'm trying to convince myself to wear the green one and I know it.

"I know you aren't talking down about your body because you are a bombshell. You've dealt with a new medical diagnosis as well as some creeper in your DMs this year." I haven't told her about the escalations and I wince internally at the last bit of the comment. I really should tell her, but she has enough to worry about. She comes close so she can hold my hands and make eye contact with me before she continues. "No matter if you are a size six or twenty, you are beautiful. If anything, the weight gain has helped you fill out those dresses a little bit, and not in a bad way. Your body is going through stresses and adjustments right now, it's keeping you going, it's keeping you here with us. And I want you to focus on that. Focus on what your body can do and is doing. Not what it isn't. Wear the red one, Ashley. And stop telling yourself that you have to make yourself smaller. You take up as much space as you deserve." She squeezes my hands again as a tear falls from my eye and I look up to avoid doing the same. I spent way too much time on my makeup to cry it off before we even leave this room.

"Thanks, Sasha. I needed that. Okay, let's get this red one on." She smiles at me and helps me step into the dress and then adjust the zipper. It's a one shoulder dress that doesn't show off any cleavage, but it has a subtle slit that goes up to mid-thigh. It's classically elegant and I feel like a trophy wife in it.

"Should I tape it a bit on the side without a strap to avoid it moving around?" I ask as I assess the full look in the mirror.

"I think you're good, hon. I don't think it's going anywhere. That dress was made for you." We take a few mirror selfies and then we are off to meet Matt outside in the hallway. The gala is happening in our hotel this year, so we just need to make our way to the ballroom. One elevator ride and a walk across the lobby, that's all I have to do until I'm back in my element—talking about what we get to do with our organization and making the connections needed so we can keep growing.

I take the ride down to get in the right headspace. I am no longer depressed Ashley or nervous Ashley—I am outgoing, happy, knowledgeable, capable, friendly, enough, mine. I can do this. We are wanting to launch our own products in the new year. And to do that we need financial backers and the space to do that. Logistics, fulfillment, so much is going to go into this new branch of the company. And with us selling products, we will be able to give our supporters another avenue to support us and our mission. Yes, we will be selling a physical product, but we will be able to continue to give back in practical ways to local organizations as well as be able to give a portion of profits to those same organizations.

My job tonight is showing the faces behind the organization. Matt is going to be with Sasha as her support. But I can do this on my own. I'm good at this part. And I can put my doubts and my insecurities on the back burner for a few hours. This is what I'm good at. I can do this. After the first hour, I need a quick bathroom break. Time to take a breath and make sure my lipstick is still in good shape. I put all of my social media notifications on "Do Not Disturb" for tonight because I know the tags for the company account are going to be high and I don't want my pocket vibrating all night. Yes, the dress has pockets. One for my phone and one for my lipstick.

With my phone being mostly void of notifications, I'm not surprised to just see a few email and text notifications on my screen after I touch up my lips. I decide to let the emails wait. If I open that app right now, I will be here for an hour responding to things and I need to get back out there soon. But this is a nice hotel, so there's a full-blown couch and drink and snack setup in the bathroom, so I take a seat for a moment to sip out of a small water bottle from the counter—fancy, I know!—and open the texts.

Mom: You all look lovely tonight! Have a good time. You're going to do great!

Sam: Just saw Sasha's story posts. You look great. Wish I was with you tonight.

Tilly: Ma'am! Absolute smoke show! Go blow them away tonight.

Rowan: Promise I'm not being a creeper, but, you look amazing tonight! Hope your trip has been good.

Rowan: This is my night, so I think you're winning here.

Rowan: <Image Attached>

I have to hold back a laugh when the picture loads. He has a stack of papers in front of him on his desk along with the syllabus for one of Professor Williams's classes. Plus, a cup of tea, because of course he does. The man hates coffee. Weird, I know.

Me: Have fun with that. Yeah, I think I win tonight.

Me: And thank you. It's going well so far, but I'm ready to be home. A week of corporate meetings and then the gala tonight is going to leave me so drained by tomorrow.

Rowan: I can see that. Enjoy your time and we'll catch up when you get back.

Me: Thanks, Rowan.

I stand and drop the empty water bottle into the recycling container before making one more stop in front of the mirror to make sure there's no lipstick on my teeth or chin. All good.

"Okay, Ash, time for dinner, then speeches, then a bit more chatting with all the people and then you get to go to bed. And a massage tomorrow at the spa. You've got this," I give myself a little pep talk and then head back out into the space.

The night goes amazingly well. And I don't start feeling it until the very end, after Sasha has gone up to accept two more awards for her work with Pink Every Day and other women-owned organizations this year. With each award, we get a little more credibility as a company and the work we are doing. Some people still see us as influencers or "little girls with a silly hobby," but more people are looking at us legitimately. Especially with the partnerships we have already curated.

"I think I'm going to head up to my room. Everyone I needed to talk to has already left and I connected with them at the beginning of the event. I will see you all for brunch or something tomorrow?" I check in with Matt while he watches Sasha talk to Natalie at the next table. The admiration in his eyes is astounding and I love watching them together. He is so gone for that girl and I love it.

"Yeah, that sounds like a plan. Do you want me to walk you up?" Matt looks over at me for a minute to check in fully.

"I should be okay. It's a pretty straightforward walk and I don't want to cut her conversation short." I give him an awkward side hug as I stand and then have to correct myself so I don't fall over. "Probably shouldn't have tried that while I was trying to stand up," I laugh at myself a bit. I'm tired and can tell. He just smiles back and tells me to get some sleep.

The walk back to my room is easy enough. I know I'm starting to come down from the adrenaline rush of everything tonight. My temperature is dropping and I'm getting tired. I need to get changed and get in bed. And probably avoid setting an alarm for tomorrow. My room is just as I left it, the green dress still laying on the bed. I hang it back up in the closet and thank the designers of this dress when I'm able to unzip it myself and step out. I do a simple nighttime routine; I'll shower tomorrow, so I just take off my makeup and add some moisturizer and lip balm. I turn the heat up in the room before burying myself under the extra blankets on the queen bed. I want to take this mattress home with me, it's so comfortable.

I text Matt to let him know that I'm not setting an alarm and that I'll see them tomorrow. A response comes back before I set the phone on the nightstand next to the bed.

Unknown: I wish I could have escorted you to the gala tonight. You looked incredible. Seeing you in your element is a beautiful thing to watch, Ashley.

Me: Seriously, who is this? This isn't funny.

Unknown: I'm yours, Ashley. I'll see you when you get home and we can have a chat then about me being with you for the next event.

Me: I don't think I want to see you. I don't know who you are or what you are getting at, but this has to stop.

Me: Don't text me again. Don't try to contact me. I'm done.

**<Blocks Number>**

I turn on the TV to give some background noise so I can go to sleep. Just as I'm about to drift off, I hear a light knock on the door. I'm not sure if I imagined it or if it actually happened, but it's after midnight. I'm not getting out of bed for whoever that was. The knock comes again and I get ready to call my brother. He's just in the room across the hall. If they knock again, I'm going to call him. But there isn't another knock. Just an envelope slid under the door. I wait a good ten minutes to make sure that whoever it was had gone before I get out of bed.

The envelope isn't sealed, just tucked into itself. I open it to find two pieces of paper. The first is an appointment card for the spa in the hotel. I hadn't been able to get an appointment this week, so I was going to just wait until I got home. This letter says I have a ninety-minute hot stone massage and a sixty-minute pedicure starting at eleven tomorrow. The second piece of paper is a handwritten letter in a script I haven't seen in a few weeks, but one I immediately recognize from the others he's sent.

Good evening my love,

I didn't mean to upset you tonight. I will give you a few more days, but I am done pretending that you don't take up every one of my thoughts. You were stunning tonight. I hope you know that. Take some time tomorrow to enjoy a day for yourself. I will see you at home. Sleep well,

Yours.

Ashley

# Chapter Forty-Five

## MARCUS

**AUTUMN FOG LATTE**

*Social Post: Reminiscing on Christmas last year in the UK with friends that feel more like family. #christmas #scotland #uk #winterwonderland*

*Image Description: Snow covered rock walls and evergreen trees outside of a home.*

Christmas break always starts with a flurry of activity in a college admin building. We have to get everything submitted and finished from the last semester and then finalize everything for the upcoming semester. Add in the fact that I am heading up the mentorship program, and my week is totally swamped. I have to finalize placements for the new TAs, and then determine who is moving up to the mentor roles for the spring semester. It's six weeks off from teaching, but only a few days where I'm not actually working.

I like being busy. It keeps me focused on the task in front of me, but not worrying about all the things I could be doing. I miss my family. And while I love independence, I am growing tired of going home to an empty apartment most nights. A few of the other professors and admin staff have asked me to join them for coffee or drinks or weekend brunch, but I've had reasons and excuses to turn them down. I'm not here to be best friends with these people. It's hard to make those attachments if I'm just going to be moved to a new campus in a year or two.

Making friends means putting down roots. And then it's that much harder to walk away. I was able to stay mostly detached while I was in the UK, except for the few relationships that I had already established before I went there. I've known Rowan and his family for over a decade. I connected with Rowan's dad in an online community and then we quickly became friends over similar interests—literary interests, as well as business interests. He was able to help a few non-profit community events turn into growing organizations that were able to pay their partners while continuing to grow their community outreach. It's possible to do both. So I became his apprentice in a way. Learning his methods for helping these business owners grow was fascinating. And now I get to do it too.

He still offers consulting for these organizations in the UK. And I get to help them in their early stages by partnering with the leaders while they are still on a college campus. There are over fifty organizations around the world that we have had a hand in. Everything from low income housing partnering with a coffee company in Vegas to single moms partnering with a ski resort in Switzerland—these organizations have a very practical piece into their communities.

I need to wrap up the newest legal documents from my colleague who teaches at Yale to see what is changing soon for nonprofits and government restrictions on donations, and then I am clocking out for the next week. Christmas is coming soon and I need some time to not think about reports and spreadsheets and market trends before I do this all over again. I won't be able to go see my family this winter break with all of my other commitments, but I hope to make some time this summer.

My phone dings, alerting me to an incoming message, and I wince when I see I've been staring at my computer for two hours. I rub my eyes and shut down the screen before sliding my notes and folder into my bag. The text is from Rowan reminding me about meeting up tonight. He's staying on campus for the break, no point in going home for just a few weeks when the weather is so unpredictable. He may get stuck in the States or in the UK and miss the beginning of the semester.

> Me: I will be at the dorm to pick you up in fifteen minutes. Pizza still okay for tonight?

> Rowan: Sounds good. You aren't allowed to work while we eat though.

> Rowan: That's from my dad, not from me, by the way.

I laugh before giving the text a "like." His dad was always big on the whole boundaries thing. He did a great job having a balance between work and home life and it's something I admired. Did I actually bring much of it to my own life? Not yet. Once I have someone waiting for me at home, I hope I can make the shift though. Right now, it means putting devices away during meal times and spending time conversing with people. Once a week, Rowan and I get dinner or lunch. I promised his dad I would make sure he's doing okay. And it's harder to lie face to face rather than through a device check in. Plus with the TA position, I see him almost daily, but that's more "work" than "leisure."

I pull up in front of his building and idle in a guest parking spot while I wait for him to come out to join me. He found a local pizza place that is apparently the oldest in Fort Collins and has been a favorite since it was established. I've heard a few other colleagues mention it, so a Wednesday night during the school break should be less busy than some of the wait times I've heard mentioned. It isn't far from the campus and we are able to find a spot outside easily enough. It's in a pretty basic strip mall, but the amount of people making their way to the door is surprising. It's five in the afternoon.

Opening the doors, I see why this is the place to be. The smell of fresh dough, homemade sauce, and spicy sausage hits me right as the warmth of the space does. The talk is happy and comforting, but not too loud. There're obviously groups here meeting up after work, but also friends that get together here regularly. Is that a group playing Dungeons and Dragons at that back table? I chuckle and shake my head lightly.

"This place feels like home," Rowan turns his head to tell me and I nod in agreement. It has a pub feel to it. Good food, good drinks, good company.

"Do you want to get a couple slices or a whole pie?" I ask him as we wait for our turn to order.

"Is this your first time here?" the man in front of us turns to ask.

"First time. Heard good things around campus and wanted to check it out," Rowan responds as he continues looking over the options on the board mounted behind the counter.

"I'd start with a couple slices then. It's more than you think it's going to be. And make sure you grab some honey."

"Honey?" I know I look confused. For what?

"Drizzle it on the crust. It's a special treat that many of us do here. Let me know what you think." I nod in thanks as he orders a few slices and then takes his number and heads back to the table where the group of men are finishing setting up for their DND session.

About thirty minutes later, we are enjoying our slices at a side table, in a position to watch the different groups in the space. We are both people watchers, and this type of environment is perfect for that.

"So is everyone pretty much staying in their TA placements next semester or are you moving people around?" Rowan has just as hard of a time staying on non-work talk as I do.

"I think everyone is staying put. I need to review a few more things once I finalize the mentor positions. Once the rotation starts and I've been here for a little longer, it will be easier to figure those out. Why? Do you not want to stay working with me?" I tease him. I know he doesn't want to go anywhere else. He just laughs and then picks up the honey bottle.

"Are you actually going to try that?"

"Why not?"

A few hours later, I have Rowan back on campus and am just getting ready to head to my empty apartment when I see another car pull up. Ashley is in the front seat with her brother. I recognize him from a previous meeting and the few photos Ashley has shown me during meetings. I need to see about connecting with him about some additional tools I want to teach our business majors. What he has been able to do with Sasha's platforms is incredible and I would love to learn how we can duplicate that for our students.

I argue with myself for a moment about approaching, they must just be getting back from New York. I hope that all went well. I decide to go over and see if I can help with bags and maybe exchange contact information with Ashley's brother, if it seems like a good time to ask. I call out when I'm still a bit away, not wanting to startle them.

"How was the trip?" Ashley turns quickly and grasps her hands in front of her chest like I just threw a spider at her. "I didn't mean to startle you, I am so sorry. Can I help bring anything inside for you?"

"That would be great." Ashley steps aside so I can come over and see how bad the luggage situation is. "I'm only dropping off a few things before I head home. I'm staying at my parent's house for a few weeks and then I'll be back on campus the week before classes start."

Ashley makes quick work of formal introductions and then we are on our way inside the building. Ashley's suite is on the second floor of the building and has an excessive amount of Christmas décor for a dorm room. I must make a face because Matt chuckles next to me.

"Our family really loves Christmas. Mom must have stopped in while we were out of town."

"Yeah, Tilly mentioned that Mom stopped over to drop some things off. I thought it was just some freezer meals for her—I was not expecting this, but I'm not surprised." Ashley shakes her head before heading to the side of the suite. I'm assuming she's grabbing a few things before heading home.

"Well, I'll let you get back to it. Matt, can I connect with you later about maybe some guest lectures or resources for students?" I hear a loud laugh from over my shoulder. And I can't help but smile. I turn to see Ashley's bright pink cheeks and her hands over her mouth. Like she's embarrassed for her reaction.

"And why is that so funny, Miss Carter?"

Her hands immediately drop and she breaks the eye contact before bringing her eyes back up to meet mine. "I just don't know how beneficial a guest lecture would be from my brother. He likes being behind the scenes."

"That doesn't mean he won't have important insight into current market trends and needs. The collaborations and visibility he was able to achieve with Sasha in just a few months is astonishing. I'd love to hear more on how you positioned her content and the strategy for reach outs. I'm sure there's strategies that we can apply to what we teach in the classroom."

"Can I think about it?" Matt answers. "We like to unplug as much as possible over this break since we just did the big trip. And the second week of January we are back in office to do it all over again."

"For sure, can I connect around January tenth?" I pull out my phone to input a reminder in my calendar.

"Absolutely. Email me so I have the information in my phone. I look forward to chatting with you." Matt holds out his hand to take a bag from Ashley as she shoulders her backpack. "Ready?" he asks her.

"Yep, thanks again for your help, Professor Williams. I'll see you in a few weeks. Have a Merry Christmas."

"You too. Let me know if you need anything and I'll see you soon."

Marcus

# Chapter Forty-Six

## ASHLEY

**HOT CHOCOLATE COLD BREW**
*Social Post: I'm dreaming of a White Christmas... #christmastime #familyday #snowflakes #jackfrost #sassyashleysmiles*
*Image Description: Frost patterns on a window pane.*

We are heading over to Matt's house for dinner tonight. I think he's getting ready to propose. But he won't tell me for sure and wants us to be surprised when he does it. I think he's nervous that I am going to spill the secret. I can keep secrets better than he thinks. I'm getting ready to fix my hair and makeup before we head over to Matt and Sasha's when my phone buzzes. Repeatedly. I groan to myself, already knowing what I am going to see when I pull it off of the charger next to my bed.

Unknown: The red dress that you wore to the gala was stunning on you, baby.

Unknown: Do I get any pictures of you in it that weren't taken by the press?

Unknown: How was the trip home on Tuesday?

Unknown: I wish you wouldn't keep ignoring me. You look so sad when you pretend I'm not yours.

I block the number.
Again.

I just need to get through the holiday break and then I can immerse myself back in the new semester. Less time at home means less time where I let my mind wander about who this is and what they want. After the holidays, if this guy doesn't actually back off, I'm going to see about getting a restraining order or something. Can you get a restraining order from someone unknown?

I finish getting ready and head to my car to drive over to my brother's house. My parents are already over there so they could help finish dinner, giving me some quiet time at the house to rest after our recent New York trip. I'm starting to really regret turning down the garage parking spot when I see the envelope taped to my windshield wiper. Of course, it's not just tucked under it. I pull it loose and then quickly get into my car and lock the doors.

*Aren't you tired of ignoring me yet, baby girl? I'm getting tired of you pretending I'm not here.*

I look around but don't see anyone on the street.
Okay, deep breaths.
This may not be the same person.

This was meant for someone else or is a harmless prank from the teenage boys down the street.

I am fine.

I am safe.

This isn't happening.

I turn on my car and get ready to back out of the driveaway only for the car Bluetooth to pick up a notification because I forgot to set it on "Do Not Disturb."

> Text message from Unknown contact:
> You look beautiful in green baby girl.
> Have fun at your brother's tonight.

This isn't happening to me. I fight back tears until I make it the five minute drive to my brother's house. When I finally put my car in park, my body releases the tension it's been holding back and I start sobbing. Uncontrollable. Ugly cry. My entire body is shaking and I can't stop. Every time I start calming down, I remember the messages, the notes, the red marks on my leg. What do I do?

I must be out here for longer than I intended, because my phone dings and my Bluetooth picks up the message.

> Text message from Mom: Hey hon, are you
> okay? Let me know if you need anything or if
> you just needed a moment before coming in.

I take a few more breaths, slowing my breathing, getting back control of my body and my reactions.

"Control what you can and leave the rest, Ash. You've got this. I can control my reactions. I can control how I approach this. I'm safe. Everyone I need is right inside. I can do this."

> Text message from Dad: Love you baby girl.
> I'm going to give you another couple of
> minutes and then I'm going to come out to
> make sure you're okay. You're worrying us,
> but I want to give you the space you need. Let
> me know how I can help honey. Love you.

I decide to text him back.

> Me: Can you come out and walk me in? I need a minute and a Daddy hug I think.

> Dad: Sure, Ash. Be right out.

Dad is at my door less than a minute later and I turn off my car and grab my things before unlocking the door and stepping out. He takes in my face and I know he can tell I've been crying, hard.

"What do you need?" is the only thing he says. Four words and I'm a mess again. He pulls me into his arms as I start crying again.

"I'm just scared, Daddy. And I don't know how I can fix it." He smooths my hair and rubs my back gently as he holds me, letting me have the space to figure out what I'm going to say and when.

"What's scaring you, hon? What's happening?" He looks down at me to meet my eyes and searches for answers I don't know how to give.

"I think someone is following me."

"Are we talking about more than the online messages? I thought Matt took care of that." I can tell he's worried. And now I'm worrying that he's going to be upset that I didn't tell him sooner. I'm an adult. I should be able to handle this on my own. "I can't help if you don't tell me what's going on, Ash. Please, let me help you." I take a deep breath, trying to find the words to tell him what else has happened.

"Dinner is ready, are you guys coming in or do you need a bit?" Mom hollers out the front door to us. I take another shaky breath before looking over my shoulder to her.

"We'll be right in, Mom, thank you." I turn back to my dad, "I'll fill you in later, let's do dinner and enjoy some time together."

"Promise you'll tell me what's going on?"

"I promise."

I didn't tell Dad what was happening. I ended up brushing it off as being concerned with the heightened messages and nasty comments about my weight gain. And I mentioned I would ask Matt to increase the filters on the security walls he put up on my social channels.

Part of me feels guilty for letting it go this long and this far. Maybe part of me liked the attention. I mean, I did respond to him sometimes. That's on me. I could have stopped this. Couldn't I? Dinner went well at Matt's and it was nice seeing everyone after the New York trip. Being in family mode instead of work mode makes a big difference in the feeling of a get together.

That night, I lay in my bed, staring at the fairy lights in my space. I fight back the tears again. Why do I feel so alone even with all of these people that love me and want to help me? Why don't I let them help me?

"Tonight is the last time I feel sorry for myself over this. I am a big girl and this has gone on long enough. I didn't ask for this, but I can also put my foot down and make it stop." I whisper to the ceiling, glancing over to the beautiful photos on my wall. I know they're from him. And maybe this is the first thing I need to do to show him, and myself, that he has no control over me and no claim on me.

I am not his.

I am mine.

# Chapter Forty-Seven

## MARCUS

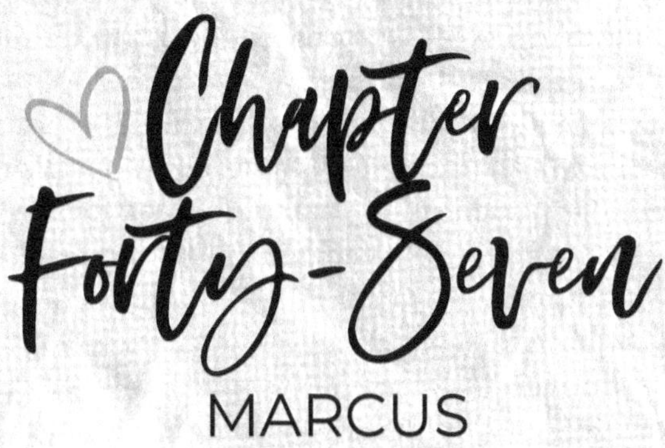

**MOON MILK TEA**

*Social Post: It may not be the tea I'm used to, but finding this tea shop downtown has been the perfect piece of normalcy that I needed over the break. #teashop #fortcollins #downtown*

*Image Description: Tea menu board for a shop in Old Town Fort Collins.*

This is the last year that I am on my own for Christmas. I am not a big holiday person. I don't enjoy endless parties or events. But being by myself over the holidays just isn't right. I will have to see about going home to Maine next year. Which means, I need everything set with the program at CSU. Having that goal in place, I determine to get as much done over this break as possible. Mapping out the next few semesters, businesses to partner with and reach out to, seeing which professors would be interested in joining the program in the coming months—it's a full few weeks. By the time we are approaching the week before classes resume, I am ready. I'm ready to get back into these routines, but also to help these students take their next steps. We are one semester closer to making an actual impact in their communities. And it is even more fulfilling than lecturing a group of 500 students.

Today, I'm meeting with Ashley and Rowan, as well as two new TA students, Marshall and Claire. Rowan will be taking on the mentor role, Ashley will be lead TA, and then the two new students will be doing the more basic work like grading, scheduling, and research. All of the other participating professors have a similar setup. Ideally, their lead TA will take on the mentor role in the next semester. This will allow the space for those who may drop out or need a break. Or just don't have what is needed for this program. Not everyone graduates with the same goals and desires as when they started college.

I had gone to school for History of American Literature with a minor in Journalism. By my junior year, I saw an opportunity to expand my impact, but that meant I needed a change in major. I still love classic literature and take every opportunity to explore the indie bookstores throughout Colorado—yes, there's plenty and they are so eclectic and wonderful. But being able to bring a literacy program to our small community of Maine by partnering with a publishing house—I was able to bring my passions together. I may not be actively involved in the business anymore, but I'm still on the board. And I get to be a part of several events both virtually and in person throughout the year.

My brothers run the publishing house now along with their wives and a few other employees. What went from a small non-profit now employs twenty people full time and a handful of others on a part-time or contract basis. And we have been able to provide resources for ten of the local elementary schools and after school programs. I have an entire bookcase in my office dedicated to the books we have published on both sides of the company. Looking over the bookshelf now while I wait for my students, I can't help but be proud of what I've built. This is why I do what I do. Will we publish the next great American novel? I have no idea. But we publish romance novels that provide escape, beginner readers that allow families to connect, and thrillers that keep the reader engaged. And that's a pretty incredible feeling.

I'm reshelving one of our thrillers published at the end of last year when I hear a knock on my door. "Are you busy, Professor Williams?" It's Professor Johnson. He is not looking that great. His hair is slightly disheveled and he looks flustered.

"Are you okay? Do you need me to meet with your students today so you can head out?" I make my way to my desk so I can review my calendar for the day and see what I can move around. If he's sick, he cannot be on campus right now. We still have a few days before the semester starts, and it's better for him to take the time off now than miss the first few days of classes.

"Oh, no I'm fine. I just wanted to confirm Ashley's schedule with you. Since I'm her advisory professor and you are her mentor professor, I figured we could coordinate and make sure we are on the same page with her schedule." He comes in and takes a seat that wasn't offered before pulling out his phone.

"I believe all of the students in the program had their schedules finalized last week, correct?" This man bothers me and it is getting harder to be civil with him. I don't know what he wants or why he wants it, but I don't like it. He reminds me of those gentleman callers in the beginning of an early 20th century novel who wooed and wined the family members of the one they wanted to court, only to show their true colors in the first days of the marriage. They're either dismissive of their partner or abusive toward them. Addictions show and compulsions aren't able to be hid any longer. And the wife is stuck because all her family ever saw was the polite gentleman that promised her the world. I feel like he is at the end of the wooing stage. And things aren't going his way. And I don't know where the fallout is going to hit.

"Yes, but Ashley is going to be doing product development at Pink Every Day, and I think she needs to take a chemistry class to help her prepare for that."

"Is she going to be the one actually making the products? Does she enjoy chemistry? Or does she need to have an understanding of ingredients, sourcing opportunities, ethical manufacturing, and the branding that will help sell the product?" I push back. She isn't the one making the products. Professor Johnson doesn't have an answer ready for me and my time is growing short before my students will be here.

"I am already in talks with Miss Carter and Miss Sloan about their future needs. I have invested financially in the company and have an opportunity to guide them in their hiring and consulting needs. We are already in talks with a skincare and makeup chemist—someone who already knows the ingredients and the needs of this type of product. Miss Carter does not need to waste her time with this. It's not a needed credit and it will just take up time that she does not have. I trust that you aren't pushing your other students to take useless credits. Now," I stand and motion for the door, "I need to prepare to meet with my students and you need to do the same. And possibly take tomorrow off to rest, you look like you may be catching something."

I offer my hand in a clear sign that this discussion is over. He shakes it without holding eye contact and then leaves my space. I'm not even back to my desk when there's another knock on my door. "Professor, if you are going to waste my time with more ridiculous questions, please save it for later. I do not have the energy to remain polite about such requests." It's quiet behind me and I make myself peer over my shoulder, expecting Professor Johnson to be standing there with his mouth agape at being called out. But it's not him. It's my students. And now I feel like an idiot.

"I apologize. Please come in and find a seat. I am almost ready for you. I apologize for my outburst, that was uncalled for and you didn't need to hear that." I pull out the folders I need from my desk and join the students at the table by my space heater. I'm not shocked that Ashley is in the seat closest to the heater. At least she looks sufficiently bundled up today.

"I feel like we missed something fun," Rowan prompts and I just shoot him a look that conveys my lack of patience. He shakes his head and chuckles but doesn't press it. He's mentioned before that he thinks Professor Johnson doesn't like him very much but has no evidence to back the claim or specific instances that can be asked about. And I know he will just take the conversation from earlier and use that as further evidence in the "we don't like Professor

Johnson" folder. Which just isn't a good use of anyone's time or energy.

"Let's get into it. I am teaching five classes this semester and we have a lot to go over before we call it a day. Here is a packet for each of you on the class syllabi, overviews, and needs. We also have the job fair later this spring, so you will find pertinent information on planning stage items you will be responsible for in there as well. I've also taken the time to set up an email and text conversation for this group. Use it for actual needs, please, or I will be forced to mute the conversations, and that defeats the purpose of having them in the first place." I begin my talk with the four students at my table.

The next hours fly by. We go through so much content as well as some of the larger roles that Rowan and Ashley will be taking over. By having the other two on the team now, we will be able to delegate things even further. Rowan and Ashley have lighter course loads this semester. This will allow them to focus on the hands-on aspect of the program. And being able to start taking on more practical pieces of their respective companies means an easier transition when they go full time after graduation. My two new students don't have placements for after graduation yet, so we will be working on finding their passions and needs this semester. I like my students to know where they are going by the beginning of their junior year, if possible.

Rowan will be working remotely on a project basis with his dad who has a similar setup to my company out of Maine. Mr. Masters has the literacy/publishing program as well as consulting for the nonprofits growing their branches. Rowan hasn't quite found his official spot yet, so we need to work on finding his role within that company. Garrett, Rowan's dad, spoke to me last week about a few positions they are looking to fill, so I will be reviewing our students in the program to see who may be good fits.

"Do any of you need anything before we finish out for today? I'd like to meet again at the end of the week to get everything prepared for the first week of classes. That way you have time to finalize your own schedules and get settled into campus." Everyone just nods in agreement. They are tired, and it shows. The first day back after break is usually a lot—another reason why we do this meeting the week before class starts. I want to give them the chance to rest and get acclimated to the schedules before they have to balance their own classwork too.

I send out the first email and text as they leave my office so it's at the top of their notifications. Inevitably, someone will have a question as soon as they leave this room. I chuckle as I get the first buzzes of text messages within moments and then have to shake my head when I see it's just a variety of "hi" and "hello" gifs from each of them. This is going to be a fun group.

Marcus

WED    THU    FRI    SAT    SUN         DATE

# Chapter Forty-Eight

## ASHLEY

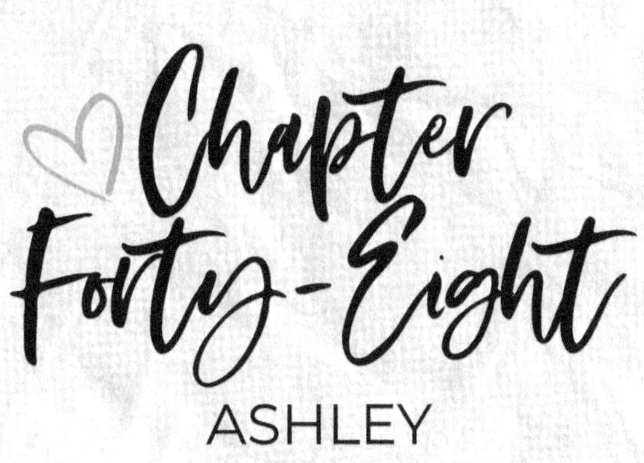

**VENTI ICED CHAI TEA LATTE**

*Social Post: Still solidly in my pink era this semester and I have zero regrets about that decision. #pinkeveryday #sassyashleysmiles #officesupplies #schoolsupplies #csu*

*Image Description: Flat lay on my pink patterned bedspread of notebooks, planner, pens, and cosmetic bag all in varying shades of pink.*

The first weeks of the semester are a run together of settling into new routines, new classes, and new roles. I'm enjoying taking on the additional responsibilities of working with Professor Williams and getting one step closer to being ready for my position at the company with Sasha. It's the first week of February before I realize I haven't gotten a text from "him" in a little while. Did he finally get the hint and decide to leave me alone? That I'm not interested?

I settle into my dorm room to sort through some of my papers

I got back and keep working on the next assignments that are due in the coming weeks. One perk of college is having the full list of projects at the beginning of the semester so I can plan accordingly. And with my meds finally leveling out properly, I am focusing better in class and sleeping better at night too. It's always surprising to me how much it affects me when I don't sleep well the night before. I am shocked when I flip through my papers to see a note on a mini-assignment from Professor Johnson.

> Come see me about this at your earliest convenience,
>
> Professor Johnson.

What's the matter with it?

I check through the requirements again and mentally go through the list. Everything is there, what did I do wrong? There's no grade on the paper, so I'm confused about this. I decide to send him an email to check in and get something scheduled. There's no point in me walking all the way to the admin building if I don't need to.

> Me: Good afternoon, Professor Johnson. Can you let me know what you need to discuss regarding my paper? And when will you have space to meet with me if that is still necessary?

He doesn't make me wait long for a reply and my anxiety comes back quickly with the response.

> Professor. Johnson: Hello, Ashley. I have availability later this afternoon if you can make it over here for my 5:00 slot. I would prefer to discuss it in person. Does that work for you?

> Me: Yes, sir. I will see you then.

Now I just need to wait the two hours before the meeting. And try not to spiral over the unknowns in the meantime.

Turns out, I can have a complete panic attack, shower, and moderately put myself back together in two hours. Don't recommend a repeat performance, but it's possible. I make my way over to the admin building at 4:30. I really hate being late, and I would rather sit in the lobby for a few minutes so I can try to settle my breathing and my anxiety before my meeting with Professor Johnson. I really hate cryptic emails. Am I in trouble? Did I get nominated for an award? Or something in between? See? This is why it's important to state at least a little bit of the expectation before a meeting.

After checking in with the receptionist, I sit down on one of the oversized leather chairs outside Professor Johnson's office. At least it's warm over here. I'm able to slip my gloves off and pocket them after just a minute sitting inside. My hair is up in a messy bun because I just honestly didn't have the energy to blow dry it after my shower. I did put on a touch of makeup and my diamond stud earrings before heading over here though. I may be fresh off of another panic attack, but no one else needs to know that.

"Come on in, Ashley." Professor Johnson stands in the door frame, smiling reassuringly at me—I guess this isn't a bad meeting then. "Go ahead and hang up your coat and have a seat. I have a few things to go over with you. I just need to run to the restroom and pick up a file from Professor Jackson and then we can jump into what we need to discuss. Make yourself comfortable, I'll be right back."

"Okay," I acknowledge what he's said and head into the office.

I'm here almost every week and enjoy the coziness of the space. The small electric fireplace is running in the corner and I love that he always has it running before I come meet with him. I have no problem hanging up my coat because I know I'll be warm enough.

He's going to probably be a few minutes, so I send a quick text to the group chat I have with the other TAs for Professor Williams to give the daily update. We've started checking in daily to let each other know what has been done and what our remaining task list looks like. I had to prep a few research topics to be presented to class tomorrow and I'm glad I finished those before I got the note from Professor Johnson. I attach the link for the document so it can be printed or sent off to the students tomorrow. I mentally go through the rest of my list while I wait for him to return.

I send a text to Tilly letting her know where I am and that I'll be back in a little while. I hover over Sam's text string next. It's been weeks since we've actually spent time together. I feel awful over how distant I've been. But I can barely keep myself going right now, much less a grown up relationship. I don't want to end things with him, but this isn't fair to him. I can't ask him to wait until I'm better. I need some serious girl talk with Tilly, Sasha, and maybe Kylie because I don't want to talk myself into another spiral. I send them a quick text on our group string.

Me: Brunch soon?

Sasha: Absolutely! How does this Saturday look for everyone?

Tilly: I'm free until noon so if we can do something close to campus, I should be able to make it happen.

Kylie: I'm in. I got gifted a coupon for a West Coast Swing lesson tomorrow night. Do any of you want to go with me?

Sasha: That's the fun dance stuff you've sent me the videos on right?

Kylie: Yeah. It looks like a lot of fun, but I don't want to go by myself.

Me: What's Carter doing tomorrow night?

Kylie: He has a wine class he has to attend for the restaurant so he can't make it this time.

Tilly: I'm free, but I can't dance to save my life. LOL.

Kylie: I don't think I can either, but it'll be fun. I can pick you up from the dorm at six, does that work?

Tilly: Perfect.

Sasha: Have fun you two! We need pictures!

Me: I will chat with you all soon. Have a quick meeting with Professor Johnson and then I'm calling it an early night.

Sasha: Sounds good.

I silence and then pocket my phone once I hear the door closing behind me. I take a deep breath to steady myself. There's no reason to stress over this. He's my advisor and we meet regularly about a whole bunch of stuff.

"I grabbed you a hot cocoa from the cart while I was out there, I know you are trying to cut back on the caffeine in the afternoon." He hands the to-go cup to me before sitting in the chair next to me, nursing his own cup. "How are you liking working with the new group of assistants with Professor Williams this semester?"

I take a sip and hum when the peppermint of the cocoa hits my tongue. "This is seriously incredible, by the way. I'm really enjoying it. It's a good group and it's been good to work with Rowan again. How are your students doing?" I'm not sure how long I'll need to maintain the small talk before I can ask why he needed to see me.

"I'm glad you enjoy it. It's the same cocoa they served at the hotel in New York and I knew you liked that. I was excited to see we could have it on campus for you here as well. And yes, my group is working well together. I wouldn't say I wasn't disappointed when I didn't have you in my group, though. I think we would have worked well together." He glances down to adjust something on his watch before making eye contact with me again. Something isn't sitting right, and I'm not sure what it is. I quickly replay his words while taking another sip to fill the silence.

"I don't remember saying anything about the cocoa at the New York hotel. Did I share something on social media about that?" I know I look as confused as I feel and I hope that didn't come across rude.

"No, you didn't post about it Ashley. But I like making sure you have what you need. And what makes you happy." He sets his cup on the desk in front of him and then reaches for my cup to do the same. I don't respond. I don't know how to. I feel a chill down my back and am suddenly very uncomfortable.

"Um, okay, what did you need to go over with me? Or do you just want to send me an email? I'm not feeling well all of a sudden, I think I need to head back to my room." I adjust myself in the seat so I can stand up, but his hand braces on my knee, holding me still.

"You can wait here, Ashley. If you aren't feeling well, I'm here to take care of you now."

"I don't understand." My words are shaky and I force the tears back. This isn't happening. His hand keeps its grip on my knee, holding me steady, gripping me in place. It hurts, but I don't dare try to pull away. I can walk away with a bruise, I don't need this to get more intense though.

"I think you do, love. It's time for you to let me take care of you. I'm going to need your cell phone now please." His voice is steady, calm. I shake my head and glance down at my lap. My words aren't working anymore. But the tears I was managing to hold back track down my cheeks. I feel his other hand move up to my face and brush the tears away.

"None of that now, the tears turn your face all red. And then you get cold easier. Now, where is your phone, Ashley?" I still can't respond, but he doesn't wait for my words. He reaches into my pocket and grabs my cell. I'm not even surprised when he unlocks it on the first try. How did I miss this? He messes with a few things on my phone while I keep my eyes locked on the floor in front of me. The pattern that looks dark grey from a distance is actually a mix of taupe, green, and black. How does something so intricate look so simple? At least it's not a thick carpet, easy to clean. I hear my phone vibrate, signaling that it has been turned off.

"Are you going to let me take care of you now, my love?" My chin is gripped and turned gently to meet his face. Gone is the soft and gentle nature of Professor Johnson. Instead, I see the man who has been behind the lens for the last few years.

"I'm not yours to take care of." I'm barely able to get the words out, but the grip on my leg tells me that he doesn't agree with my statement.

"That's where you're wrong, Miss Carter." I shiver at his tone. It's too controlled. "You've been mine for a very long time. I'm just done sharing." I don't even have time to decide how to respond because all I feel is a pinch on my knee and then everything goes cold and quiet and still.

WED    THU    FRI    SAT    SUN        DATE:

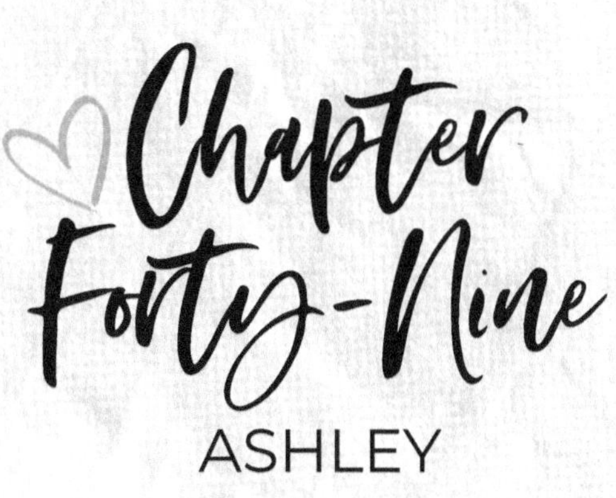

# Chapter Forty-Nine

## ASHLEY

I don't want to open my eyes. Everything hurts and if I can just stay asleep for a little while longer, I don't have to think about what's on the other side of unconsciousness.
Just a bit longer and then I'll wake up and deal with reality.
I'm not ready yet.

# Chapter Fifty

## MARCUS

### APPLE CIDER SANGRIA

*Social Post: The mix of rain and snow we've gotten this week reminds me of home. #weatherreport #oncampus #winter*

*Image Description: Shoveled pathway on the CSU campus with snow covered trees on either side.*

Something is wrong and I don't know what it is or how to fix it. Ashley didn't check in with the group today, and she always checks in. I got her work last night and was able to have what I needed for the class today, but we had a meeting scheduled thirty minutes ago, and she isn't usually late. I send her another message privately to see if everything is okay. If I don't hear from her soon, I'll reach out to Sasha or Matt to see if she is okay. She has some health concerns that she doesn't always pay the best attention to. That's to be expected with her current life stage and the fact that they are recent diagnoses. But still, I'd be lying if I said I wasn't worried.

# SAM

The text I got last night doesn't make a ton of sense, but I knew it was probably coming. Ashley has been juggling a lot, and I know I have been too. Maybe in a different life stage, we could have made things work. I'll give her the space she asked for. I just hope I can still be her friend after all of this is settled. She may not be the love of my life, but she is my soulmate and my best friend. And I won't let her walk away from me completely.

Marcus

WED   THU   FRI   SAT   SUN        DATE

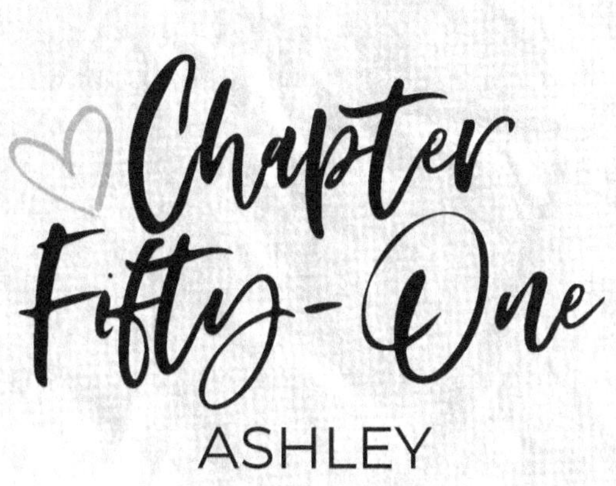

# Chapter Fifty-One

## ASHLEY

I can't hold off waking up any longer. I don't know how long it's been, but I know it's been long enough that I'm cold and hungry. And me being cold to this level is never a good sign. I can't feel my toes and my fingers ache.

*"So much for taking care of me,"* I grumble internally while trying to bring awareness back to the rest of my body. I'm not in my room. I don't recognize the smells around me and it's way too quiet. I seriously can't hear anything. No traffic outside, no footfalls, no music—absolutely nothing. I force my eyes open to blackness. I blink to allow myself time to adjust and still, it's just black. I adjust to try to bring my hands to my eyes, but I can't. Everything is tight and I realize I must be restrained or tied up somehow. I can't feel enough or move enough to determine how. I can't feel half of my body and I don't know if that's because of the cold or whatever drugs Professor Johnson used on me.

Oh God, Professor Johnson. I cannot believe he was the one doing this. There's no way. I force the tears back. I cannot start crying about this again. I don't have the energy. Despite my efforts, I feel the tears track down my face, the cool air hitting the path they leave behind.

I must cry myself to sleep because suddenly I'm waking up again. I hear footfalls approaching me and only have a moment to decide if I'm going to pretend to be sleeping or if I'm going to wake up fully. He decides for me.

"Did you sleep well, my love?" His voice is soft and gentle, completely at odds with how anxious I feel. I don't want to answer him. My weight shifts as I realize I've been laying on a bed and he is now sitting next to me. His body is up against my hip, one arm stretched over my body, bracing himself up. I feel his hand brush the hair out of my face. The touches are gentle and I hate that I feel the comfort he is trying to give me. I don't have the energy to pull away from his touch.

"I'm going to remove the wrap on your eyes. It's not too bright in here, but keep your eyes closed for a minute to adjust," he instructs me, and I listen. I don't want to get hurt more than I probably already am. I feel the fabric move and don't know why I didn't realize I had been blindfolded. But I listen and keep my eyes closed so I can adjust. I feel his hands move to my hands, untying them and then rubbing them with his own. Bringing warmth back into my fingers. I almost sigh in relief when he places gloves on them and then something warm into my palms. I really do hate being cold.

"Let's see how those feet are looking." His voice is still gentle and calm. He's talking to me like I'm his sick or hurting wife and not the student that he just kidnapped. I don't stop him though, because I really do need him to look at my feet. Raynaud's means I am incredibly susceptible to frostbite because of the low circulation. I watch as he pulls my socks off my feet and shake my head because I can't feel the motion of the fabric leaving my skin. My toes are literally blue right now. At least he seems to understand the severity of the situation.

"I'm sorry, Ashley. I got held up at my last class and couldn't make it here sooner. I brought some things to try to help warm you up faster." His hands move to my feet as he just holds them for a minute. I really don't want to get frostbite. I focus on the warmth returning to my hands as he focuses on my feet. I don't even realize that I've fallen asleep again, until I feel his hands move up my calves, massaging, rubbing. I press my legs together and try to roll on my side.

I don't want to be here.

I don't want him touching me.

I can't bring myself to say anything though.

I can't say anything.

Why can't I say anything?

I begin to have a panic attack and curl in on myself. There's not enough things to focus on because I can't open my eyes or voice anything. I feel stuck within myself. I know Professor Johnson is here with me. But where I normally can find comfort and reassurance in those around me, there is no comfort in his touches. I want him to stop. I can't breathe.

He must realize something is wrong because he stops. Instead, he lays down behind me and just holds me close. The steady pressure of his hold works to steady me, even though I know I shouldn't like him touching me. But I need it right now. If I can't control my breathing, I'm going to pass out, and this is going to start all over again. I try focusing on his deep citrus and amber scent. I feel the scruff of his beard against where my neck meets my hair line. I finally can make sense of the words he is whispering.

"I don't want to hurt you."

"I'm here to take care of you."

"You don't have to be scared."

"It's going to be okay."

Why can't I talk? I don't want to work myself up again, but why can't I say anything?

"Don't fight it, baby. I gave you something to calm you down a bit. Once I know you are okay and you understand what is happening, I will lessen the dose. I brought a small heater and layered up your feet. Get some rest," he places a kiss on my temple and I hate that it feels good. It's not supposed to feel good.

"I will be back in a little while to see if you're ready to eat something." His weight leaves and I feel another blanket being draped over me. And I can't fight it anymore, so I let sleep take me under.

The next time I wake up, I'm able to open my eyes right away. And I wish I wasn't able to. I'm on a king size bed. The bedding is comfortable and honestly, something I would have probably picked out. It's a really pretty lavender floral pattern that complements the green and white pillows and throw blankets. There's a white rug on the floor, contrasting with the hardwood floor. Two space heaters are positioned toward the foot of the bed to keep me warm. The room feels like it's out of one of my own dreams.

Until I get to the walls. There are no windows. The walls are painted in a light green and are absolutely covered in photos. Water droplets blur them all. And I hate that they're beautiful. I hate that I love them. I hate that I recognize so many of them from the Instagram account. And I hate that I know which ones have me in the background. I force my feet off the bed and then my body to stand. I want to look at them closer. As I get closer to the wall, I realize there are so many photos that were never shared online. Some of these are from the summer before I started at CSU. Some of these are from our first NYC trip. I'm transfixed, moving from moment to moment. It's like a scrapbook of my life for the last three years. Good memories and bad – all are now seen through his lens. And now they all seem tainted. How long was he following me for?

I must be focusing pretty intently on the pictures because I feel his hands on me before I hear him approach. I jump in surprise and try to jerk away, but his hands on my hips hold me steady. His grip is harder than it needs to be, but it does the job of keeping me still.

"I've been admiring you for a while, Ashley. I do hope you will allow me to photograph you now that you are here," he whispers in admiration in my ear. His lips brush over the skin there, making goosebumps travel down my spine. His arms snake around my waist to pull me closer and I turn my head away. I don't want to feel his lips on my skin. I pull at his hands but can't get a grip on his fingers. I start pulling frantically, trying to get away, all the while he just holds me tighter. He's hurting me. I don't want to be here. I start sobbing, the only sounds I can make myself make. I still can't voice what I'm thinking, what I'm feeling, and I hate being trapped like this.

I barely make out the blood on his hands from me breaking the skin with my nails before he's spinning me around and pushing me into the wall, into the collage of photos that make up the space. His breathing is as labored as mine, but the anger in his eyes is a stark contrast to the comfort he usually tries to convey.

"You need to understand that you are not getting out of here, Miss Carter. You are mine. You will be with me. I cannot care for you properly outside of these walls. It's up to you how comfortable and easy your time will be. I want to make you feel good. I know I can make you feel good. Will you let me?" His voice drops at the end as he leans in and begins kissing and nipping at my neck. It's all wrong. I don't like his touch or the intimacy he thinks we share. I shake my head and try to pull away. He doesn't stop though. I push him and pull my hands free from his grasp.

He grasps my hair into his fist to anchor me in place. The sting when I try to pull away causes me to yell out. So, I can make noise. I can call for help. I can't form words, but I do my best to yell again. There has to be someone close by, right? I lose my footing and fall to the floor, clawing and doing my best to crawl away. He is grabbing at my legs, using his size and weight to hold me down. I can't kick him or push him away. I bang my fists on the ground, doing everything I can to make noise. Until my hands are jerked behind my body and clicked into a restraint – did he seriously just handcuff me? They are tighter than they should be and I feel the pinch in my skin. I don't think I have any more tears to cry. My body is tired and my mind is shutting down.

He rolls me over and climbs on top of me, pressing his hands into the floor on either side of my head, glaring down into my eyes. He's angry. Why is *he* angry? I'm the one that should be angry. I'm the one that's lived in fear for literally months because this creepy old man doesn't understand that I don't belong to him. I'm the one that has to get out of here. I'm the one that's going to get out of here. I am mine. Not his. I wait until his eyes drift away from mine and take a deep breath. I'm lying on my hands so I don't have many options to try to get away, but I can try.

His body moves off of mine and goes to my shoes, beginning to untie them. I can't run with untied shoes, I'm going to need to wait. I can wait a minute. It's okay. I talk myself through the breaths, knowing this is going to be okay. I will get out of here. He finishes with the laces and then gently pulls off my shoes.

"You are so beautiful, my love. I've been waiting so patiently to have you before me like this. And I'm going to make sure you enjoy this too." Yeah, that's gonna be a 'no' from me there, buddy. I jerk my foot away from him and kick as hard as I can, making contact with his nose. The crack I feel and the blood that comes tells me I hit him right and he is not happy. He brings one hand to his nose while the other grabs my foot, anchoring me. I use the new angle to kick again—this time to his crotch. I make contact again and he doubles over in pain.

I am so thankful for all of those yoga classes now because I'm able to use my core strength to roll over and maneuver my hands to my front, still restrained but now usable. I run to the door and silently thank my lucky stars that it's unlocked. The door leads to outside—cold and wet. It's dark and raining, and I have to focus hard on not slipping on the ground. At least it isn't snowing, but it's only a few moments before I am completely soaked.

I run until I begin noticing things outside of the ground in front of me. I'm on a residential road, there's houses here. I need to ask for help. I don't know how far I've run or how long I have until Professor Johnson comes after me again. I take a chance and run to the next building I see. The door is locked. Of course, the door is locked. There's five doorbells by the house number and I frantically push them all. Over and over again.

I hear feet running on the sidewalk, my name being called. He's angry and he's coming. I keep pushing buttons, knowing I don't have the time to find another spot. The fatigue is catching up with me, and I can't run anymore. I use my fists to bang on the door once, twice, and then a third time before my knees finally give out.

My eyes are closed before I hit the porch, but I hear my name one more time.

And this time, I actually do feel safe.

# Chapter Fifty-Two

## MARCUS

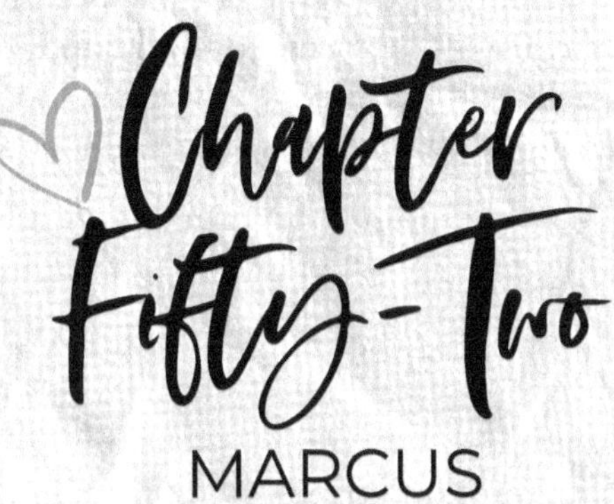

**PUMPKIN CREAM CHAI LATTE**

*Social Post: Even though the days may be dark, the sun always shines, and fate always brings about beautiful things. Reminiscing on a favorite poem from Longfellow today as I listen to the rain outside my window. #poetry #henrywadsworthlongfellow #rainyday #fate #soothingsounds*

*Image Description: Cup of tea sitting on the dining table in the foreground, the window covered in rain droplets in the background.*

Going to sleep listening to the rain on the roof and the wind blowing through the bare trees outside my window reminded me of my time in Scotland. And home in Maine too, if I'm being honest. I think we had more rainy days than sunny days in my years back east.

What I wasn't expecting was to wake up to the doorbell ringing over and over again. What is going on? I slide on my house shoes and robe over my sleep pants and make my way to the window overlooking the street. I don't see anyone, but the ringing continues. If it was kids, they would have rang once or twice and then run away. This person is staying on the porch, under the overhang so I can't see who it is. I do notice a man running up the road though. I can't see any features of who it is, just that they are moving fast, and with a bit of a limp.

I don't like the way this looks. I pocket my cell phone and race down the stairs. Hoping I get to the door before the angry man running toward my front steps does. I open the door to the sounds of the man's footfalls splashing on the pavement, the rain pouring from the overflowing gutters, and Ashley's sobs at my feet.

"Ashley?"

Two hours later I am sitting in a hospital waiting room with Ashley's parents, her brother, and Sasha. Ashley didn't say anything to me while I held her in the foyer of my building, she just quietly cried. The ambulance and police arrived, and still, she didn't talk. Her eyes were blank, staring ahead, and all I could do was hold her hand. Why were they so cold? They were tinged blue and I knew her feet had to be in worse condition. Who knows how long she was running outside before she collapsed on my porch.

After getting her checked in, I was escorted to the waiting room. The doctors came to speak to her parents and I hated the words I was hearing: PTSD, rape kit, significant bruising and dehydration, borderline hypothermia and frostbite. It had only been two days. What had this guy done to her in two days? Kept her in a freezer? I was angry, almost irrationally so. I had emailed in to ask for class coverage until the end of the week. I didn't know why, but I needed to be here. I needed to make sure she was okay. There was plenty of faculty available that could pick up the slack with me being out of the classroom. And Rowan was more than capable of teaching my freshman level course.

It felt like days before we were allowed back into the room. I'm sure it was only another hour in reality. Ashley's parents went back first, and then Sasha and Matt joined them. They were only there for about thirty minutes before they came back out. The time was approaching five in the morning and I knew we were all feeling the fatigue.

"How is she doing?" I stand to meet Mr. Carter as I wait for an update—anything they are willing to share with me.

"She still isn't talking. The doctors said the shock of the event is still very present. They're hoping a day or two of rest and knowing she is safe will help. She was borderline hypothermic, but they don't expect any lasting damage to her fingers and feet. The Raynaud's is probably going to be worse for a while because of that though." Her dad updates me as his wife goes to the desk to make sure her daughter is taken care of while they go home for a little while. "They are going to give her enough medication that she will stay asleep for a while, let her body and her mind rest," he continues.

"I hate asking this, but what about the other tests?" I lower my voice. I don't want to worry the others, but I need to know she is okay.

"Rape kit came back negative. She has some nasty scratches on her body where I think she was fighting to get away. And she had some skin and blood on her that wasn't her own that they are submitting to the police department. Hopefully, we get a match and they can catch this guy." I breathe in a sigh of relief, knowing that while she probably went through the hardest couple of days in her life, part of her dignity remains intact.

"I think I want to stay here, if you're okay with that." My voice is barely above a whisper, but I know he hears the conviction in my voice. "We don't know who this guy was, and I want to make sure someone is with her. With her not talking and the state she is in, I don't want her waking up to see someone that shouldn't be here. I don't think she knew she ran to my apartment when she did, but she knew who I was in the ambulance. I think me being here if she wakes up before you get back will help with some of the uncertainty." He thinks for a moment before nodding his head.

I'm taller than he is, but he still rests his hand on my shoulder in a reassuring gesture. He's passing off the responsibility of his daughter to me, even though he doesn't say the words. "Let me give you my number in case anything happens. We will be back in a few hours. They said they wouldn't start bringing her out of the medication until tomorrow, so it should be quiet." I input my information into his phone and then call my number so I have his as well.

"I took the day off so I'm good to stay here until you get back. Do we have any idea who this might have been so the hospital security can be looking for him too?"

"We don't know. Matt is going through her phone, computer, and social media now to see if he can find this guy. For now, we are keeping this small. No other visitors. If her roommate comes, that should be okay, but we need to keep it close. Once the DNA tests come back, we can go from there. Right now, the focus is on her resting and coming back to us." I nod in agreement and shake his hand.

Walking down the hallway to her room, I'm reminded of how oblivious we tend to be. Would I have known who it was? Was it someone on campus? Was it someone who she trusted? She must have thought she was safe to some degree, but the bruises that are visible on her body show that she fought hard. Whoever this was, they were bigger than she is. There are visible handprints on her arms and a harsh ring where the handcuffs were before the paramedics removed them.

I take my seat next to her, putting my phone on silent except for notifications from her parents and Rowan. No one else needs to get in touch with me right now. For now, I will hold space for her and be here with her. Ashley was brought into my life for a reason, and while I value her position as my assistant, I know she is destined for incredible things. I want to be around to see what she accomplishes. It's in these quiet moments that I allow myself to see her beauty and her strength—side by side. This woman is absolutely remarkable. And I know this isn't going to stop her.

"You need to rest and take the time you need, and then you need to come back to us, Ashley. You aren't done with the work you have started," I whisper to her. I don't know if she can hear me or not, but I don't want her to think she's alone here. Her heart monitor blips a bit and I can see her heart rate rising. She's stressing or hurting, even in her sleep. The nurse steps in and adjusts some things on her IV and before long, she's settling again.

"Oh, Ashley, who did this to you?"

# Chapter Fifty-Three

## MARCUS

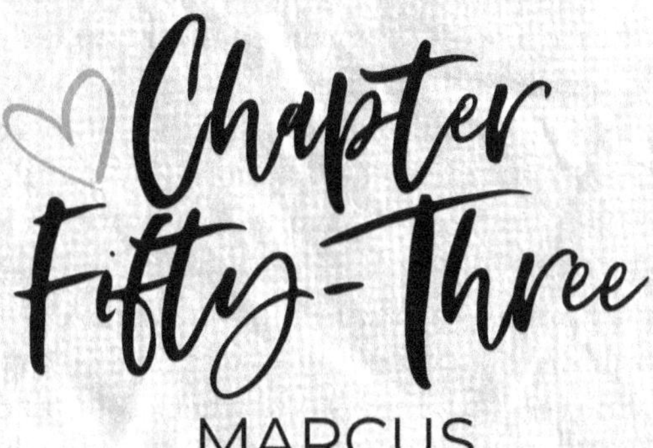

**VANILLA CINNAMON MILK TEA**

*Social Post: And indeed there will be time*
*To wonder, "Do I dare?" and "Do I dare?"*
*Time to turn back and descend the stair,*
*With a bald spot in the middle of my hair —*
*(They will say: "How his hair is growing thin!")*
*My morning coat, my collar mounting firmly to the chin,*
*My necktie rich and modest, but asserted by a simple pin —*
*(They will say: "But how his arms and legs are thin!")*
*Do I dare*
*Disturb the universe?*
*In a minute there is time*
*For decisions and revisions which a minute will reverse.*
**An excerpt from The Love Song of J. Alfred Prufrock by T.S. Eliot*
*#poetry #tragedy #classiclit*
*Image Description: Blank notebook paper with a black ink pen resting on top of it.*

The next several days begin to blur together, and I am reluctant to return to campus, but I do have to see to my responsibilities there. The DNA tests are taking longer than expected, and we are all on edge. Campus security is on high alert and those on campus have been urged to walk in pairs until the perpetrator is identified and caught. Ashley remains sleeping. They've begun weaning her off of the medication, but she just isn't ready to come back to us yet. Something is keeping her in the space between sleep and awake. I'm only planning to be back on campus to teach my two classes for the day, meet with Rowan, and grab some work that I can do from her bedside.

I can't explain the draw I have to her. I just know that I'm supposed to be taking care of her. I've known her for about a year, but something is telling me she is important to me. And someone else has broken her trust. I hate the feeling that I know who her attacker is. I am going to be devastated when those results come in, especially if it's someone I knew, or do know. I had only seen her as a student, as someone I was mentoring, and now I wish I had spent more time getting to know her. Maybe I could have seen some of the signs.

Rowan is waiting for me outside of the classroom when I arrive on campus. A quick shower and change at my apartment, and I am back in the professor's headspace and not the worried man sitting next to the woman I barely know as she sleeps. "How is she today?" Rowan asks as we make our way into the classroom and begin preparing for the lecture.

"About the same. She's off of the meds enough that she should be waking up. She just isn't ready yet." I shake my head and sort through the papers in front of me. "Thank you for getting this done for me. I don't want to pick up another assistant, but we may have to. I want her to have her spot when she comes back, but I also don't want to put too much on you, either."

Rowan just shakes his head and lets out a small chuckle. "It really is okay. Ashley had most of this done already, I just needed to print it out. She got a lot done in the first few weeks of the semester. The three of us can manage for a while. Besides, you found the four students on campus that aren't put off by your grumpy exterior, don't push it by trying to add another one."

"Who says I'm grumpy?"

He just levels a look at me that tells me all I need to know. I'm not grumpy. I just have a procedure for things and get annoyed easily when people don't follow that procedure. I'm a college professor—keep it professional. Is that too much to ask? The students file in and find their seats. The chatter is quieter than usual. Everyone knows what happened. And the mood shows throughout the space. Ashley is a girl that everyone knows. She talks to everyone and jumps right into a new situation. Hearing what happened was devastating to those who know her. Class goes smoothly. No stupid questions or unnecessary interruptions.

I have my next class in this same room, so I settle in behind the desk to wait until it's time. Rowan will be in that one with me as well, so he leaves for a minute to grab us some tea from the coffee cart. They broadened their tea offerings once I told them I love a good London Fog Latte and now there are some suitable teas to choose from. The time goes by quickly, and before long, I have just about ten minutes before students should start shuffling into the room.

"Do you have a moment?" The voice from the door startles me a bit, but I quickly refocus to greet Professor Johnson, waiting just inside the threshold of the room.

"My next class will be in soon, but I have a few minutes. How can I help you, Professor Johnson?" I stack the papers in front of me and sip on my tea, enjoying the bergamot undertones of this blend.

"Have you heard how Ashley is doing? I haven't had the chance to go visit at the hospital and didn't know if she's woken up yet." His voice trails off, not finishing the statement. His hands are shoved into his pockets and his glasses are smudged a bit.

"Are you feeling okay? You're looking a little rough today, Professor." I don't hide my disdain. I don't like this guy. And I really wish I knew why.

"I'm okay. Just worried. Ashley has been with me since she started on campus. I'm worried."

"You said that." I am only a few steps from him now, holding my cup in one hand, the other resting lightly in my pants pocket. I had left my suit coat unbuttoned and I don't miss the way he sizes me up a bit. Yes, I know I'm tall. And I think he's used to being the bigger man in a conversation. I don't use my height to intimidate, but I have no problem using my status on campus to make him feel inferior. He deserves to be brought down a peg or two.

"Right, well, I may try to stop by after my class today. Thanks again, Marcus." He turns to leave but I don't let him leave the conversation yet.

"It's Professor Williams."

"I'm sorry?"

"We are in a professional setting, Professor Johnson. You may call me Professor Williams when we are in a classroom setting or in front of students." I hear Rowan trying to stifle a laugh behind me. The man in front of me doesn't have a response for me, and I revel in it for a moment.

"Have a good afternoon, Professor Johnson." I extend my hand to his. After all, we are gentlemen. He extends his hand to mine and I immediately see red. "What happened to your hand, Professor Johnson." My tone conveys my growing anger and I hear Rowan come around the desk and walk closer to me.

"Do not make me ask you again, Professor. What happened to your hand?" His hand is in mine and my grip is growing to the point of pain, evidenced by his face. My phone dings and I know it has to be one of Ashley's parents. Everyone else is silenced when they reach out to me right now. "We were waiting on DNA testing to come back about Ashley's attacker. That text message should be the results. But I bet you already know what they are going to say, don't you?" His eyes search everywhere, trying to avoid my gaze. I pass my phone to Rowan.

"What do the results say, Mr. Masters?" I pray I'm not right about my thoughts right now.

"There was a 95% match to Charles Johnson, professor at Colorado State University. Blood and skin samples were enough to issue a warrant. Police should be on their way to arrest him now. And Ashley is still asleep." Rowan's voice is low and steady as he reads the message.

I don't think, I just react. And I'm pretty sure my hand is going to be bruised after I finish laying into the piece of dirt in front of me.

WED   THU   FRI   SAT   SUN
DATE      /     /

# Chapter Fifty-Four

## ASHLEY

**STASH HONEY ORANGE GINGER TEA**

*Social Post: Hey all, this is Sasha. Ashley is going to be taking some time away from social media for a few weeks. She'll still be working behind the scenes with Pink Every Day and on her classes, but is stepping back from this platform for a bit to rest, recover, and focus on healing. Please give this post some love so she knows you are here and will be here when she comes back. Comments are off, but feel free to leave all the hearts. Thank you all so much for supporting Ashley and her account as well as the work we are doing @pinkeveryday #sassyashleymiles #pinkeveryday #socialmediabreak #control #iamenough #iammine*

*Image Description: Throwback photo of Sasha and Ashley at the New York Gala in December.*

He's at my bedside again. I am not aware of much outside of the beeps of the heart rate monitor, the footfalls outside my door, and Professor Williams sitting in the chair next to me. His hand is bandaged up today. He doesn't look hurt anywhere else, but he's holding tension in his shoulders. He really should probably get a massage or something. Sleep takes me under again before I'm able to tell him I'm awake and ask for my parents. My body still hurts so much. And I don't even want to think about how many of my classes I've missed.

The next time I am aware of what's happening, my parents are in the corner. My mom is sitting, holding Matt's hands, and my dad is talking to a police officer. Where is Professor Williams? I force my eyes to stay open for a minute and try to hear what's being said. I can't make sense of the words, but they aren't angry. I don't think I'm in trouble. Why would I be in trouble? Why am I here? Why is everything so fuzzy? I take a breath and everything comes rushing back and I suddenly can't breathe. My mom makes eye contact with me and runs over to grab my hand while my dad runs into the hallway yelling.

I can't understand what Mom is saying, but she holds my hand and runs her hand over my head. I know she's trying to be soothing, but he did that to me too. How do I tell her that she isn't helping? It's just bringing back memories of him doing the same. I shake my head and try to tell her to stop. Why can't I say anything? What's wrong with me?

Mom has tears in her eyes and I finally hear what she says. "They got him, Ashley, you rest, you're safe."

I'm safe.

I can sleep.

I'm safe.

I can sleep.

And then Professor Marcus Williams is in the door frame again, holding a to-go cup that probably has tea in it. I look at his hand again and know that he helped lock "him" up. I can't even think of his name. But he's here now, so I can sleep.

The days start becoming reality with more time awake and less time in my sleepy haze. I've been able to force myself to respond to a few questions. Basic things. Simple answers. I don't want to talk anymore. The memories hurt and I blame myself every time I get asked something else. Why didn't I see the signs sooner? Why did I keep responding to him? Why didn't I ask for help? Why did I go to his office that night? Why did I let him take my phone? Why did I not pay better attention?

The spiraling usually happens after the police or the doctors ask me questions. Sometimes I'm alone and sometimes I have either my mom or dad with me. It doesn't make it easier though. I got my phone back yesterday and saw the message he sent to Sam. And then Sam responding when he heard about what happened. I had Mom help me text him again yesterday to tell him that I hadn't sent the initial message, but I think I do need to call things off. It isn't fair to him. He understood and Mom held me while I cried. Part of me hates that I can't say I'm his girlfriend anymore, but I haven't been that title for a while honestly.

Professor Williams stops by every day too. He doesn't ask me questions or demand answers from me. He just sits next to me and works on his laptop while I watch TV or doze off again. He brought me a book today. Anne of Green Gables. I haven't read this book since I was a little girl, but I find comfort in the story. Normally I like suspenseful romance stories and I want to stay away from that for a while. Living it, at least the suspense part, is enough for a few months. I forgot how much I enjoyed this story and find myself smiling at the different familiar chapters. I catch Professor Williams staring at me as I finish the dance scene.

"You look better," he remarks softly and I just nod in agreement. "Can I get you anything else?"

I think for a moment before responding, "Another blanket for my feet? I know I'm not actually cold, but my feet don't know that and they hurt."

"I'll see what I can do." He stands and makes his way to the cabinets at the end of the room, sorting through them in an orderly fashion to see what's there. And I am staring at his ass. His very nice ass that fills out his dress slacks way better than a professor should be looking. And I need to dial it back on the meds apparently because why am I thinking that literally days after my kidnapping and assault? What is wrong with me?

"I found one more in there. Do you want it layered up or just one layer on your feet?" His tone is gentle and even and I can listen to him talk all day. In the days before I fully woke up, I could hear him reading to me sometimes. His mellow tone keeping me grounded, giving me something to focus on. I couldn't always understand what he was saying, but I liked that he was there.

"Layered up, please." He adjusts the blanket and then comes back to his seat next to me. "Have you brought on a new assistant to take over for me yet?"

"No. I wanted to check in with you first about it. That spot was for you and I have things lined up for you this semester. I didn't want you to think I was taking it away from you. And when you are ready to come back, I'd love for you to continue working with me, Ashley."

"When I come back? Not if?"

"Not if. I haven't known you for very long, Ashley, but I know you are determined to finish what you started. And I'm going to help you do just that. You are getting discharged tomorrow, right?"

"Yes, sir." I try to put more cheer in my tone than I actually feel. "As long as everything is okay overnight and tomorrow. Then I get to start working on therapy sessions and trying to avoid freaking out any time someone tries to talk to me." I hate how scared I feel to leave these walls. There's security and cameras and locked doors here. I don't have all of that at home. And I don't think I can go back to campus. But home is safer, and Matt has installed some additional cameras and alarms on the property.

"You're going to do great. And you aren't alone. You have friends and family who are here for you. Let us help, okay?" His eyes are pleading and I can almost feel his sincerity. I nod in agreement as more tears fall down my cheeks. Always crying. I can't seem to stop now. He doesn't tell me to stop or even hand me a tissue, he just sits with me, and we go back to our books.

Being back at my house is harder than I thought it would be. My brother found some sort of device that finds cameras and trackers and went through my room before I got home. The guy seriously had trackers in my earrings – the pretty pink diamond ones I wore almost every day. Apparently, Sam didn't give me those. I haven't even let myself think of all the gifts I've received over the last few years. How many more of those were from him?

My mom, Tilly, and Sasha completely refreshed my room for me though. New bedding, new curtains, new pillows. I didn't want to think of the nights that he watched me in here. And I now have blackout curtains on my windows. I don't spend much time in my room. Most of my awake hours are spent on the couch in the family room, facing the fireplace. A book on my lap and a cup of tea on the coffee table next to me. And Professor Williams sitting quietly in the chair on the other side of the table.

He's been the constant I didn't know I needed. He comes over after classes and gets his grading done here. He's started giving me small things to work on too. Papers to review or brand proposals to check before we give them back to the students. I like feeling useful. I don't know if I'll be ready to go back on campus this semester, but at least this gives me some normalcy. Rowan and Tilly come over sometimes too. The family dining room table has turned into a workstation most evenings. And I think my parents secretly love having more people over here. I know my therapist does. We've discussed how I tend to spiral when I'm alone for too long. I get stuck in my head and then struggle to stay on top of things.

I also haven't been back on social media. Matt and Sasha went through and pulled everything that the lawyers needed for their case. Since I deleted many of the messages, they don't have as much concrete evidence to show the premeditation. Apparently, he completely scrubbed all of his devices after he took me. He didn't get rid of the pictures though. They even found some in his office on campus. He was using them as bookmarks in his textbooks. I hope I don't have to be there during the trial, but my therapist and lawyer said we will work on that when it comes. For now, I'm focusing on getting better physically and allowing those that are here for me to do just that—be here.

"When we are not on campus or with students, I think it's okay if you call me Marcus, Ashley. You asked that I call you by your given name, and I feel kind of silly having you continue to use my professional title when we are grading papers." It's just the two of us working tonight. Midterms are next week, so there's a lot of papers to review. I love this part of what we get to do. Tonight, it's reviewing submissions for his Understanding Community Needs section of the Business Startup Class. It's a fascinating study. Students had to choose a community, do a deep dive into the community needs, and then create a business pitch for something the community has a need for and how to make the business profitable while not adding burden to the chosen place.

"If you're sure, Marcus," I try out the name and he smiles back at me, adjusting his reading glasses before going back to the papers in front of him. I spend way too much time thinking about how attractive he is. He's here to help me. To be the authority figure. Not because he likes me. That would be absolutely ridiculous.

I go back to reviewing the packet in front of me. It's for a pretty remote town in Maine, one that has a growing need for after school activities for the kids. The parents are working, so they have several hours that are spent getting into trouble rather than getting to enjoy being kids. The proposal is to set up a café/library that has licensed teachers and caregivers on site. The kids would be able to come and work on homework and can start working a few hours each week once they turn fifteen. They would be partnered with a literary and publishing company out of a neighboring town to provide resources. This is amazing.

"You have to check this one out." I pass the packet over to Marcus. He skims over the title and synopsis pages and smiles.

"This is great. I spoke to this student earlier this semester. He is from a town close to where I am originally from. The publishing company he talks about is mine. It's something he is actually looking to do when he graduates. I love that he took the time to work through the logistics already. It's a solid idea and we may be able to get that started." He owns a publishing company? What?

"How did I not know any of that?"

"I don't share much about my personal or business life, Ashley. I enjoy what I get to do. The right people find out when they are supposed to." He smiles back at me and then gets up to get the kettle started for more tea. I am down to only one cup of coffee in the mornings, then I switch to tea. Marcus may have gotten me hooked on a few different blends and I love the art form that the blend masters have.

"I'm not keeping you from business responsibilities with you being here babysitting in the afternoons, right?" I just had the thought and feel awful at my selfishness.

"Not at all. I'm where I need to be. And where I want to be. I enjoy spending time with you. And it helps me stay focused on my work too. No reading until we get the grading done." He smirks a bit and then returns to the table with fresh cups of tea for the both of us.

"It smells spicy–what's this one?" I ask as I blow gently on the mug, enjoying the warmth seeping through the double walled ceramic.

"Ginger and orange." He sips his cup and then hums in satisfaction.

"It smells like you." I feel the blush creep up my cheeks. I cannot believe I just said that out loud. I take a sip and know this is going to be my new favorite tea. I'm gonna need more of this please and thank you. I sneak a glance to see the smirk back on his face.

"I know what I like." He shrugs it off and then we get back to our comfortable silence, only hearing the shuffling of papers until my eyes grow heavy and I wish Marcus a good night.

# Chapter Fifty-Five

## MARCUS

**BLACKBERRY EARL GREY ICED LATTE**

*Social Post: Some cultures see the process of making and serving a cup of tea to be an art form. And it's not hard to see why that is the case. #tea #blendmaster #teacup #morningbrew #localblends*

*Image Description: Loose-leaf black tea leaves on a white cloth tea bag.*

I had to hold back a chuckle when she said that the tea I gave her last night smelled like me. She's not wrong. I've used this cologne for years and love the way it smells. My mom actually gave it to me about ten years ago, and it's become my "signature scent" as my sister-in-law calls it. It's a classic combination for a reason. I am bringing a few boxes of some of my favorites to her house today. That girl was drinking way too much coffee, and I'm glad she's enjoying the teas I've brought for her. She seems to be getting better but is still very withdrawn. She doesn't let many people in on her feelings or her thoughts.

Ashley has taken to some very minute facial expressions or reactions to show what she is thinking. I think it's going to be a while for her to find her confidence and voice again. The asshole that was following her showed her she can't trust freely. She has to rethink her choices. And I hate how much he took away from her. So much I didn't truly get to see as she was stepping into her position with Sasha and on campus. I hope this doesn't permanently derail her or her passions.

I approach the front door and knock gently, waiting just a moment before the door opens to Ashley's mother. She reminds me so much of my mom, even with me being closer in age to Martha Carter than she is to my mom. I'm not going to think about that right now.

"I brought a few more teas for your cabinet, Mrs. Carter," I pass the bag to her with the teas and honey sticks in it.

"You really can call me Martha and you don't need to bring tea every time you come over," she shakes her head but takes the bag from me as I follow her inside, leaving my shoes by the front door next to the rest of the pairs.

"If you're sure. How is she doing today?" I set my bag down on the table and look around the space, surprised that Ashley isn't down here already. She usually is waiting for me when I get here. "Is she okay?" I turn to look at Martha as she sets the bag I gave her on the counter.

"She's having a rough day. I'm not sure what triggered it, but she hasn't wanted to get up. I didn't want to tell you not to come, because having you come here to work is a point of consistency for her. I don't know what to do except give her space and let her know we are here." She fights back some tears and I can tell she's hurting, but I understand her feelings.

"Has she eaten anything today?" I try to tackle one problem at a time. She just shakes her head at me in response. "Can I try?"

"Of course. Feel free to use whatever. I have baked ziti planned for dinner, but that may be too heavy for her. You're more than welcome to stay for dinner or bring some home with you when you're done working this afternoon, though."

I spend a few minutes in the kitchen, getting a cup of tea steeping and a bit of broth warmed up on the stove while I make a toasted turkey and cheese sandwich. Something warm, some protein, and something that smells good. Hopefully I can get her to at least sip on something. Martha is reading in the living room when I pass by her with a tray and my bag over my shoulder. "I'm going to sit with her if she's okay with it. I'll text you if I'm able to get her to eat anything."

"Thank you, Marcus. Holler if you need me. We appreciate you being here for our girl."

"Of course. I want to be here," I reassure her. Why isn't that a strange thought? Would I be like this if it was any other student? Probably not. So why her?

I get to her door and knock gently. The door wasn't latched closed so it pushes open slightly when I knock. "Hey Ash, I brought you some tea. May I sit in here and get some work done? Your mom is baking dinner downstairs and I figured it might be calmer up here."

As I step into the room, I see her curled up in her bed, under the covers. Her blonde hair has started growing out a bit, so it must have been a while, even before the attack, that she got it colored. The messy strands are falling out of the bun on top of her head and only a little of her face is showing. I set the cup of tea on her nightstand and then the tray on her desk in the corner. She only has a small work space since it was primarily for makeup content, so I make myself comfortable on the floor. Away from the door so she doesn't feel trapped at any point.

I'm not sure if she's sleeping or awake, but I focus on getting my work done. Reading the papers out loud and commenting on them. She had mentioned she could hear me reading to her when she was in the hospital, so I'm hoping this may have the same effect. Maybe it will let her find that point to anchor to so she doesn't stress about everything else. After about twenty minutes, she starts to stir until she rolls over to look at me. I continue to read to her after making the briefest of eye contact.

It doesn't take much longer until she slowly sits up and grabs the tea. "Do you want to eat anything? It's not anything fancy, but I have some broth in a coffee mug and a sandwich for you," I prompt her with my request. I don't want to upset her by asking too much, but she really does need to eat.

"Well, as long as it's in a coffee mug." She hints at a smile and I can't help replying with my own. I stand and grab the mug, thankful that it's still warm. I pass it to her after she sets the empty tea mug on the night stand.

"Would you like more tea?"

"No, that was good. Thank you." She sips on the broth and then looks at my little makeshift workspace on the ground. "Maybe we can get a chair up here so you don't have to do that when you come over?" I like that she says it like it's going to happen.

"Whatever you want, Ashley," I keep my voice steady, not wanting to push. "Do you want to get up or are we calling today a chill day?"

"Definitely a chill day. I just couldn't make myself get out of bed today. Nothing sounded good and I didn't even have the energy to go pick out a book to read. So, this is where I've been all day." She seems almost upset at herself over it. Like she failed at a task but doesn't know what the task is.

"Do you want to try something with me?" I have an idea and it may not work, but maybe it will help.

"Sure," she doesn't even hesitate.

"What if I give you a few things to do for the days when you have a hard time getting out of bed. That way you have a list to follow, easy and simple tasks to do, but it will give you something to check off of a list. And then we can check in later in the day. That way even on your 'stay in bed days' you don't feel like you completely wasted the day." I don't even realize that I've sat on the edge of the bed. But it's easier to talk to her when I'm only a bit above eye level and not standing next to her.

"I think I would like that. Can we try for tomorrow though? I don't know why, but I'm exhausted already." The hopefulness in her voice is quickly replaced with disappointment and I hate that she is so hard on herself.

"Absolutely. Do you want me to bring everything back downstairs?" I stand and go to grab the mug from her to set it out of the way.

"No, can you sit in here with me, at least until I fall back asleep?" She's already settling back into the covers and I have to fight the urge to tuck her in.

"I can do that. Sleep well, Ashley." The content smile on her face matches my own. And I head back to my spot on the floor to spend my time watching her rest rather than grade the papers in my bag.

Me: Good morning, Ashley. How are you feeling today?

Ashley: Better than yesterday, but still not great. I'm always really sore the day after a bad depression day.

Me: That's actually pretty normal – one of my brothers deals with pretty significant depression and he always had to take a day to come back to things slowly.

Me: Would you like a few things to work on today or do you want to take another full day off to rest?

Ashley: I think I would like a few things to do, if you don't mind.

Me: I can do that.

Me: Take a shower and change into your comfiest pajamas after.
Pick out a comfort read – something that you've already read and know you enjoy that you can take your time reading because you already know how it's going to go.
Spend twenty minutes working on the project for Professor. Erickson's class.
Sound good?

Ashley: I think I can do that.

Me: Text me as you finish each thing so you can pace yourself throughout the day. I may not be able to respond right when you text me, but I will as soon as I can between classes. I'll be over around four today.

Ashley: Sounds good. Thank you, Marcus. I'll see you this afternoon.

Me: You're welcome.

That began a daily pattern of me sending her a task list each morning. Depending on how she was feeling, sometimes it included outside time, cooking with her mom in the kitchen, or even meeting up with Sasha to complete an errand together. We talked about the parts of her "old normal" that she wanted to bring back into her life and we gradually worked on bringing those back into her routines. Before long, we were only a few weeks away from the summer, and from when I was supposed to go back to Maine for a month to visit my family. I found myself torn on what to do. I had seen Ashley every day since the end of January. Now it seemed like too long to even miss a weekend, much less an entire month.

Rowan was heading back to the UK for the summer. His brother was getting married and it was a good chance for him to get back there for a little while. I know my mind is preoccupied when I get to the house that afternoon. I had stopped to pick up some sushi and miso on my way so we could have some "feel good food" as Ashley calls it. Her definition of comfort food is very different from mine, but I love the quirky things that make her who she is. And I'm seeing more and more of it every day. Ashley meets me at the door before I even have a chance to knock.

"Did you bring me sushi?" she asks excitedly as I step inside and toe off my shoes, carefully balancing the containers in my hands so I don't ruin the rolls.

"Did you get everything done today?" I teasingly ask her back. On days where she has completed everything before I get to the house, I do my best to bring her something as a "treat." Sometimes it's a new pen or a box of new tea to try. And on Wednesdays, it's sushi.

"Yes, sir. Of course. It's Wednesday." She tells me in a "how dare you question me" tone. I smile at her as we walk to the kitchen. I set the sushi out on the island and she grabs the plates, chopsticks, and soy sauce bowls. I take a quick look at her work from today, making sure it is done and then I pass over her favorite roll. The happy dance she does when the spicy tuna roll passes her lips makes me laugh. I'm seeing my Ashley back. Wait, *my*? Where did that come from?

Her eyes shine in happiness as she looks at me. "Wednesdays are my favorite days now. Thank you, Marcus. Are you ready for the semester to wrap up so you can go see your family?" Her voice dips a bit at the last question. Is she not looking forward to the change in routine either?

"I'm excited to see them, but in all honesty, I'm going to miss coming to see you in the afternoons." She seems absolutely shocked at my confession.

"Really?"

"Yes, really. Does that honestly surprise you?"

"I guess part of me thought that you may be doing this as a

professional obligation to the school or to the program. That it wasn't going to be a big change in your day when you no longer had to come see me every day." Her eyes are focused on the soy sauce swirling in her bowl as she uses her chopsticks to play with it, avoiding looking at me so I can't clearly see the hurt on her face.

"Look at me, Ashley." My voice is steady with the statement— not quite a command, but a plea. "I *want* to be here every day with you. It started as me checking in on you, wanting to make sure you were okay, but I enjoy our time together. I enjoy getting to know *you.* This isn't a collegiate requirement. I'm here because I want to be here. Don't diminish your value in my eyes by dismissing my motivations." She nods her head in agreement and I can tell she doesn't know how to respond. *I'm* not sure how to respond to that. "Let's finish dinner and then we can put on a movie for some background noise while we finish grading these papers. It's the last batch of this assignment before we switch into finals prep."

"Okay. Can I pick tonight?"

"Of course," I smile at her. She picks every night, but I love that she asks. And I love giving her what she wants.

Marcus

WED   THU   FRI   SAT   SUN
DATE :

# Chapter Fifty-Six

## ASHLEY

**YOGI BLUEBERRY SAGE TEA**

*Social Post: Taking the social media break was really necessary for me, but I'm excited to be back. What's everyone doing for the summer break? I can't believe it's only a few days away! #imback #iamenough #iammine #control #sassyashleysmiles #coloradogirl*

*Image Description: Partial self-portrait, showing my hair down and over my shoulder, only a bit of my face is in the frame, light purple wall shows in the background.*

"I don't want him to go." I can't believe I said it out loud, but it's true. I'm sitting cross-legged on my bed, sorting through photos for our next brand collaboration with Tilly and Sasha. Tilly is kneeling on the floor next to my bed and Sasha is sitting opposite me so we can all see the photos and lay it out how we want on the website. This is our second collaboration this year, and with our biggest brand partner, so a lot of thought goes into the layout and the photos we will finalize today. This may be my favorite part of my job. And I love that I get to do this again. There were weeks where I didn't even look at makeup. I'm still not where I was, but at least I can do this again.

"Who? Professor Williams?" Tilly asks as she pulls out a photo and sets it in the "definitely not" pile. "When does he leave for Maine?"

"He leaves this weekend. And he's going to be gone for a month. He's been here every day since the hospital. It's going to be weird not seeing him and being on a time difference. Does everything stop once school is out for the summer? Does he just go back to normal and forget about me once he leaves?"

"Do you want him to forget about you?" Sasha voices the question that I've been thinking over for literally weeks as she puts another set of photos in the proper sequence. We will do this all again digitally once we finalize the layouts, but it helps to see them physically too.

"No. I don't want him to forget about me. And I don't want him to go, is that horrible of me? He hasn't seen his family in years and I want him to keep coming over for afternoon tea and Wednesday sushi." I toss my current stack into the 'maybe' pile and stand up to go look out the window. My curtains are pulled back today. I've started letting the sunshine back into my room, and the warmth of the rays on my face is grounding and calming. I hear a car door close outside and I glance down to see Marcus leaving his car and making his way to the front door. He glances up to my room and sees me watching and gives me a little wave before he heads to the front of the house. I hear the knock on the door and then my mom letting him inside.

"Why don't you go with him?" Tilly asks. "I mean you can work remotely on everything that needs to happen for Pink Every Day, weekly and daily check-ins as needed. And we were planning to take the first week of June off anyway, right? You meet with your therapist virtually and the trial isn't starting for another couple of months. You're a grown up, Ashley. See if you can go with him, it sounds like he wouldn't be opposed to it."

"We haven't talked about that at all. And again, I'm his student.

Is that appropriate?"

"I think 'appropriate' went out the window when you got kidnapped by the crazy professor, Ash. He cares about you. Maybe being away from campus and where everything happened will help you guys see what can happen." Sasha is the voice of reason here and I don't hate the idea of spending more time with him.

"There's a ton to figure out with that. Where would I stay? I'm not ready for a cross country trip? How do I tell him I want to go with him? Would that be weird?"

"Now you sound like me with the overthinking," Sasha laughs a little. "Just see what he says, maybe bring it up today when you guys finish with the last of the finals grading. He may have been thinking about this too."

"Do you think so?" I know I'm hopeful with my asking, but I kind of hope she is right.

"I know so," I hear his voice behind me and turn to see him standing in the doorway to my bedroom.

"What do you know?" I ask him, hoping that I'm right with my assumptions.

"I've been thinking about asking you to come with me to Maine." He says it matter-of-factly, steady, like he always talks to me. No second-guessing. It's obvious it's what he wants.

"Are you sure?" I hate that I'm hoping he confirms it. He pulls something out of his back pocket and places a piece of paper in my hand.

"Very. Your mom is pulling your luggage out of the craft room now so you can pack. Here's your list of what needs to be done before we leave on Saturday. I'll come pick you up for the airport at nine with a coffee in hand." He waits for me to digest the words and look back up into his eyes before he continues, "that is, if you want to come with me to Maine."

"I'd love to come with you, Marcus," I hear Tilly squeal behind me and I blush at the response. Marcus just chuckles.

"Now, go finish the layouts so we can get these grades submitted and can officially start enjoying our break." He motions to the bed where we have the photos laid out.

"Yes, sir. I'll be downstairs once we finish." I wait until he leaves the doorway before turning back to my friends, "I guess I'm going to Maine with Marcus."

Why do I keep forgetting that airports are cold? And why has Maine not learned that it is May—not February. I dig another pair of gloves out of my purse while Marcus heads to wait for our luggage. I am absolutely freezing. I knew it was probably going to be colder here than at home, but the wind and the humidity make it so much worse. When he comes back with our luggage, I am sufficiently annoyed at the cold. He just shakes his head and laughs at me.

"I promise we don't have anything outside planned for next week. And I have a huge wood burning stove in my place here so you'll be nice and warm and cozy." We begin making our way to the doors and I brace myself for the wall of cold that I know is coming.

"How old is your house? And you have your own place out here?"

"Yeah, it's about ten minutes from my mom's place and my brother's too. About the same amount of time from town too. Far enough away that there isn't a bunch of traffic outside, but close enough that I can pop out for sushi on Wednesday." He winks at me at the last one as he pulls out his phone to see where our ride is. He decided an Uber would be better for this one and then we will grab his car from the house and meet his family for dinner in a few hours. "And my house was built in the 1930s. It's on the small side, but I love all of the character of old houses. I think you'll like it. My mom went by yesterday to bring over clean linens and stock the fridge a bit. So, we should be able to get settled so you can take a nap or rest for a bit before we go to dinner."

"Old man with all of his old things," I joke with him a bit as our car pulls up and the driver gets out to help load up the bags.

"Be careful who you call old, sweet girl. I may be almost as old as your parents, but I can keep up with you just fine," he holds my gaze for an extra moment and I have to bite my bottom lip to hold back from saying something else snarky. Why was that so hot? And I guess my libido is finally waking back up. This is going to be an interesting vacation.

We end up driving through the bigger town of Camden on our way to the small town where Marcus lives. It's the perfect mix of small town and luxury homes and I know this is probably going to be an amazing spot for morning walks, if it ever warms up that is. When we get to Marcus's house, I know that I found my new happy place. There are flowers beginning to blossom outside the house, and a huge oak tree on the edge of the property. It's in a cul-de-sac neighborhood of similar homes, a few kids are playing in driveways, and a dad is mowing the lawn at a house down the street. It's quintessential Americana and very Marcus.

"This fits you," I tell him as we make our way to the front door.

"How do you figure?" He motions me inside as the lock gives way. I take in the character of the house as I do a cursory glance. All of the built-in bookshelves and cabinets are incredible.

"Um, is that an ironing board built into the wall?" I motion to a small cabinet door that is hinged in the middle. Marcus laughs and joins me next to the space I'm looking at. He pulls the door open and then lets the ironing board down.

"Welcome to a house older than your grandparents. They definitely were efficient with the space they were given." He puts the board back and fastens the door closed. I'm fascinated with the space. The ceilings aren't as high as a modern home, which means Marcus looks even taller comparatively. It's an eat-in kitchen, but the gas stove is just screaming at me to use it. And he has vintage appliances! I squeal and run over to the mint green fridge.

"How on earth did you get these?" The stove matches too and now I'm noticing the accents of the linens and tchotchkes throughout the space that complement the appliances.

"I got them at an estate sale a few years ago and have worked to maintain them. I love the classic feel of them. And I have a freezer in the canning room for extra food I may need since this doesn't hold as much as modern appliances do."

"Wait, you have a canning room?"

"Do you want to see it?"

"I think you may have just found a stupid question, Professor Williams. Yes, I want to see it!" I'm practically giddy with excitement. I can't wait to see all the things that make up this house with Marcus. I grab his hand and start pulling him toward where I hope is the canning room, and then have to stop and wait for him to lead because there are way too many doors in this hallway and I have no clue what I'm doing. He seamlessly takes over and opens a door to his right then leads us down an incredibly narrow staircase.

At the bottom is a large wood stove and it already smells amazing down here. The wood and then the oil used to maintain the stove is like a perfect memory. We walk around the stove to a back space where a larger door is already opened. There's a single light bulb hanging from the ceiling and Marcus walks over to pull the string to bring more light to the space. Shelves and shelves of dried pasta, canned goods, and empty glass jars line the walls. There are also two stand up freezers on opposite ends of the room, assumedly on different breakers.

"One for meat and one for everything else," he explains as he notices me glancing between the two. "I have a buddy who hunts each deer season, so I buy some of the meat off of him along with some chickens from one of the farmers a few blocks over."

"We are only blocks from some farms?"

"You grew up in a very agricultural area, this shouldn't surprise you," he chuckles as he grabs a jar of tomatoes from a shelf and then turns off the light, "let's head upstairs so you can get settled before we head out for dinner."

Back upstairs, he leads me to a room at the end of the hall. "My room is directly across the way if you need anything. The bathroom is the door between the basement door and my bedroom. There's just one, so we may have to coordinate shower times a bit. If it's too cold in here, let me know and I can get out a space heater. My mom brought over a few extra quilts that she's made for the bed. But, let me know."

The room is perfect. One wall is covered in bookshelves, books ranging from classic literature to children's favorites. And then a separate bookshelf with a very random conglomeration of titles. "What's the thought process behind these?" I ask him. He is so methodical with everything else and I don't get this one.

"Those are all titles from the publishing house I am on the board for. We do a little bit of everything, as you can see." I glance back at the books and then notice the logo at the bottom of each of the titles.

"This is incredible, Marcus. Are these for reading or just for looking at?"

"All books are meant to be read, Ashley. Enjoy." He smiles down at me before reaching for a title at my eye level. "Maybe start with this one." He hands me a romance novel before making his way back across the room. "I'll be in the kitchen if you need me. I need to make sure the Wi-Fi is working okay and check in with Rowan before we head out."

"Thank you, Marcus, for all of this. I appreciate you."

"You're welcome, Ashley." And then he smiles and gently closes the door behind him to give me a little bit of privacy. I could get used to being here with him.

WED   THU   FRI   SAT   SUN        DATE :

# Chapter Fifty-Seven

## ASHLEY

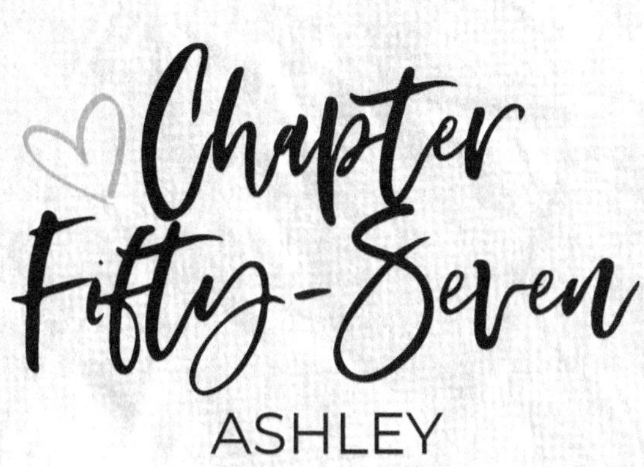

**STONEWALL KITCHEN WILD MAINE BLUEBERRY TEA**
*Social post: Classic, eclectic, vintage—I cannot get over how cute everything in this town is. #mainevacay #ceramics #vintageamericana #ontheshore*
*Image Description: Ceramic duck figurine with a bonnet on its head.*

Marcus's mom reminds me so much of my own. She may be old enough to be my grandmother, but she has all the best qualities of a mom. Her house smells like sugar cookies and she has little vintage ceramic ducks everywhere. Not in a weird way, in a cute design choice way. His brothers, Connor and Charlie, along with their wives, are incredibly welcoming. And no one makes a comment or looks down on Marcus for bringing a student home. They treat me like they would a girlfriend or colleague, not someone who is almost twenty years younger than Marcus. I thought it would be a little awkward, but it's a seamless conversation.

Stacey is married to Connor and they're expecting their first child in the fall. And then Clarissa is married to Charlie and they have a gorgeous little girl named Marie. Marcus points out that my middle name matches little Marie and then we make the connection that my grandmother and Marcus's grandmother also had the same name. It's a classic for a reason. Dinner was a fabulous chicken cutlet dish from Lynne, Marcus's mom, a salad from Clarissa, and fresh bread from Stacey. Plus a few other sides that I got to help with when we got here a bit before dinner.

When Marie starts fussing, we decide to call it a night. It's been a long day, and I need to get some rest. Tomorrow we get to stay at the house, but I'm starting to feel the fatigue of the day. Lynne gives me a hug and places a glass container in my hands once I'm bundled up to go. "A few leftovers to stick in the fridge, so you two don't have to order takeout tomorrow if you don't want to. Not sure how long until you'll be able to head to the store to get what you want for cooking or meal times. I want you to enjoy some time off, not stressing about meals." See? She seriously would be besties with my mom.

"Thank you, Lynne. Dinner was fantastic and I so appreciate this. I'm sure we'll see you soon." Marcus picks up the diaper bag for his brother and we make our way outside with the others. It's definitely easier to all leave at the same time. I'm thankful that we keep goodbyes short, because it's cold out here and I only have on one pair of gloves. I don't want to drop the Pyrex in my hands. I almost whoop out loud when the car starts as soon as we step outside.

"Please tell me you have remote start on your car and it's already warming up." I am giddy over the possibility. It's something I've wanted to get in my car since my diagnosis and it is going to be amazing if he actually has that already set up.

"Why don't you go climb in and I'll be there in a moment. I just want to make sure Charlie didn't forget anything inside for the baby. She comes with more stuff than you do." He winks at me before walking away.

"If you didn't have a magic car that warms itself I would take offense to that statement," I holler across the driveway to his back and just get a headshake in return.

We stop to get gas on the way back to the house, and I must fall asleep, because I'm woken gently when we park outside the house. "Hey, we are back home, you can crash on the couch or your bed, but let's get you inside." His voice is gentle and I just want to curl up into it. But I force myself to wake up and head inside with Marcus. I take a quick shower and get ready for bed while Marcus answers emails at the kitchen table. I peek out to say goodnight before I go back to my room. He's sipping a cup of tea and closing his laptop when I get to the end of the hallway.

"I'm going to call it a night. Water was still warm when I got out of the shower, if you take showers at night. Or if you shower in the morning, let me know. I don't want to take up too much of your space." I'm rambling, I'm tired and need to go to bed before I embarrass myself further.

"Have a good night, Ashley. I'll see you in the morning."

The stairs to the basement are so steep, and dark. I'm not sure why I neglected to find a light switch before I started coming down here, but I woke up and wanted to explore. Marcus must still be sleeping and I didn't get a chance to take a look at the canning room very closely earlier. I pad over to the room, my socked feet feeling the texture and the cold of the concrete floor. I can't tell if the ground is wet or just cold because of the temperature difference, but my socks don't look wet, so I'm assuming I'm okay.

I get to the doorway and search for the light switch before remembering that it's a string on the bulb in the middle of the room. I don't remember it being so dark down here before. I try to measure my steps until I am in the middle and start reaching for the string. It has to be around here somewhere. I feel someone up behind me, reaching up to grab the string to turn on the light and I take a deep breath when I can finally see.

"Thank you, Marcus. I hope I didn't wake you up, I just wanted to explore," I turn around to smile at him but lose all of my words when it isn't Marcus behind me…it's *him*. I can't even scream, I just collapse on the ground directly under the light.

# MARCUS

Waking up at two in the morning to blood-curdling screams is never a fun time. But when it's coming from Ashley's room and I know there shouldn't be any reason for her to be screaming like that, I'm immediately on high alert. I race into her room, not even thinking of the fact that I'm only in a pair of boxer briefs, to see what is happening.

She's thrashing in her bed, absolutely drenched in sweat, and her face is soaked in tears. A nightmare. By the looks of it, a pretty horrible one, but she's okay.

"Ashley, honey, it's okay," I talk in an even tone as I approach the bed. I don't want to set her off, but she needs to wake up. She is not making any sense with the words she's saying, but I know she is seeing *him* right now. She's scratching at her hands and arms and if I don't stop her soon, she's going to hurt herself. I sit on the bed next to her and pull her body up so I can hold her in my arms. I use some light compression to hold her close and smooth her hair down gently, all while speaking to her quietly.

Before long she settles, and I realize I had switched from trying to soothe her to quoting poetry to her from my days teaching high school literature. "Do you like daffodils or just Williams Wordsworth?" she sniffles finally when I get to the end of the piece.

"Maybe a bit of both. How are you doing?" She wraps her arms around me and just holds me tight, her breathing finally evening out with my own.

"Better. Thank you. I haven't had nightmares like that in a

while.”

"I'm sorry for grabbing you without talking to you about it first, but I didn't want you to hurt yourself.”

"It's okay. I like it." I smile, because I do too.

"What do you need, sweet girl.”

"Can I come sleep in bed with you? My sheets are kind of sweaty now and I don't want to be alone.”

"Of course." And I don't even hesitate in picking her up bridal style and carrying her across the hall to my bed.

WED  THU  FRI  SAT  SUN
DATE

# Chapter Fifty-Eight

## ASHLEY

**PUMPKIN CHAI**

*Social Post: The sound of rain falling on a window may have been replaced with the sounds hitting the shore. #asmr #prettysounds #soothingsounds #mainevacay #calm*

*Image Description: Snapshot of the beach in Maine near where I'm staying.*

Waking up being held may just be the best thing ever. Waking up knowing that I'm safe and cared for, makes it even better. Feeling arms wrapped around me and the smell of cinnamon and tobacco still lingering on his arms and his pillow—I am winning at life. By the even cadence of his breaths, I think he's still sleeping so I allow myself the space to look around the room. It's so cozy. There's a smaller wood stove in the corner of the room with an oversized armchair across from it. Bookshelves have tastefully arranged titles along with several degrees and recognition certificates on the wall. I see a variety of classics as well as some modern favorites. I even spot a few romance novels mixed in there.

I feel the arm around my waist tighten a bit and Marcus's nose moving up my neck, is he smelling me? And why do I kind of like that?

"Good morning, sweet girl," Marcus murmurs in my ear. "How did you sleep?"

"Amazing once I was in here with you. Is that weird?" I roll over so I'm on my back and can look at him better. He's propped up on one of his elbows, resting his head in his hand so he can look down at me. His other hand gently plays with my hair, now completely loose from the messy bun I went to bed with.

"Not at all. I slept really well too. I haven't had someone stay with me in this bed before," he confesses, continuing to play with my hair, and letting his eyes drift over my face, taking in everything.

"Really? No crazy summers at home for you while you are visiting? Didn't you live here full time before you went to Scotland?" I let my hands reach for his chin, the little bit of stubble prickling my fingertips. He's usually clean shaven, so I'm guessing he shaves each morning. I like the texture on my fingers and have to stop myself from thinking about feeling it elsewhere on my body.

"No crazy summers. I was busy with the publishing company and helping my mom after my dad passed away. I'm not opposed to waking up like this though," his eyes that had been exploring my face and my hair return to my eyes, and in that moment, I see nothing else, there is nothing else, just the two of us here.

"Kiss me?" I whisper. It's a request, not a statement. But I want it so badly right now. I don't move my hands, continuing their slow perusal of the shadow of a beard on his face, my eyes bouncing back and forth between the ones glancing back at me.

"I'm going to need you to say that one more time, sweet girl. I need to make sure I heard you right." His grip has gotten just a bit stronger on me, nothing too much, a steady pressure that lets me know he is touching me on purpose.

"Kiss me, Marcus." And then I move my hand to the back of his neck and let my thumb go back and forth a few times before gently drawing his head down toward mine. The first touch is tentative, like we both aren't sure what we are doing. What we should be doing. Mouths stay closed but the touches return. It's slow and gentle, but also, I feel so incredibly safe with him. I feel beautiful and seen and taken care of with Marcus. And I want to kiss him. I don't want to freak him out by pushing too far, but I need to be kissed by this man. Like, actually kissed.

So I grab the back of his head a bit harder, pressing his mouth to mine, letting me turn my head just a little so I can slip my tongue through his lips. I need him to let me in. He doesn't make me try more than once. I can tell he's letting me have the control here, letting me set the pace. But I know at any moment, I can surrender to him and what he wants, and I want to do that. Maybe not today, but soon. He playfully nips at my bottom lip and I automatically arch into him, oh, that felt good.

"Did you like that, Ash?" His voice is breathless as he moves just enough to start trailing kisses away from my lips, along my jawline to where my neck starts, before leaving a kiss there.

"Yes, you kiss pretty good for an old man." I smile up at the ceiling while reveling in the way he is worshipping my exposed skin with his lips. He abruptly stops his exploration and props his body completely over mine at that statement.

"Who are you calling old, Miss Carter?" Okay, I like that way too much.

"Well, your hair is turning a bit gray, you've got a few little wrinkles when you smile big or when you are concentrating hard on a paper or trying to hold back from scolding a student for repeating a question you've already answered," I let my fingers touch the spaces I'm referencing as I speak, seeing those lines differently now that I'm close to him. So close to him.

"And does being old mean that you're surprised that I can make you feel good?"

"Not surprised. I knew you would know how to make me feel good."

"You knew, huh? What else did you know?"

"I knew that I was hoping I'd get to kiss you on this trip. And that I was hoping you would want to kiss me too." My voice is shy with my confession. How can I go from having a professor completely cross the line with me just a few months ago to wanting another one to absolutely claim me as his own? He must see my flickering emotions in the moments I'm quiet because he rolls onto to his back and positions me so I'm cradled in his arms, holding me close.

"I'm not *him*, Ashley. I have no intention of breaking your trust or your friendship. Yes, I am your professor when we are on campus. But I would be lying if I said I didn't want to explore more with you. Getting to know you since the beginning of this year was something I didn't know I needed. And I don't want to lose you. I am happy to take this as slow as you need and want to. But I need to tell you, I like spending time with you. I like you, Ashley. And I would love to explore a relationship with you. At your pace. On your terms." I grip him tight as his arm gently rubs up and down my back in a soothing gesture while he talks.

Even with how insanely broken I feel, he wants me? It feels so perfect here in his arms. And I don't feel guilty for it. I feel taken care of. He isn't trying to wield his position as a manipulation like Professor Johnson did. This is different. He is different. I am different now too. I may be more guarded, but he has been by my side every day for the last four and a half months. Every day. Being just what I needed – there, present, consistent, steady. I just lay in his arms for a few more minutes before I feel a gentle kiss on my forehead.

"What do you want to do today, Ash?"

"Can we go explore the town a bit?"

"Do you want to go see the lighthouse?"

I spin around so fast to look at him to confirm what I just heard. "A lighthouse? Like we can actually go see a real one?"

He smiles at me before replying, "We can actually go in it and see the whole thing if you want."

"Um, that's an absolute 'yes' from me. Let's go!" I jump off the bed and race to my room to get dressed. It's still kind of chilly out so I wear a pair of jeans and a cute tee under an oversized sweater. Layers are my go-to wardrobe now, and I like how I can change it from casual to office ready with just a few adjustments. My hair is up in a ponytail so it won't get in my face with the wind by the water. I meet Marcus a few minutes later in the kitchen. He is looking all kinds of classically handsome in his dark wash jeans, pullover blue sweater, and the white tee he's layered under it visible with the zipper pulled down just a bit.

"Ready to go?" he asks as he passes me a travel mug.

I take a quick sip before doing a little happy dance. "You made me coffee?"

He just laughs. "I may not drink it, but you do. And I know how you like it. We'll grab breakfast in town, but I wanted you to have something to sip on before we get there." He helps me with my jacket and then we are on our way to go explore the little town that Marcus calls home.

Okay so, lighthouses are way bigger than I thought they were. Which is kind of silly to think about when you realize that their light had to keep an entire harbor safe. But they're massive! And built so well. The caretaker of this one gave me a brief history lesson of the lighthouses along the Northeast coast. So many of them are still standing after literally hundreds of years. The caretakers had to live in them and were responsible for use and upkeep. They may not be used practically anymore, or not much anyway, but they still show a big piece of coastal history.

Marcus just smiled and held my coat once I started warming up as I looked through the pictures and documents at the lighthouse. It is almost a mini museum now, and it was so fascinating to see. Downtown was no different. A mix of new businesses and buildings that were built in the 1800s dotted the town. I thought I loved old architecture, but after seeing it, I know I love it. Especially the churches and schools. The attention to detail and the fact that they are still standing is amazing. I take way too many pictures and send them to my mom and to my group chat with Tilly, Sasha, and Kylie. My photo app is going to look like a digital memory book of today and I can't wait to go through them later.

By the time we head back to the house, I have a small bag of goodies from several shops. And there's about five paper sacks in the back of the car from the grocery store. It may only be May, but there are already a few things from local farmers and families. Fresh jelly, jams, and salsas, as well as local sausage and eggs make up several of our purchases.

"Beginning in June, there will be a farmer's market set up downtown. And there will be even more to choose from," Marcus lets me know as we put the groceries away in the kitchen.

"Really? Are we going to be able to go?" I so badly want to go. I love farmers markets.

"We should be able to make that happen. We are set to go back to Colorado June 20th. So the market should be up and running for at least a week or two before we leave."

"Perfect. Thanks again for today, that was amazing." I go up on my tiptoes to brush a kiss on his cheek. He didn't shave this morning so I let my fingers play with the stubble on his jaw line as I stand in front of him.

"Sorry, I don't usually shave when I'm home. No classes or meetings, so I give my face a rest."

"Don't apologize, I kinda like it." I smile up at him and then have to force back a yawn.

"I hope that was for you just needing some rest and not that I'm already boring you." He smirks down at me and I laugh back at him.

"I think I may need a nap before we tackle dinner. It's been a long few days."

"Well, how about you go take a little nap and I'll get the stove going so the house stays warm. It's supposed to get a little cold tonight and I want to get ahead of it. Then we can figure out dinner when you get up."

"Sounds good. Don't have too much fun without me?"

"Never."

And I head to his room to take a nap—in his sheets that smell like the two of us, like home.

Ashley

# Chapter Fifty-Nine

## MARCUS

### CHERRY EARL GREY MILK TEA

*Social post: Being home automatically helps me transition to a slower pace and a calmer mindset. This month is needed, but it's going to go by way too fast. #maine #coastalliving #vacation #summervacation*
*Image Description: Photo of the chairs on the porch facing the water.*

Dinner has been done for fifteen minutes, but I don't want to wake her up. She's resting peacefully, and seeing her at rest, not worrying about anything, it may be my new favorite thing to see. I shift my feet and the old wooden boards of the floor let out a creak. She begins to stir and I smile at her when she notices me standing in the doorway.

"Didn't want to sleep in your room?" I tease her a little.

"It smells like us in here, I kind of like it." She smiles sleepily back at me. Her ponytail has come loose, and her hair is absolutely everywhere. She hadn't been wearing much makeup today, but she was wearing some, and now her mascara is smudged a bit on her face. She is perfect. "What's that smile for?"

"You are beautiful. And I like having you in my bed," I state matter-of-factly. I have my hands resting in my pants pockets because we really need to go eat dinner. And I don't want to get distracted by thinking of eating something else in my bed. And now that's where my mind is. I start naming 19th century American poets while I wait for her to get up.

"Well, I like being in your bed." She takes a quick pause before continuing, "What smells so insanely good?"

"Dinner. I'll go get things plated up and meet you out there in a minute." I'm thankful for the brief reprieve to get a handle on myself while I bowl up the stew. It's a simple dish my grandmother used to make with whatever was handy—meat, vegetables, tomatoes—using up food before it went bad. She had called it *chambot*, but I have since learned that the proper Italian name is *ciambotta*. It's a comfort meal for me and makes for incredible leftovers too. I pour myself a glass of red wine and then one for Ashley as well. Only to remember that she isn't twenty-one yet and I probably shouldn't be serving her alcohol.

What the heck am I doing with a woman that isn't even twenty-one? And a student at that? I stare out the back window over my sink, holding the wine in my hands, trying to decide what to do, when I hear her footsteps coming down the hall. I cannot get over how gorgeous she is, and I know my face doesn't hide the admiration I have for her.

"I poured us wine and then realized I wasn't sure if you drank yet or not," I start to tell her.

She comes over and rests her hand on mine before she finishes my sentence for me. "And then you started freaking yourself out because of the age difference."

I nod at her and reply with a simple, "Yeah."

She smiles at me knowingly and then shocks me with her response, this woman. "I was drugged with a soda at a party last year. Since then, I have been incredibly wary with what I drink. I trust you, but I don't like the feeling of not being in control of my thoughts or my body. So, I don't drink alcohol. That may change when I'm older and have healed from all the trauma that 'he who will not be named' left me with. But for now, I will politely decline. And, before you freak out more, I am not concerned with the age difference at all. Actually, I think I kind of like it. And I don't want you second-guessing this. It happened naturally. We aren't at school right now. And we are both consenting adults. I have one more year until I graduate. I want to do this with you, Marcus. As long as you still want to do this with me." Her eyes are hopeful as she says the last bit. She isn't doubting me, more like she is questioning her own words, unsure if she overstepped.

I set the wine bottle on the counter and then pour the wine from both glasses down the sink before I turn and hold both of her hands in my own. Her hands fit perfectly in my own and I love that her fingertips begin to warm in my hands. "I want to do this with you, Ashley. So much. If this ends up being something we want to pursue after the summer is over, we will have to make some adjustments on campus. But I want you. And if you are choosing to be alcohol free, I will back you in that for as long as you want to—whether it's until you're twenty-five or forever. I'm all yours, sweet girl." Her eyes glisten with emotion and I catch the tear with my lips, placing a kiss on her now makeup-free cheeks.

It seems to be the reassurance she needs at the moment, because she gives me a smile and then we are at the table enjoying dinner and the sounds of the water hitting the rocks outside the house.

Darkness falls early, but the warmth from the wood stove in my room and the main one downstairs help keep the house at a comfortable temperature. For me anyways, Ashley is bundled up and has apparently found my old college hoodies because she's wearing one on top of her leggings. I had laughed a little when she came out of the bathroom after her shower. I had been in my room, putting away a few books on my shelves that had arrived this afternoon, when she walked in to plug her phone in next to the bed.

"Are you sleeping in here tonight?" I ask her hopefully.

"Where else would I sleep?" She's sassy tonight. I have a feeling this is how Ashley was before everything happened. She is so sure of herself and what she wants. And I love that in this moment, she wants to be with me.

"Did you find something you liked in the closet?" I ask as I plug in my own phone, silencing the ringer—no one is going to need me tonight.

"Yep," she lets the 'p' pop and it's the cutest thing ever, "and I don't think you're getting it back. It's warm and cozy and it smells like your cologne."

"Whatever you want, sweet girl." I sit on the end of the bed, watching her peruse the titles on my bookshelf. She brings up one hand to her mouth and puts the cuff of the sweatshirt between her teeth. That may just be the cutest nervous habit and I smile at her reaction while she reads the titles, head tilted to get a better look at the options before her. She finally chooses one and turns to look at me, looking at her, and smiles at me. Gripping her selection to her chest, she hugs it close, so I can't see which one she chose.

"Anything I want?" she taunts me with the question. She knows what she wants, I just haven't been made aware of it yet.

"Within reason," I answer back to her, placing my hands on her hips as she settles between my legs.

"So, if I wanted to read a scene out of this book," she pauses to show me the title—one of the steamiest romance novels we've released recently: masks, primal play; murder mystery—a good one, but not what I was expecting from her right now, "and act it out with you, you'd be okay with that?" She swishes her hips in a mini turn, playing into the cuteness she knows she is exuding right now.

"That one may be a bit much for our first time 'playing' together, but if that's what you want, I'm open to trying." I let my hands wander from her hips to her thighs and back up again, enjoying her curves under my touch.

"Is there something that you enjoy when you 'play' with someone in your bed, Professor Williams?" Oh, we are shifting a bit, this could be fun. I bite the inside of my cheek to avoid grinning like a teenager. I'm her professor here. The mature one. The one in charge.

"There may be a few things that I enjoy. If you're up for a hands-on lesson with me, Miss Carter," I let the offer sit there a moment, wanting to see where she takes this.

"Teach me?" She sets the book on the bed next to me. "Teach me what you like, Professor."

"You're my student, I am fifteen years older than you, Miss Carter. Once I have you in my bed like that, it's going to be very hard to walk away. Are you okay with that?" I need to give her this out—with or without the game we are playing, she needs to know she has a choice.

"I am a fully consenting adult and I know what I'm asking for, Marcus." She steps back half a step from me and places her hands on my shoulders, angling her body a little so her face is closer to mine. "I want this. I want you."

"Are you sure?" Last chance. I know at any point the PTSD may trigger and I will stop this game we are playing, but I need her words now so I can fully enjoy the process of making her feel good. Of making her mine. Because she wants to be. Because she wants me. I need those words.

"I'm sure. Teach me, Professor Williams. I'm all yours." And with that she places her hands at the hem of her sweatshirt and pulls it over her head, leaving her in a simple pink camisole, obviously without a bra because I can clearly make out her hardened nipples, a darker shade than her top, aching for my fingers, my mouth.

My hands are back on her hips and I allow my thumbs to brush under the hem of her camisole to feel the warmth of her skin. She is so smooth. And the breath she inhales tells me that is enjoying the hint of a touch as much as I am.

"I want to make you feel good, Miss Carter, can I do that?"

She nods down at me as I place a kiss on her belly, over her camisole, and then pull it up just enough to expose a few inches of skin so I can kiss her skin there.

"Words, Miss Carter," I scold her. "One day, we will play without words, but right now, I need your words, sweet girl."

"Please. I want you to make me feel good. For a little while, I don't want to think. I just want to be here with you. I want to be yours, Marcus. Please. Please make me yours," the pleading in her voice is intense and all I want to do is help her turn her brain off for a little while and focus on how good she can feel. I know I can answer that request. I stand up and face my body to hers, cupping her cheek in my hand, and tilting it up so she is looking in my eyes.

"At any moment, if you are uncomfortable, or are getting overwhelmed, please tell me. Am I right in that this is the first time you've been with someone since everything happened earlier this year?"

"Yes," she whispers to me.

"I will go slow, but I don't know where your lines are yet or what potentially will trigger you. So I need you to talk to me. And I need you to understand that if we don't get very far tonight, I'm willing to wait. And you aren't going to disappoint me. Okay?"

"Okay, I think probably nothing with me on my stomach with your full body weight on my back, I can't think of anything else, but that's something I still have nightmares about."

"Thank you for trusting me with that. Can I kiss you now?"

"You better." There's that sassiness again. I lean down to seal my mouth over hers, waiting until she is breathless and fully focused on my lips before I firmly pick her up and lightly toss her onto my bed. She giggles in response and then zeros in on my body as I pull my T-shirt off over my head. I may be thirty-five, but I run almost every day. And yes, I do yoga at home on the weekends. I take care of my body. And it's obvious that she sees just how much effort I put into taking care of myself. She bites her bottom lip and I chuckle at the response.

"See something you like?" I unlatch my belt and slowly pull it out of the loops. I'm not sure if the sound would be triggering, so I take it slow, setting the belt on the floor next to the bed.

"I knew you were hot, but seeing you right now, you're definitely giving off all kinds of Daddy vibes." I unbutton my slacks and take those off as well, setting them on the end of the bed, before I begin crawling up to be closer to her.

"Daddy vibes? And you're sure you mean that in the 'you're

hot' way and not 'you're so old' way right?" I tease her as I begin placing kisses around her exposed collarbone and up her neck. Goosebumps break out where my lips have touched and I love how responsive she is.

"Definitely in the 'you're hot' way. Not sure how I feel about calling you Daddy in bed, but I may be convinced to do the whole professor/student thing if you ask nicely."

"Is that something you want to do?"

"Maybe one day. Right now, I just want it to be Ashley and Marcus. No games. No extras. Just us."

"I can do that, Ashley." I begin kissing her again, delving into her mouth and enjoying the way her body squirms under my own. I'm about a foot taller than her, and it's enough for me to be able to touch every part of her with myself. When she begins arching her hips into me, I know she is looking for more. I position my thigh in between her legs, giving her something to grind up against.

"Take what you need, Princess. I'll have you coming on my cock soon but let me see you grind on my leg." My voice is husky and my cock is so hard, I know if she touched it right now, I would come in my underwear, and that just won't do. I move my mouth down to her breast, teasing her hardened nipple with my tongue, my teeth, using my other hand to anchor my body, allowing myself to put my pressure on her clit where she needs it. I know she's close because her head tips back and her entire body tenses.

"Let go for me, Ashley. I've got you, let go." And she does. And it's the most incredible thing I've ever seen.

As she comes down from the high, the tears that had been in her eyes track down her face. I quickly move off of her body, but don't move far, waiting to see what she needs from me. "What do you need, pretty girl? I'm right here." I let my hands trail up and down her arm, letting her know I am here, giving her the steady touch without crowding her.

"That was so perfect, and I so want more, but I was not expecting that level of emotional release. Is it okay if you just hold me for a little while? And we can try again tomorrow?" I settle a kiss on her forehead and hold her close.

"I would love to hold you, do you want to call it a night and get under the blankets or go watch a movie?" I want to give her some options so she still feels in control of what's happening. PTSD and intimacy after trauma shows up differently for everyone. And Ashley needs structure and consistency. This is a brand new situation for her, and I want to give her the freedom to explore without overwhelming too much.

"Movie, please. I think a reset would be good."

"You got it, Ashley. Thank you for communicating that with me."

She just smiles at me before kissing my cheek and jumping off the bed, putting my hoodie back on and then skipping to the main room of the house. And I very happily go after her.

Ashley

# Chapter Sixty

## ASHLEY

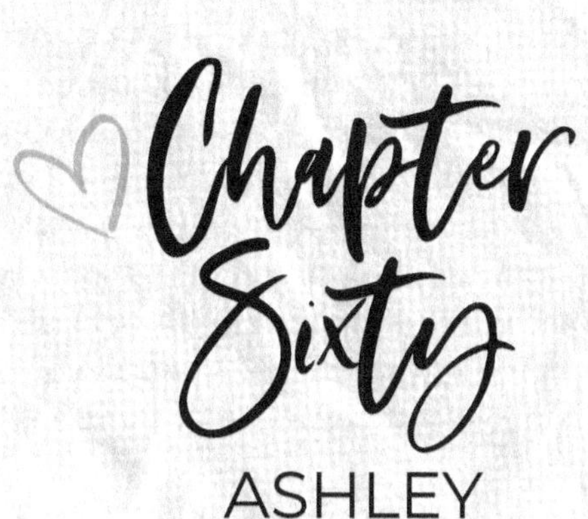

### GINGER PEACH TEA

*Social Post: Sometimes it's the littlest things that let you know that someone is thinking of you. And in those moments, everything is enough. #thelittlethings #seashellsandsunshine #mainevacay #beachvibes*
*Image Description: Seashells in the sand.*

Maine in early summer may just be my favorite thing ever. It's a small town, so things are quiet. We go on walks along the beach in the mornings, and yes, it's insanely cold with the wind coming off the water, but the views are incredible. And every morning, I've found a pretty shell to give to him and he finds one to give to me. It's become a little way to say, "I see you and I'm here." And while I haven't been ready to try having sex again, knowing he's okay with growing this type of closeness has been amazing.

I've been able to sit on the porch and watch sunsets while

reading a book on the outdoor couch next to Marcus. We've been here for a week, and I don't ever want to leave. But then Marcus reminds me of what winter is like here, and I firmly told him that we can only be here from April-September. The other months we need to live somewhere else. He just laughed at me for planning out our lives together already. But it doesn't feel silly to me. I'm his.

It's the first time I've thought about myself with someone else since the incident online started. That's why I had gotten the "I am Mine" tattoo. I needed to remind myself that I belonged to myself. I got to control the narrative. I got to control who was in my life and who I gave my time, energy, and space to. And now, I want to give that to him. Probably because I know he will treat it well. He treats me well. He cares for me in a way that I didn't know was possible. It's that storybook and fairytale kind of magic you hear about when they fall in love at first sight, experience true love's kiss, and then get married in the middle of the woods with all of the animals in attendance.

I'm not ready to say I love him. And I know it wasn't overnight. It's been a process. But he saw me at my literal worst—mentally, emotionally, and physically. He saw me get better. He saw me get back to myself. And grow into the new version of Ashley. The one that went through literal nightmares and is now enjoying her own kind of fairytale. Her knight in shining armor just happens to also be her professor. But he's mine. And I'm his.

Memorial Day weekend in a small town is a big deal. And I am not disappointed by all of the activity leading up to the holiday. Marcus let me know that this is the official start to any tourist activity that may happen, and to expect some more people coming into town the next two weeks that we are here. Part of me hates that we have an end date on our time here. It's been wonderful. I've gotten to get a peek into the behind the scenes work that Marcus does with the publishing company—both here in Maine and in the

UK. We are halfway through our time here, and I already can't wait to come back.

Sitting on the porch, with my book and my morning cup of coffee, I take in the beauty of the moment. It really is absolutely beautiful here. I can hear the giggles of a family playing on the beach just outside of my line of sight. The waves breaking on the rocks provide a cadence I know I could fall asleep to. And because of the breeze from the water, the bug activity is minimal. The hydrangeas will be blooming soon and those should attract some butterflies and honeybees. And I can't wait to see those.

"Are you up for a little adventure this afternoon?" Marcus pokes his head out of the open sliding glass door to ask me and I grin up at him.

"What kind of adventure?" I close my book and stand to head inside with him.

"Do you want to see the area from a different view?"

"Are you going to take me for a helicopter ride, Professor?"

"Would you like that?"

I literally squeal before jumping up to place a kiss on his lips. "I would love that! When do we need to leave the house?"

"You've got a few hours, I need to finalize the reservation. I wanted to confirm with you before I booked the spot. I wasn't sure about your comfort level in a smaller aircraft."

"Have I told you today how much I appreciate you?" I make my way to the bedroom to begin figuring out what I'm going to wear to a helicopter date.

"Not yet, but you don't have to." He comes up behind me, resting his chin on my shoulder and his arms around my waist. I love it when he holds me. I haven't been able to do much in the way of sex or physical intimacy yet, I get triggered and end up crying in his arms. But I love how he holds me. And I love that he doesn't push me or my comfort level. I know he's going to be ready for me when I'm ready for him. And it's going to be amazing once my body finally decides to cooperate.

"What do I need to wear for this?" I rest my hands on top of his, anchoring myself to this moment.

"Probably something warm. It'll get windy and a little cold. The sides are closed off, but it's going to be cold. So, plan for layers on your hands and feet, and maybe the lap blanket on the chair in the main room too. I've got your hand warmers plugged in and charging too." He kisses the top of my head and then slowly pulls away. "I need to go send a few emails and then we can get ready to go." He winks at me and heads out to the main part of the house. He doesn't have a full office here, choosing instead to utilize the spaces in his room, the kitchen, and main living area, as well as the porch for work. The publishing house has extra office spaces that he can use when he's here if he wants, but he's chosen to do the little work tasks from the house since we've been here.

When I head back into the kitchen, extra socks and gloves in hand, I can tell Marcus's mood has shifted. He's staring at his laptop, reading glasses on, lines on his forehead showing his frustration. I set my things down on the edge of the table and then sit next to him, where I can see his face and not the screen. I want him to look at me and tell me what's going on.

"Everything okay?" I prod him a little bit.

"Not great. There's a couple things I just got answers to and they weren't exactly what I wanted to hear." He gently closes his laptop and then puts his glasses on the lid of the device. Looking up at me, I know he's about to break my heart, and I brace myself for what's about to come.

Ashley

# Chapter Sixty-One

## MARCUS

**BLUEBERRY PEACH GREEN TEA LEMONADE**

*Social Post: Back in another place that brings me joy. I never get tired of the views from the other side of this glass. #helicopter #flymaine #flying #helicopterpilot*

*Image Description: Controls and front windshield of a helicopter, looking out onto the tarmac.*

Could this have waited until after the helicopter ride? Absolutely. But that isn't fair to Ashley. She deserves to be treated like the woman she is. And I will not be accused of keeping anything from the woman I know I'm going to spend the rest of my life with. I take a deep breath and hold her hand before I dive into the details of the emails I just opened.

"So first, everyone back home is fine. I don't want you stressing over that." I can practically see the weight being lifted from her shoulders. Yeah, my mind would have gone there too with my demeanor when she first came out here.

"The trial has been moved up for the initial hearing. So, if you want to be there for that, we need to leave Monday. I will go with you if that's what you want to do, or we can stay here for the scheduled time. But the hearing is going to be on Tuesday and I want you to have the option to be there if you would like." I give her a moment to digest that. Knowing that was the easier of two pieces of news I had to share with her today.

"I think I want to go back. I love being here with you, and I was serious when I said that I expect to make summers out here a thing after graduation, because I love everything about this place. And I may change my mind on Tuesday and not go into the courtroom, but I want to give myself that choice." I nod and smile at her.

"You are so incredibly strong, I hope you know that. I'll get the return flights booked once we finish going over everything here."

"What else is going on?" She thought that was it. And now I feel horrible all over again.

"I got one more email that we need to talk about...from the university."

"The university? What's going on?" She grips my hand tighter and I can tell she's already overthinking. I don't want to make her wait before I tell her this so I dive right into it.

"The admin staff was lenient with the time we spent off campus because of everything you had gone through and how I was working with you on TA responsibilities as well as helping you with your core classes. But someone must have passed along that we are vacationing together right now. I got an email with the policies and procedures highlighting that professors and students are not to be in a romantic relationship while the professor is employed by the university. They've said that things need to be broken off until you graduate or I need to step down while you are a student. And they need to know our decision before we get back from our trip. I have meetings to begin preparing for the new semester the first week of July, so we have until then to finalize everything. And I wanted to give you the details and the time to think through this."

The tears in her eyes mirror my own. This is not how this was supposed to go. I thought we would be able to downplay our closeness while on campus, but that I could continue seeing her off campus. I was wrong.

"So, either we break up for a year or you lose your job?" she repeats what I just told her in the simplest way possible. Accurate, but simple.

"Yes."

She sits back and takes a deep breath before leveling her eyes on my own.

"I can wait."

"Excuse me?"

"I can wait for you. It's less than a year. We will both be busy with classes and I'm sure there's another professor I can TA for these last two semesters. We start transitioning now into our professional roles. And then graduation happens and we pick up right where we left off."

This woman amazes me. "Or I can resign my position and work remotely for another university until you graduate." She practically cuts me off with her response.

"Absolutely not. You are not putting your career on hold for me. We are literally months away from me having a degree and a full time position with Sasha. You are approaching milestones to be able to share this mentorship program with other universities and majors. It's not forever, it's just a few months. It gives me some more time to focus on healing and therapy and then we get to spend forever together."

"Are you sure about this, Ashley? I promise I will wait for you and there won't be anyone else. And I selfishly want to ask the same of you but feel awful for it."

"There won't be anyone else, Marcus. You're it. I love you. And I have no problems avoiding frat boys on campus because I get to come home to you in just a few months."

"No one else?"

"No one else."

"Good, because I'm the man for you." She comes to sit on my lap and kisses me deeply, pouring everything she has into the kiss, into my soul. I am going to miss holding her so much. I only have two more nights where she can sleep in my bed before we have to put a huge pause on our relationship.

"This might just kill me, Marcus." She holds me tight and whispers into my neck as she begins crying softly.

"We can do this, Princess. You've been through hell and back. We can survive a few months of waiting. Can I take you on an amazing last date in the sky now though?" She moves her head to look up into my eyes.

"I would love that."

Marcus

# Chapter Sixty-Two

## ASHLEY

**BUTTERBEER LATTE**

*Social Post: About to close this chapter of my life and begin another one. Thanks for the degree CSU. #csugrad #graduationday #prettyinpink #pinkeveryday #sassyashleysmiles*

*Image Description: Graduation cap laying on top of my pink dress on my bed.*

If you would have told me at the beginning of my college career that I would be excited about the possibilities and promises after graduation, I probably would have believed you. If you would have told me that I would be doing something related to makeup, skincare, and supporting other women-owned businesses, I would have believed that too. But if you would have told me I would deal with a stalker, both virtually and in person, who would kidnap me and attempt to assault me, I would have told you that you were crazy. If you would have told me it was one of my professors, I would have asked what book you were reading. And if you would have said that I would fall in love with a different professor but have to wait to be with him until after graduation, I would have asked for the book title so I could read it too. I never would have thought that this would be my life. But here we are.

It's a beautiful Sunday morning in northern Colorado and I'm wearing a beautiful pink dress that showed up in my closet this week. I know it's from Marcus, even though we haven't been able to talk more than a "hello" in the hallway or a few sentences on a feedback form over the last eight months. He still found ways to let me know he was waiting for me, and I found ways to let him know as well. Seashells became our quiet "I love you" this year. I have a pair of earrings that are silver little conch shell studs and I wear them almost every day. A charm bracelet that started out as a simple silver chain is now full of charms—shells, a lighthouse, a lipstick charm, a book, more shells, and a pair of gloves. I got a new charm on the first of every month. Another month that we had completed on our pause. Another month closer to being together.

I have one more milestone and then I can officially and fully be with Marcus again. And my therapist has been working overtime with me to help me get in the right headspace. He's waited for me too. And Professor Johnson took way too much from me. I won't let him take any more. And with his jail sentence having him behind bars for the next twenty years, I won't give him any more of my mental space either. I am hours away from walking across that platform, hours away from being back in Marcus's arms, and a day away from walking into my office at Pink Every Day as Head of Product Development.

A light knock comes on my door and I turn to see Sasha and Tilly waiting for me. "You ready for this?" Tilly beams as she asks me. I smile and then quickly look up to avoid the tears spilling down my face and smudging my makeup.

"Don't you have a dance competition to get to?" I ask Tilly. She's taken up West Coast Swing Dancing with Kylie since they took that class over a year ago together. Kylie has started competing and is thoroughly enjoying herself. There's a local competition happening this weekend and I'm pretty sure Tilly was supposed to compete too.

"Not this time around. Kylie doesn't have her performance scheduled until tonight, and it's only a two-hour drive, so Sasha, Matt, and I will head down after the graduation. Since I'm guessing you will be all kinds of occupied tonight." She winks at me and then moves to my back to help me with my zipper.

"Literally LOL right now." But I smile at her over my shoulder. She isn't wrong.

"Are you staying at his place tonight?" Sasha asks as she glances at my overnight bag sitting on my bed and then gives me a knowing grin.

"He actually got us dinner reservations and a hotel for tonight. My boss was a meanie and I have to be at the office for my big girl job at nine tomorrow morning. So, I do need to try to get some sleep tonight." I stick my tongue out at her. She had offered to give me the week off to just be able to spend time with Marcus, but I want to find my new normal as quickly as possible. And with October being our busiest month as a company, June and July are insanely heavy prep months. I have two weeks to get everything ready that I can before we have to start production of our October campaigns and collaborations. And I can't wait!

Tilly comes around with my lip gloss in hand which promptly goes into the secret pocket of my dress. "Let's go get you graduated, beautiful."

It feels like hours later when I'm standing on the grass, diploma in hand, posing for pictures. Rowan and Tilly are giving the group of us that graduated ridiculous prompts so I have no clue if any of these will be anything but us laughing at each other. Sam, myself, and Brock are posing for one last group shot when my parents come over. We do the obligatory family photos, and I'm reminded again how insanely grateful I am for their support. My brother and his fiancé, Sasha, join us for some of them too. Matt brought me in contact with Sasha and she is now one of my best friends and technically, my boss. But I'll get to call her my sister soon enough.

I hand off my flowers to my mom, giving her another deep hug. "Thank you again for helping make this happen. I know my college journey wasn't easy and you had to watch a lot of hurt. But you were always there for me, and I can't thank you enough for helping me get here." She squeezes me tight before resting her hands on my shoulders to push me back a bit, making eye contact with me.

"You are the strongest person I know, Ashley. Now you get to show everyone else the amazing person that you are." My dad comes up behind her with my bag in hand, "I'm guessing you put this in the car for a reason," he prompts and I can't help the blush that creeps up my cheeks.

"Yes, sir, she's going to be needing that." I know it's him before I even turn around, but I love seeing his hand extend to shake my dad's hand and then take the bag from him. And then I'm in Marcus's arms, being kissed like a proper lady in a mid-century romance novel, graduation program being held to cover our faces from my family while he dips me low and kisses me deeply.

"I've missed doing that so much, Princess." He smiles down at me and I can't help placing my hands on his chest and then his face.

"You didn't shave today," I whisper to him, "I like it."

"Or yesterday. Wanted to get a jump start on the summer beard. Are you ready to head out?" He offers me his arm and I gladly accept. I know this isn't saying goodbye to my family, but it feels like a big moment, so I glance over my shoulder to wave to them as we make our way to his waiting car.

I don't remember what restaurant we went to or what I ordered for dinner. I don't remember the waiter's name or how long we had to wait for the check. I remember getting to hold hands with the love of my life, getting to look into his eyes for as long as I wanted without worrying about what others would say. Marcus jokes about the tattoo I chose for this year, a simple seashell on the inside of my pointer finger on my right hand. So I can see it every time I pick up a pen, a makeup brush, or my lipstick. It's my reminder that he loves me. That I'm his.

"Can I give you something before we head out for the night?" Marcus asks me as he signs the check and then turns his attention back on me.

"Of course, I like presents," I practically beam up at him. I am so ready to start my forever with this man. I am not expecting the jewelry box he pulls out of the inside of his suit coat. Not small like a ring box, bigger like a bracelet or necklace. I take the dark blue velvet box from him and wait for his nod before I open it up. Inside, I find the most beautiful pearl bracelet. They're pink pearls. And they match my dress perfectly, because of course it does.

"Oh, Marcus, this is stunning!" I gasp as I pull the string out of the box. "Can you help me put it on?" I give him the bracelet and my left wrist so he can put them on me.

"Last summer, we started giving each other shells as a sign of our relationship. A way to say, 'I'm thinking of you,' 'I love you,' and 'I can't wait for forever.' Pearls are another beautiful thing that can be found in the ocean. They don't wash up easily for anyone to grab, they have to be worked for. And to find enough that go together to create a piece like this," he pauses to place a kiss on my wrist, "takes many hours, days, and even weeks to create. We have been through a year of waiting to be together and that was after months and months of healing and progress being made after the attack. I want you to have a daily reminder of the beauty I see in you and the work I am willing to put in to be by your side for the rest of our forever." I have to choke back a sob because that was beyond beautiful.

I stand and come around the table to hug him and hold him close, "I love you so much, Marcus. And I really, really hope you wrote that down somewhere so I can read it again because that was beautiful." He rests his thumb under my chin and then lifts it so I can make eye contact with him.

"Of course, I wrote it down. Are you ready to go?"

"Now that's a silly question." I reach for my cardigan on the back of the chair and practically pull him out of the restaurant with me.

WED    THU    FRI    SAT    SUN         DATE

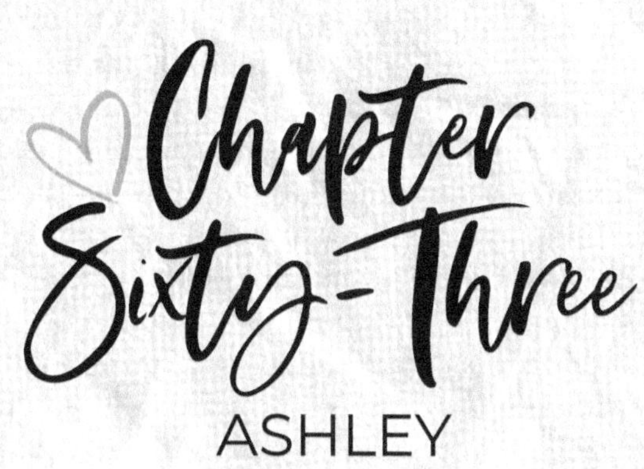

# Chapter Sixty-Three

## ASHLEY

**POMEGRANATE RASPBERRY TEA**

*Social Post: Head of Product Development has a nice ring to it.
#pinkeveryday #corporatebarbie #sassyashleysmiles*

*Image Description: Name and title placard on the door to my office
at Pink Every Day*

I'm kissing Marcus before we even fully make it into the hotel room. My shoes are off as the door latches closed and I grab his hand to come with me to the bed. My cardigan and his jacket find a home on the chair next to the bed and his tie follows. Marcus comes next to me, glancing over my face like he's trying to memorize the lines that are there. Every freckle. Every spot. He moves my hair gently to expose the back of my neck and then my zipper is being slowly pulled down. Part of me loves that he's taking this slow and part of me wants nothing more than for him to rip my dress off and ravage me. Respectfully, of course.

He must sense my lack of patience, because as my dress falls to the floor, he traces his hands up the sides of my waist until he's cupping my breasts, holding their weight in his hands. "Can I see you, Ashley?" he whispers in my ear before placing a gentle kiss just below the spot.

"Yes, please." I whimper. Yes, whimper. I need this man so badly right now.

He removes his hands just for a moment so he can undo my bra. And I'm not even sure when he removed his shirt, but I can feel his bare skin against my back and it is the best feeling ever. His solid build behind my own. His hands resume their exploration of my breasts, feeling, teasing, kneading. And I know I'm already so wet for him. "I need more, Marcus, please." I tilt my head back so it's resting against his shoulder and all I want is to feel his body on mine all night long.

Before I realize what's happening, he's spun me around and lifted me off of the ground, carrying me the few steps to the bed. His slacks are pulled down and lain on top of the rest of our clothes and then we are both just in our underwear. We make eye contact as we both rid ourselves of the cotton and I finally get a good look at what he's been hiding in those perfect pants of his. The head of his cock is so hard, it's already almost purple, and I can see the moisture glistening on the tip. I quickly sit up and maneuver closer to him.

"May I?" I look up at him, standing there at the end of the bed. I reach out to touch his hip then run my fingers so they cup his balls, when he finally grunts out a yes, my hand goes to his throbbing cock and I grip him. I draw my hand up once, twice, and then I let myself taste what he's already leaking. His hand immediately goes to my hair, whether to hold me still or control the pace, I don't know. But his grip is steadying while I explore as much of him as I can. I can't quite take all of him into my mouth before I'm gagging, but it's something to work toward. As I begin to suck and am rewarded with a little more of a taste of him, he pulls me back gently.

"The first time I come with you is going to be in that beautiful space between your legs, sweet girl, not down your throat. You can explore that more later." I smirk up at him, trying to decide how much of a brat I want to be tonight. And then decide that I really don't want to wait much longer, I need him inside of me. "I apologize in advance how fast this first time might be," he whispers as he begins crawling up my body, placing kisses along the way. I'm not sure when he grabbed a condom, but he rests it on the bed next to me as he begins exploring my mouth with his own. Using the time to trail his hand up and down my body.

Feeling his hands on me is incredible. And I'm glad we took this year to focus on me getting better so I can be with him without any triggers popping up. At least not yet. His fingers keep moving down until they reach my thighs and then they move inward. I gasp as he touches around my opening, knowing he's finding me wet. I am literally aching for this man. I arch into his touch, desperate for more. And he doesn't make me wait. Two fingers slide into me as he presses the heel of his hand into my clit. The steady pressure keeps me anchored as he continues his worship of my body. It feels like minutes but it might only be seconds until I explode underneath him. The silent cry that leaves my mouth is quickly swallowed by his kiss and then the fingers that had just brought me to pleasure.

I'm surprised at the taste, but then moan into his mouth as he removes his fingers and resumes kissing me. "I can't wait to taste you directly from in between your legs, Ashley. But right now, I need to be inside you. How do you want to do this?" He's still so gentle with me.

"Can we try with you on top? And then if something happens, we can move, but I really want you in control of this."

"Are you sure?"

"Absolutely. Please, I need to feel you." I fumble around my head until my fingers touch the foil packet resting there and then I open it and slide it onto his length.

"I'm going to pretend you are just an expert at that your first time trying," Marcus chuckles before he gently lays me back down on the bed.

"Well, I think that was like my third time, so, close." I spread my legs as far as I can for him, giving him the space to run his length through my wetness before he looks down, watching the space where he slowly enters me. The stretch is more than I was expecting, which is silly because it's been years since I've done this, but the slight discomfort quickly stops as he massages my breast and kisses the other one. He worships my body. It's more than an exploration, he is kissing and touching, like he needs to be in contact with me. And it is amazing.

Finally, I feel so incredibly full as he pushes all the way inside. I look up to see Marcus glancing down into my eyes. "How are you doing, beautiful?"

"So good. You feel so good, Marcus." I can't help the way my body pushes up into him, needing movement or pressure or something. I need more. Marcus doesn't make me wait as he starts moving back and forth inside of me, grinding his pelvis along my clit, the pressure doing wonders for the next orgasm that is already building. I can feel how wet I am around his cock every time he pulls back out. I trail my hand down so I can feel where we are connected, where he and I join together as one. My fingers come away coated in my arousal, and I use it to trace a circle around my nipple and then the other one.

"Are you wanting something, Ashley?" he teases me gently.

"I want you to clean up the mess I just made."

"Gladly," is the only thing he says before putting his mouth on one nipple, licking and sucking until the only wetness that remains is from him. By the time he is finishing with the second one, I am so close to coming again. He must sense it too, because his fingers trail down to put light pressure on my clit, right as he pushes in again and again.

"Come with me, Ashley. I'm right there with you. Let me see you come on my cock." And that's exactly what I do. Once he finishes pulsing inside of me, I watch as he goes to dispose of the condom and then happily fall asleep, completely sated in his arms.

Ashley

#  Epilogue One

## MARCUS

Having Ashley back with me in Maine for a few weeks has been incredible. Timing wasn't exactly the way we originally planned because of responsibilities at Pink Every Day, but we've been able to slip away for a little bit at the end of July. Her busy season for content and sales is about to start, so having this small break away was incredibly needed. It's like we didn't miss any time at all during the pause months. If anything, our relationship is stronger. And I know she is stronger.

This sassy girl is mine. And she chose me. And I don't think I will ever get over that.

"I have a surprise for you," I whisper to her as she places her coffee mug in the sink. I still haven't been able to convince her to give up that morning cup of coffee. But she is learning how to appreciate (and prepare) a good cup of tea.

"What is it?" Her eyes sparkle with mischief, knowing that I can't keep a secret from her even if I tried. I pull a small box from behind my back. Wrapped with the lavender design that she saw in the local shop last week and couldn't stop staring at. I may have bought a few rolls to stash for later presents for her. "Can I open it now?" she asks excitedly.

"Of course, Princess." I smile at her and then grab my tea before finding my seat at the table. She follows and sits opposite me so I can see her face as she opens the gift. Inside is a book. A navy cloth-bound hardcover book. The only thing on the cover is "my Princess."

"What is this?" She runs her hands gently over the textured cover and then opens to the first page.

"To the one that reminds me to look for the beauty among the seashells and the footprints." She whispers quietly but turns the page again to the first passage in the book. A typed out version of what I told her the day I gave her the pearl bracelet.

"This is what I did over the last year. It's my love letter to you. Poems, passages, mini stories—all things I wrote down while thinking of you. This is for your eyes only. So on the times where we can't be together, you have a piece of me with you." She's crying now and I have to fight the urge to do the same.

"This is absolutely incredible, Marcus. Thank you." She gets up to come hug me, but I stop her.

"That's not all." She looks at me confused before I can continue. "Turn to the end of the book and grab the envelope that's in there." She flips to the end and finds the envelope. I nod, telling her it's okay to open it up.

Her eyes go wide as she registers the tickets she's holding. "Are you taking me to Scotland for Christmas?!" She is practically screaming right now and I love how excited she gets over every little thing. It makes me want to give her absolutely everything.

"Would you like that?" She plops herself down in my lap and begins pecking kisses all over my face and neck all while saying "yes" over and over again. I laugh and tickle her to get her to stop. She finally pulls away laughing.

"I figured it was time to show my Princess what a real castle looks like."

"Who do you know that has a castle?"

"Rowan's dad. And we are going to get to stay there for two

weeks at Christmas. If that's okay with you."

"That's very okay with me.

451

# EPILOGUE TWO

# CONTENT WARNINGS

MYSTERY PREGNANCY TEST,
MENTION OF PREGNANCY
IMPLIED CHEATING

# Epilogue Two

## SASHA

"Okay, so we have the next campaign starting in two weeks, is everything ordered for that?" I glance up from my notebook to Ashley, waiting for confirmation before I check this off of my list. Only to have my notebook gently taken out of my hands and put into my fiancé's bag on the floor in front of him.

"We are here for lunch, a double date, it is not a work meeting. You two can clock out for a few minutes." Matt places a gentle kiss on my forehead and I immediately feel bad. We are supposed to be hanging out together for a little while. It's early September, so Tilly and Marcus have school requirements, and Ashley, Matt, and myself are swamped getting ready for our October campaigns and product launches. It's my favorite time of year. Add in the fact that I'm getting married in early November, there's just a lot happening right now.

The guys suggested we take a mini break today and do a late lunch together. With how busy we all are, if we don't literally schedule things together, it doesn't happen. Add in the fact that my old roommates, Carter and Kylie, are busy with job promotions and new hobbies, and if it's not in my phone calendar, it doesn't happen. I hate that life gets busy and the people that I want to spend the most time with, I don't get to see unless we intentionally move other things out of the way. Priorities though, right?

As soon as our appetizers come to the table, Ashley's phone rings. I instinctively check mine to see if it's work and notice I have several missed calls and text messages all from the same person. What the heck? I look up to see Ashley answering her phone and know it's probably about what's waiting for me on my phone as well.

"Hey hon, what's up?" Ashley answers, holding up her hand in a 'give me a sec' motion.

She's quiet for a minute and then looks at me.

"You haven't been over to the apartment recently, right?" Ashley directs her attention to me.

"My old one? No, why, what's up?" I respond, now really confused. I've been living with Matt in his house for over a year now. It's been weeks since I've been over to the apartment. We go over there sometimes to record content or for dinner with Kylie, but we haven't been able to make the schedules all work recently.

Ashley turns back to her phone. "Nope, neither of us. What happened?" She's quiet for another beat before her eyes go wide. "In the bathroom? What did it say?" What the heck is happening?

"No, hon, I don't know. Do you need us to do anything?" Another pause and then she nods, even though whoever is on the phone can't see her. She closes her eyes and rubs her temple as if to relieve the stress building in her forehead.

"Okay, keep me updated. You're welcome to come over tonight to either my place or Sasha's. I'll let her know what's happening." I unlock my phone to see what all the notifications were from. This doesn't sound like a good news phone call. I cover my mouth instinctively at the picture message that immediately downloads.

Ashley gets off the phone and just looks at me.

"Did she send you the picture?"

"What's going on? Is everything okay?" Marcus rests his hand on Ashley's shoulder, sensing her concern.

"That was Kylie, wanting to know if either of us had been to the apartment in the last few days while she was out of town for the West Coast Swing competition," Ashley steadily answers him.

"Why did she want to know that?" Matt is the one that asks this time. I slide my phone to him, still not sure how to answer.

"Please tell me she took that before her trip or the second she got back." He practically pleads with me to answer him.

"Nope. She found that in the trash can when she got home just a bit ago. It's not hers."

"So, if neither one of you were over there, and the test isn't hers, who is pregnant, and why are they taking a test at her apartment?" Matt asks both of us.

And honestly, I have no idea.

# KYLIE'S STORY COMING
## Spring 2025

# The End

# THANK YOU SO MUCH FOR READING ASHLEY AND MARCUS'S STORY.

Subscribe to my newsletter at nikkigrantwrites.com to hear first about when Kylie's story will be released as well as bonus scenes from this book!

# OTHER BOOKS BY NIKKI GRANT

Makeup and Mochas
The Funnel to You
The Man for You
Book Three (Summer 2025)
Book Four (Fall 2025)


Untitled Romantic Tragedy (Fall 2025)


Check nikkigrantwrites.com for other updates on future projects.

# ACKNOWLEDGEMENTS

I can't believe this is the end of book two. This process would not be possible without so many amazing people supporting me. Going from reader to writer to published author has been absolutely mind blowing and I can't believe this is my life right now.

To my husband, thank you for being there to bounce ideas off of, for taking care of things around the house and with the kids so I can write, and for celebrating me every step of the way.

To Bookish Bubbly PR - thank you for your support in my role as an author and for everything you did to help share this book with other readers!

To the authors that have allowed me into their circles and encouraged me along the way - whether it was help writing the blurb (Jamie), help in some of the fun inspiration for the pieces of the story (Jolie - did you catch them all?), or help in seeing if what I wanted to make happen actually worked.

Charly - you did incredible work as always. And I am so glad I get to work with you!

Chris and David - thank you for making the model cover on this one something I literally screamed over!

Kendra and Spice Me Up Editing - thank you for helping to make this the best it could be.

Justine and Bethany - you two were so incredibly beneficial in the early writing stages of this work. Having you two as Alpha readers (and beta and arc) made this process a lot easier. I am so glad to have you on this writing journey with me.

To my Beta team: Alyssa, Tea, Ely, Amy, Katie, Rebecca, Jamie, Tiffani, Teia, and Tori. The feedback you provided and having your "live feedback" was amazing! You each played an important role in bringing The Man for You to publishing day.

All the ARC readers - the messages, posts, and video reactions were amazing! I'm so glad you were able to enjoy that late Christmas present from me.

My author inspo for this book was Jolie Vines. Getting to travel to Scotland, dealing with stalkers that just can't take a hint, and the helicopter rides were all nods to her. Jolie, I have loved your books so much and appreciate the friendship and the encouragement along the way in my author journey. And the tea of course!

# IF YOU OR SOMEONE YOU KNOW NEEDS HELP, HERE ARE SOME RESOURCES THAT MAY BE ABLE TO HELP.

National:
info@stalkingawareness.org.
Victim Connect: 1-855-4VICTIM(1-855-484-2846)
National Domestic Violence Hotline: 1–800–799–7233or TTY
1–800–787–3224 En Español.
The National Sexual Assault Hotline: 1-800-656-HOPE (4673)

Stalking Awareness and Prevention
https://www.stalkingawareness.org/contact/

RAINN
https://rainn.org/news/resources-survivors-stalking-and-cyberstalking

For depression

In Colorado, dial 988.

National Network of Depression Centers
https://nndc.org/resource-links/

Digital depression resources
https://www.nimh.nih.gov/get-involved/digital-shareables/
shareable-resources-on-depression

# COFFEE DRINKS TO TRY

Mocha Mud Puddle (submitted by L. Clara)
Combine frozen blend of chocolate and vanilla with Columbian coffee and milk
Top with whipped cream


Sweet Vanilla Cookie Butter
Iced shaken espresso with 2 pumps macadamia syrup
2 pumps white chocolate sauce
Toasted cookie crumble topping
Almond milk


Nutella Cold Brew
1 pump mocha
1 pump hazelnut
3 sugars
Splash of cream


Hot Chocolate Cold Brew
Combine Mocha and White Mocha
Add vanilla sweet cold foam
Top with cocoa powder


Pumpkin Cream Chai Latte
Chai tea latte
Pumpkin sweet cream cold foam

HAVE A COFFEE OR TEA DRINK THAT YOU WOULD LIKE TO SEE FEATURED IN THE NEXT BOOK? CONNECT WITH ME THROUGH MY WEBSITE NIKKIGRANTWRITES.COM OR INSTAGRAM! I ALSO HAVE A COFFEE DRINKS BOARD ON MY PINTEREST PAGE IF YOU ARE LOOKING FOR SOME NEW THINGS TO TRY.